HOSTAGE ZERO

"Jonathan Grave, my favorite freelance peacemaker, problem-solver, and tough guy hero, is back—and in particularly fine form. *Hostage Zero* is classic Gilstrap: the people are utterly real, the action's foot to the floor, and the writing's fluid as a well-oiled machine gun. A tour de force!"
—Jeffery Deaver

"This addictively readable thriller marries a breakneck pace to a complex, multilayered plot. . . . A roller coaster ride of adrenaline-inducing plot twists leads to a riveting and highly satisfying conclusion. Exceptional characterization and an intricate, flawlessly crafted story line make this an absolute must read for thriller fans."
—*Publishers Weekly* (starred review)

NO MERCY

"*No Mercy* grabs hold of you on page one and doesn't let go. Gilstrap's new series is terrific. It will leave you breathless. I can't wait to see what Jonathan Grave is up to next."
—Harlan Coben

"John Gilstrap is one of the finest thriller writers on the planet. *No Mercy* showcases his work at its finest—taut, action-packed, and impossible to put down!"
—Tess Gerritsen

"A great hero, a pulse-pounding story—and the launch of a really exciting series."
—Joseph Finder

"An entertaining, fast-paced tale of violence and revenge."
—*Publishers Weekly*

"No other writer is better able to combine in a single novel both rocket-paced suspense and heartfelt looks at family and the human spirit. And what a pleasure to meet Jonathan Grave, a hero for our time . . . and for all time."
—Jeffery Deaver

ALSO BY JOHN GILSTRAP

ZERO SUM

A JONATHAN GRAVE THRILLER

JOHN GILSTRAP

PINNACLE BOOKS
Kensington Publishing Corp.
www.kensingtonbooks.com

To Joy

Chapter 1

As Jonathan Grave jogged along River Road, past the swaying masts in the Fisherman's Cove Marina, he replayed in his head the conversation he'd had this morning with Boxers, his longtime friend, who made linebackers look puny.

"I'm telling you up front, Boss, so you don't get mad," he'd said. "You're gonna get attacked today, but it's nothing personal."

Jonathan had barely cleared the shower and wasn't fully dressed yet. "What are you talking about?" he asked into the speakerphone.

"You'll know when it happens."

"Is it your intention not to make any sense?"

"It'll make sense sometime today." There was a smile in Boxers' voice.

"Where will this attack be coming from?"

"Just live your life as normal," Boxers said. "Go about your day as you normally would."

"You know I don't like games, Big Guy," Jonathan said, invoking Boxers' call sign.

"That's why I'm giving you this heads-up."

"I don't like practical jokes, either."

"This isn't a practical joke," Big Guy said. "Think of it as an experiment."

"It sounds like we can add experiments to the growing list of things I don't like."

That's when Boxers disconnected. Almost two hours ago.

Jonathan knew that Big Guy wouldn't hurt him, but the sense that something or someone was coming for him had ignited an unfamiliar sense of paranoia in his gut. The thought of it had kept him from finding that Zen place in his head while he ran.

His Spidey-sense tingled. A noise he'd never heard before had invaded his head. It sounded like a big insect, but it didn't register as natural. He was away from the water now, flanked by trees on either side of the roadway, and the buzz seemed to be coming from everywhere. He didn't wear sunglasses when he jogged because he didn't like them sliding down his nose, so when he looked to see if he could pick up a threat, he shielded his eyes with his left hand, keeping his right hand free to draw from the elastic holster around his midsection.

Nothing.

He turned and jogged backward for a few seconds to see if something was sneaking up from behind.

Still nothing but the incessant buzz.

"Goddammit, Box," he muttered.

Then he saw it—a tiny propellered drone, maybe six inches in diameter, circled overhead, bobbing and weaving as if to avoid an obstacle that Jonathan couldn't see. Seconds later, it darted straight to Jonathan's chest, faster than he could move to dodge it.

"Ow! Shit!"

After the impact, the plastic whirligig clattered to the sidewalk and went still.

"Dammit!" Jonathan cursed. "That hurt." Nothing like getting shot or stabbed, of course, but he expected to find a bruise when he returned to the firehouse that also served as his home and office.

This had to be what Big Guy had been talking about. The coincidence was too perfect otherwise. He stooped, picked up the toy, and turned it over in his hands. It looked like a four-rotor helicopter. It weighed nearly nothing but featured a tiny lens in the middle of the body. Just above the lens someone had applied a piece of Scotch tape on which was written the word *Boom*.

Jonathan pulled his phone from its pocket in his running shorts and pressed a speed dial button.

Boxers' voice nearly vibrated with excitement as he answered with, "Did it find you?"

Jonathan couldn't help but smile. "What the hell does *boom* mean?"

"If you'd been a real target, Little Roxie would have blown you up."

Boxers loved his toys, and he loved his explosives more. "You're telling me that this thing can be fitted with a bomb?"

"Well, a grenade. Or a flash-bang if we didn't want shrapnel. But that's not the headline. Big Roxie can deliver explosives, too, so the payload is old news."

Jonathan had never asked who in Big Guy's life had been named Roxie or why he'd chosen some form of that name for each of the UAVs—unmanned aerial vehicles—in his collection. "Okay, I'll bite. What's the headline?"

"The one that found you and hit you was on its own. I wasn't controlling it."

Jonathan walked to a deadfall on the edge of his running path and took a seat. "Who was?"

"It was controlling itself," Boxers said with a giggle. Jonathan had never heard him giggle before. He found the sound unnerving.

"You're going to tell me, right? You're not going to make me ask all the questions?"

"It's cool technology," Big Guy said. "I just loaded a digital image of you onto its internal memory card and entered the rough GPS coordinates. I told it to find you on River Road, and it did."

"I'm the only person out here. How hard can that be?"

"But you're not the only person she flew over. She rejected ten or twelve other folks before she zeroed in on you."

Jonathan was impressed. He had no idea what the practical use for such a toy might be, but he was impressed.

"It gets better," Boxers said. "This is amazing technology. The more identifying factors I load onto the card, the easier it would be to find you. If I chose a hundred people off a social media page and loaded the obvious stuff, I could program it to kill the first marching band drummer it finds. Or, if I had a swarm of them, I could tell them to find and kill every math major, or everyone who's vacationed at Disney World."

"You're playing with assassination tools now?"

"It'd be tough to defend against."

More like impossible, Jonathan thought. He wondered if the creators of social media had foreseen the myriad ways that their brainchildren would ruin lives and screw up the world.

"Was I your first experiment?" Jonathan asked.

"For now, yes."

"Lucky me."

"Can you bring her back when you're done with your run?"

"You can't fly her back to you?" *Jesus, I'm calling it a she.*

"It's a safety thing," Boxers explained. "I call it a kamikaze drone. It goes out, does its thing, and then goes dead. With a real munition on it, I didn't want a bad guy to be able to return the favor and send it back. It'll have to be reprogrammed before it can fly again."

"You designed this?"

"I had some help from Venice, but yeah." Venice Alexander (pronounced Ven-EE-chay and don't ask why) was one of the world's great computer geniuses.

"Did you tell her what it was for?"

"Hell no. I don't think she would have approved."

Jonathan's call-waiting beeped, causing him to look at the screen. "Speak of the devil," Jonathan said. "There's Ven now."

"Don't forget to—"

Jonathan had already pressed the disconnect button and moved on. "Hey, Ven, When did you become an early riser?"

Her tone was urgent. "Digger, you need to come up to RezHouse." Resurrection House was a residential school for children of incarcerated parents. No one paid tuition because Jonathan paid all the bills.

"What's going on?"

"Not on the phone. You need to come up."

"Don't toy with me, Ven. Tell me what's happening."

"A student died," Venice said. "Overdose."

Jonathan's stomach flipped. "Shit. I'll be there as soon as I can." He clicked off with her and reconnected with Boxers. "Big Guy, I need you to come and get me."

RezHouse sat on the property that once had served as Jonathan's childhood home. He'd deeded the estate—mansion included—to St. Kate's Catholic Church for the sum of one dollar, on the condition that it be used for the purpose it now served.

It was supposed to be a safe place for children who'd seen too much violence and experienced too much pain to learn and grow in a peaceful setting. Now a monster had introduced narcotics into this safe haven and taken a life. When Jonathan found the sonofabitch, it would get very ugly very fast.

A Fisherman's Cove police cruiser had positioned itself to block access to the grounds. As Jonathan and Boxers approached, a skinny teenager with a badge and a ballistic vest that weighed more than he did stepped from the vehicle to block Jonathan's path.

"I'm sorry sir, but—"

Jonathan slowed, but he did not stop. "Out of my way."

The cop winced a little as he prepared to physically intervene.

Jonathan cut him a break and pulled up short. "Officer, do you know who I am?"

"You're Jonathan Grave, sir. I have specific instructions to tell you that I can't let you pass."

"And so you did. Be proud of a job well done." He pressed past the kid.

"I'll tase you if I have to."

"I'll punt you like a football," Boxers said. "If I have to."

Jonathan spun on the kid, causing him to recoil.

"What's your name?"

"Hoffman, sir. Kurt Hoffman."

"Officer Hoffman, I know you're doing your job as you've been told to do it. Now I'm going to do mine."

"You know it's not the flight through the air that's unpleasant," Boxers said as he went with his boss. "It's the landing."

Hoffman gaped. He looked like he didn't want to be there anymore.

Jonathan turned away from him and started walking again. As he continued up the hill toward the mansion and the dormitories that lay beyond, he wondered what it was going to feel like when he rode the lightning bolt from Officer Hoffman's Taser.

Ultimately, it wasn't an issue.

Jonathan and Boxers skirted the mansion and walked straight toward the dormitory farther up the hill, where the presence of an ambulance told him where the action was. They'd barely passed the halfway mark when a fireplug of a man in a police uniform with a gold badge vectored in from the right to intercept them.

"Digger, Box, you need to stop." The approaching cop was Chief Doug Kramer, whom Jonathan had known since their shared boyhoods. Kramer held his hands to his sides, cruciform, to block the pathway.

"Officer Hoffman already threatened to tase me," Jonathan said. He stopped when he came nose-to-nose with Kramer.

"I'm trying to stop you from committing a felony," Kramer said. "You need to calm down."

"I'm not spun up yet," Jonathan said. "Venice said somebody died."

"Yes."

"A student."

"Yes."

"Then get out of my way."

"Please, Dig. Just wait, will you?"

Jonathan took a step back and crossed his arms.

Kramer inhaled noisily and stuffed his thumbs into the top of his Sam Browne belt. "The patient is, indeed, a student. Was. His name was Giovanni LoCicero, and he was twelve years old."

Jonathan's heart sagged. "How the hell does a twelve-year-old overdose in a secure facility?"

"How did you know about the overdose?"

"Venice told me. She left out the part about the age. What happened?"

"We're still—"

Jonathan held up a hand. "It's just us, Doug. You're not on the record. Nobody's going to quote you."

Kramer shifted his weight from his right foot to his left. He had something to say that he didn't want to articulate.

"Screw it," Jonathan said. "I'm not doing this." He moved to push past the chief.

Kramer grabbed his biceps.

"Be careful, Doug. We haven't exchanged blows since we were twelve. I've gotten a lot better at it since then."

Kramer coughed out a laugh as he released Jonathan's arm. "You *really* want to know what Tasers and nightsticks feel like? Throw a punch at the police chief in front of his troops. Let's not do the dick knocking thing."

"I've seen his dick," Boxers said. "Not much there to knock."

Jonathan ignored him. "I've got to get up there, Doug. Ven said—"

"You can't go all vigilante," Kramer interrupted.

"I don't even know what that means."

The chief took a few seconds to sort his thoughts, then he set his shoulders. "It was fentanyl," he said. "Disguised as candy."

Jonathan felt heat rising in his ears. "So . . . What was the dead boy's name again?"

"Giovanni LoCicero." Doug spoke to his feet. "He went by Jonni."

"So, Giovanni died for eating what he thought was

Pez?" Jonathan felt the kind of anger building that was never helpful and often harmful. Fentanyl was the Chinese Communist Party's cash crop du jour. It found unlimited distribution throughout the United States courtesy of President Tony Darmond's protracted dereliction of duty.

"Who were Giovanni's parents?" Jonathan asked. Every resident of Resurrection House was a product of a criminal household where violence was often the rule. Harm to one student posed a threat to all.

"Rocco LoCicero will never see freedom again," Kramer said. "Among other crimes, he's serving a life sentence for killing Priscilla LoCicero, Giovanni's mother."

"Is Rocco connected to the mob?"

"I don't know that yet. Why?"

There was always a chance that something like this was retribution for something else. "Where are Mama and Venice?"

Kramer pointed up the hill with his forehead. "In the dorm."

"How are they?"

"About like you'd expect. Distraught."

"I need to go and be with them."

As he moved to pass Kramer, the chief grabbed his biceps again.

"I thought we already danced to this tune," Jonathan said.

"There's more," Doug said. He shot a nervous glance at Boxers. "Venice's boy, Roman, took some, too."

Jonathan felt his neck and ears turning red while Big Guy swelled with anger.

"He's okay. He spit it out, but it was close."

"Please make a hole and get out of my way," Jonathan said.

"Dig, this is a police matter. You need to understand that. You need to *accept* that. There's no room for vigilante justice."

Jonathan cocked his head. "That's the second time you've used that word. What are you suggesting?" He had long suspected that Kramer knew more about the clandestine side of Jonathan's business dealings than he had a right to know. While Jonathan and his team had a long history of bringing justice to people who had hurt others, they did not, and had never considered themselves to be, vigilantes. He waited for Kramer to make the rest of his point.

"You're a hothead, Dig. You run a detective agency, and you have more money than all the police forces within a hundred miles put together. You need to stay out of the way and let us do our jobs."

"Duly noted. Now, either arrest me or let go of my arm."

Kramer released his grip, and Jonathan resumed his walk up the hill.

"Someone's gonna die," Big Guy said.

"Oh, yeah."

As far as Jonathan was concerned, Kramer had no worries about him getting in the way of any official investigation. Kramer and his cops would proceed at their typical glacial pace. Evidence would cool as every effort was made to ensure that the perpetrators' constitutional rights were carefully protected. The chief would have no idea when Jonathan and his team would be running high-speed circles around him.

Kramer stayed with Jonathan and Boxers step-for-step, but three paces behind. The police officer standing guard at the dorm's main entrance seemed confused by what he saw. As Jonathan approached, the guard's eyes focused on the chief. Whatever transpired in the silence prompted the cop to step aside.

"Thank you, officer," Jonathan said as he passed. He wouldn't swear to it, but he was pretty sure that this was the same cop he'd seen cowering behind the front wheel well of his cruiser not too long ago as Resurrection House was under fire.

The activity in the dormitory's foyer was a study in unfocused meandering. Uniformed cops and plain-clothed detectives postured and chatted among themselves as the housemother and the senior students, all in the same issued pale-blue pajamas, tried to corral and comfort the younger children and themselves.

Somewhere in the swirl of activity, Jonathan was confident that he would find Father Dom D'Angelo, the pastor of St. Katherine's Catholic Church. In addition to his doctor of divinity diploma, Dom also carried a Ph.D. in psychology, which allowed him to provide counsel and comfort to the traumatized children of RezHouse.

"Where are Venice and Mama?" Jonathan asked the first non-cop he saw.

The woman he presumed to be the housemother pointed to a closed door along the foyer's right-hand wall.

He pushed it open and there they were. When Jonathan saw the distress in their eyes, he found himself transplanted back decades. Jonathan's mother had died when he was just a little boy, and Mama Alexander—the family's housekeeper—had stepped in as his chief disciplinarian and soother of wounds. Venice was Mama's daughter. Jonathan had known her as a cranky baby and toddler long before she became one of the most feared hackers to haunt cyberspace.

The ladies stood together from the cramped love seat they'd been sharing. Mama got to him first and encased him in a massive hug. As soon as they made physical contact, she started to sob.

"Oh, Jonny, this is awful." Exactly one person in the world still called him by that name. "I saw him there in the hallway. So young. Lordy, it tore my heart out."

Jonathan wasn't much of a hugger. He'd hang in there in a pinch—and this was a pinch—but he'd rather be putting a fork in his eye. He shot a plaintive look to Venice, who was only a click and a half more composed than her mother.

After thirty seconds or so, Jonathan lightened his embrace and eased Mama away. "We'll get through this," he said. "*You'll* get through this." He kissed her forehead and accompanied her back to the love seat and helped her sit down. Venice joined her.

Jonathan pulled the ottoman away from the over-stuffed chair on the other side of the room so he could sit directly in front of Venice. "How's Roman?" Responding to her look of confusion, he added, "Doug Kramer told me."

Venice's fourteen-year-old son resided at RezHouse, placed there not because of his parent's indiscretions but for security concerns. "Medics say he's fine. No need to go to the hospital. He spit it out in time."

"Thank God," Boxers said.

"He was ready to eat it when he saw Giovanni collapse."

Mama reached over and grabbed her daughter's thigh. Gave it a little squeeze. "Go ahead and tell him the rest, Venny."

Jonathan waited for it.

Venice cast her gaze to the floor. "Roman says he knows where the drugs came from."

"You've talked to him, then?"

"Of course. He was very upset."

"How long ago did this happen?"

"Right before I called you."

"Where is he now?" Jonathan asked.

"In his dorm room. That's where he wanted to be."

Mama looked unhappy. "You should've brought him here."

"He wanted to be with his friends," Venice said. "I understand that. The other students don't have anyone to hold their hand. He doesn't want to be that different."

"So, you went to his room?" Jonathan asked. "He didn't come here?"

"I needed to be sure that he was okay."

"How long ago?"

Venice scowled. Her unease deepened. "Is something wrong that I don't understand?"

"Can I have an answer, please?" Jonathan pressed. "How long ago were you with him in his room?"

"I don't know, ten, maybe fifteen minutes ago."

"Before or after the police came?"

"While they were on their way."

"And what did he tell you, exactly?"

"Your tone is scaring me, Digger."

Jonathan set his jaw and waited.

"I didn't memorize the exact words. He said that Giovanni brought a tin of candy to his room. He said it came from his mother in a care package."

"Did you see the container?" Jonathan asked.

"I saw it, yes. It was on Roman's desk in his room."

"What did it look like?"

"It was a little metal tin. You've seen FreshAir Mints before."

He had, indeed. In fact, he kept a tin of them in his desk and the center console of his car. They were great for getting rid of coffee breath. "Why did he bring it to Roman?"

"I don't know," Venice said.

"Did he bring it just to Roman, or did he bring it to a bunch of kids?"

Mama leaned forward. "Jonny, are you suggesting that Giovanni was trying to hurt Roman?"

"I'm not suggesting anything yet, Mama. I'm just trying to gather information."

"It never occurred to me to ask," Venice said. "I was so relieved that he was okay."

If this was a targeted attack against Venice's son, it wouldn't be the first time. Though it would certainly be the most brazen. "We need to know more details," Jonathan said. "I need to speak with Roman."

"*I* need to speak with Roman," Venice corrected. "He's been traumatized enough already. He doesn't need the third degree from you."

Chapter 2

Jonathan stood at the window behind his desk, watching the forest of masts in the marina across the street sway with the currents and eddies of the river beyond. Something about the perpetual randomness of the movement soothed him. Autumn hadn't quite won the day from summer, but it was getting close. Even though the temperature still topped eighty on most days, the nights were chilly and the trees were beginning to turn.

Behind him, the door to the Cave—the secure wing of offices dedicated to the clandestine side of Security Solutions—opened and shut. Vibrating floorboards under his feet told him exactly who was approaching his office before he turned around.

A voice that was equal parts baritone and bear boomed, "Who are we gonna kill?"

Jonathan turned and watched his friend Boxers close the distance to his office door. Pushing seven feet tall and built like a linebacker, the giant man's given name was Brian Van de Muelebroecke, and he was the most lethal operator Jonathan had ever known.

"We need to do a little research first," Jonathan said.

"How the hell did fentanyl get into RezHouse?"

"I don't know that yet."

"With the gajillion dollars of spyware Mother Hen's got, how can we not know this?"

"Good morning to you, too," Venice said from Big Guy's six o'clock.

Boxers looked instantly repentant. He stepped aside to make room for her to enter.

She stayed on the other side of the doorway. "I'm set up in the War Room. There's not much but there's something." Without waiting for a response, she turned on her heel and walked away.

"She's pissed," Boxers said.

"Probably." The bar for pissing off Mother Hen was set low on any given day. That Big Guy had impugned her research prowess would be treated as an exceptionally low blow. "I like it that you're afraid of her."

"I'm not afraid."

"You're a little afraid." Jonathan gestured out the door with an open palm. "Lead the way."

In the world of hackers, Venice was known as FreakFace666—respected and feared as one of the most adept wranglers of ones and zeroes in the world. The War Room was her playground, outfitted with every electronic toy that she'd ever requested. The latest and greatest of these was a cache of top-secret software developed by the NSA to crack into pretty much anything she wanted to see. The Puzzle Palace had broken the law to develop the software in the first place, so even the FBI was unaware of it.

Venice sat in the command chair at the head of the teak conference table, surrounded by her electronic children. Jonathan took his usual spot at her left, facing the door, while Boxers sat on his left in the Aeron chair that was specially built for his massive frame.

"Is Gunslinger coming?" Boxers asked.

As if on cue, the door to the Cave opened and Gail

Bonneville entered the suite. "I'm here," she said. As usual, she sat across from Jonathan, on Venice's right. A former member of the FBI's elite HRT—Hostage Rescue Team—Gail held a law degree and most recently was the sheriff of Samson County, Indiana. Her call sign—Gunslinger, which she despised, making it all the more entertaining for Jonathan—came from her ability to drive nails with an M4 carbine from a hundred yards.

"All settled in?" Jonathan asked. Not too long ago, Gail's house had been torched by bad guys. She'd gotten stabbed in the fight, but the bad guys had gotten dead. That made her the winner. She'd lived in the firehouse with Jonathan while she recovered and the house was rebuilt, and as of only a week or so ago, she was back in her own place.

"Settled in overstates it," Gail said. "But I'm getting there."

"Let's get started," Jonathan said. "How the hell did drugs make it through our security? Ven, you said that Roman has an idea. Have you spoken with him about it?"

"Not much," she said. "I know that he went over it with the police this morning. And on further reflection, I thought it best if we all heard it straight from him. He's waiting outside if you want me to bring him in."

Boxers made a noise that could have been a subtle growl. Given the nature of their work, OPSEC—operational security—was essential. They'd been forced to tip their hand to Roman a while back after he'd been the target of an 0300 mission—a hostage rescue—but there were limits to what a fourteen-year-old boy should know. The contents of the War Room ranked right up there with unreasonable security risks.

"I think it'll be okay if we keep the computers off and watch what we say," Jonathan said. He nodded to Venice, who picked up the landline and punched the intercom button.

"Let the record show that I think this is a bad idea," Boxers said.

"Duly noted," Jonathan replied.

"He's already seen the genie out of the bottle," Gail said. "He's a good kid, and he's loyal to his mom, certainly, if not to all of us. Maybe the more we trust him, the deeper the loyalty will set in."

"It's not like I'm going to toss his skinny ass out," Big Guy said, blushing a little. "I just think this is a lot of grown-up shit to process."

While they had been friends for years—way back to their days with the Unit—there was something about Boxers' past that Jonathan had never understood and Big Guy had never shared. A merciless killer and operational genius when the occasion called for it, he also had an inordinate soft spot for kids and a murderous intolerance for people who would hurt them.

Venice returned the handset to the cradle. "He's on his way. Charlie knows it's okay to let him in." Charlie Keeling and Rick Hare were the armed guards who kept looky-loos from entering the Cave.

A minute later, they all watched through the glass walls of the War Room as Roman entered the Cave. Venice waved him into the War Room with a broad gesture. He'd grown two inches and reduced his 'fro since Jonathan had last seen him. He finally was beginning to look his age.

Jonathan pointed to the chair next to Gail. "Have a seat. Tough morning. How are you holding up?"

"Seeing a guy get beat to death with a sledgehammer was a lot worse," Roman said, with what he tried to sell as a knowing smirk, but he couldn't quite pull it off. Sadly, it was all true. It happened in Mexico during the time he'd been kidnapped by a cartel.

"This isn't a time for humor," Venice said. "Giovanni LoCicero was a friend of yours."

"Okay, let's stop that shit right here and now," Jonathan said. "Teen angst gets checked at the door." He shifted his eyes to Venice. "It goes right next to the motherly angst. We're here to get information, not to light fuses under each other's asses."

Roman couldn't suppress the giggle triggered by Jonathan's choice of words. That had sort of been the point.

"Can you walk us through what happened?" Jonathan asked. "Take your time."

Roman lifted a blue pen from the cup in the center of the conference table and spun it between his thumbs and forefingers. "Giovanni ate a piece of candy and he died."

Jonathan looked to Gail for relief. She had a way of pulling information out of people without the intimidating side effect that he seemed to bring to the table.

"Start at the beginning," Gail coaxed. "Don't start with the only detail we already know."

"Where's the beginning?"

"Where did it happen?" Gail asked.

"Outside my room. Mom already knows that."

Jonathan put his hand on the table but didn't slam it the way he wanted to. "Come on, Roman, you know how this works. You've seen it work before. You're going to hear a lot of questions you've heard and already answered because that's how we piece together the larger puzzle. It's not that we don't trust you or that we think you're not telling the truth. By asking over and over again, each telling brings out more details or cleans up details that are fuzzy. Please don't make us fight over each one."

So much for being the nonintimidating one.

"How did that come about?" Gail asked. "Paint the whole picture. Why were you outside your room instead of inside? Was it just the two of you, or were there others? You know, that sort of thing."

Roman made real eye contact for the first time. "You know, Mateo and I have become kinda tight over the past few months."

"He lives across the hall from you, right?" Venice asked.

"Right. After morning alarm and before breakfast, we usually shoot the sh—" He stopped himself.

"For our purposes here," Venice said, "You can let those filters down. Just say it as it comes to you."

Given all the shit the kid had been through, Jonathan thought he'd earned the right to cuss like a longshoreman.

"So, before breakfast we usually talk about stuff. Nothing important, just stuff. It's usually just the two of us, though sometimes others poke in."

"Is Giovanni LoCicero a usual part of the discussion crowd?" Gail asked.

"He's not a regular part of any crowd," Roman said. Then he looked down. "I mean, he *wasn't*. He was too new. He was only there for a few days. He seemed nice enough. Richard Goldsberry didn't like him much, so when that happens, you don't get a lot of friends."

"Did you try to include him in your group with Mateo?" Venice asked. "That would have been the nice thing to do."

Jonathan swallowed his urge to moan. Mothers, he'd decided, should not be a part of their son's interrogation.

"It's not like that, Mom. Everybody's got to find

their way. I didn't like him or dislike him. He was just there. You know, quiet. He kept to himself mostly."

"But this morning . . ." Gail prompted.

"But this morning, when me and Mateo were talking about candy—what's good and what's bad—Giovanni came out of his room with a tin of FreshAir Mints. You know, those breath mints?"

"I use them to get rid of coffee breath," Jonathan said.

"Right. Those. Anyway, whose favorite candy are those? I mean, they're not bad, but they're really minty. So, Giovanni comes out and says that he just got a fresh tin of these things, and he offered to share it with us."

"He was being nice," Venice said.

Jonathan was *this close* to asking Venice to leave the room.

"Yeah, I guess. Or at least trying to be relevant."

"And then what happened?" Gail asked.

"Giovanni opened the tin, passed it around to Mateo and me, and then took one for himself. Apparently, he really likes them. He popped it in his mouth, chewed it, and then went down. Like, just collapsed. It was so fast."

Roman shifted his gaze back to the pen. "That was scary."

"What did you do?" Gail asked.

"I spit mine out. So did Mateo."

"And then?"

"I called for help. And then I did CPR." His voice caught in his throat. "But nothing worked."

Jonathan wanted to keep the emotions at bay, so he redirected the conversation. "Let's move back a bit," he said. "Do you know where this tin of candies came from?"

Roman shook his head. "No."

"Had you seen them before?"

"No."

"Wait a second," Gail said. "Those candies usually come wrapped in cellophane—or whatever they use instead of cellophane these days. Do you remember if Giovanni had to unwrap it before he came to you?"

Roman scowled as he rummaged through his memory. "No, I don't think so."

"Was the tin full the first time you saw it?" Jonathan asked. If the fentanyl candy was just a random tablet among many normal ones, this would be a different investigation than if the tin was full of only poison.

"I don't know if it was *full* full, but it was close."

Jonathan looked to Venice. "Any word on ICIS about that?" As soon as the words left his mouth, he realized that he'd been the first in this meeting to violate the security standards. The look he got from Venice told him that she'd drawn the same conclusion.

"Forget I asked," Jonathan said.

"What?" Roman asked. "What's going on?"

"None of your concern," Jonathan said. He modulated his tone to make it clear that the subject was dead. "Do you have more that you need to add? More that you think we need to know?"

Roman sensed the change in demeanor, and his expression darkened. "I suppose not."

Jonathan looked to Venice, who looked equally uncomfortable. "Do you have anything?"

"Thank you for coming," Venice said. "How about you come to the house for dinner tonight?"

"I'd rather be with my friends." He stood. "Are you going to get the people who sent the poison?"

Jonathan could feel the heat of Boxers' glare without looking. "You know the drill, Roman. You'll know what we think you need to know when you need to know it."

"What are you going to tell people you've been doing this morning?" Boxers asked. "You know, in case someone asks."

"I'm going to say I've been here, talking with my mom about what happened." He gave a knowing smirk. "It's the truth, isn't it?"

Boxers wasn't sure how to answer. Which Jonathan figured was exactly what the boy was going for.

Venice stood and joined her son at the door. "Are you sure you're all right, sweetie?"

"I really am. I promise." He allowed himself to be hugged, and he exited through the Cave.

Venice watched after him for a few seconds, then spun on her heel to address the others gathered at the table.

Jonathan recognized the look in her eye. She had a presentation that she wanted to get to, but he had thoughts at the front of his mind that he wanted to get to first. "Buzz the guard station," he said. "I want to talk to Charlie."

"Now?" Venice asked.

"In here?" Gail added.

"In here, right now," Jonathan said.

Eyebrows scaling her forehead, Venice did as she was told, and thirty seconds later, Charlie Keeling was standing at the door of the War Room. "What can I do for ya, Boss?"

Charlie was as New Yawk as anyone Jonathan had ever known. Maybe five-five, with an ample gut that looked like it was made of concrete, his accent sounded more Brooklyn than the Bronx he claimed to hail from, but it sure as hell was not Virginian.

"You know about the incident in the dorm this morning, right?" Jonathan asked.

"Sure. Terrible thing. I hope they catch the sonsabitches who sent that shit and turn 'em on a spit."

"How dialed into the RezHouse security program are you?"

"I helped to write the book. Like, literally."

"Do we examine incoming mail to the residents?"

"We photograph it," Charlie said. "But we don't open it or nothin'."

"Do we keep those records?"

"Only till forever."

Jonathan said, "I want to know every bit of correspondence Giovanni LoCicero has received since he first arrived."

Charlie pursed his lips as he rested both hands atop the pistol grip of his slung M4 rifle. "Shouldn't be too hard, I don't think. I mean, he ain't been here but so long, right?"

"Less than two weeks," Venice said.

"Let me make a phone call or two," Charlie said. "The mail's processed down at the mansion. Rick Hare's workin' down there today. He'll take care of it forthwith."

"Thank you."

"That all you got?"

"That's everything."

"Right. I'm on it." He was already keying the mic on his radio as he turned and crossed the Cave's lobby toward the door most recently used by Roman.

Jonathan tapped the table with both hands. "All right, Mother Hen, the floor is yours."

Venice pushed a button as she sat. The lights in the War Room dimmed by half as a 106-inch projection screen came to life at the far end. Two images of a young boy appeared on the screen side by side. On the left, a sullen and angry kid stared into the lens for his arrival photo. On the right, the same kid stood arm in arm with two other boys in RezHouse soccer kit, filthy and sweaty and beaming with joy.

"Meet Giovanni LoCicero," Venice said. "Twelve years old, now dead." Her voice caught in her throat for the last two words, but she got past it. "He arrived here at the school two weeks ago."

Venice clicked her laptop, and the image changed to a mugshot of a slightly built white male in his fifties with a well-trimmed goatee. According to the height chart in the photo's background, he was five feet, eight inches tall. The guy could have been a banker.

"This is Rocco LoCicero, Giovanni's father. He's serving a life sentence in Big Sandy for killing Priscilla LoCicero, Giovanni's mother." The screen flashed and displayed a suburban-looking mom with curly blond hair and the same smile that she'd willed to her son.

"Wait," Gail said. "Big Sandy is in the federal system."

"Yes," Venice said.

Jonathan asked, "Did Rocco kill Priscilla on government property? What brings the feebs into a murder case?"

"I'm confused by FBI involvement, too," Venice said. "The murder happened at their home in Louisville, with Giovanni as a witness. The local police opened the investigation, but the FBI took it over within a couple of days."

"Rocco was a goombah?" Boxers guessed.

"Gold sticker for Big Guy," Venice said, shooting her forefinger at him. "He was muscle for the Schillaci crime family."

"Was Pricilla's murder a hit?" Gail asked.

"He never shared a motive with the Louisville cops," Venice said with a smirk.

"You're making your face," Jonathan said. "There's a *but* coming."

"But he did come clean for the FBI."

"Feebs gotta be involved before Rocco can come clean to them," Boxers said.

"Rocco requested their involvement." Her smirk morphed into a smile.

Jonathan felt his patience fraying. A quirk in Mother Hen's personality dictated that she reveal the results of her research in the manner of a Texas Hold'em dealer— never all at once and timed for maximum drama. "Okay, Ven, this is the one and only time I'll play along today. Why did Rocco request to have the FBI involved?"

"Because Kentucky has a death penalty," Venice said.

"So do the feds," Gail said.

"But Rocco had information to share," Venice said. "He made a deal. He'd burn the Schillacis on the condition that he get federal time."

Jonathan scowled as he leaned his elbows into the conference table. "My bullshit bell is clanging. The Kentucky prosecutor isn't going to give a damn about a federal rackets charge. He's gonna want the win. He's gonna want an arm to stick a needle in."

"You're exactly right," Venice said. "Except for the part about the needle. The local prosecutor was fine with life without possibility of parole. Rocco confessed to Priscilla's murder, and with that, the US attorney's office took over. Rocco sang like an opera star, and the FBI hoovered up all corners of the Schillaci operations."

"Don't think I missed that thing you did there,"

Jonathan said through a grin. "Feds. Hoover. As in, J. Edgar. Nicely done."

"Why did he kill his wife?" Gail asked.

"Do we care?" Boxers asked. "I mean, does it matter?"

Jonathan invoked the motto of Faber College: "Knowledge is good."

Venice typed some more, and a police report appeared on the screen. "Young Giovanni testified at the time that his parents hadn't gotten along for months. In his words, *It was something about work.* Rocco later confirmed that Priscilla had been threatening to go to the cops with what she knew of his involvement with the Schillacis. He said he only wanted to cuff her around a little bit—those were his words—but she fell wrong."

"So, it was her fault," Gail said.

"Something like that," Venice said. "The Louisville prosecutor saw it as murder one. But it gets better." More clacking of keys. The screen filled with what appeared to be an advertising brochure for a law firm. Slater, Meeks, and Bardot. "Rocco LoCicero miraculously was able to afford to hire Stanley Meeks, one of the big names, at nine-fifty an hour."

Jonathan knew that was supposed to elicit a response, but he had nothing. He waited for the rest.

"Three months later, after Rocco spilled his guts, care to guess who represented Giuseppe Schillaci?"

"Not really," Jonathan said through a groan.

"Stanley Meeks," Boxers said. Then, to Jonathan, sotto voce: "It goes faster if you play along."

"Exactly," Venice said. "Stanley Meeks."

"So, Meeks is a mob lawyer," Gail said. "Why is that important?"

"I think it's pretty safe to assume that Mr. Meeks did

not arrange Mr. LoCicero's transfer to the federal system," Jonathan said.

"Exactly the opposite, in fact," Venice said. "It's no surprise that Meeks is no longer LoCicero's lawyer."

Jonathan connected the dots aloud. "We're all just guessing here, but it seems reasonable that the Schillaci family was unhappy with their man who turned state's evidence."

"So, they retaliate on his only child," Gail said. "I wish I could say that sounds outrageous and unbelievable."

"It gets better," Venice said. A picture of two men appeared on the big screen. One was LoCicero, and the other was a Latino in an expensive-looking suit. It looked to Jonathan like a surveillance photo taken from a great distance. "I lifted this from the FBI file on LoCicero. The narrative identifies the other man as Paco Gomez, the son of Rolo Gomez, the president and CEO of the Los Muertos cartel."

Jonathan leaned forward, fully engaged. "Now *that's* interesting. Did we know that the Schillaci gang is linked to the cartels?"

"I'm not sure I knew they existed before today," Venice said. "I haven't had a chance to go through the whole file yet, but if they are—assuming they are— that would explain retaliation via fentanyl."

"It's not like the mob to retaliate against family," Gail said.

"But it's very much like the cartels," Jonathan countered. "We've seen them wipe out entire villages in retribution for the actions of one resident. They're animals. And they need to be put down."

"It ain't for lack of trying," Boxers said. "Those

assholes are like worms. You cut 'em in half and they just grow back."

"Nice image, wrong animal," Jonathan said. "They're not worms, they're snakes, and snakes have heads. We just have to find them and cut off a few."

"What are you suggesting?" Venice asked. Her face was a mask of concern.

"I'm suggesting that we turn the tepid fifty-year-old *drug war* into something that looks a lot more like real war."

"We've killed a lot of drug dealers and blown up a lot of shit already," Boxers said. "I'm not saying I object to more of that—hell, it's like my favorite thing to do—but if we haven't made a difference already, what makes you think we can make a difference now?"

"Because we have to," Jonathan said. "We can't afford not to. Especially since we know who the head of the snake is."

Venice rolled her eyes. "Here we go again. *The Darmond crime family.*"

"Damn straight," Jonathan said. "The Darmond crime family. Tony and his step-spawn Nicky Mishin, both of them butt-buddies with the cartels, all of them with a license to print money."

It was a conclusion months in the making as bits and pieces of information glued themselves together to form a smoking gun linked directly to the Oval Office. The case was decidedly circumstantial, but it was incontrovertible. The problem was that every bit of evidence had been derived by Jonathan and his team through extralegal means during extralegal activities, using intelligence-gathering means that they had no right to own.

"So, you're going to assassinate the president?"

Venice asked. Just speaking the words made her look horrified.

"Of course not," Jonathan said. "We're not in the murder business, and we're *certainly* not in the assassination business. There are other ways to bring down a tyrant. We've got all the intel we need to make it happen."

"Wolverine told you herself," Gail said, invoking the call sign for Irene Rivers, director of the FBI. "And more than once. Knowing it's true doesn't mean anything if we can't prove it."

Boxers added, "And even if we roll over and show our throats on the means and methods by which we got the evidence we have, it still wouldn't be admissible because of the ways we got it."

"We'll shift gears, then," Jonathan said. "Through LoCicero, we've got a direct line to the head of the cartel snake. We can take the fight directly to them and come home with the head of that snake in our rucksack."

"I thought you said we're not about murder," Gail said.

"Murder and justice can look a lot alike," Jonathan said. "But they're fundamentally different."

"Unless the justice is being wrought outside the law, and the target is, say, your father."

Boxers cocked his head. "Whose father?"

"Even cartel captains have families," Venice said.

"This is the wrong day to sing that sad song," Jonathan said.

"What's the plan?" Boxers asked.

"I don't have one yet. All I have is a goal, and that is to kill the Los Muertos cartel."

"What good will it do?" Gail asked. Her voice

showed anger. "All that risk, all that blood, and even if you succeed, another one will just rise up in its place."

"She's got a point," Venice said. "The American government is protecting these monsters. The politicians need the talking point and the campaign contributions, the federal law enforcement community needs the budget justification, and every department in the Darmond administration is tasked with making sure the snakes survive. You can't do this alone."

"I don't have to be alone. I'll have Wolverine with me."

"Oh, hold on now, Boss," Boxers said. "She reports to the attorney general, who's been running interference for President Numb Nuts since they were in college. She's got no official pull. And the second she tries to pretend she does, hers will be the head in somebody's pocket."

"It's time for her to step up, then," Jonathan said. "After that last op in Venezuela—when we learned that the cartels had enough clout to get American flag officers to turn off spy satellites to make us blind for a few hours—Wolfie and I had a sit-down. We talked about all the shit we knew but couldn't bring to trial, and we swore to each other that we would scuttle the Darmond administration."

"You *swore*?" Boxers scoffed. "What, like kids taking a blood oath?"

"We shook hands," Jonathan deadpanned. "Like adults trying to make things right."

"What does that even mean?" Gail asked.

"I don't know that yet, either. But I trust that she'll be good to her word."

Jonathan fell silent as he thought it through, and the rest of the team gave him the silent space to work the problem. As the solution formed in his head, he realized that no matter how it went, when they pulled the trigger on this op, there'd be no going back. A clean win was the only viable option.

The old Emerson quote came to his mind: *"When you strike at a king, you must kill him."*

Chapter 3

Rocco LoCicero could tell from the rhythm of the footsteps in the hallway outside his cell that something was wrong. There was a staccato urgency to them instead of the usual disinterested stroll. It wasn't the Shock Team either, on their way to toss a cell or beat up an inmate. If it had been them, there would be a dozen or more and they'd be stomping in step, stormtrooper style. Rocco guessed that these footsteps were driven by the kind of urgency that had less to do with discipline and more to do with delivering a message.

When the steps ended outside his cell door, his blood pressure spiked. The steel door opened on the far side of the barred wall to reveal Corrections Officer Morgan Earp. No shit. Apparently his parents—presumably Mr. and Mrs. Earp—had a sense of humor. Rocco had named him Ratface in his mind. In profile, the guard's weak chin and prominent nose formed a lopsided triangle. To his face, Rocco called him sir, same as every other CO who had the power to make an otherwise lousy life something truly awful. Seeing Ratface wasn't a surprise. But seeing Captain Hite in the same frame was a real shocker.

"People to see you, Rocco," Ratface said in a reedy

voice that Rocco imagined a real rat would have if rats could speak. "They need to talk to you."

"What about?"

"That's not a question I'm allowed to ask. Now turn around, present your hands, and approach the bars. You know the drill."

He did, indeed, know the drill. While he'd been in Big Sandy for only a few days, Rocco was no stranger to prison life—starting with juvie as a kid, followed by three separate, multiyear stretches in various state prisons. This was his first gig for the feds, though, and they seemed damned happy to see him. Serving in isolation might get old, he supposed, but for now, he found it ten times better than general population at the state level. He enjoyed the quiet, giving him lots of time to read, and the food didn't suck. It was a hell of a lot better than taking a needle in the death chamber.

Letting muscle memory be his guide, he laced his fingers behind his back and shuffled to the front of his cell, where Ratface opened the food tray door in the wall of bars, guided Rocco's hands through the opening, and applied the cuffs as gently as was possible under the circumstances.

"How do I rate the VIP service, Captain?" Rocco asked.

"I'm just here to watch," Hite said.

"Am I in trouble?"

"You talk a lot, don't you?" Hite asked.

"Don't mean no harm," Rocco said. "You know how us cons get jumpy when traditions or routines change."

"All the questions will be answered in time," Ratface said.

"You talk a lot, too, come to think of it," Hite said.

With his hands secured, Rocco stood to his full

height and turned to face the bars. At a whisper, he said, "I think the boss is in a bad mood."

"The boss'll lay your head wide open if you don't get your shit together and shut up," Hite snapped.

Rocco remembered the day when threats like that could be considered promises—a day when blood slicks on the floor were common. Now, though, even corrections officers had drunk the snowflake Kool-Aid.

"I am in your hands," Rocco said. "Literally."

Ratface grasped his left biceps while Hite grabbed his right, and together they turned left out of his cell and headed down the expanded metal hallway deck toward the heavy steel door on the far end. On his right, he could see the rest of the third level past the expanded metal grated wall that kept prisoners from taking a header over the edge of the four-foot railing. They walked in silence and, ultimately, in step.

The silence was another break in tradition. For the most part, Ratface exhibited good humor. Not friendly, exactly, but cordial and conversational. The presence of Hite had taken all of that away.

At least, that's what he hoped it was. Truth be told, they seemed to be dreading what lay ahead.

Once at the door, they waited for the lock to buzz, and together they crossed the threshold into an eight-by-eight-foot steel-walled mantrap. Until the door behind them sealed shut, the door in front of them wouldn't open. After ten seconds, the door in front opened, and they entered another cell block. Rocco knew from previous experience that two more of these lay in his future before he got to the uber-secured interview room.

If a Schillaci assassin with a death wish wanted to take him out, this would be the time to do it. Being escorted through the general population section of the prison by guards armed only with sticks and pepper spray, with pinioned arms that kept him from defending himself, Rocco's unprotected gut felt awfully vulnerable to a blade attack.

"What did you do, put them on lockdown in the middle of the day?"

"It seems that you're a very important man to the FBI," Hite said. "Important enough to inconvenience all of these people."

Rocco leaned left and whispered, "I've never met him before, but he does seem very grumpy."

A second later, he found himself being flung by his right arm against the steel wall. He hit hard, his elbows and wrists taking the bulk of the impact. "Shit!"

"Listen to me," Hite snapped. He'd jammed the webbing of his thumb and forefinger into the soft spot under Rocco's jaw and squeezed. "You're not the class clown. You're inmate number one-seven-four-four-three-two. You don't even have a goddamn name. You're a snitch and a murderer, and I don't need to hear you saying a goddamn word. Not good morning and not some funny banter." He let go of Rocco's throat and pulled him away from the wall by the front panel of his shirt. "I hope I've made my opinion clear on this."

The temptation to pop off just to get the last word was nearly overwhelming. It also felt insane.

Six or seven minutes later, they entered the secure interview space of the prison. This was the one prison cliché that Hollywood mostly got right. It was dimly lit—presumably to hide the filth of the place from the outside world—and a steel wall with impossibly thick glass separated him from the visitors' side.

With nobody left in his life to visit him, Rocco's trips to this space had been exclusively to speak with his attorney about his admittedly dim future. Even from those few experiences, he knew that not all of the

chatting slots were created equal. One in particular—
second one from the wall on the right—was so scratched
that it was nearly opaque. Verbal communication happened through a thick wire screen that had been set
into the bulletproof window. If confidentiality were an
issue, you had to press your mouth against the screen
while the party on the other side pressed their ear.

"Booth number four," Ratface said, pointing to one
of the better stations.

Rocco waited while his hands were released and then
recuffed in front, then he walked to the round metal
stool that was bolted to the floor, and sat down.

He'd expected to see Peter Silveri on the other side
of the glass, his teenaged public defender who took
over his case after Stanley Meeks bolted. Instead, he
saw FBI Agent Thomas Caine—the special agent who'd
been managing Rocco's transition to stool pigeon—and
another fed-looking guy whose skin would break if he
cracked a smile. Both men looked dour.

Ratface and Hite had moved in closer than he was
comfortable with.

"You're crowding me a bit, gentlemen," he said, shooting them a look. Then, through the glass, he addressed
his FBI handler. "What can I do for you, Agent Caine?"

"I'm afraid we have bad news for you, Rocco."

Somehow, he knew what was coming. "Is something
wrong with Jonni?"

Caine's stern expression became even more stern.
"I'm afraid there is. He's dead."

Time stopped.

The air grew too thick to breathe.

His vision blurred.

His jaw clenched tight, and he squeezed the edge
of the table as if to throttle the life out of it. "What
happened?" As if he didn't know.

"It was an overdose, Rocco. Fentanyl, we think, but we won't know until after the autopsy."

The image that raced into his mind triggered a chill. His little boy, naked on a steel table, cut open, with strangers' hands removing his organs and weighing them. "No autopsy," he said. "I won't have it."

Caine stared, unmoving and unmoved.

"Say something, you sonofabitch!" Rocco leapt to his feet, and strong hands pushed him back down.

"Keep control," Hite said.

"Is this why you came along on this?" Now it made sense.

"People take bad news in different ways," Ratface said. "We needed to be cautious."

Rocco turned back to Caine. "How the hell did drugs get into Resurrection House? You assholes told me it was a secure facility."

"We don't know that yet," Caine said. "We're working on that."

"I'll tell you exactly how it happened," Rocco said. "Give me two minutes in a room with Giuseppe Schillaci and I guaran–goddamn–tee you I'll have a confession from him."

"Couldn't be him," Caine said. "That's the one person we can tell you with certainty that it was *not*. He's in custody. *Our* custody."

"What, you think he can't run his world from behind bars? I can also tell you that the drugs came from the Los Muertos cartel." He started to stand again, but the hands returned to his shoulders. In that instant, Rocco wanted to kill both Ratface and his boss. He wanted to smash their heads together and watch the brains spill out. He torqued his shoulders to break their grasp. "Keep your mitts off of me."

"Keep it together, Rocco," Hite said, "or you'll find

yourself in the kind of isolation that you *really* won't like."

Hite was not his fight. Not now, anyway. His fight lay with the thugs he'd dedicated his life to.

After all these years of loyalty, who the hell did Schillaci think he was to take this sort of revenge against his *family*? Where were the days of honor? Yeah, Rocco had broken his vow and morphed into a government witness, but that was between him and the Schillaci mob. Families had always been off-limits. Sons do not have to pay for the sins of their fathers. That had *never* been acceptable behavior.

"What are you expecting me to do?" Rocco asked to whoever wanted to answer.

"You needed to know," Caine said. "I wanted you to know."

"Your wife might have told you, instead," the unknown fed said. "You know, if you hadn't murdered her."

Rocco felt Ratface and Hite move closer as Caine whirled on his partner. "That's uncalled for," Caine said.

"Imagine how his wife felt," the asshole replied.

"He's being a dick," Ratface said softly. "You can't do anything about it, so don't let him spin you up."

A thought bloomed in Rocco's head so quickly and clearly that it startled him. If this is how Giuseppe Schilacci wanted to play, then Rocco was going to go all-in.

"Have a seat, Special Agent Caine. I have a story I want to tell you."

"Listen, Rocco, I know you're upset, but I don't have time for bullshit."

"This ain't bullshit, my fed friend. This is friggin' earth-shattering. This is upend-the-world-and-change-everything shit."

Caine sighed theatrically, looked back at his asshole

buddy, and lowered himself onto the padded stool on his side of the glass. "You've got five minutes, Rocco."

"I'm gonna want protection for this one," Rocco said.

"That's not a thing I can negotiate up front. Actually, I can't authorize that at all."

"I can," the asshole said. "Allow me to introduce myself. My name is Stephen Hirsch, and I am supervisory agent in charge of the Louisville field office of the FBI."

"Why are you here?" Rocco asked.

"Because I want to be. That's really all you need to know."

Rocco looked at Caine through the window and saw the eye roll that reassured him. "He *is* the boss," Caine said.

"So, do I get protection or not?"

"You put that cart about three blocks ahead of the horse," Hirsch said. "What is this earth-shattering bit of gossip that you've got to share?"

Rocco shifted his gaze from one man to the other, trying to gauge their trustworthiness. Then there was the matter of Ratface and Hite. "Is there a way we can talk in private?" Rocco asked. He didn't direct the question to any one person because he didn't know who among them had the authority to grant the request.

"This is as private as it gets for you," Hite said.

"You're not here when I speak to my lawyer," Rocco said.

"And you're in leg shackles and a belt when you do that. Plus, these folks ain't your lawyers."

To Caine, Rocco said, "What about you guys? Can you scare up some privacy?"

"You're a murderer, Rocco," Caine said. "And I'm

not talking just about your wife. I'm talking about all those others you've hit. That doesn't come with a lot of favors."

"I know about thousands more murders," Rocco said. To hell with it, he decided that he had to throw out a baited hook to get this thing moving.

Hirsch laughed. "*Thousands*? We don't have *thousands* of open cases, LoCicero."

"That's because you misclassify them. Or whatever the hell you call it. And it's *tens* of thousands."

"The hell are you talking about, Rocco?" Caine said. "You're not making sense."

"Drugs," Rocco said. "All of 'em, from pot to fentanyl. I know where they come from, how they get into the country, and why no one can stop any of it."

Hirsch laughed again, a high-pitched, derisive cackle that seemed overwrought, too loud for the moment. "That's ridiculous."

"Like hell it is. I'm the man who ran the program for Schillaci. I've got evidence that your guys with badges are getting paid to look the other way when the mules cross the border, and that trail goes all the way to the White House. I can set this whole country on its ear. How's that? Is that enough for some consideration?"

Something passed between Caine and Hirsch—a worried glance. Then they turned their attention to Ratface and Hite.

"Yeah," Rocco said. "I've got it all, man. For the price of freedom for *moi*, you can get credit for bringing down—"

"This interview is over," Hirsch said.

Caine stood. "This is outrageous."

Then why does your face show fear? "Why would I lie?" Rocco asked with a chuckle. "I'm offering to confess to more murders here. Why would I do that if it were a lie? On the other hand, why would I do that without guarantees for my own future, if you know what I mean?"

Hirsch pointed a finger through the glass at Captain Hite. "You two. Get him out of here. LoCicero, shut your mouth."

Rocco felt the first slice of fear. "What's wrong with you guys? I'm trying—"

From behind, Hite cleared his throat. "Um, Rocco? I think you need to heed their advice."

"What's happening here?"

"Don't let him talk to anyone," Hirsch instructed. "LoCicero, keep your mouth shut."

Rocco felt hands on his arms.

"You need to get up now, Rocco," Ratface said. He had one arm in his grasp while Hite had the other. "You need to get back to your cell."

Rocco had barely found his feet when he saw Hirsch whip his phone out of his pocket and press a button. Before the call could possibly have had a chance to connect, the two agents were hurrying toward the door.

"Hey, take it easy," Rocco said as the guards' hands clamped down hard and pulled him away from the partition. "Somebody want to tell me what the hell is happening?"

"Please stop talking," Ratface said.

"It's for your own good, Rocco," Hite added.

"What—"

Hite jerked him to a stop, turned him by his arm, and stared him straight in his face, so close that Rocco could smell the coffee on his breath. "Shut. Up." Hite hissed. "You've got to learn to read the room, Rocco. You need to know when the time is right to say something and when the time is right to listen to the people who are trying to keep you from stepping off a cliff."

"What cliff?" The heat of Hite's glare froze the words in Rocco's throat. He didn't have a clue what was going on, but clearly, it was something. And whatever it was, was scary-important. He decided to let it go.

They hadn't taken a dozen steps when Hite's radio crackled, "Captain Hite, Captain Hite. Call control immediately. Captain Hite, call control immediately."

The captain reached to the microphone that was clipped to his epaulette. "This is Hite. I copy."

"I can take him from here," Ratface said. "You'll behave yourself, won't you, Rocco?"

Rocco didn't bother to answer. He didn't think the question required one.

"Straight to his cell," Hite instructed, and then he peeled away, leaving Rocco alone with Ratface.

"Do you understand any of this?" Rocco asked.

Ratface didn't even look at him as he said, "You talk too much."

A point that had been made forcefully and repeatedly. As they retraced their steps through the walkways and mantraps, Rocco replayed the conversation through his head. They weren't upset that his boy had been killed—no, they didn't give a shit about that. If it had been the original team of agents, they would have—

Wait. Why weren't they the original team of agents? What happened to Caine's usual partner, Berkin? They were the lead agents on the Schillaci investigation. They were the ones he'd been negotiating with from the very beginning of all of this. They were the ones who'd arranged safe passage for Giovanni to Resurrection House. Those guys were hard asses, but at least they had hearts.

That interview with Caine and Hirsch had been wrong from the beginning, from their demeanor to their words.

And why would Captain Hite go along in the first place?

Southern Hammer.

That had to be it. These guys who didn't give a shit about Giovanni being poisoned—didn't give a shit about the cartels poisoning thousands of others—suddenly gave a shit about Rocco opening his mouth about the flow of money across the border.

Don't let him talk to anyone. Those were Hirsch's words.

"Did I just sign my own death warrant?" he asked aloud.

"Never implicate a federal agent," Ratface whispered. "They take care of their own."

As they entered the final mantrap and the gates closed, the guard who oversaw that patch of real estate was just placing the black handset of a telephone into its cradle on the wall. "Is this Rocco LoCicero?" he asked.

"The one and only," Rocco said.

The guard never looked Rocco in the face, choosing instead to direct his words to Ratface. "Just got off the phone with Control. There's been a change in plans. He doesn't go back to his cell. Take him directly to the administrative wing."

Rocco's stomach knotted. "Solitary?"

"They said right away," the guard added. "No stops."

"What the hell?" Rocco said. The rise in the pitch of his voice annoyed him. "This isn't right."

"Don't fight it, Rocco," Ratface said. "Orders are orders. I've got to take you there, but I'd prefer not to break any bones to make it happen."

Chapter 4

Harold Standish, special assistant secretary for the Department of Homeland Security, looked up from the statistical report on border interdictions that he was pretending to read. His executive Suburban crawled through the afternoon traffic on the Francis Scott Key Memorial Bridge. The Potomac River flowed below, Arlington, Virginia, lay ahead, and the cesspool that was Washington, DC, grew smaller in the rear windshield.

"You said the Iwo Jima Memorial," Special Agent Missy Dolan noted, glancing at him in the mirror. "Any particular spot?"

"As close as you can get to the statue," he said. "It's an inspiring place to take a walk."

"Yes, sir." The extra two seconds that her gaze remained locked on him showed she questioned the cover story. It was the best he could do on short notice.

He turned the page on the report he wasn't reading and closed his eyes. This meeting was a mistake—a confab that should never happen. He blamed it all on Trevor Mosby, the commissioner for CBP—the US Department of Customs and Border Protection, or more commonly, the Border Patrol. Standish had tried to dodge his incessant phone calls, but Mosby finally ended the game of chicken with a threat to visit the headquarters building on the campus of St. E's—the now defunct mental hospital that had been converted to house one of the largest bureaucracies on the planet.

Standish tried to ignore the irony that St. Elizabeth's not only traced its origins to craziness but had also been built atop—wait for it—a swamp.

If the meeting had been held at HQ, it would have been on the record, easily discoverable by congressional overseers and the media—though he'd stopped worrying about media coverage a long time ago. President Darmond had them sewn securely in his pocket.

Mosby had petitioned for an indoor meeting, but Standish preferred to be outside. He had no reason to believe that he was being surveilled, but neither had any of the other high-end criminals who had started their careers in the political, intelligence, and law enforcement worlds and had been caught in the acts that would send them to prison forever. It paid to be careful. While an outdoor environment made it easier to be overheard by disinterested tourists, the open air made electronic eavesdropping orders of magnitude more difficult. Throw in the massive stone structure that was the Iwo Jima Memorial itself and its effects on radio waves and line-of-sight listening devices, and this was a winning location.

"Do you want to use the emergency lights for special access, sir?"

"Thank you, no, Missy. The mission today is to stay as incognito as possible."

"Yes, sir."

Five minutes later, they'd broken free of DC traffic and had blended in with Northern Virginia traffic. A native West Virginian, Harold Standish had never fully divorced himself from the peace and quiet of the

Mountain State. He'd signed on with the Darmond administration for his friendship with Tony the Man. And, let's be honest, for the money.

Which was why this meeting should never be happening. Trevor Mosby knew that the risk was unreasonable.

Now that he thought about it, maybe Standish should have given Mosby the benefit of the doubt after the first call. If Mosby wanted a face-to-face meeting over an "urgent matter," perhaps Standish should have conceded the urgency from the get-go. He so, so dreaded the paper trails that could one day hang him.

Tourism in the DMV—District-Maryland-Virginia, the trendy new term for the Washington Metropolitan Area—was a seasonal business for the most part, but Standish had noticed that the foot traffic around the Iwo Jima Memorial remained constant throughout the year. Never the top priority for visiting families of four from Ottumwa, it remained a consistent destination for those who considered a visit to nearby Arlington National Cemetery to be a priority.

As Standish's Suburban climbed the final hundred yards of the casual incline that led to the memorial, Missy gave it one last shot. "All civilian vehicles have to unload here," she said. "Are you sure you don't want to—"

"Here is fine, Agent Dolan." By invoking her title instead of her first name, Standish hoped to forestall any follow-up questions.

As they pulled to a stop, Missy opened her door in preparation to come around and open his, but he thumped the arm rest on his door with his fist. "Nope, stay put. Let's draw as little attention as possible."

Standish opened his own door and stepped out into the sunny chill. If he had been his boss—Barton Wills—he might have drawn attention thanks to the countless hours of narcissism logged on the Sunday talking head shows, but Standish had never been recognized in public as far as he knew. And that was fine.

From the moment he started to walk around the memorial, his every move was an ad lib. His conversation with Trevor Mosby had ended with the commissioner saying, "When you get there, I'll find you."

Standish decided to take the man at his word and not demand more detail. At six-two, one ninety-five, with an East African complexion, Mosby was the very opposite of below the radar. The Darmond administration had spared neither electrons nor ink in promoting the former NFL running back as their symbol of inclusion and racial consciousness. Lost on all of them in the satellite tours was the reality that Mosby was very damned smart, and his skin color had nothing to do with it.

As Standish strolled up the incline toward the stone monument, he stopped for a few seconds to take in the famous moment that had been captured forever on film by Joe Rosenthal, in which six Marines raised the American flag over Mount Suribachi in February 1945. A detail lost to most modern Americans was the fact that by the time the battle had ended, three of those Marines had been killed in action.

Harold Standish walked the entire circumference of the memorial, sticking to the walkway, casually scanning faces for the one that belonged to Trevor Mosby. The fact that he hadn't shown up yet pissed him off. He was a busy—

"Pardon me, mister," someone said, pulling on his pants leg. "Can you spare some change for a disabled vet?"

Hite jumped and looked down to see a man dressed in Vietnam-era fatigues sitting in a squatty wheelchair, his legs canted to the side in the way of a longtime paraplegic.

"Any little bit will help."

Hite's initial reaction was to pull away and walk away, until he noted the broad shoulders, coal black skin, and familiar voice.

"Trevor?"

Trevor Mosby used his left forefinger to push the camouflage boonie cap higher on his forehead. "You walked by me once without noticing," he said. "Pretty good disguise, yeah?"

"What the hell?"

"Stay stealthy, Harold," Trevor said. "You said yourself that I'm too identifiable."

Hite smiled. Yeah, it was a great disguise. Disabled people made Americans uncomfortable. Disabled veterans made them feel guilty—*thank you for your service.* But disabled vets from the Vietnam era made them feel *ashamed.* It was the perfect plan to make sure that no one made eye contact.

"Nice threads," Standish said.

"Wheel me around to the back," Trevor said. "Try to look like you don't want to kill a cripple."

That last comment hit home. Standish eased the tension in his face, hoping to make himself look less *pinchy,* as his wife would have called it.

The low handles on the chair made Harold hunch at the shoulders as he pushed Trevor around the statue toward a cleared spot on the back side.

"I'm all ears," Standish said.

"About damn time. Have you heard about the collapse of the LoCicero issue?"

Hite stopped short. Naming names was beyond inappropriate. It was suicidal.

"Keep pushing," Trevor admonished. "Some news can't be soft-pedaled. He's been arrested."

"For killing a family member, if I recall correctly."

"His wife."

They stopped at a low stone wall, where Standish helped himself to one end of a concrete bench. Now, they were eye to eye. "His arrest is a glitch," he said. "An inconvenience. Our Italian friends will find a way—"

"The FBI got to him," Trevor interrupted. "Murder is a state crime with a death penalty. The feds created some kind of racketeering charge to get him transferred to federal custody."

Standish felt his face getting hot as he listened.

"They want to milk him for information to bring down the Schillaci family."

"That would be suicide."

"As opposed to the death penalty," Mosby reminded. "In the federal deal, LoCicero pled down to a manslaughter charge in Kentucky, with a minimal-slash-nonexistent punishment. In return, LoCicero agrees to turn rat. It's a done deal."

Standish's head hurt as he processed the ramifications. Once thugs started selling each other out, the rush for special treatment became a tsunami. "When did this happen?"

"When did you ignore my first phone call?"

Shit.

"They've moved LoCicero to protective custody at Big Sandy. If he plays along and lives through the process, he'll get immunity."

Standish took a deep breath to settle himself. How bad was this, really? There'd never been any indication from the feds that they suspected the Schillaci outfit of their connection with Operation Southern Hammer, the administration's arms-length relationship with the cartels. Hell, the DOJ was hip deep in continuing the flow of narcotics. It was no more in their interests to poke the cartels than it was in the White House's.

Standish lowered his voice to barely a whisper. "LoCicero can do all the damage he needs to do on the Schillaci family without touching Southern Hammer, right? He wouldn't be stupid enough to lock it up with the cartels."

"You'd think so, wouldn't you? It'd be suicide to cross Los Muertos, right?" Mosby said.

"Absolutely. Those guys are freakin' monsters."

"And they're experts in intimidation," Mosby said. "Their smart move would be to kill LoCicero outright or just lay low and trust him to leave Los Muertos out of play."

"Exactly." Standish felt his gut relaxing a bit.

"Yeah, well, not all cartel members are smart," Mosby said. "Paco Gomez—son of Rolo Gomez, a.k.a. Crooked Man, a.k.a. top of the pyramid—apparently had a temper tantrum and sent a warning shot to LoCicero."

"Meaning what?"

"Meaning they killed his son."

Standish felt as if he'd been slapped. "What? Why would they do that?"

"You know, Harold, as much as I wish they'd include me in their decision-making processes, they just refuse to do it. They're assholes that way. After LoCicero got arrested, Paco sent fentanyl-laced candies to the boarding school where the kid was sent after his father's arrest. The son died, a couple of others got sick."

"That doesn't make any sense."

"Do you read the reports I send to you?" Mosby said. "We've known that Paco is Mad Hatter–crazy since he took over operations south of Brownsville. Yet here again, Los Muertos doesn't seek my input on personnel matters."

"You're sure it was him who did it?"

"You mean, did he send me a memo? No. But it has to be him. More importantly, who do you think LoCicero is going to think did it when he finds out the cause of death?"

Standish sat back against the concrete of his bench. This was huge. This was a freaking shitstorm.

Mosby continued, "The executive branch pulled strings to get Giovanni LoCicero placed into Resurrection House in the first place. It's got great security—or so everyone thought—and it set Rocco's mind at ease that at least his son would be safe from mob retaliation when he was ratting them out before disappearing into WitSec for the rest of forever. What would you do if you were Rocco?"

Standish stood, laced his fingers behind his neck, and stretched. "I'd do as much damage to as many people and institutions as I could."

"And if you died in the process, so what, right? Apparently, that's what he's thinking."

Standish sensed that more awful news was on the way. He waited.

Mosby explained, "When a contingent from the FBI went to his prison to break the news of Giovanni's death, he went to suicide mode. He told the agents that he had evidence that could knock the whole country on its ear. Those were his words. He specifically mentioned the flow of narcotics across the border. He said he would name names."

"How do you know this?"

"Because I got a panicked phone call from Steve Hirsch, the supervisory agent in charge."

Standish cocked his head. Something here wasn't right. "Why did he call you? Does a supervisory agent in charge of a field office know about Southern Hammer, too?"

"Yeah, but don't worry about it. He used to run the El Paso office, so he had to be read in. His hands are as dirty and his pockets are as fat as anyone else's. He's not a liability."

Standish sat back down, his hands still clasped behind his neck. "Everybody's a liability," he said, startled that he'd spoken that thought aloud. "What did your guy Hirsch do when he heard the news?"

"He shut it down. He stopped the interview, had LoCicero moved to administrative custody."

"What does that mean?"

"Solitary."

"Can he do that?"

Mosby bobbled his head. "Not on his own, no. But I made a call to people who answer their phones. The top of the FBI talked to the top of the Bureau of Prisons, and stuff happened."

Standish's head whipped around. "Director Rivers?"

"Oh, hell no. The Girl Scout? Are you kidding me? No, it was one of her deputies. Dylan Bishop."

That was a good choice, Standish thought. As a handpicked political appointee, his reporting chain to Irene Rivers was at best dotted-line. If Standish wasn't mistaken, Assistant Director Bishop was a longtime family friend of the Darmond family and a former business partner with Nicholas Mishin, the president's stepson. As far as Standish knew, Bishop's main contribution to Southern Hammer had been to use the powers of his office to play the national security card to shut down any talk on social media platforms that hinted of corruption within the administration. With the rumors quashed at birth, the media gave itself reason not to report on stories that might make their chosen incumbent look bad.

Standish closed his eyes, hoping to somehow make it all go away. There were way too many people involved in Southern Hammer, yet the program was growing so quickly and making so much money, he didn't know that there was a way to shut it down. "What's the plan from here?"

"You tell me," Mosby said. "This shit is at best stabilized right now. LoCicero can't talk to anyone, and no one can talk to him. But that can't last forever."

"It can't last for *hours*," Standish countered. "The other agents are going to want to build their case around Schillaci. They're not going to sit idly while LoCicero hides in solitary."

Mosby snapped his fingers. "There it is," he said. "How well do you know Dylan Bishop?"

Standish wobbled his hand. "We've crossed paths a few times. Under the circumstances, we try not to spend a lot of time in the same frame, if you know what I mean."

"Do you know him well enough to get him to transfer the agents off of his case?"

"I have no idea how that works," Standish said. But he did have a related thought. While he imagined it would be difficult to transfer agents off the Schillaci case, there was no reason he could think of why Assistant Director Bishop couldn't dispatch a reliable agent or two to figure out what, exactly, LoCicero might be willing to share.

Or what might be necessary to keep him from sharing at all.

Chapter 5

Senator Roland Jackson of West Virginia was in a tough spot. During his decades in the Upper Chamber, the political views of his state's population had spun one hundred eighty degrees while his rhetoric had remained rooted in the old ways that had led to his election back in the day. He'd survived four terms on smiles, hearty handshakes, and a war chest larger than a Third World economy. Now, however, he was a member of a party that had shifted wildly away from the priorities of his constituency, leaving him stuck with the wrong letter in the parentheses after his name. As an election loomed in the all-too-near future, he was desperate for damage control, and somehow, he'd determined Irene Rivers to be an ally.

She was not, and she was enjoying the display of senatorial groveling.

"I really need your support on this police bill, Irene," he said as he burdened a cold-boiled shrimp the size of a small lobster with a wad of cocktail sauce and dangled it over the white tablecloth. "Actually, more than your support, I need your endorsement." He scarfed the entire shrimp in a single bite.

Irene pulled at her grilled halibut with the tines of her fish fork. "Doesn't that sauce burn your sinuses?"

This was a not a conversation she wanted to have in a public place, and she couldn't figure out Jackson's reason for conducting it there. She knew there was an angle because that was the way he rolled. If she waited long enough, he'd reveal it.

"I love this place," Jackson said around the mouthful. "Best seafood in DC."

He needed to get around more.

"Don't forget, Reeny, I voted for your confirmation back in the day."

Reeny? What the hell? "I remember," she said. "You helped me squeak by with a unanimous vote."

"It ain't about the number, and you know it. It's the fact of unanimity. It only takes one vote to deny that bragging right."

"Of course. How rude of me not to thank you."

"I'm sensing some sarcasm, Reeny. What's going on in that pretty little brain?"

Irene ate her bite of halibut. It was damn good, but nowhere near the best in the city. "If I'm being honest, Roly-Poly, I'm thinking about shooting you in the face if you ever call me Reeny again."

Jackson threw his head back and guffawed at the ceiling. It was too loud for the room and drew attention that Irene didn't want. "Touché, Madam Director. Touché. Roly-Poly, indeed." He dipped another shrimp and stuffed it down his gullet.

"To your point, Senator, you know that I don't endorse candidates for head custodian, let alone United States senator."

"A nod from you would go a long way. Hell, even a mention of my name would go a long way."

"You mean, do a campaign ad."

"No, no. Nothing like that. But you get a lot of airtime

on the various networks. Just a quick mention that I was
doing a good job would be a nice step."

Okay, she'd had more of the bullshit than she could
handle. He'd picked this fight, so the consequences
were all on him. "Why on earth would I do that, Senator? Do you think that people weren't listening when
you toured the country campaigning to abolish police
departments? I can't undo that for you. Nor can I undo
your unfathomable desire to inflict homelessness and
poverty on the already impoverished constituents in the
coal industry that's more or less headquartered in your
state."

"You're exaggerating, Irene."

"If you think that to be the case, so be it," she said.
She didn't play the card that Jackson didn't know she
had. When Tony Darmond was running for reelection,
Jackson was still two years out from having to face his
own constituents at the ballot box. On the promise of
an ambassadorship to the Court of St. James, he'd fallen
in with Darmond's political drumbeat of hating everything that America had stood for for two centuries and
willingly screwed over the residents of his own back-
yard. Irene knew because even senators have to endure
background checks for appointments at that level.

When Darmond's promise turned out to be a lie—as
most of his promises turned out to be such—Jackson
was left with a damning voting record and no political
base.

"Let's be honest, Roland. We've known each other
for a long, long time. The very reason you think a nod
from me would be a boon to you is because I've never
taken a political stance publicly and, as a result, people
still trust me."

"Bullshit they trust you. The FBI has turned into a
steaming pile of betrayal under your leadership."

Irene smiled as she turned her attention back to her meal. "You have an interesting way of currying favor."

"I just don't want you climbing up on your high horse. We all have skeletons in our closets after this much time in the arena."

Irene gritted her teeth, upset at herself for letting Jackson's gratuitous shot get under her skin. The issues with the Bureau—the leaks, the lies, the disregard for the crimes of the elite—while occurring on her watch, had little to do with her leadership. None, if you could ignore the cliché of where the proverbial buck stopped. The attorney general, members of Congress, and the president himself had done everything they could to stymie her efforts to restore honor to the federal government. When she refused to let the FBI spy on the president's enemies, Darmond turned to his appointees at CIA and NSA. During his brief time in office, POTUS had even been able to turn institutions like the Joint Chiefs of Staff into political mouthpieces.

Sensing no upside to a response, she decided not to rise to the bait of the high horse bullshit. Her biggest challenge now was to figure out a way to break this meeting off.

"You know, Irene, I'm a better friend than I am an enemy."

Irene let the words settle in her mind to make sure she'd heard them right. She gently placed her fork on her plate and folded her hands on the table. "It takes a certain moxie to threaten the director of the FBI."

"No threats, just reality. The US government is a big beast, and not everyone can get the budget approval they'd like. As an agency head, I don't think you want to get on the wrong side of decision makers."

Irene offered a tight-lipped, humorless smile. "It's

hard to be fearful of a budgetary process that hasn't produced a real budget in what—six years? Omnibus spending bills are just expressions of cowardice."

Her words darkened Jackson's expression. "I sense that I'm wasting my time here," he said. "I ask for a simple favor, and you insult me."

"The favor you ask is anything but simple," Irene said. "As the director of the FBI, I cannot pick political favorites. The perception would be one of me putting my thumb on the scales of justice. If this agency were perceived to favor one political party over the other, the American people's belief in a fair and just government would evaporate."

"I'm not asking you to make a speech, Irene. I'm asking you to seed a few good words."

Irene breathed deeply to settle her thoughts. "Look, Senator Jackson. Roland. Personally, I think you're a nice guy. I'll be happy to say good words about your record so long as the words are true. If, for example, you were to renounce your efforts to slash funding for police and your demonization of police officers, I'd sing your praises to the high heavens. As it is, I find your voting record to be abhorrent, and I'd find it difficult to publicly praise you for a good haircut. Which you need, by the way."

Jackson reflexively smoothed his coiffure with both palms. "So long as you don't take sides," he scoffed.

"This is a one-on-one scolding," Irene said. "I would never say such things in public."

Beyond and behind Jackson's head, back by the door that was flanked by her security detail, Irene saw a familiar face arrive at the maître d' station. Jonathan Grave made eye contact and gave a little wave that seemed to upset her detail. While the volume remained low, the body language said that Digger was giving them the hard time that was his custom.

Jackson shifted his attention back to his meal. "The next course is going to be awkward."

"It's not, actually," Irene said. "I have to go."

Jackson followed her eyeline to the door. "Is there a problem?"

"Probably." She stood and placed her napkin on her chair. "Thanks for lunch."

"Your bodyguards can handle—"

She was done with him. Soothing her pink blazer to rid it of wrinkles or crumbs, she weaved through the tables filled with other noontime diners and made her way to the front.

It was rare for a five-minute period to pass in Rolo Gomez's life without him cursing himself for that day in his youth when he took the dare that left him a cripple. The horse was too big and too ornery to be ridden even by an adult, let alone a thirteen-year-old who hadn't yet had his growth spurt. The fear when they told him and his parents that he had broken his back was that he'd be paralyzed, but that fear never materialized. Now, as he approached his seventieth trip around the sun, he wondered if paralysis might not have been a blessing.

The pain had always been present, had always been a factor in his life, but he'd been able to deal with it until the past two decades, as arthritis exacerbated the pain of bulged and dislocated disks, leaving him in a state of perpetual discomfort. Painkillers helped him through the nights, but during the day, he needed to

keep his head clear to deal with the controlled madness
that was his business.

He knew that behind his back, his friends and enemies
alike referred to him as Hombre Torcido—the Crooked
Man—but never to his face. Never twice, to be sure. To
do so would be to learn why those who feared him
whispered his name as El Diablo, the devil.

Over the past ten years—the years of his greatest
agonies—Rolo had built Los Muertos from one low-
level, hand-to-mouth dealer in street narcotics to a
multibillion-dollar multinational conglomerate whose
products were pleasure and fear. The world in general
possessed an unslakable thirst for narcotics and sex,
and Los Muertos provided both in many different
forms. He'd single-handedly perfected the supply chain
logistics of shepherding dope from the growing fields
in Colombia and Venezuela, through the processing
operations here in Mexico, outside Reynosa, and on
through the wide-open borders of the United States.

Gone were the days when the American DEA would
even pretend to care about the open spigot of drugs.
That was old news, a business that had been thriving
for generations. What surprised Rolo was the American market for boys and girls to serve as sex slaves.
There'd been a time when Americans would have declared war to prevent such privations, but times change,
and when they do, more opportunities arrive to make
money. The explosion of pornography in all of its forms
had generated a demand for flesh-and-blood services
that generated so much cash that the American political class could not help but fall in line.

Never again would Rolo wonder why American
politicians would borrow and spend millions of dollars
for a Senate seat that paid only $174,000 per year. In

addition to the perks and the guaranteed millions to be made on K Street when their terms were finished, they got to live fat off their incentives to look the other way.

During their election cycles, when federal-level politicians in Washington needed some bragging points, Rolo Gomez would provide intel to the American *federales*, who could make arrests with network television crews in attendance. None of the arrests affected Rolo's profits, of course. In fact, the elimination of competitors at the hands of American agents only served to strengthen Rolo's monopoly.

He worried, though, about the influx of Chinese fentanyl into the business model. With over one hundred thousand Americans killed every year from fentanyl poisoning, it wouldn't be long before the citizenry of the United States realized that the Chinese Communists were deploying weapons of mass destruction as part of an ongoing war that Ma and Pa Mainstreet were not yet aware of. The political class and the once-vaunted Fourth Estate made sure that voice was never given to the inconvenient truths. Together, the American establishment had made even a hint of the obvious interference by foreign actors a declaration of racism, a label that ruined careers and led to universal shunning and shaming.

Even the most heroic defenders of what had once been the American way of life would rather remain silent than be vilified on social media platforms.

Who would have dreamed ten years ago that it would be such an easy task to topple a giant?

As the thought passed through his mind, he checked himself. It never paid to become complacent. A major upset in Washington could change many things. It was always possible that an outsider—a Boy Scout—could rise to power and stay there long enough to learn how the system had been working for so long and then determine to change things. Once the decision to change was made, along with a sweeping upheaval in personnel, not only would the illicit trade pact known as Southern Hammer fall apart, but many people also would be bound for prison.

The continuing bloodshed had always been troublesome to Rolo. In the early days, it was necessary to flood the gutters with blood to seal his control over the marketplace. His rivals would not surrender peacefully, and their murders prompted the murders of their families so that generational blood feuds could be stanched before they began. And, periodically, as younger, healthier caballeros made the mistake of challenging Rolo's authority, spectacles had to be made of them.

Police and soldiers who tried to interfere needed to be dealt with as publicly and horrifically as possible. It would not be enough to poison such people in their beds, or even to fire a bullet through their brains. They needed to be humiliated and tortured, their naked dismembered bodies hung high so that their families would have to cut them down and pick up their pieces.

Power was fragile, and without fear, there could be no power. When violence came to Los Muertos, it needed to be returned in kind tenfold. A hundredfold. Such retaliation always worked.

Almost always worked.

Over the past months and years, Rolo's operations had been repeatedly terrorized by *los gringos yanquis*, a small team of American soldiers—Jonathan Grave and the giant Dutchman, Brian Van de Muelebroecke— who had cost Rolo millions of dollars in product and equipment and who had killed some of the best leaders of Los Muertos.

Those attacks had infuriated Rolo and his lieutenants, leading his hotheaded son, Paco, to launch assassination squads to the United States to kill the American terrorists. But the Americans had proven to be indestructible. On their home soil in America, there was only so much retribution that could be meted out.

And then the Americans had returned to obliterate a joint operation between Los Muertos and the Russian government to install ballistic missiles on Three Sisters Island off the coast of Venezuela. There would be no repairing or replacing those installations. The Russians insisted that the Three Sisters attack was the work of the Central Intelligence Agency, but Rolo's sources told him otherwise. The Darmond administration made sure that spy satellites were turned off to facilitate the movement of the ballistic missiles into their launch bunkers. It made no sense for them to likewise dispatch a commando team to destroy them.

No, the Three Sisters incident had to be the work of *los gringos yanquis*.

And *los gringos yanquis* would soon be forced to pay the price.

A knock on the door brought Rolo out of his head and back into the present. "Come."

His favorite girl, Angelina—his trusted girl—opened the door. "Excuse me," she said. "Your son is here. Paco."

Ah, yes. Paco, the idiot son whom he loved too much to kill for his incompetence. "Have him wait in the sitting room," Rolo said. "I will join him in a moment."

"Do you not want him to—"

"I will join him in the sitting room in a moment," Rolo repeated. When the door closed again, Rolo began the arduous process of rising to his feet. With his cane in his right hand, he pressed himself up with his left until he found the balance point. He wavered a few seconds until he was comfortable and stable, and then he took his first step forward. As his vertebrae shifted, lightning bolts of pain shot through his buttocks and down the backs of his legs, all the way to his heels. This was the transition that he wanted no one ever to see. He moved like a crippled old man—because he *was* a crippled old man—but his sense of dignity required that he hide the most obvious evidence of his disabilities from others. More than that, his very *survival* depended on that.

Hombre Torcido, indeed. The crooked man whose back could never straighten, who walked as if perpetually examining his shoes.

The crooked man who'd best never be crossed.

Rancho de Oro—the Golden Ranch, Rolo's expansive hacienda—was designed in the image of a hotel he'd stayed at in Marathon, Texas, not far from the northern edge of Big Bend National Park. What would have been a long stretch of single-story bungalows for travelers here served as housing for his staff and bodyguards. They stretched in parallel lines, perpendicular to the main house, which itself was nestled two kilometers from the nearest road, surrounded by stone walls around the entire three thousand acre estate. He raised his own cattle and sheep and goats—or, more accurately, he had staff who did such things. Video and electronic sensors littered the entirety of the property as insurance against attackers. He navigated his estate via Razor ATVs, and on the rare occasion when he left the property altogether, his motorcade rivaled that of the president of Mexico.

Paco sat on a sofa with his back facing Rolo's office, staring out at the vast expanse of desert and expensive landscaping. In the far distance, Alejandra, the lead housekeeper, was using a long wand to sweep the bottom of the pool, her body clad immodestly in a bikini so tiny as to qualify as no bathing suit at all.

"I see you are enjoying the view," Rolo said.

Paco turned in his seat and stood. "Hello, Papa." As usual, Paco wore expensive clothes of a brand Rolo wouldn't recognize even if he'd been told. His silk shirt hung open to his muscular abdomen, and a gold crucifix dangled from a chain at his chest. His two-toned laceless shoes glistened in the light through the window, and Rolo had no doubt that his feckless progeny had spent hundreds if not thousands of dollars for them.

"You shouldn't sit with your back to the room," Rolo admonished him. "Your enemies can sneak up on you."

Paco smiled. "I'm sure I have no enemies here."

"We all have enemies, son. I have many, and therefore so do you. As I get older and our *friends* see opportunity, they may easily become your enemies, as well." Rolo leaned heavily on his cane as he moved around the overstuffed leather sofa and eased into a padded rocker designed specifically to ease the pressure points on his mangled back.

Paco seemed confused as to whether or not he should help his father settle into his chair.

"I'm fine, I'm fine," Rolo said. "Sit."

Paco sat back into the sofa but chose a spot close to his father. "The message you sent sounded urgent," he said. "I was concerned about you."

"As I was concerned about you," Rolo said. "I've been troubled as I try to figure out how someone such as you—raised in affluence, gifted with the finest in education—could be so immensely stupid."

Paco's back straightened as his smile faltered. "Be careful, Papa," he said. "I am not a boy anymore. I have allies of my own."

"All of whom are terrified of me," Rolo said. "What possessed you to send poisoned candies to an orphanage?"

Paco recoiled from the question. "How did you know about that?"

"So, you confirm that you did."

"It had to be done. Rocco LoCicero, our go-between with American authorities—"

"Was arrested," Rolo interrupted. "Yes, I know. But how does that explain your stupidity?"

Paco's face reddened. "There was nothing stupid about it, Papa. He had to be warned to remain silent about our arrangements down here. I believe Señor Schillaci is pleased that I did so."

"You believe he is happy that you killed a child?"

"The intent was not to kill, Papa. Merely to—"

"What difference do your intentions make when you kill the child of the man whose silence you are trying to enforce?"

Paco waved the words away. "Accidents happen."

Rolo slapped the wooden arm of his rocker and bellowed, "That was not an accident! That was an act of supreme carelessness!"

"Papa, we cannot risk having someone like Rocco LoCicero exposing the details—"

"The details of our arrangements with the American administration in Washington? You have guaranteed exactly that," Rolo said. "My sources tell me that LoCicero has already offered to expose everything as part of his plea agreement with the federal prosecutors."

"Then he has to be dealt with," Paco said. His tone was businesslike, devoid of emotion.

"You speak of murder as if it were nothing," Rolo said.

"We have built an entire industry on murder, Papa."

"We built that industry on strategic moves, Paco. Not on cold-blooded murder."

"This is not the first time I have killed a child," Paco reminded him. "Would you like to hear the list of children you have *ordered* me to kill?"

"Always for a purpose! Always for *my* purposes. Young Giovanni was the only thing in Rocco LoCicero's life that was worth anything to him anymore. *Preserving* the boy's life was the only smart move. By killing him, you *created* the need to kill LoCicero, only now he is in prison."

"We have people working in every prison in North and South America," Paco said with a dismissive wave. "You are making too much out of this."

"And you are being far too dismissive." Rolo closed his eyes and forced three calming breaths to settle himself down.

"Are you okay, Papa?"

"Hush!" Rolo needed only a few seconds of silence to push his boiling anger back down into his gut where it belonged. Nothing good ever happened when acting out of anger. When his pulse had slowed to a less lethal rate, he asked, "What do you know about the school where you sent your toxic gift?"

Paco's face seemed to fold into itself as he considered the question for what was clearly the first time. "It was a school," he said with a shrug. "And an orphanage, I believe."

"Does the name, Jonathan Grave, mean anything to you?"

That question scored. "Of course," Paco said. "He is the leader of the American mercenaries you refuse to kill, even as he labors to kill us and destroy our business."

The sheer weight of the information that Paco didn't know, either because he was too stupid to remember or because Rolo had left him out of the loop, would sink an aircraft carrier. The American terrorists who had been wreaking havoc over Los Muertos over the past years had never had a name until very recently, when one of Rolo's associates snatched a fourteen-year-old boy off the streets of El Paso and spirited him into Mexico as a means of extorting money from the boy's parents. By pure coincidence, as Rolo understood the events that transpired, the boy revealed the name of the American mercenary leader to be a billionaire named Jonathan Grave.

But even then, the man was little more than a name. Rolo had passed the intel on to his contacts in Washington, but they were unable to find useful information on the man beyond the fact that he'd retired from the US Army some time ago and that he now ran a private detective agency out of a small town in Virginia.

Rolo explained, "The school you sent the poison to is named Resurrection House."

"That sounds familiar."

"It is owned by Jonathan Grave. He is the man who funds everything at the school."

Paco smiled. "Even better," he said. "He can suffer as well. While you cannot kill the man, perhaps I can help kill what's important to him. That was not my intent, but I am pleased that it happened."

"You don't understand, Paco. This man will come for us again. If LoCicero reveals everything he knows, Jonathan Grave and his mercenaries will have all the details they need to destroy us."

Paco cocked his head like a curious puppy. "What has happened to you, Papa? When did you become a weak and frightened man? I remember a time when you would never speak that way. I remember a time when you would be taking the fight *to* your enemies, not trembling and hiding away from them. We can kill this Jonathan Grave just as easily as we can kill Rocco LoCicero."

"No, Paco, you cannot. I have tried, as others have tried. These mercenaries are demons, unstoppable."

"Surely, our friends in Washington can do something to help."

"I have reached out, and no, they cannot." Rolo didn't think this was the time to mention the obvious, but he imagined there was concern over the questions that would be triggered in the American government if too much of an effort were made to stop the mercenaries. Why, for example, would it be considered a bad thing to eliminate the Los Muertos cartel? Wasn't that what they'd been proclaiming to be their goal for these many years?

"Then I will," Paco said. "I have just the right contacts. They are good and they are fast."

"No," Rolo commanded. "Absolutely not, and you must not argue with me on this point. The FBI will take care of LoCicero when the time comes. As for Jonathan Grave, they have people watching him, as well."

Paco made a noise that sounded like *piff*, and he raised his arms to his sides. "Then we have nothing to worry about. Everything will be taken care of."

"You are not understanding the reason I summoned you," Rolo said, wincing as he leaned forward in his chair. "None of this would have been necessary if you had not been so impulsive. You may be my son, Paco, but you have enemies who watch carefully and wait for moments like this. You do not want to be someone else's strategic target for killing."

Paco remained unmoved. Rolo changed the subject. "Are we prepared for the council meeting?" he asked. Once per month, Rolo summoned his senior lieutenants to the hacienda to discuss their various lines of business. He called the assembled group his council because they seemed to like the name.

"As ready as we always are," Paco said. "The rooms will be ready for them, and we will have . . . toys for them to play with in the schoolhouse." He winked at the last part.

The toys, of course, were the newest crop of youngsters who'd been snatched from roadsides and bars along the border, and the schoolhouse was actually a collection of adobe structures that served as a brothel. One way to assure that the council members arrived on time was to provide them with evening entertainment. Once the council meeting concluded, those whores would be shipped across various borders, where they would be delivered in fulfillment of standing orders that had already been placed and paid for.

"Do we have enough whores to serve them?" Rolo asked.

"We will," Paco said. "We still have a couple of days."

"Very well," Rolo said. He did not enjoy speaking of the human trafficking business. "You can go now."

Paco didn't move, but rather continued to watch his father.

"What is it?" Rolo asked.

"This business with LoCicero," Paco said. "It will be taken care of."

Chapter 6

Irene made a subtle slashing motion with her hand as she approached her security detail at the door to the restaurant. "He's cleared," she said.

"He's got a firearm, ma'am," one of the bodyguard agents said.

"On the plus side," Digger said, "I didn't use it. Howya doin', Madam Director?"

Irene felt heat rise in her face. This was not the way things were to be done. The nature of their relationship was such that Jonathan was never to make direct contact with her and they were never to be seen together except under the most controlled circumstances.

"I'm fine, Agent Bonner. What brings you here?" Some time ago, Irene had issued ersatz Bureau credentials to Digger and his team so that they could more effectively help her with an issue she needed to resolve. The creds came with a complete and entirely fictitious background for each of them.

Jonathan smiled when she used his covert name. "An urgent matter, I'm afraid. It cannot wait." As usual, his expression showed an amused edge, as if he were about to tell a joke but deciding against it. When his impossibly blue eyes flashed, they made Irene's heart skip. Not that they shared a romance, but there was no denying his virility. Or his lethality, when it came to that.

"All right, then," Irene said. "Let's go to my vehicle and chat."

"I'd prefer that we go to mine," Jonathan said. He cast a decidedly unsubtle glance at her security detail.

She wished that she could say that his concerns about eavesdroppers were uncalled for, but such was not the case. In fact, she had a history of disloyal agents serving as her bodyguards. Disloyalty among sworn agents and civil servants in general had become a distressing new normal.

Every detail of this meeting screamed that something had gone terribly wrong. Digger Grave was not one to create drama where it wasn't necessary. If he needed that level of privacy, then she'd respect the request.

"Can we sit, or do we need to drive?" she asked.

"Let's drive," Jonathan said. "Have your guys follow. I promise I won't try to lose them." He sold that last part with a smile.

Irene relayed the instructions to her detail and ignored their obvious displeasure. In their defense, she was directing them to do the very thing that they were to keep her from doing, but in a sense that made it a little bit more enjoyable.

They walked in silence as they passed out of the restaurant and through the hotel lobby toward the doorway that separated the peace of the lush interior from the noise of the city beyond. The doorman seemed to be expecting them and opened the door as they approached.

"We kept your vehicle waiting for you, sir," the doorman said.

Jonathan slipped the man a folded bill, thanked him,

and headed toward a gleaming sleek black sports car with red highlights. "Is that a *Corvette*?" Irene gasped.

"Yes, it is."

"You always said they looked like penises. I never in a million years—"

"This is a Z06," Jonathan said, as if that solved the hypocrisy. "Zero to sixty in two point six seconds. This is not a Stingray. Though to be honest, they're less like penises, too, these days."

The teenager who'd been standing sentry at the car handed Jonathan the keys and earned himself a stealthy tip. "Please take care of the lady," Jonathan said.

The teenager opened the passenger side door and reached out to help Irene lower herself into the world of leather. "I'm okay," she said. "But thank you."

The engine roared to life, and seconds later, they were easing out into city traffic.

"Wait for my detail," Irene said.

"In this traffic, a three-minute head start might gain us all of two blocks. We need to talk."

There it was again—his tell that something had gone terribly awry. Their meetings always started with friendly banter. This time, he went right for the serious stuff. She waited for it.

"Remember a few weeks ago when you shook my hand and we swore that we were going to flush the toilet that is Washington?"

Those weren't quite the words that she remembered, but his version captured the spirit of the conversation. "I do," she said.

"Good. Because the time has come. One of the kids at RezHouse was murdered yesterday."

"Oh, my God. What happened?"

"Fentanyl happened. Twelve years old, and he's dead because someone sent poison masquerading as candy."

"That's terrible," she said. And she meant it. But . . . "What does that have to do with me?"

"The young victim was Giovanni LoCicero. You have his father in custody, and I want to go talk to him."

"Who's his father?"

"Rocco LoCicero. He's a mobster."

In a heartbeat, she understood where Digger was going with this. "You think he can lead you to the cartels."

"That's exactly right."

"And you think we're not competent enough to get that information ourselves?"

Digger flipped his turn signal and drifted into the left lane. If Irene read his intentions correctly, he was plotting a course out of the District and into Virginia via the Key Bridge. "It's not a matter of competence, Wolfie. It's about willingness."

"I don't follow."

"Of course you do. You're going to squeeze LoCicero for his ties to the Schillaci family, and then you're going to cut him loose with a sweet WitSec retirement."

Irene couldn't believe what she was hearing. Every word that Digger just spoke was highly classified information. "I don't know what you're talking about."

"Don't, Wolfie. Not today. Not for this. You know I know tons of shit that you don't want me to know. I always have, and it's always bugged you. Just don't bullshit me."

"No one is supposed to know about Rocco LoCicero turning state's evidence."

"Well, there you go. I do and I don't care. The mob means nothing to me. I want to get the cartels, and your guy has the contacts."

"If he's got information on the cartels, we'll get it from him," Irene said.

"Why would you?" Digger didn't bother to look at her as he asked the question.

Irene was tired of his bullshit. "Dig, if you've got a speech in your head, go ahead and deliver it."

He moved his hands to ten-and-two on the steering wheel and took a deep breath. "I'm trying to figure out which approach will work best," he said. "Ah, screw it. I go for all of them. First, the FBI doesn't give a shit about a murder in a small town like Fisherman's Cove. Because it won't be a big story, you can keep the back-lash down, so the media won't pursue it for more than a day or two. That makes the case not important. Certainly not as important as flipping a mobster."

Irene felt anger rising. "Now wait a second, Dig—"

"Second, the murder happened on private property, making it not a federal crime to begin with. You have no real jurisdiction. You have the one witness who could make the case for the local constabulary, but you're going to shelter him so that he won't get spooked and clam up on you."

Irene opened her mouth to object, but Digger was on a roll and wouldn't let her.

"Don't object, Madam Director, because you've already done it. You're already sheltering Rocco from prosecution for murdering his wife."

"How can you know this?"

"Thanks for confirming," Jonathan said. "And as spot-on accurate as all of the above is, it's totally trumped by what we—you and I—know the truth to be. If you open a line of questioning about the cartels, your boss will cut the legs right out from under you. The AG knows that all roads lead to the Darmond crime family, as Big Guy likes to call them. They're not going to let that information leak out. If LoCicero even tries, you know as well as I do that the chances of him living to see the next sunrise will be next to zero."

The level of vitriol stunned her. "Good God, Digger, how corrupt do you think the government is?"

"We've *talked* about this, Irene. Are you seriously going to tell me that your guys don't whack people in prison? Really? What about the pedophile with his private island and steaming black book? Would you like me to show you the evidence we have on that?"

Irene fell silent. She had nothing to do with that hit, but she was made aware of it immediately after the fact.

"The order came directly from the attorney general, am I right?" Jonathan said.

Holy shit.

"And you guys used assets arranged through the Agency."

He nailed it squarely on the head. Every detail.

"Don't look so stunned, Wolfie. Mother Hen's research skills know no bounds. Plus, you know the kinds of people I hang out with. The kind of people I know. If you've used them, then there's a very good chance that I know about it."

Irene didn't know what to say. Her head was a jumble of thoughts and images triggered by Digger's words. There was no possible way for him to know the things he was talking about. Yet, clearly, he did.

Jonathan navigated the confusing spiderweb of turns and lane changes to put them on Interstate 66 on the way to Falls Church and points west. Irene thought she should object but couldn't figure out why. *How the hell could he know?*

"Wolfie, look," Digger said. "This is a once in a life-time chance to get these guys. LoCicero has it all. Or, if he doesn't have it all, he has most of it. If I can talk with him, he can put us on the right track that will lead to pulling to cork out of the cartel's bottle."

"I suppose you want to do this as Special Agent Neil Bonner."

"I don't know of another way to get inside."

"But you're not a real agent, Dig. None of the evidence you uncover can be used in court."

"I don't give a shit about court. I give a shit about justice. All I need is names. I can take it from there."

"To do what?" Irene heard the squeak in her voice, and it annoyed her. "You going to go kill people and blow things up? Is that your solution?"

Jonathan fell quiet before saying, "Don't ask questions you're not sure you want the answers to."

That was all the answer she needed. Jonathan Grave was not an assassin in the sense that you could hire him to kill a designated target, but she knew from personal experience that he was very good at bringing justice to victims of evil. And the cartels were evil.

"The thing is, Wolfie," he continued, "we both know where the evidence is going to take me. Take us. This is going all the way to the White House. I'll pass along to you what I learn, but from there, it's up to you to figure out the legal pathways."

"The administration won't allow it. They'll kill to protect their secrets. If I get my hands on the kind of evidence you're talking about—assuming there's a way for me to legitimize it—I'm going to have to take it to a grand jury, and investigations at this level have to be approved by the attorney general, who, in this case, is likely to be part of the conspiracy."

"C'mon, Wolfie, think outside the box. There has to be a way."

"There used to be one!" she said, nearly shouting. "Until this administration, the rule of law was real. The courts and the workers who swore to protect and defend the Constitution of the United States worked hard to be apolitical. Now, every senior bureaucrat has his thumb on the scales. I can't undo all of that by myself."

"You're not alone," Jonathan said. "I've got your back."

"You're in the stealth business," Irene said. "You can't stay in the shadows *and* have my back at the same time."

"Of course I can. I've been protecting people from the shadows my whole life."

"You can't shoot up the Department of Justice."

Jonathan's shoulders sagged. "I know you really think more of me than that."

"Digger, I've got nothing but admiration and good thoughts about all that you do. As annoying and difficult as you can be sometimes, you're very good at your job. But meaning no disrespect, the waters I swim in are deeper than you can imagine."

He smiled and navigated the exit into Ballston, a monument to tall steel and concrete.

"Let's get back to my original request," Jonathan said. "I want access to Rocco LoCicero. I want to have a chat and maybe convince him to come clean about the business cycle of the cartels. I need to have a target and a larger understanding."

"To what end?"

"I told you about asking questions."

"It so happens that I want to know the answer to this one."

Jonathan seemed to assess his options. "Am I speaking to Irene Rivers, longtime friend, or to Director Irene Rivers of the Federal Bureau of Investigation?"

"Now, who's thinking less of the other?" Irene said. "I've covered for you enough times to get thrown *under* the prison, right next to the hole they dig for you and your team." She meant every word. In the years since Jonathan had helped to rescue her daughters from kidnappers, they'd both benefited from each other's assistance more times that she could count.

"All right, then, my good friend Wolfie. If I get an opportunity, I'm going to escalate the so-called drug war, which is really little more than a pillow fight, into something that looks like a *real* war. Think rivers of blood and towers of smoke."

She recoiled from the words. "Are you being serious with me?"

"Serious as a heart attack."

"How are you going to do that all by yourself?"

"I don't talk about means and methods," Jonathan said. "But trust me when I say I won't be alone."

"You're raising an army?"

"Means and methods, Wolfie. Means and methods. But I'll tell you this: If I can do what I plan with the few resources that will be available, you should be ashamed of yourself if you can't take on a bureaucracy. You're America's top cop. I heard that on the news just the other day."

That had been on a local news talker, *A New Day in Washington*, starring Darren Mills and Connie Morales. She frequently heard herself described as America's top cop, and while she never corrected anyone directly, it always annoyed her that the description was wrong. She was merely a bureaucrat who led a massive agency that used to be dedicated to protecting America and her citizens but had morphed dangerously away from the purity of that mission. If she couldn't find the political handle to change the trajectory of the Bureau, where hundreds of thousands of Americans were spied upon based on their rhetoric against the administration, it would soon more closely resemble the old KGB or Stasi than it did the Bureau she'd joined so long ago.

"What makes you think you can get Rocco LoCicero to speak with you even if I could make the appointment?"

"Everybody has their sweet spot," Jonathan said. "I've been doing interviews my whole career, many with people who had no interest in sharing data with me."

"I won't let you torture him for answers."

"Jesus God, Irene. There you go again. I do not torture people. I inspire them to open up and share information."

"By breaking fingers and dislocating elbows?"

"Of course not!"

"Then how? And don't give me this *means and methods* secrecy crap. You want entry from me, I want details from you."

Jonathan turned right onto a street whose name she didn't catch, then at the end of the block, he turned left. If her guess was correct, he was just driving aimlessly to kill time.

"Okay," he said. "Boxers would not approve of me telling you this, but I will make deals with LoCicero."

"Deals?"

"I've got an FBI badge and a wallet full of credentials. Maybe you don't realize it, but those creds bring a lot of old-fashioned street cred, too."

"What are you telling me?"

"That I'll promise Rocco a shorter sentence or a more spacious cell. Hell, I'll offer him hot and cold running women if that's how I assess his greatest desire."

"But you don't have the authority."

"I'll be lying my ass off," Jonathan said. "I don't need any special authority to do that. All I need to do is make him comfortable enough to share the details I want to learn about the cartels and their American handlers."

"What's going to happen when the promises never come true?"

"Who cares? He's a murderer and a drug dealer. That makes him a kid killer. What the hell does anyone care what happens to a piece of shit like that?"

"I care and my people care," Irene objected. "Piss him off too badly and he'll clam up on the Schillaci case."

"Oh, God forbid," Jonathan said with an ostentatious eye roll. "Okay, fine. I'll tell him that none of what I offer will happen until after the other investigating agents are satisfied with his continuing cooperation on the Schillaci prosecution."

"What happens when LoCicero talks to the other agents about your visit?"

"It won't matter. By then, I'll be into the wind. You can tell them that I'm special and that they need to mind their own business."

Irene turned away from him to look out the side window. It was a crazy idea and unethical as hell. Not only was Digger proposing to manipulate a witness, he was also talking about committing acts of war in a foreign nation.

Not that he hadn't done similar things in the past. Then, however, she hadn't been a part of the conspiracy.

Something did have to be done, and perhaps this really was the once-in-a-lifetime opportunity to succeed where others had failed over dozens of years.

"I can keep you out of it if it's that important," Jonathan said. "I just want to kill the cartels. If you don't want to take a flame thrower to the administration, I understand."

"That's exactly what I want to do," Irene said. "I've

been dealing with this corruption for far too long. I can't imagine it will be too long before Darmond demands my resignation, anyway. I might as well give him good reason.

Jonathan looked at her and smiled. "I'm proud of you, Wolfie."

"Don't patronize, Digger. It's not becoming. Now, pull over and let me make a couple of phone calls. When my detail catches up, try not to start a gunfight."

Chapter 7

Grayson Buchanan paused outside El Gallo Azul—the Blue Rooster—before reaching for the front door handle. Two blocks off the main drag, on the shaded edge of a bustling side street, the place looked like it might be closed.

"Are you sure this is the place?" asked Sissy, his seventeen-year-old twin.

Grayson fished the card back out of the front pocket of his shorts and looked at it again. "Right name, right address," he said. "Looks kinda spooky." The front window had been rendered opaque with black paint. The wooden double doors had a medieval look to them. Maybe even Middle Eastern. They weren't of a design they'd seen before in Cancun.

"And you're sure this is the place that Juan recommended?" Sissy had hit up their butler at the resort for the name of a place where they could get away from their mom and her boyfriend, Clifford.

"This is the card he gave me." He grabbed the door and pulled it open.

Inside, El Gallo Azul looked like it had been put together by someone who built sets for the 1970s-era cop shows that their mom liked to watch. Underlit and made of dark wood, the interior smelled like cigarette smoke and spilled beer.

Sissy held back. "I don't know, Gray."

The hesitation embarrassed Grayson. They'd come this far, and now they were taking up space in an open doorway in front of everyone. "Juan is not going to send us to a place where we'll get hurt." He stood to the side and held the door for Sissy to enter past him.

When the door closed behind them, Grayson felt a little like he was being swallowed. A few people sagged in the stools along the bar, and he could see three couples engaged in separate conversations at separate four-top tables.

A few steps inside, his eyes adjusted to the light. Perhaps someone had spun a rheostat a quarter-inch to the right. This place could not have been more different than the various bars inside Pelican's Perch, the resort where they were staying down the street. The floors in here felt sticky, and the wooden serving bar itself looked as if it had survived a war, with severe white scars torn into the nearly black surface.

"You don't have to be afraid," said a voice from close behind.

Sissy made a little *yip* as they both jumped at the sound out of nowhere. Grayson turned to see a man in his thirties dressed in a slick green suit with a lighter green shirt undone to the third button.

"It's not pretty to look at, but this is what you get with a neighborhood bar." The man spoke perfect English, no trace of an accent. His smile seemed genuine, but Grayson got a predatory vibe from him.

If he backed off now though, he'd look scared, like a pussy. "Thanks," he said. With Sissy at his side, he approached the short side of the L-shaped bar and raised two fingers to attract the bartender's attention.

Maybe twenty-five years old, the bartender wore his hair in a man bun and clearly worked out. Equally clear was the fact that he was hitting on the underage brunette at the far end of the sticky, once-polished, wood-paneled serving surface. The bartender raised two fingers of his own.

I'll get to you when it's your turn.

"Mom and Clifford are going to kill us when they find out," Sissy said.

Grayson scoffed. "Mom and Clifford are enjoying each other far too much to give a shit what we're doing. Did you hear them last night?"

"The whole Riviera Maya heard them," Sissy said through a scrunched face. "It's disgusting."

"Won't argue that," Grayson agreed. "But with all the grunting and the '*yes, yes*'"—he mimicked orgasmic breathlessness—"I don't think they'll be wondering if we went out to a bar."

The man from the door chuckled behind them.

Grayson heard a tremble in his own voice when he said, "Could you give us a little space, please?"

"*Lo siento, hijos,*" he said. "I don't mean to eavesdrop. It's just quiet in here."

The whole thing was feeling like a mistake now. They'd been forbidden to leave the resort, but Grayson couldn't stand the prospect of listening anymore to their carnal bliss. Why did they even take Sissy and him along on this stupid getaway? It wasn't as if he and his sister couldn't take care of themselves at home. If they were going to spew their love for each other twenty-four seven, including the kids was downright rude.

He waved to the bartender again and got another motion for him to hold his horses.

"I think you're doing it wrong," Sissy said.

"Doing what wrong? How many ways are there to get someone's attention?"

Sissy's eyes flashed. "Let me try." She undid a button on her shirt, shook her hair to poof it up, and then pressed her arms in to emphasize her cleavage.

"Jesus, Sissy, you know I'm here, right?"

"Oh, for God's sake, we used to bathe in the same tub."

"I don't remember that."

"Your pee-pee was very small."

"Jesus."

She winked at him and leaned into the bar top. As if drawn by a magnetic field, the bartender's head turned, and he flashed a very white smile.

I bet this guy gets laid every friggin' night, Grayson thought. He didn't think his own chosen career path as a cop would bear the same benefits.

As Man-Bun oozed closer, Sissy said, "*Me llamo Sissy. Como te llamas?*"

"My name is Javier," Man-Bun said. "I speak English. At least better than you speak Español."

"We'd like two tequilas," Grayson said, leaning in closer.

"I'm talking to the lady," Javier said. Then, to Sissy, he added, "Your skinny date is rude. He should learn some manners."

Grayson felt himself flushing.

"He's not my date," Sissy said. "He's my brother. And he thinks he's always in charge." As she spoke, she gave Grayson a wink. "But he's right about the tequilas. Do you think you could find some?"

A smirk formed on Javier's face. Grayson couldn't tell if he was genuinely amused or merely mocking them.

"*Quieren Blanco, Reposado, o Añejo?*"

Sissy looked stunned and Javier laughed.

"You were right about my Español," Sissy said. "What did you say?"

"I asked if you wanted the Tequila Blanco, Tequila Reposado, or the Tequila Añejo. Blanco is about what you Americans would call white lightning, the Reposado has been aged in oak barrels, and the Añejo is more expensive than two American teenagers can afford to buy." He waited for his words to hit home, then added, "Even if they can afford to stay at the Pelican's Perch."

Grayson knew his face had gone bright red. The drinking age in Mexico was eighteen. They were a year short. And how did he know—

"Juan sent you here from the Pelican's Perch, did he not?" Javier asked.

Grayson forced himself to remain impassive, but in his peripheral vision, he saw Sissy nod.

"I keep telling him that he shouldn't do that. Do you have any identification?" Javier's smirk remained in place.

Sissy looked to Grayson. They had passports, but the birth dates would only make things more complicated.

Javier's smirk bloomed to a grin. "Okay," he said. "We'll pretend that you showed me a passport. What would that document show your age to be? Remember, you must be eighteen to drink. So, whatever you tell me needs to be over eighteen."

"We're twenty-one," Grayson said.

"*Vientiuno* it is," Javier said. "Two Reposados on the house."

"I can afford to pay," Grayson said. The instant the words left his mouth, he realized he was being stupid.

"What are you doing?" Sissy said.

"Sorry. I had a flash of honesty."

Thirty seconds later, the drinks arrived. They were doubles, with wedges of lime balanced on the rim.

Once the glasses were on the bar, Javier produced a saltshaker from somewhere below and set it down between the glasses.

"Where are you from?" Javier asked. "Other than from the Pelican's Perch?"

Sissy answered for both of them. "Holland, Michigan."

"Where is that in America?"

"Almost Canada," Grayson said. He sipped the shot, winced against the burn.

"There you go being rude again," Javier said. "When I am speaking to a beautiful woman, I do not want to be interrupted by a skinny baby brother."

Grayson didn't get why this guy was trying to pick a fight, but he was *this close* to getting his wish.

"Ooh, I see that look," Javier mocked. "Be careful, baby brother. You don't want to start anything that you cannot finish. The *policía* are my friends, not yours."

"Now who's being rude?" Sissy said. "And he's not my baby brother. We're twins. In fact, Grayson is three minutes older."

Javier laughed as if that were the funniest thing he had ever heard. "*Discúlpame, entonces.* Forgive me for not seeing that you are three minutes older than your very fine, very hot sister."

Grayson felt the pressure of strangers closing in around him. He pivoted his head and saw a tall and trim Mexican standing too close to his right side. Soon another joined on his left.

"We don't want any trouble," Grayson said. He wrapped his hand around Sissy's biceps and gently tugged. "C'mon, Sis, we should get back."

"You have drinks to finish," said the man on Grayson's right. Beyond that man, Grayson saw someone slide the lock closed on the front door.

Grayson wanted to pull away, create some distance

from which to operate, have a little room, but the others wouldn't allow it.

"L-look," Grayson stammered. "We don't have any money. Well, we've got some, and you're welcome to it, but we're not rich or anything."

The man got very close—so close that Grayson could smell the nicotine exuding from his pores. "Are you calling me a thief?"

Grayson tried to take a step back, but another man had moved in too close to allow it.

"Javier," said Nicotine Breath. "What did you tell me it costs to stay in the Pelican's Perch for one night?"

"It depends, Lobo," Javier said. "Big suites go for ten thousand American dollars. The cheapest rooms, though, are nine hundred dollars per night."

Lobo pressed his face even closer to Grayson's. "People who can afford those kinds of moneys must be willing to pay *really* big money to get their twin babies back, don't you think?"

Grayson's mouth felt as if it were filled with dust. Even if he could think of something to say, he doubted that he could form the words. Then his guts exploded in pain as Lobo's enormous hand grabbed a fistful of Grayson's genitals. He squeezed and lifted with one hand while the second hand grabbed Grayson's collar to keep him from falling.

Grayson yelled and Lobo pulled harder, lifting him to his tiptoes. "Swallow the pain, *hijo.* Yelling will only make it worse.

Javier reached across the bar and touched Sissy's blouse with the tip of his forefinger. "You really are a beautiful young lady," he said. "I may just take you home with me."

He leaned forward for a kiss, but Sissy recoiled.

ZERO SUM   91

"You are feisty," he said.

"I like women who fight back," Lobo said. He released his grip on Grayson's testicles and shoved him into the edge of the bar. "*Eunoco*."

Grayson's knees started to sag.

"No, no, you stay on your feet. Try to be as manly as your baby sister."

"W-what are you doing?" Sissy asked.

"What's your plan?" Grayson added.

"I think I won't tell you," Lobo said. "Because I think you won't like it."

"Please," Sissy said. "Just let us go. I promise I won't go to the police. Neither of us will, right, Gray?"

"I promise," Grayson said. He worried that he might throw up.

Javier and Lobo both laughed. "Go ahead and tell the police," Javier said. "In fact, I can call them for you if you would like. I told you that they are my friends."

"Then what are you going to do?" Grayson said.

Lobo eyed him for a long five seconds. "Finish your tequila," he said. "Both of you."

Grayson shook his head. "It's poison, isn't it?"

"Drink it and find out."

"No."

Lobo moved with speed that looked impossible because of his size. He lunged at Grayson, this time closing his talon of a hand around the young man's throat, right at the spot where his neck met his lower jaw. Within seconds, Grayson's world started to lose color.

"You will drink the tequila you ordered, or your parents will find your bodies in tiny pieces scattered around the swimming pool."

Grayson tried to say okay, but his voice wouldn't

work. Soon, nothing would work. His head twitched in a motion that simulated a nod.

The pressure went away, and the pressure of returning blood made Grayson's head swim in a different way. It took one huge gasp of air for him to learn that he hadn't been breathing. Or that he'd apparently gone deaf for a few seconds because Sissy was begging for Lobo to leave her brother alone.

Lobo reached past Grayson, picked up the shot glass filled with amber liquid, and handed it to him. "I won't ask again."

Grayson looked to Sissy through clouded vision. She was holding her own glass.

"I love you," she said.

"You too, Squirt," he said.

Certain that he was about to die, he shot the whole contents down his throat.

He was still choking against the burn when the world went away.

Chapter 8

The United States Penitentiary Big Sandy in Inez, Kentucky, was invisible from the prying eyes of passersby on Route 3, in a part of the state that defined the middle of nowhere. The prison was accessed by a narrow, hidden lane carved through a hardwood screen of trees. Boxers had fitted the Batmobile—their heavily customized and armored Suburban—with US government license plates, and he and Jonathan both wore polo shirts emblazoned with the shield logo of the FBI.

Once they were through the corridor of trees, the vista opened up to reveal the sprawling walled complex of white concrete and razor wire. Towering gun turrets marked the corners of the roughly rectangular complex.

"Did the Corps of Engineers design this place?" Boxers quipped. "It kinda looks like their design aesthetic."

"It's supposed to be a nasty place," Jonathan said.

"I think I want it to be," Big Guy said. "The people who go to the big house like this have earned a little misery."

"Pretty bold talk from a guy who's afraid of small spaces."

Boxers had long been on the record that he would

die before ever being taken as a prisoner. Uncharacteristically, he let Jonathan's jab go unchallenged. Not even a witty riposte.

Prisons are designed to be intimidating places. In every prison Jonathan had visited over the years, he'd found the outside of the place to be oversized to such a degree as to make mere humans feel small and insignificant. Inside, the opposite was always true, with the passageways two sizes too small and the overheads far too low. Common areas were defined by heavy fences, and movement from one place to another inside the concrete walls was interrupted by multiple security checks and body searches. He'd be surprised if he found something different behind these walls.

"I don't see any signs for where law enforcement vehicles should go," Boxers said, slowing to nearly a stop outside the massive gates, not quite to the guard shack.

"I guess we just follow the signs for visitors," Jonathan said. "I mean, what the hell? We're visitors. Even with the feebs gambit going, we're still new."

Boxers eased the vehicle forward, all the way up to the guard shack, where a no-bullshit, ruddy-complected security guard with a big belly made of stone stepped out into the sunlight and waved for them to stop.

Boxers rolled down his window and showed his badge. To his right, Jonathan leaned forward and presented his, as well. "Agents Cantata and Bonner," Boxers lied. "We have an appointment to interview a prisoner."

"They're called inmates here," the guard said. The nametag stitched to his ballistic vest read Miller. "Which one is Cantata and which is Bonner?"

"I'm Bonner," Jonathan said.

Miller scowled and shielded his eyes as he peered around Big Guy's big form to look at Jonathan. Satisfied (but maybe not really), Miller pulled away and strolled back into the guard shack. "Let me check the record," he said. "I don't remember no fibbies comin' in. Not at this gate, for sure."

As Miller busied himself at a computer atop a standing desk, Boxers said, "I told you we should have looked for a LEO entrance." Law enforcement officer.

"You literally did not say that," Jonathan said.

"I was thinkin' it pretty loud, though."

Through the doorway, Miller seemed confused. He leaned closer to his screen, then leaned away before reaching for a landline telephone handset. As he lifted it to his ear, he pushed the door to the guard shack closed.

"That's interesting," Jonathan said.

"Looks like they're not expecting us," Boxers said.

"That's the better possibility. I worry that they *are* and that they have unfortunate instructions for us."

"I can't think of a shittier place to have a shoot-out," Big Guy said. "If it's bad, I figure every guard in every tower has eyes on us."

"You're letting the paranoids get too close," Jonathan said. "We've done a lot of stuff on a lot of days worthy of being shot at for. But this isn't one of them."

"Give it time," Boxers mumbled.

When the guard shack door opened again, Miller's face looked pinched, some combination of confusion and annoyance. He whirled his finger at Boxers, a silent order to roll down his window again. "I just called upstairs," he said. "Warden Cooper told me he wanted you to pull over there and wait. Somebody will be out to see you in a few minutes."

"We're not even allowed into the parking area?" Jonathan asked.

Miller stooped to see past Big Guy. "If you could park in the lot, would I be telling you to wait out here?"

It was a solid point, Jonathan supposed.

Boxers dropped the transmission into gear and crept the Batmobile fifty yards to a spot behind a concrete security barrier. "This doesn't feel right at all," he said. "Think we should turn around and leave?"

Jonathan thought through the options. Their FBI creds were both the blessing and the curse here. The fact that they held them had brought them this far. The fact that they were counterfeit left them exposed to explanations that he was not prepared to deliver.

"We're in this deep," Jonathan said. "We'll keep playing the bluff till it runs its course."

Eight minutes later, Jonathan caught sight of a tall man in a white shirt, black tie, gray slacks, and gold badge exiting the front entrance of the prison building and walking with purpose directly toward the front gate.

"Think that's our guy?" Boxers asked.

"I'm guessing supervisor of the guards," Jonathan observed. "Notice how conscientiously he's looking everywhere but toward us," Jonathan observed.

"Maybe Wolfie doesn't have the clout we thought she had."

Jonathan pulled on the release and opened his door. "If we're going to chat, it's going to be on equal footing," he said.

Boxers did the same, unfolding his huge frame. Together, they moved to the front bumper and waited.

"Excuse me, gentlemen," Miller called from the guard shack. "Wait in the car, please."

Jonathan ignored him. "This isn't the conflict they want," he said to Big Guy.

"If those were supposed to be encouraging words, they fell a little flat."

As the white shirt approached the man-sized gate to the side of the massive vehicle gate, Miller stepped back into his booth. Jonathan heard a buzz, and the white shirt stepped out into the open.

Finally, there was some eye contact. And a smile. The humorless kind that could have been either condescending or smug. Maybe a bit of both.

Neither Jonathan nor Boxers moved, letting the guard make the entire trek to them. "Agents Contata and Bonner, I presume," he said, offering his hand after he'd closed to within a couple of feet.

Jonathan went first. "I'm Bonner," he said. They shook.

"And you must be Sasquatch." White Shirt's attempt at humor fell flat. Boxers didn't like being teased about his size.

"Special Agent Contata," Boxers said. "My friends call me Special Agent Contata."

"Captain Hite," White Shirt said. "I'm the corrections supervisor for this shift. I'm afraid I have bad news for you. The inmate you wanted to see is not available."

"And which inmate would that be?" Jonathan asked. "I don't remember dropping a name."

"Rocco LoCicero, right?"

"Yes. And why can't we see him?"

"Warden's orders."

"We've come a long way," Jonathan said. "I was told this meeting was arranged in advance at the highest levels."

Hite chuckled and ran his hand through his hair. "I don't know what that means, exactly, but in my world, the warden is the highest level that I concern myself with."

"How about we speak with him, then?" Jonathan pressed.

"Alas, he's out of pocket, too."

"Didn't you just talk with him? Isn't that why you're out here to piss in our Wheaties?"

Hite recoiled from the words. "Colorful phrase."

"We'd really like to chat with the warden," Boxers said. The rumble of his voice seemed to vibrate the pavement.

"We'd all like many things that we can't have," Hite said. "Unfortunately, such is life."

"How about a little courtesy here, Captain? We killed a whole day getting out here. It seems to me, the least you could do—"

"Tell you what," Hite said. Something flashed behind his eyes that Jonathan couldn't quite make out. "How about you give me your business card and I can pass it along to the warden. Perhaps he can give you a call later."

"We don't want to talk to the warden at all," Boxers said. "We need to speak with LoCicero himself."

"About what, if I may ask?"

"You may not," Jonathan said.

"Then we seem to be at an impasse."

"No," Boxers said. "We seem to be at a place where you're blocking us from doing our job."

Hite seemed to be making a point of keeping his eyes on Jonathan. He held out his hand. "Your business card would really help quite a lot," he said.

Boxers started to object again, but Jonathan subtly held up his hand, silencing Big Guy. He reached into his back pocket and withdrew his creds case. He flopped it open and fished around for his FBI business card. The phone number was fake, but it ran through cloaking software that would ring at Venice's desk for the first three rings, then on to Jonathan's cell phone.

"Here," he said. "Is there a chance that the warden might change his mind?"

"I doubt it," Hite said. "But we'll never know unless we try." He glanced at the card. "You're out of the Manassas office?"

"That's correct," Jonathan said. A computer check would prove that to be true, even though Neil Bonner didn't really exist.

"I presume you're heading back tonight?" Hite asked.

"Any sense in us sticking around?" Jonathan asked.

"Not if you ask me," Hite said. "Plus, decent accommodations are hard to come by around here."

Something about Hite just wasn't right. It manifested itself in the way his eyes kept darting to the sides and down to his feet. "Is there something I should know?" Jonathan asked.

Hite pocketed the business card. "Nothing I can think of," he said. "And sorry for the confusion. Y'all drive safely now." He pivoted on his heel and walked back toward the gate.

"What just happened there?" Boxers asked.

"For one, we got jilted." Jonathan led the way back into the Batmobile. As he was buckling into his seatbelt, he asked, "Did you notice anything strange in his demeanor?"

"Strange how?" Boxers fired up the engine.

"I can't put my finger on it. He seemed nervous."

"I didn't see nervousness," Boxers said as he threw the transmission into reverse. "I just saw assholery."

"You see that in everybody."

"Because that's where it resides," Big Guy said. He carefully backed out through the concrete barriers.

After a couple of hours had passed, Boxers asked, "Are we going to bed down somewhere for the night? It's been a long day. I'd like to catch a few hours of sleep before we do the eight hours back."

"I don't have a problem with that," Jonathan said. "I'm not sure what we'll find out here, but if it's got a bar and a bed, I'm good with it."

Forty-five minutes later, they were pulling into the parking lot of McWhorter's Tavern, an old-school roadside motor court whose iffy neon assured them that there was a VA ANCY and that the rooms were AIR COND TION D. Moreover, the bar was open and apparently served the OLDEST BEER IN KE TUC Y.

"This is where we pray they're missing a *C* in *oldest*," Boxers said.

"Oh, I don't know," Jonathan said. "Kentucky's been around for a long time. Might be interesting to taste their oldest beer."

Jonathan led the way into the squatty little office, where a bell slapped against the glass door to announce their arrival. After some words exchanged from the apartment beyond the desk, a boy of about thirteen wandered into sight, rubbing his eye with one hand and scratching his mop of disheveled hair with his other. He was barefoot and dressed in a T-shirt and flannel pajama bottoms.

"Welcome to McWhorter's," the kid said. One look

at Boxers brought him fully awake. "Oh, crap," he said, taking a step back. "Sorry."

"No need to apologize," Big Guy said. "I get that a lot."

"Good evening," Jonathan said. "We'd like two rooms for the night."

"Just so you know, you've got to pay for the whole night no matter when you leave."

"Jesus," Boxers mumbled.

"That will be just fine," Jonathan said through a smirk. "How much?"

"Cash or credit?"

"Jemmy!" a voice yelled from the wings.

"Customers!" he shouted back, clearly answering an unasked question.

"Are we interrupting dinner?" Jonathan asked.

"Nah, Ma just don't like it when people come this time of night." He dropped his voice to a whisper. "It interrupts her drinkin'." He tried to sell the line with a laugh, but the words seemed too real.

"You okay here?" Boxers asked the boy.

"Oh, yeah. Cash is ninety dollars, credit is one-ten."

"We'll do cash," Jonathan said, pulling his wallet from his pocket.

"Everybody always does," Jemmy said. "Do you need adjoining rooms?"

"Doesn't matter," Jonathan said. He handed over two one-hundred-dollar bills. "Keep the change."

The boy winked. "Don't you worry. We're discreet here." He opened a flimsy cash box, deposited the money, then reached under the desk for two keys, each dangling from a diamond-shaped piece of plastic.

"Rooms fourteen and fifteen." He pointed through the doors. "About halfway down."

"Aren't you going to write down our names?" Boxers asked.

Jemmy laughed. "What's the point? Nobody gives their real ones, anyway."

Jonathan handed one of the keys to Big Guy. "Let it go," he whispered as he led the way back to the Batmobile. The lights on the walls of the motor court were mostly burned out, and from the few that worked, the illumination was dim and yellow.

"That's no way to grow up," Boxers said.

"He's fed, he's dry, and he's got a roof over his head," Jonathan said. "That's better than most of the places we visit."

Jonathan had opened his door and was climbing into the shotgun seat when movement across the street caught his eye. It took him a few seconds to figure it out, but then it became clear. A dark SUV had stopped along the opposite side of the road, about fifty yards distant.

"You see 'em, too?" Boxers asked.

"Just now," Jonathan said. "Were they here when we pulled in?"

"If they were, I didn't notice them."

Less than a definitive answer, but Jonathan couldn't do any better.

"What do you want to do about it?" Boxers pressed.

"About a vehicle minding its own business along a public highway?"

"About a government-looking Suburban spying on us."

Jonathan pulled his door shut. "I say we move into our rooms and then go exploring."

* * *

Rooms fourteen and fifteen did, indeed, connect, and the latch between them didn't work. Boxers had backed the Batmobile into the space in front of his room—fourteen. From there, they unloaded their luggage, which included two duffle bags loaded with battle gear. Big Guy grabbed the one with weapons and ammo, while Jonathan grabbed the one with the night vision and electronics gear. They entered their rooms, locked the doors, and met in the middle.

"You closed your curtains, right?" Jonathan asked.

"Of course," Boxers said. "Not that the windows are clean enough to see through, anyway. Whatever you do, don't shine a black light on any surface of this place. I've already seen too much shit in my life that I can't unsee."

Jonathan chuckled. In a perfect world, he'd much rather spend a night on the road in a real hotel, but he'd spent enough nights in rain-soaked drainage ditches to appreciate the simple pleasures of a roof.

But Big Guy was right: if you didn't see the accumulated splashes of body fluids on the walls and bedspread, you could always pretend that everything was recently cleaned.

Boxers pulled two rifles out of his duffel. He handed the M27 to Jonathan and kept the HK417 for himself, while Jonathan pulled two NVG arrays—night vision goggles—out of his duffel and handed one to Big Guy.

"Do we have a plan?" Boxers asked.

"Of course not," Jonathan said. "Not a real one, anyway. I figure there's only a few ways for this to go. One, this is all innocent, and we have nothing to worry about."

"I'm not buying that one," Boxers said.

"Neither am I. Two, they're going to wait until they think we're down and out for the night and make whatever move they're planning to make."

"What do you think that move will be?"

"What's most likely is that they're just surveilling. Keeping an eye on us."

"I don't like that one, either," Boxers said. "I don't want to wait for them to make the first move."

"Assuming there's a first move to be made," Jonathan said. "That leaves us with them springing an ambush."

Boxers held his forefinger high. "Ding, ding, ding! That's the one."

"I agree. And offense beats defense every time." Jonathan lifted his ballistic vest out of the duffel, slipped it over his head, and closed the Velcro fasteners. The ammo pockets in the vest held eight thirty-round magazines. He removed one from its sleeve, slid it into the M27's mag well, and thumbed the bolt closed.

"I never get tired of hearing that sound," Boxers quipped.

As Big Guy kitted up, Jonathan reached back into the electronics duffel and produced two radios. He slid his into its designated pocket at his shoulder and handed the other to Big Guy. "To be clear, our primary mission is to surveil *them*. In a perfect world, there will be no gunfire."

"The perfect world *always* has gunfire," Big Guy said. "We goin' with full comms? Bringing Mother Hen into the loop?"

Jonathan looked at his watch. "I don't want to wait the time it will take for her to stand everything up. If we need her, we can always call her."

He placed his tiny transceiver into his right ear, turned the radio on, and said, "Test, test."

Boxers gave him a thumbs-up. "Test back at you."

They were good to go. "Let's keep it on VOX," Jonathan said. Voice-activated transmission. When only two operators were in the mix, VOX often worked best because it kept your hands free and you knew who was talking. When ops got larger, PTT—push to talk—often made more sense just to keep the channel clear of heavy breathing and curse words.

With all the lights off inside the room, Jonathan donned his NVGs and toggled the switch that turned the darkness to daytime. During his time in this line of work, some of the most impressive technological advancements had come in the arena of night vision. Being able to see while others were blind in the dark brought huge tactical advantages.

The first critical challenge was to get across the parking lot to the trees at the far end on the right-hand side. While all but two of the outside lights were dark, there was plenty illumination to keep them visible.

"Go slow," Jonathan said. Though counterintuitive, one trick to remaining invisible in the night is to make no sudden moves. Human beings had missed out on the part of evolution that granted nocturnal vision. We compensate by becoming more sensitive to sound and movement after the sun goes down. Jonathan thought it ironic that at least his caveman ancestors could hear the saber-toothed tiger before they became the main course.

Jonathan moved in a low crouch, his carbine at low-ready as he inched across the pavement, scanning constantly for any signs of trouble. Three feet to his right and two feet behind, he heard Boxers keeping up with him step for step.

In the distance, from the other side of the trees—

the roadway side—they heard the crunch of gravel as a vehicle moved.

"Is that our friends?" Big Guy asked.

"If it is, we'll know soon enough," Jonathan said. He picked up his pace to get behind cover. "If it is, they're either making their move or going home."

"I'm not gonna lie," Boxers said. "I'm kinda hoping it's the former. It's a good night for a gunfight."

Big Guy wasn't homicidal, but he was a violent and deadly man. Jonathan wondered sometimes what would have happened to his friend if he hadn't joined the military and gotten to blow stuff up for the forces of good.

Taking care not to trip over the parking blocks on the far side of the lot, Jonathan led the way into the tree cover before pivoting and taking a knee.

Ten seconds later, the black SUV from before rolled silently into the lot, lights off. The driver parked it in the shadow of the office, and all four doors opened at once, disgorging six figures identically dressed in black and all carrying AR15 variants. In what appeared to be a practiced motion, they moved in a wide arc toward the Batmobile and the rooms beyond it.

"They've got NVGs," Boxers whispered.

But they were of a previous generation, just two-tube arrays that would give them less detail than Team Good Guys and none of the peripheral vision provided by Jonathan's and Boxers' four-tube arrays.

From the way they moved, Jonathan guessed that this was not the team's first op together.

"SWAT team?" Boxers guessed.

"I don't see any police markings," Jonathan replied. These guys were dressed for anonymous warfare. "I'm thinking hit team," Jonathan said.

"Only six of 'em? I'm insulted."

The presence of night vision with the other team did

put some limitations on Jonathan and Boxers beyond the mere fact of being visible. The infrared flashlights and laser sights that Jonathan normally used would be as visible to the opfor—opposing force—as they would be to them, with the effect of revealing their positions to the bad guys.

Anything that shaved away even a tiny advantage was a serious problem.

The opfor fanned out into a perimeter focused on the Batmobile in the center. By the time they stopped, one of the bad guys was only fifteen feet away from Jonathan, close enough for Digger to hear him breathing.

Once in position, on a signal that Jonathan could not hear, they collapsed their circle onto the door to Room Fifteen. They placed a breaching charge against the lock and then did the same to the lock on Boxers' door.

This was Big Guy's kind of hit team. Why knock when you can blow a hole?

This was a delicate moment for Jonathan. If these were law enforcement officers, about to breach the doors with a warrant, shooting them would be a capital crime. On the other hand, if they were a hit squad, this would be the time to take them out.

"I'm calling an audible," Jonathan whispered. Then, without waiting for a response from Big Guy, he called out in full voice, "Hey! Can I help you folks?" He was reasonably sure that Big Guy and he were far enough behind cover that the bad guys couldn't see them.

The opfor didn't hesitate. They spun on their axes and shot into the woods at the sound of Jonathan's words. Big mistake. Not only were they five or ten degrees off on their aim, they'd also shown their hand as non-LEOs. In the quiet of the dark night, their unsuppressed rifle reports sounded like hand grenades.

"Take 'em," Jonathan said.

He and Big Guy had been through enough of these operations to understand each other's strengths and anticipate each other's actions. Jonathan took the three on the left, moving from near to far. He kept his shots north of the ballistic armor, drilling his targets two in the head and one in the throat. The throat shot hit the attacker with the detonator. It was a kill shot, but not an instant one, so Jonathan followed up with a second round to the guy's left eye.

To his right, he heard Big Guy's suppressed HK417 pounding at the night, and he was dimly aware of the others dropping in their own shadows.

"Three down," Big Guy said.

"Three here, too. Total of six." As soon as the words had left his mouth, he pivoted and headed for the motel's office. "You check these guys for identification," he said. "Take photos of their faces and get fingerprints. I've got to go talk with the owners."

Jonathan sprinted across the parking lot and arrived at the front glass doors just as Jemmy was about to throw the deadbolt.

Jonathan hit the doors with his full weight, launching them open and sending Jemmy sprawling backward into a rack of travel brochures. As the boy rebounded, Jonathan caught him and eased him onto the floor.

"Jemmy!" The same voice as before called from the back room. "What the hell is going on?"

"FBI!" Jonathan boomed. "Federal agent! Show yourselves and be sure you are not armed!" He kept his hand on Jemmy's shoulder to keep him from getting up.

"Is that your mom back there?" Jonathan asked.

Jemmy nodded as best he could. "Please don't hurt us."

"I don't intend to. Does she have weapons back there?"

Jemmy hesitated.

"You need help, Boss?" Boxers asked over the air.

"This is the time to tell the truth," Jonathan said. "It would be a very bad idea for her to come out shooting." Shifting gears, he said, "Big Guy, that's a negative."

"There's a shotgun. Twelve-gauge pump."

Jonathan started to say something, but Jemmy beat him to the punch. "Mom!" he yelled. "Don't come out with the gun. Leave it where it is."

"I'm not here to hurt you," Jonathan said, louder this time. "I do need to talk with you, though."

After ten seconds, Jonathan asked Jemmy, "What do you think is going on?"

"She probably passed back out," the boy said. "Can I get up and check on her?"

It was Jonathan's turn to hesitate.

"I'm not stupid," Jemmy said.

Keeping his M27 at low-ready, Jonathan took his hand away and let Jemmy rise to his feet. As the boy made his way behind the counter, Jonathan followed.

The living area behind the check-in desk was a study in Danish modern furniture. At least that's what Jonathan thought it was. As much wood as there was cushion, and both the wood and the cushions were too thin to be comfortable. A woman sat in the far left-hand corner of the room, a short glass of dark whiskey perilously balanced on her thigh. She looked up as they entered, but Jonathan didn't see any recognition.

"Is she all right?"

"She will be in the morning," Jemmy said. "She gets like this when she drinks too much." He dutifully strode over to her, but as he touched the glass, she snapped awake.

"It's just me, Mom. You don't want to spill."

And then she was gone again.

"This is worse than usual," Jemmy said. "Don't call CPS or social services, okay? We don't need them assholes—" He looked down.

"You can say whatever you want," Jonathan said. "Just because people are public servants doesn't mean they can't also be assholes. Sometimes it comes with the territory."

"Scorpion, Big Guy. How about a sitrep?" Boxers didn't like it when Jonathan was out of sight for more than a few minutes at a time.

"We're fine here," Jonathan said. When Jemmy gave him a strange look, Jonathan held up a finger for patience and said, "Move our friends into our rooms."

"Way ahead of you," Boxers said. "And I've got a bag full of IDs."

"Come up to the office, then, and bring the cash pouch."

"Are you talking to someone?" Jemmy asked.

Jonathan flipped the switch on his radio over to PTT. "My big friend," he said.

"What happened?" Jemmy asked. "Was that shooting?"

"Yes," Jonathan said.

"And you're with the FBI?"

"Yes." Jonathan couldn't put his finger on why that lie felt so bad.

"Anybody get shot?"

"Six men are dead," Jonathan said.

"And you guys killed them?"

Jonathan nodded.

"What, were they like bank robbers or something?"

"Or something. Listen, Jemmy, are we the only lodgers here tonight?"

"For now." The boy looked at the clock on the wall, where the analog hands showed it to be 21:35. "The hookers don't start coming till after ten. Then it'll be pretty busy for a few hours before it slows down again."

There was something about this kid that Jonathan found to be very engaging. There was an honesty and world-weariness about him that reminded Jonathan of himself. By most estimates, the kid was living a shitty childhood, but somehow he was making the best of it.

"Do you have to be awake all night, then?"

"Nah, we lock the doors at two-thirty. I can go to bed then."

"School?"

"Mostly home school," Jemmy said. "I can read and do math better than most of the kids I run into that are my age. Mom and me make stuff work. We're a team."

Jonathan forced a smile and felt relief when he heard the Batmobile arrive at the front doors. The bell slapped on the glass and Boxers boomed, "Where you at, Boss?"

"Back room."

When Big Guy entered, he gave perspective to just how low the ceiling was in this place. In the corner, Mom hiccupped, sounding like a goose, and readjusted herself in her chair.

Boxers shot a curious look to Jonathan, who said, "They're a team."

Clearly, that clarified nothing for Big Guy, but he didn't pursue it. Instead, he handed over the green cashier's bag that he'd removed from under the Batmobile's center console.

Jonathan unzipped it and then sat on the edge of one of the undersized chairs. "Have a seat, Jemmy. We need to talk."

"What's that?"

"We need to talk."

"Should I be afraid?"

"Are you?"

"Not especially."

Jonathan scowled. "What about the dead men?"

"Did they shoot, too?" Jemmy asked.

Jonathan nodded.

"Then it was a fair fight, right?"

"Yeah, I guess it was," Jonathan conceded.

"It's not like I haven't seen dead bodies," Jemmy said.

"Really?"

"Hookers and their friends are mostly junkies, too. They shoot shit into their veins and then just go to sleep and don't wake up."

Jonathan didn't know what to say to that, so he changed the subject. "Okay, well, I'll be honest with you. There are a bunch of dead bodies in room . . ." He looked to Boxers.

"Fifteen."

"There are a bunch of dead bodies in room fifteen. It's important that they go undiscovered for a while."

Jemmy looked confused.

"Keep the door locked and don't tell anyone."

"How long?"

"As long as possible," Jonathan said. "Tomorrow at least, but even longer if you can make that happen."

"Why?"

"Can I leave it at *because I asked you*?" Jonathan said.

Jemmy's eyes narrowed. "You're not really with the FBI, are you?"

Boxers made his growling noise.

Jonathan weighed the options in the space of three heartbeats. The kid was smart and street savvy. He didn't seem prone to panicking. Sometimes, telling the truth was the best option. It was also guaranteed to piss Boxers off.

"No, Jemmy, we're not FBI agents. But we *are* special agents who are working for the FBI. I know that sounds confusing, so welcome to government-speak. We're the good guys. Those men out there were the bad guys."

"Who were they?"

"I don't know yet. All I know is that they tried to kill us."

"Why?"

"I don't know that, either."

"Why aren't we calling the police?"

Jonathan liked the honesty of the question. "I know that seems like the right thing to do, but in this case, it's really not."

"Why?"

"Jesus, kid," Boxers said. "Give it a rest."

"He has every right to ask whatever questions he wants," Jonathan said. He reached into the money pouch and withdrew a strapped stack of $100 bills. "Here's another reason to keep our secret for a while."

Jemmy's jaw fell open, and his eyes grew wide as he took the money with just two fingers. "Seriously?"

"That's ten thousand dollars," Jonathan said. "I'm guessing that you and your mom can put that to really good use."

"Holy shit."

"It's a lot of money," Jonathan said. "All you have to do is agree to keep people out of rooms fourteen and fifteen.

Jemmy riffled through the bills, his eyes wide.

"Did you hear what I told you?"

"This is what ten thousand dollars looks like? I expected it to be bigger."

"And why did I give it to you?" Jonathan prompted.

"To keep quiet about the bodies."

"Right. And to keep quiet about us, too. We were never here."

Jemmy broke his own spell and looked away from the bills. "People are going to find 'em no matter what. What do I tell them? The police are going to come sooner or later."

The kid had a point. "Tell them that you don't know anything," Jonathan said. "It's more or less the truth."

"How do I explain that they ended up dead in one of our rooms?"

"It's going to be pretty obvious that they were shot," Boxers said. Jonathan thought he meant it as sarcasm, but it fell short.

"What the hell?" Jonathan said. "Tell them mostly the truth. Two people checked in tonight, and then you went to bed. When you got around to cleaning the rooms, you found the bodies."

"But then they'll know about you."

"In all honesty, I'd be happy if you could lie a little bit about that. Particularly when it comes to our physical appearances." He looked at Big Guy. "And size."

"Oh, man, then the police will be all over us," Jemmy said.

"That's a given," Jonathan pointed out. "That ten grand will help you with any lost revenue."

Jemmy's eyes returned to the bundled cash.

"By the way," Jonathan said. "Don't tell anybody about the cash. If the police find out you have it, they will take it away like this." He snapped his fingers. "They'll consider it to be evidence."

"But it *is* evidence, isn't it?"

Jonathan shrugged with one shoulder.

"Don't you get in trouble for hiding evidence?"

"All the more reason not to say anything about it."

"Do I need to tell my mom?" Jemmy cast a cautious glance at his snoring mother.

"That's entirely up to you," Jonathan said. "She for sure can testify that she doesn't know anything."

"What about video?" Boxers asked.

Jemmy scowled. "What about it?"

"Do you have any security video of the office and parking lot?"

Jemmy coughed out a laugh. "Hell no. For the same reasons we don't ask for people's names."

Outside, the sound of an approaching vehicle drew Jonathan's attention to the front lobby. "Sounds like you have more customers." He produced one of his FBI business cards from his pocket. "There's a telephone number on there for you to call if you need anything."

Jemmy cocked his head as he read the card. "I thought you said you *weren't* FBI agents."

Jonathan reached out to ruffle the kid's hair, but Jemmy pulled away.

"What can I say? A lot of the world just doesn't make sense."

Jemmy petted the money bundle a little more. "I think I won't tell my mom about this," he said. "She'd ask too many questions and then spend it on stupid shit."

"Suit yourself," Jonathan said. He offered his hand.

Jemmy took it and shook.

"Sorry for all the excitement," Jonathan said.

"I'm almost for sure going to have to tell the police tomorrow. We clean the rooms every day, even if it don't look like it. If we skip those rooms, people will wonder why."

Jonathan let go of the handshake. "Good thinking, Jemmy. Smart thinking."

"I told you I was smart."

"And you didn't lie," Jonathan said.

Chapter 9

Jonathan and Boxers decided to leave the bad guys' vehicle where it was, but only after they'd helped themselves to the limited contents of the glove box and center console.

They drove straight through the night, arriving in Fisherman's Cove shortly before dawn. Jonathan carried the contents of the dead men's pockets and the detritus from their Suburban up to the office and left a note for Venice to work her magic to figure out whatever she could about the attackers. Then he went back down to his residence, where he could hear Boxers already snoring a hole into the darkness from the guest room.

Jonathan made his way to the master bedroom, lay on his bed, fully clothed atop his covers, and was asleep within seconds.

By ten o'clock, Jonathan was showered and ready for a belated start on the day. When he entered the Cave, he realized he was last to show up.

"You and Big Guy were busy last night," Gail quipped. "Is there a reason I wasn't invited to come along?"

"You're upset that you missed a gunfight?" Boxers asked with a chuckle.

"I thought two were enough," Jonathan said. He

neither owed a rationale for his thinking nor intended to deliver one. Gail went through periods from time to time when she proclaimed to feel like a lesser member of the team. She was very good at what she did. She displayed courage under fire, shot better than most operators that he'd known, and was very, very smart.

But not every operation required all three of them to be on triggers, and yes, he tended to be protective of her. In recent months and years, Gail had endured more grievous injuries than any other member of the team. She always came back, but to Jonathan's eye, the returns were progressively less enthusiastic and more cautious. That concerned him. The reasons behind the success of Security Solutions' operations had everything to do with the team's supreme confidence that they could pull off the impossible when the impossible was the only remaining alternative. If that confidence faltered, even for a second, the results could be catastrophic.

Her recovery from a wicked stab wound inflicted by the man who'd burned her house had left Gail significantly changed, Jonathan thought. She spoke less often and appeared distracted. When he'd suggested that maybe she consult a shrink, she'd stormed out of the room. When he'd asked Father Dom to talk with her, the priest had resisted. "It doesn't work that way," he'd said. "Patients have to come to the doctors, not the other way around."

Jonathan was Gail's boss, friend, and occasional lover, but he was not her keeper. She was a grown-up who would figure things out for herself. Or not.

Venice looked up from her keyboard and held up her hand as Jonathan passed the door of her office. "War Room," she said. "Right now."

While he was Venice's boss, too, it often didn't feel that way.

Jonathan spun on his heel and reversed course, heading back toward the teak-and-glass War Room.

Within two minutes, all the players were in their normal seats, and the projector was fired up.

"Pictures of dead people and bloody fingerprints," Venice said as she settled into her command chair. "What a lovely way to start the day. I take it that your trip to Kentucky proved to be exciting?"

Jonathan took two minutes to relay the events in the parking lot of McWhorter's Tavern.

By the time he was done, Venice was tapping away on her computer. "I'm pulling up ICIS," she said. Pronounced EYE-sis, the Interstate Crime Information System was a post-9/11 computer program that allowed police departments to share details of ongoing investigations in real time. Like most of her other workarounds, she had no legal authority to access the system. "I don't see any activity about a shooting there," she said.

"Doesn't surprise me," Jonathan said. "I trust the kid to do the right thing."

"Lord, I hope not," Boxers said. "For most people in the world, calling the police to report a mass murder would *be* the right thing to do."

"How sure are you that the people you shot were not the police?" Gail asked.

"Since they're all dead, let's pretend that I'm very sure," Jonathan said.

Venice tapped and two pictures flashed onto the screen: one of a corpse that was missing most of his head and the other of an athletic man in his forties with blond hair, thin lips, and a sharp stare. "This is Dmitri Korta," she said. "Ukrainian by birth, Russian by choice.

The most recent data shows that he was part of the Wagner Group in Russia."

"That's their private army," Jonathan said.

"I knew that," Venice said. She still didn't like to be interrupted. "The point is—and I believe you'll see it as the beginning of a trend—he was a mercenary."

"Definitely not police," Boxers said, looking straight at Gail.

Another set of pictures, one dead, one alive. "This is Ivan Alexandrovich Gagarin—no relation to the cosmonaut. He disappeared off the radar about four years ago, but he was previously aligned with—you guessed it—the Wagner Group. He was kicked out of that organization for reasons I haven't been able to uncover yet."

"Wow," Boxers said. "You know you've reached a new low when you're not good enough for a group of rapists and murderers."

More pictures. In this set, the corpse still looked much like the live photo. "Now, this one is interesting," Venice said. "He's Richard Petcovich. American by birth, Russian by ancestry, and formerly a special agent for our very own Federal Bureau of Investigation."

Jonathan sat taller in his seat.

"I knew him," Gail said. "HRT, right?" Hostage Rescue Team.

"Exactly."

"That was a long time ago," Gail said. "He washed out on a disciplinary thing."

"I haven't been able to hack in that far yet."

Gail nodded as she remembered. "Yeah, he wasn't right for the job. He liked shooting too much." She cast her eyes at Big Guy. "Like some other people I know."

"I make no apologies," Boxers said.

"Is he still with the Bureau?" Jonathan asked.

"No. His separation date was two years ago, three years short of retirement."

"That's unusual," Gail said. "I left early because I wanted to do other things. But Petty loved the badge and authority. Even if you're a total screwup, the Bureau will do what it can to protect your pension."

"Maybe he got a better offer to play with the Russian mercs," Jonathan said. Back to Venice. "What about the others?"

"More of the same," Venice said. "Petcovich was the only American. The others were all Russian paramilitary." She pushed back her chair and crossed her arms. "All right, gentlemen, what did you do to anger a bunch of mercenaries?"

Jonathan thought it was obvious. "The last few months have brought a recurring theme," he said. "We've got the Los Muertos cartel and Russian mercs."

"Think they still haven't gotten over us blowing up their launch facilities in Venezuela?"

Not too long ago, Jonathan and his team had deployed to the jungles of Venezuela to rescue ten Baptist missionaries who had been taken hostage by the Los Muertos cartel. Once in-country, they'd uncovered a cooperative effort between the Venezuelan government, the cartel (as if there was a difference), and Russian special operators to install missile launch facilities that could lob nuclear warheads to more or less anywhere in the continental United States. None of that could have been done without the cooperation of highly placed and influential players in the American government.

"Why now?" Gail asked.

"Because today's the day we tried to visit Rocco LoCicero," Jonathan said.

"You think they wanted to scare us off from visiting again?" Venice asked.

"I think they wanted to kill us for knowing enough to formulate the questions that would end them," Boxers said.

Gail tried to find a bright spot. "At least they paid a high price for it."

"They'll be back," Jonathan said. "And with a better team next time. We need to get ahead of this."

Venice cocked her head. "What does that mean?"

"That means we bring the fight to the bad guys while they're regrouping to bring it to us."

"I don't know what that means, either," Gail said.

"You lost me there, too, Boss," Boxers said.

"I'm tired of these drug mule assholes just strolling across the Rio Grande with their pockets full of poison," Jonathan said. "I'm tired of having my government— the one I fought for and for which countless of my friends gave up their lives—turning the other cheek to make a profit."

"You can't prove any of that, Digger," Gail said in a soothing tone.

Jonathan caught the attempt at cooling him down, and he appreciated it. "We never really tried to prove it before," he said. "I mean, we always saw the dots that needed connecting, but we never really busted our asses connecting them. Think about it. When the Los Muertos worker bees were moving nuclear launch platforms from their hiding spots to their new reinforced concrete homes, *somebody* at the NCA level turned off the spy satellites to keep the ops off the record." NCA referred to the National Command Authority, which translated to the president, vice president, and secretary of defense, along with their immediate senior staffs.

"What does one thing have to do with the other?" Gail asked. "Are you suggesting that the Los Muertos cartel is trying to develop nuclear capabilities?"

"Wouldn't be any worse than the Iranians getting it," Boxers scoffed.

Jonathan thought he had a point, but said, "No, I don't think the cartel is trying to go nuclear—though like any other terrorist organization, they'd be delighted to have them. The main data point we have from that operation was that the Russians and Los Muertos are working together. I wouldn't be surprised if they were already hard at work fixing the facilities that we blew up."

"Wait," Venice said. "I don't understand how you can glibly assume that the president of the United States and his SecDef are committing treason."

"Because they are," Boxers said.

"You're reading the evidence the way you *want* to read it," Venice said. A rarely discussed fact among the Security Solutions team was that Venice had voted for Tony Darmond. "Even if someone in his administration is responsible for this, that's not the same as Darmond himself."

"The buck stops where it stops," Jonathan reminded. "If you consider that—"

The shrill ring of an old-fashioned telephone interrupted him. It came from Venice's computer. She swung in her chair to address it.

"What the hell was that?" Jonathan asked.

Venice's eyes grew wide. "Oh dear," she said. She looked at Jonathan. "It's a call to your FBI number." The contact information on the business cards Neil Bonner handed out was all fictitious in the sense that neither the phone number nor the email address actually went to the FBI, but very real in the sense that it went to Venice's computer, which scrambled and anonymized the signal. "It's coming from a Kentucky number."

"This should be interesting," Boxers said.

Jonathan pointed to Venice's computer with his forehead. "Answer it."

Venice donned a headset, coded in office background noise, then pressed the connect button. "Federal Bureau of Investigation, how may I direct your call?" She listened for a moment. "Special Agent Bonner is out of the office at the moment. May I take a message?" Another moment of silence. "I understand, sir. Hold for a moment and I'll transfer you to his cell phone." She put the call on hold and pointed at Jonathan. "Do you have your cell phone on you?"

Jonathan lifted it from his pocket and held it high. "I'll put it on speaker so everyone can hear, but no one else talk." The phone buzzed and he connected the call. "Bonner."

A hesitant, gravelly male voice said, "Is this Special Agent Neil Bonner?"

"Who's calling, please?"

"You first. I have to know."

"I'm Bonner. Now, it's your turn."

"Agent Bonner, we need to meet. This is Captain Michael Hite of USP Big Sandy. We met at the gate yesterday."

"I remember. How can I help you?"

"Not on the phone. We need to meet ASAP. Face-to-face."

Jonathan scanned the War Room for reactions. Nothing but facial question marks.

"I'm afraid I need more than that, Captain Hite. I've

already wasted too many hours trying to deal with your prison and its policies."

Silence.

"Captain?"

"People are going to try to kill you, Agent Bonner."

Boxers sat taller in his seat.

Jonathan's mind raced to decide his next move. Should he express surprise or tell the truth? "Why would they do that?"

"That's why we have to meet. I can't talk about this on the phone."

"When people are trying to kill me, why can't *you* talk about it on the phone?"

Silence.

"Captain Hite?"

"I don't know what to tell you, Agent Bonner. This is a very serious matter, and the FBI needs to know about it."

"There's a field office in Louisville," Jonathan said. "Go talk to them."

The expressions in his staff's faces cried out in unison, *Are you crazy?*

"I can't."

"Why not?"

"Because they can't be trusted. I can tell you this. Remember who you came to speak to yesterday? Don't say the name."

"Of course I remember. And why not say the name?" Jonathan thought he knew, but he wanted to hear it from Hite.

"Because to say it will trigger listening algorithms."

Just as Jonathan thought. In recent years, the CIA, NSA, FBI, and any number of other alphabet agencies had thrown citizens' Fourth Amendment protections onto the pyre of natural rights that had been shredded

ZERO SUM 125

under the guise of improving security. If people used certain words or phrases, the computers that listened passively to every phone conversation and passively read every email correspondence would click into active mode and not only start recording the conversation but also alert federal law enforcement personnel of a possible impending threat. It was no accident that citizens who did not toe the president's party line found themselves the subject of grand jury investigations and IRS audits. Given the events of the past forty-eight hours, mentioning the name of Rocco LoCicero did seem like a bad idea.

"Okay," Jonathan said. "Here's the deal. I'm not going all the way back to the prison."

"Neither am I," Hite said. "Not ever. I can't. Not with what I have."

"What is it that you have?"

More silence. Finally, "For reasons already mentioned, I cannot tell you that. But I can tell you that it's everything you were hoping to learn from your visit, plus much, much more."

Boxers held up a piece of paper on which he'd written a question for Jonathan to ask.

Jonathan nodded. "How do I know I can trust you?"

Hite's tone changed abruptly. "Goddammit, can we please stop playing games? This is important, and you know it is. It's important enough to sic a hit team on you. And that was good shooting, by the way."

Jonathan recoiled. He hadn't expected that. "Excuse me?"

"Games, Bonner. Let's stop playing them. I know about what happened at the motel. That's when I knew it was time for me to get out of town and stay there. Now, what do you say? Are we doing this or not?"

Jonathan found the change in Hite's approach to be startling.

"Look, Bonner, I'm not going to beg, okay? Do you want to flush the toilet that is Washington, or don't you? One way or the other, I don't expect to be alive for more than a day or two. Neither should you. Consider this the last time I ask the question."

This new approach was more convincing, Jonathan thought. Somehow, anger seemed like the better emotion.

"All right," Jonathan said. "Where do we meet?"

"Are you familiar with the Hilltop Manor Resort in West Virginia?"

"I am." He was very familiar with it, in fact. He doubted that anyone else understood that if the threat of a nuclear war ever tipped past a certain point, the resort's underground conference facilities would become the US Government Relocation Center—the spot where the Senate and the House of Representatives would hunker down to continue to run the government.

"Good," Hite said. "If you leave now, how long would it take you to get there?"

Jonathan shot a look to Venice, who was already consulting her computer. After five seconds, she held up five fingers.

"About five hours," Jonathan said.

"I'll give you seven," Hite said. "Come to the lobby at five o'clock this afternoon. There's a sofa along the front wall. In case you don't remember what I look like, I'll be sitting there drinking a bourbon and reading the front section of the *Wall Street Journal*. I'll be wearing jeans and blue tennis shoes."

Jonathan found the amateur tradecraft amusing, but he kept that out of his voice when he asked, "Do we have a pass phrase?"

The line went dead.

"I don't want you going alone," Boxers said within seconds.

"Shouldn't be a problem," Jonathan said. "Hite didn't say I had to be alone." He looked to Gail as he added, "I think all three of us should go. We'll treat this as a real op."

Chapter 10

Along the curb outside of the Paisano Hotel in Marfa, Texas, Paco Gomez watched in silence from the driver's seat of his Ford F-150 as residents wandered by, seemingly oblivious to his presence. He scowled at the memory of his time with the new girl last night—the one named Sissy who had been brought in along with her twin brother. Personally, Paco had no use for the boy, but others on the hacienda would. Plus, the field bosses could always use another young back and a pair of strong shoulders.

But Sissy. She would be special tonight. He had the highest expectations.

Paco had heard rumors that Marfa once thrived as a business hub, but given what he saw today, it was hard to imagine. The impressive courthouse loomed in his rearview mirror with its rounded dome, which no doubt provided a spectacular view of the utterly flat surrounding countryside, but what on earth could an observer hope to see?

Paco sat behind the steering wheel, facing Texas Street—more specifically, the entrance to Kathee's Koffee Kup, the tiny diner that he'd chosen as the venue for this morning's meeting. He expected that Harold Standish would be late, and the man did not disappoint.

What was it about powerful Americans that made them feel more powerful by making others wait? Paco sat in his observation spot specifically to deny Standish the satisfaction of seeing him biding his time at a table alone.

The thought occurred to him that perhaps Standish was playing the same game—hanging out and observing until Paco arrived, but he rejected it as unlikely. From where Paco sat, all sightlines were covered. Outside of commandeering a window in one of the businesses with a view of the street, there was no spot from which to observe Kathee's that would not be visible to him.

So, he waited.

Kathee Hafer held a special place in Paco's heart. A devoted wife and mom at heart, she saw right away the infinite upside to the business proposal that Paco offered her nearly three years ago. Located as close as she was to the courthouse, her clientele included some of the most reputable professionals in this part of the state. It was the last place anyone would suspect to be a distribution hub for Los Muertos. Rolo Gomez had discovered many years ago that try as they might, gringos could not see past their prejudices and preconceived notions about the drug business.

Gringo lawmakers imagined that cocaine and fentanyl and methamphetamines were manufactured in the back rooms of ugly *barrios* by tweakers who were so high on their own product that they could barely function in society. It never occurred to them that the executives of a billion-dollar operation like Los Muertos would operate their business like, well, a billion-dollar operation. Cartel kingpins were also church elders, Masons, Lions, philanthropists, and members of the local chamber of commerce.

It only made sense that people like Paco would dine

at will with people from the courthouse. Paco dressed as they did, but better. Where their boots were from Justin or Ariat, his were Lucchese. His clothes were tailor-made, as were the six-thousand-dollar hats he wore. He was richer and smarter than those lawyers and cops and court officers would ever be.

And politicians? They were the same on both sides of the Rio Grande. They could smell a man with money, and they would literally sell their souls for surprisingly few dollars. And once you had a politician in your pocket, the world belonged to you. Once politicians accepted their invitation to join your world of unlimited, untaxable income, they became your protectors.

Kathee Hafer's building was one of few in Marfa that had a basement. She'd been using it as a place to store her dry goods—ground coffee, paper towels, condiment jars, that sort of thing. Access to the basement involved opening a hatch in the kitchen floor and walking down a steep flight of stairs to an expanse that at one time ended at the base of the foundation along the back wall of the restaurant. More recently, over the course of the past two years, Paco's construction team had turned that back wall of the basement into the entrance to a tunnel that burrowed over one hundred yards to another basement, this one in a tiny bungalow that Paco owned through a nonexistent firm called Oil Resources.

No one questioned the presence of trucks unloading at a restaurant's loading dock, even in the wee hours of the morning. Kathee understood that the crates and boxes with the blue labels were not to be touched by her, even though the labels identified the contents as meat or eggs or cheese.

Kathee had been paid very well not to notice the construction that had led to the tunnel, and she continued to make good money not to ask questions and to be absent from the basement when those boxes and crates were shuttled through the door she was paid not to notice. Paco had even camouflaged the door as a bed frame propped up against the wall so that she might have plausible deniability if anyone asked questions that should never be asked. Finally, if anyone did ask, she was paid to send security camera footage of the questioner to Paco, who would decide that person's fate.

In the years since their special arrangement had been secured, Kathee had spent a good chunk of her illicit income to beautify the interior dining space and make the exterior façade to the Koffee Kup look three times more inviting than any of the other restaurants downtown. The ruse was made all the more believable by the fact that Kathee's skills as a chef were really very good.

Harold Standish's car approached from behind Paco's Ford and rolled to the curb directly in front of Kathee's Koffee Kup. The front door opened, and a pretty young lady stepped out of the driver's seat. She walked to the left rear door and opened it. Standish took his time climbing out of the seat. He stretched, said something to his driver, then disappeared into the restaurant while she returned to the driver's seat

What a narcissistic prick, Paco thought. *I wonder if he'll even bring her something to eat?*

Paco counted to sixty in his head and then let himself out of the Ford. As he strode toward the door, he settled his hat just so on his head. An invisible bell dinged as he pulled the door open and stepped into the over-chilled bistro. Gringos loved their air conditioning.

Kathee acknowledged him with her eyes but made no physical move to say hello as he strode to the back of the dining room, where Harold Standish had been seated.

Paco imagined that the Food Network shows he

liked to watch would consider the décor inside Kathee's to be dated and in need of replacement, but he liked the old-style faux leather booths and four-tops with cane-back chairs. As was the case of pretty much every structure in Marfa, pictures of Rock Hudson, Elizabeth Taylor, and James Dean dominated the walls, along with behind-the-scenes photographs from the production of the 1956 film *Giant*, which, for reasons Paco neither understood nor cared about, was shot there.

Standish gave a subtle wave when he saw Paco approaching. He sat in the left-hand bench of the booth in the back-right corner.

Paco didn't return the wave. As far as he was concerned, this wasn't the kind of meeting that warranted a wave. He was still ten feet away and closing when he took the offensive. "Why on earth would you bring a driver with you?"

Standish's face remained impassive. "Good afternoon to you, too, Paco."

"It's a serious question," Paco said as he slid into the bench opposite the other man.

"I'm sure it was," Standish said. "I don't owe you an explanation, but suffice it to say that being without my driver would raise far more eyebrows than bringing her along. This is what she does. She thinks that I'm meeting a business contact. She's paid to accept compartmentalization of information."

Paco realized that he didn't care. "Let's get to it, then," he said. "Your people are incompetent. You know that, right?"

"How 'bout you dial it back a little?" Standish said. "I presume you're speaking of that incident in Kentucky?"

"Goddamn right that's what I'm talking about. You said you were going to send your best team."

Standish *piff*ed, his face a mask of studied boredom.

"What I said was, I was going to send the best team I could assemble. We didn't have a lot of time."

"If you weren't ready, then you should have waited," Paco said. "Now, Director Rivers's team has been alerted. You've said yourself that she could be a problem."

"She's only a problem if she has information that can hurt us," Standish said. "I have a greater concern, Paco. I've heard rumors that you and your father are not getting along. I've heard rumors that you are trying to take over control of Los Muertos." He rested his forearms on the table and leaned in. "It makes sense to me that you might stand to profit if Operation Southern Hammer were to come undone. You could point to the old man and say, *See? He's the wrong guy for the job.*"

Paco absorbed the words as he watched Standish's eyes. The eyes, after all, were the windows to the mind—to a person's true intent. For whatever reason, the American was trying to get a rise out of Paco. He would not grant satisfaction.

"You would be wise to focus your concern on matters that you can control," Paco said.

Standish smiled, and then he chuckled. "You've got a lot of nerve, my friend. I'll give you that. After you create the mother of all screwups, you try to blame me for dropping the ball. If you hadn't had a temper tantrum like a little baby and sent poison to a little boy, none of this would be happening. That takes *cojones grande*, for sure. It also makes me wonder if you're not a little *loco en la cabeza*." He made a swirling motion at his temple with his forefinger.

"Crazy in the head," Paco translated. "Is that what you think of me?"

"That's what everybody thinks of you, Paco," Standish said with a chuckle. "But that's what keeps your enemies on edge, right? I mean, if you're willing to kill an enemy's only child, without regard to what we call collateral damage, a person's got to ask himself what else would you do? That was the whole point, wasn't it?"

Paco didn't like the way this conversation was going. He was supposed to be chastising Standish, not the other way around.

"You called this meeting," Standish said. "What are we here to talk about?"

Paco felt his resolve faltering. He held up his hands, as if to surrender. "Perhaps my actions against Rocco LoCicero were a bit ill-considered."

"Ya think?" Standish scoffed. Then he retreated. "I'm sorry. That was rude."

Paco tried to organize his thoughts. "I have a feeling," he said. "Sometimes, you know, things don't feel right, but you can't exactly articulate why?"

"Those feelings keep us alive sometimes," Standish said. "I know exactly what you're talking about. In general, anyway, but not in this circumstance."

"Are you aware of who runs the school where Giovanni LoCicero was enrolled?"

"You mean where he was *killed*," Standish corrected. Again, he retreated. "Sorry."

"I didn't know this at the time, but my father informs me that the school's benefactor is a very rich man and a former elite soldier. His name is Jonathan Grave, and we have strong reason to believe that he has been involved in extensive violence against Los Muertos in recent months and years. It's entirely possible that he was one of the men who wanted to interview LoCicero in prison."

Standish's jaw dropped as his skin turned pale. This was genuine surprise. "I thought they were FBI agents."

"Everyone thought they were FBI agents," Paco said.

"And perhaps they were. But I fear that they were *posing* as FBI agents."

Standish drew quiet as he thought through the ramifications of what he was hearing. "So, this *extensive violence* you mention . . ."

"Unbelievable violence. I don't know how many of our people they have killed. They have destroyed over a hundred million dollars in product."

Standish scowled and rubbed his forehead. "If you know who they are, why are they still walking the earth? Why haven't you killed them?"

At the mention of the K-word, Paco reflexively pivoted to scan the room in case someone had heard. "Please be careful what you say," he pleaded. "This is a small town, and all small towns have huge ears."

"The question remains."

"You saw the answer in the motel parking lot in Tennessee."

"Kentucky."

"Whatever. It's as if this team is unstoppable."

Standish cocked his head to the side. "Why didn't you tell me this before I dispatched my operators?"

"I did not yet have the information."

"Six very good operators are dead now," Standish said.

Paco allowed himself a smirk. "The fact that they are dead calls into question your assertion that they were *very good*." When he didn't get a smile in return, he knew that he'd failed to sell the laugh line. He let a few seconds pass to change the tone of the conversation. "Meaning no disrespect to your operators, I think perhaps if they had known the . . . *talents* of the men they were confronting, things might have gone the same. It's easy for very good operators to assume that their opponent is very bad. That can lead to deadly miscalculations."

Standish's brow furrowed as he cast a glance toward the floor. It was the posture of bad news.

"What are you not telling me?" Paco asked.

"I'm told that there's disturbing video camera footage from the prison in Kentucky," Standish said. His eyes stayed focused on the floor. Maybe on a place beyond the floor. "The captain of the guard there—a man named Michael Hite—spent time with LoCicero alone in his cell in solitary."

"Is this unusual?"

"The meeting happened after LoCicero had made his pitch to reveal Southern Hammer."

Paco waited. He wasn't understanding what he was being told.

"They met for quite a long time."

"What did they talk about?"

"We don't know for sure. There are no cameras allowed in the individual cells, and we're not allowed to record conversations."

Paco sensed that he knew where this was going, but he didn't want to jump to conclusions. "You're assuming that LoCicero shared his story."

"Yes, I am," Standish said.

This was the problem with secrets that are known by too many people. Even the smallest leak blossoms into a tsunami with stunning speed. "So now you need to eliminate this . . . I'm sorry, I forgot his name."

"Michael Hite. Yes, that's what we need to do. But he's nowhere to be found."

"I don't understand."

"Hite and LoCicero met for, like, twenty, twenty-five minutes, and then Hite left the cell, left the facility, and disappeared."

Again, Paco waited for the rest of the explanation.

"Disappeared," Standish said. "Poof. Gone. Didn't go to his house, didn't go to an ATM, just vanished."

"And your paranoia is telling you that he's gone straight to the prosecution to bring us down."

"I wish it were that simple," Standish said. His face grew progressively grayer. He explained, "While cameras are not allowed in the jail cells, they are all over the place at the front gate to the prison. Cameras caught the FBI men we attacked handing Michael Hite a business card."

"You've seen this picture?" Paco asked.

"I have. And here's the strangest thing. The features of the agents are blurred in the images."

"I don't understand."

"They're blurred. As if someone put a greasy thumbprint over their features."

"And why should this concern me?" Paco asked. He still wasn't quite seeing the whole picture.

"Because the men with the blurred faces took out some very good operators with extreme precision."

"You think the FBI agent is Jonathan Grave?" Paco asked. He wanted to be sure he was seeing the big picture.

"And more than that, I think Michael Hite brought Rocco LoCicero's story straight to him. Even after we kill Rocco—and we will—the story will still be out there, protected by a very rich, very talented special operator."

Yes, this was bad. Very, very bad. "You have to stop him."

Standish leaned back in his seat again. "We're working on that," he said.

"What does that mean?"

"That means you don't need to know the details," Standish said.

"Are you following him?"

"Let's say we're tracking him."

"Who is *we*?"

The smirk returned. "You worry about the things that you can control," Standish said. "You leave the rest for me. Now, let's get back to the business of business."

Paco cocked his head.

"Southern Hammer is not dead, Paco. Commitments have been made, and bills need to be paid. With the old way of doing business broken, we need to think of something else. The last thing we want is for the well to run dry. If the flow of product stops, our list of enemies will grow very quickly."

Standish realized that he'd long ago misplayed his hand in his dealings with Paco, and now that was coming back to haunt him. In the early days, he'd let Paco believe that he, Paco, was in charge of far more elements of Operation Southern Hammer than he was. Standish did it to stroke the man's prodigious ego, to keep him focused on the flow of product and the concomitant security exposures. In the end, he'd fed the Mexican's ego far more than he should have.

Could Paco really have expected the United States government to be a passive player in an operation as vast as this one? Did he really believe that Uncle Sam would entrust a bunch of tweaked-out street thugs in an enterprise that could sink the Darmond administration? Standish wrote it off against Paco's ongoing and vast ignorance about everything.

Standish would look into this Jonathan Grave person, but that was a concern for the future. The most pressing business now was to silence LoCicero and this prison guard, Michael Hite. Killing a man in prison was no harder than keeping him alive. Concrete walls and the absence of an escape route made murder easy.

Michael Hite, on the other hand, posed a greater challenge. The instant Standish got word that the prison guard had disappeared, he reached out to one of his contacts at the NSA to lock onto Hite's cell phone and track his movements. His next move was to contact Porter Granger, a former paramilitary contractor for the CIA (or the highest bidder) to assemble a team to close in on the coordinates supplied by his NSA guy and kill Hite.

Porter had been Standish's go-to guy for a long time. Given the colossal failure of the attack in the motel parking lot, this one would cost twice what a normal hit team would cost, but it was what it was, and Porter was in the mercenary/hit team business. If only the taxpayers knew where countless millions of off-the-books dollars were spent.

Actually, they wouldn't want to know.

This operation to prevent the exposure of Southern Hammer was a favor to the American people. They were tired of controversy and political infighting. They wanted to live their lives in peace, ignorant of the truths of governance. They understood and accepted that every president was a criminal at some level—whether it was planting false stories about their political opponents or lying about inconvenient truths that didn't serve their immediate needs. In the years since politics had become a team sport, where players demanded unwavering loyalty to the party line, politicians on both sides of the aisle had been granted popular immunity by their respective voting blocs. No matter how egregious the violation, political supporters would coalesce around their candidate and rationalize that a win for the team outweighed the rule of law because the win was a de facto loss for the other side. Compromise meant political suicide.

President Darmond was particularly talented at playing the game of binary politics, and he wasn't even all that subtle. Powerful people who voiced opposition to his plans or programs found themselves under investigation or even indictment for technical violations of obscure laws, the defense against which would ruin them financially. The president's team played along, with rousing support from members of the media, most of whom considered themselves part of Darmond's team.

When LoCicero and Hite were dead, there would be no story to report. Sure, there would be rumors and allegations, but without eyewitnesses, Darmond would play the card he always played and proclaim the truth tellers to be crazy conspiracy theorists. Investigations and indictments would follow. Rinse and repeat.

The less the rabble had to think about their preconceived conclusions, the more contented they would be. With luck, this matter could be cleared up in just a day or two.

But first, there was the matter of guaranteeing that the flow of product continued unabated.

Chapter 11

The Hilltop Manor Resort was the throwback to old-school Southern aristocracy. Jonathan was no expert in architectural geology, but to his eye, the edifice was constructed of stark white marble, the main entrance dominated by towering columns and a grand staircase that must have covered a half-acre of land. The stairway led to a grand foyer that featured custom murals depicting fox hunts and daily life before the American Civil War. Beyond the foyer, another grand staircase ushered visitors to the Grand Lobby, which itself was dominated by a dozen or more four- to six-person conversation groups defined by reproductions of Victorian-era sofas and chairs.

Jonathan hadn't been here in years, but back then, gentlemen in the lobby wore jackets and ties unless they were on their way back from a golf outing, in which case country club chic was acceptable so long as it was worn only in passing from the club to their lodgings, where their jackets and ties awaited. Today, people dressed as if they were visiting a bus station, with ratty shorts and flip-flops more common than neat attire.

Jonathan had tipped the doorman a hundred bucks to keep the Batmobile parked where Boxers had left it in the front circle at the base of the stairs. From that location, at a command from Mother Hen, the jammer built into the vehicle could block all cell phone signals. One of the most recent additions to the Batmobile, the ability to block outgoing communications made working in large crowds a lot safer.

He and his team entered separately, with Gail leading and Boxers bringing up the rear. They were half an hour early. Jonathan wanted to get the lay of the land and a feel for whether or not they'd voluntarily entered some kind of ambush.

"Half the people here are carrying pistols," Boxers said through the bud in Jonathan's ear.

"Welcome to West Virginia," Jonathan said.

The lobby bar they were searching for was called the Winner's Circle, and it was designed exactly to Jonathan's preferred taste in watering holes. The expansive bar and the back bar were fabricated from black walnut, and the display of scotches was one of the most extensive he'd ever seen. At twenty-plus bucks a pour, he figured this place churned money like an ATM.

Twenty-five feet over his head, the arched ceiling featured stamped copper tiles and a spectacular chandelier that may have been original to the building, though converted to electricity.

Gail Bonneville sat in a green velvet club chair, nursing what appeared to be a gin and tonic—clear liquid on the rocks with a lime. They made eye contact but otherwise did not acknowledge each other as Jonathan made his way to the bar and ordered a Beefeater martini, straight up.

"You just checking in?" the bartender asked. His nametag proclaimed him to be BARNEY.

Why is it that half the bartenders on the planet are named Barney?

"No, I'm just passing through, really. A friend of mine told me about this place, and I am something of a connoisseur of dark wood bars." As a rule, Jonathan didn't talk to strangers while on an op, but sometimes silence brought more suspicion than evasion. "I'm surprised you're not more crowded."

"Give it another hour," Barney said. "We'll be wall-to-wall."

Jonathan cast a casual glance over his left shoulder and saw that Gail was staring at him. "I believe our friend has arrived," she whispered into the invisible ear bud mic. When they made eye contact, she cut her gaze to her left, pointing him toward a man in jeans and blue tennis shoes who was helping himself to a seat at the end of the sofa by the wall. Jonathan pulled his cell phone from his pocket to give himself plausible deniability and said, "Big Guy, what's your location?"

"I'm in the lobby on the other side of the fireplace. I don't have eyes on either you or Gunslinger, but I can be on top of you in seconds if something goes bad. Is it our guy?"

"Seeing him out of context, I'm not sure," he said. The old adage was true: when you speak with a cop, all you really see is the badge. Jonathan pantomimed disconnecting from the call. The guy in the jeans hadn't yet ordered a drink, and there was no sign yet of a *Wall Street Journal*. Then again, it was early— only 4:52.

Jonathan did the phone gambit again. "'Slinger, do me a favor and see what happens if you sit on the sofa next to him."

Gail didn't reply, but she stood from her seat, collected her drink, and moved across the room to the sofa.

"Don't ask for permission," Jonathan said. "Just sit down next to him. See how he reacts."

Despite her nagging limp, Gail moved with what Jonathan thought was a dancer's grace as she glided over to the man-who-might-be Hite, placed her drink on the end table, and sat on the opposite end of the sofa from him, leaving the middle cushion open.

The other occupant of the sofa said something to her, and she replied, "I'll only be here for a few minutes."

Hite's eyes showed something north of fear yet south of panic. He said something else, to which Gail replied, "There are many other seats open. You're free to move to any one of them."

Jonathan smiled. If the man was, in fact, Hite, putting him on edge was a good idea. Jonathan scanned the room for signs of a reaction from the other patrons. If this were part of an organized ambush, this kind of change in plans would trigger a response. Nothing.

"Pretend you know him," Jonathan said. Part of this exercise was to entertain Jonathan and mess with Hite's head, but his reaction to being recognized would say a lot about the man's true intentions.

Gail cocked her head and leaned closer to the man. "I think we've met," she said.

Hite's eyes widened, and Jonathan could read his lips as he said, "No, I don't think so."

"I'm almost certain," Gail said. "My name's Jerri. Yours is Michael Hite." She pretended to search the ceiling to unlock the memory while Hite's face turned red.

"Am I right?"

Hite looked on the edge of panic.

"Go for it," Jonathan said as he stood from his stool. He left fifty bucks on the bar for his drink.

"Shouldn't you be drinking bourbon and reading a newspaper now?" Gail asked.

Hite shot to his feet, clearly ready to bolt.

Jonathan stepped into the open where Hite could see him and gave a little four-finger wave.

"You can relax," Gail said. "We're part of the same team. Agent Bonner wanted to make sure you're who you said you'd be."

Jonathan approached and offered his hand. "Good to see you again," he said.

Hite hesitated but reached for the hand anyway. "I hate this shit," he said.

"There's always a bit of theater to tradecraft," Jonathan said. "Just for grins and giggles, would you mind showing me what you said you'd be reading?"

Hite fumbled with his soft-sided case, placing it on the sofa to pull it open. He withdrew a copy of today's *Wall Street Journal*. "I just hadn't got to it yet. I should also be drinking a bourbon."

Boxers' voice in Jonathan's ear said, "Um, Boss, I think we have a problem. Teams of unsubs are gathering around the exits. They've got a Secret Service vibe to them, and their eyes are darting everywhere. They're also wearing too many layers for the weather."

Unsubs were unknown subjects, and the extra layers suggested firepower and body armor.

Gail turned to face the fireplace and the Grand Lobby beyond, while Jonathan turned the other way to look past the bartender and the wall behind the bar.

Hite sensed something was wrong. "What's happening?"

"I think we're about to have a problem," Jonathan said. "What are the chances that you were followed?"

Hite's head spun one hundred and eighty degrees as

he tried to figure out what Jonathan and Gail were looking at. "What is it?"

Jonathan didn't bother to ask again because the question was fundamentally irrelevant. Clearly, Hite *had* been followed—or, more likely, traced electronically.

"What did you bring to give me?" Jonathan asked.

"Please tell me what is happening."

Jonathan grasped Hite's left biceps and lifted. "We're relocating."

"Where to?" Unbeknown to each other, Boxers and Hite spoke in unison.

"There's a door in the wall to the left of the bar. With luck it leads to someplace useful."

"Are you talking to someone else?" Hite asked.

"I don't think they've seen us yet," Gail said. She did her best to look casual as she scanned the room behind them.

"Stand up normally," Jonathan said to Hite. "Don't make me drag you, and don't run. It appears as if you have, indeed, been followed and that the followers are here."

"Why?"

Jonathan didn't answer. Instead, he led the way to the vertical rectangle in the tapestry wallpaper that could be nothing but a door.

"Excuse me," said Barney the bartender as Jonathan turned the recessed D-ring handle. "That area is off-limits for guests today. There's maintenance work going on, and we don't want—"

Jonathan didn't care. He opened the door and pushed Hite through the opening first, then ushered Gail in second. As she cleared the threshold, he dared a look over his shoulder into the Grand Lobby.

"They're coming," Boxers said at the same instant

that Jonathan saw the men in suits converging their
way. "You take care of the PC. I'll see if I can slow a
couple of them down."

Before Jonathan could look away, he watched Big
Guy lift one of the followers by his belt and his collar
and sling him like a bag of fertilizer into one of the
other ones. While the men crashed to the floor, causing
lamps to shatter and furniture to overturn, a chorus of
screams and shouts pulled Barney's attention away,
allowing Jonathan to disappear behind the wall without
further confrontation.

The room beyond the bar looked like a cross between a ballroom and a basketball court. Polished maple
floors formed an architectural starburst as the wedges
of floorboards converged on an eight-foot-diameter
circle of polished ebony that was centered under a
massive chandelier featuring about a million crystal
baubles. Partially completed scaffolding lined the walls,
but no workers were currently on the job.

"I gave three of the suits a bad limp," Boxers said
in Jonathan's ear, "but at least three more are heading
your way. I'm moving the Batmobile to secondary exfil.
Try not to dawdle." The secondary exfiltration spot
was a door on the far western end of the hotel and one
floor down.

"We need to hurry," Jonathan said. Then, to Gail, he
asked, "Are you okay?" Her expression showed distress,
and she'd begun to favor her left side.

"Don't wait for me," she said. "I'll get there. It's not
such a bad idea for me to hang back and hold off the
bad guys."

That was bold talk, and Jonathan appreciated the
offer, but there was no way he'd leave her alone in a
fight. Instead, he brought them all to a stop at the far end

of the ballroom, where he turned and took a shooter's stance, gun drawn in a two-handed grip, feet planted, his left slightly forward of the right.

"Suppose they're cops or feds?" Gail asked. "We can't just shoot them."

This was becoming a recurring theme. "These aren't police tactics," Jonathan said. "They're being too obvious, and there aren't enough of them."

"They could always be stacking up outside," Gail said.

Yes, they could, but Jonathan chose to assume otherwise.

Three seconds later, the door they'd just passed through opened again, revealing two men in nearly identical overstuffed suits. Jonathan fired three shots from his Colt into the floor just in front of the bad guys' feet. They jumped back into the bar and became invisible.

"You missed," Hite said.

"No, I didn't," Jonathan said. He'd fired his weapon for the benefit of the noise, not the kill, and by stitching the floor instead of the wall, he didn't have to worry about over-penetration that might accidentally hit an innocent party on the other side.

"Way to ignite a panic, Boss," Boxers said over the radio. The sounds of fear and running feet crescendoed throughout the hotel.

Jonathan pushed Hite through the next doorway, which led to yet another ballroom, this one decked out floor-to-ceiling with mirrored glass. He made a note not to shoot in here. At seven years' bad luck per pane, he'd need twelve lifetimes to pay off the karmic debt.

They picked up their speed as they cut diagonally

across the dance floor to a door on the far right-hand wall.

Jonathan turned and started walking backward. "'Slinger, you take custody of Captain Hite and I'll cover our six." It was a compromise solution to leaving Gail to take the rear yet still provide a dignified reason to be moving more slowly than he'd like.

As Gail pulled open the door, the sounds of panic peaked. "We need to holster up," Gail said.

It was a valid point. When people are running from the sound of gunshots, it's best not to be seen with guns drawn. By the time Jonathan made it to the doorway of the mirror room and the hallway beyond, the bad guys still had not entered. He took three seconds to drop his partially spent magazine from the mag well and exchange it with a new one from the mag pouch on his left hip. It was always better to reload in the downtimes than in the height of a shitstorm.

Fearful people flowed like a river in the hallway as they fled the sounds of the gunshots. "Where the hell are they going?" Jonathan thought aloud. If he had, in fact, been the active shooter they feared, they were now presenting limitless target opportunities. *Morons.*

With his firearm put away, he joined Gail and Hite in the wide hallway and became part of the crowd.

"Where are we going?" Hite asked. His tone was beginning to show progressively more panic.

"We have a car waiting for us," Jonathan said.

"I'm not going with you. I have a plan of my own."

"And we'll be happy to drop you off wherever you'd like to go. But for right now, this is the primary place for you *not* to be. Agreed?"

"I suppose." He neither fought back nor ran away. Jonathan decided to call that a victory.

Sounds of distress among the hotel guests grew even louder behind them.

"Hey!" someone yelled.

"Get out of the way!"

Jonathan tossed a glance over his shoulder in time to see a curtain get pulled off its rod, punctuated by the sound of furniture falling.

"You son of a . . . Gun! Jesus, he's got a gun!"

"That's our cue," Jonathan said. "Rush him out of here." Jonathan thrust his left arm around Hite's left arm, trapping the crook of his elbow in the crook of his own, and extended his hand to the back of Hite's shoulder, causing the PC to bend at the waist and provide a less visible target. Gail mirrored the maneuver on Hite's right side.

"Federal agents, out of the way!" Jonathan called.

The panic spiked even more.

"There they are!" someone yelled. A gunshot shook the building as the window at Jonathan's right shattered and collapsed in its frame.

It had been a long time since Jonathan had done this level of personnel protection, but the instincts were still there. "PC's yours," he said to Gail as he released his grip on Hite's arm.

Dropping to one knee, he redrew his Colt. "Down!" he yelled. "Down, down, down!"

Gail kept driving Hite forward.

Two more gunshots pulsed through the hallway, and this time, Jonathan saw three people fall. *These shooters suck.*

They were trying to run and shoot at the same time, and that was their mistake.

As hotel guests fell to the floor for cover or raced by him in a panic, he finally caught a useful sight picture.

He saw a guy in a dark suit with a pistol at high-ready, and Jonathan popped him without hesitation, drilling him through the point of his chin. The guy pitched forward onto the green-and-white carpet, dead before he started to fall.

Jonathan shifted his aim but saw no one who appeared to be a target.

"I've got one down, but at least one, maybe two still around and breathing."

"'Slinger and PC are already at the stairwell," Gail's voice said.

"Scorpion, if you're alive, call it a victory and get out of there," Boxers said.

Jonathan scanned the crowd for more targets, but there continued to be none.

"We need to know who these guys are," Jonathan said.

"No, we need to di di mau right by-God now!" Boxers said, invoking Vietnam-era jargon for getting the hell out. "I'm pulling the Batmobile into position now."

Jonathan advanced on the body of the man he'd shot. Even with a good part of his head missing, the guy had a certain military bearing about him—thick neck, broad shoulders, narrow waist. He'd dropped his SIG-SAUR P320-M18 when he died. Jonathan picked it up off the carpet by the trigger guard and used two fingers to drop it into his jacket pocket. Maybe Venice could pull some fingerprints.

As the panicked crowd started to reanimate and look his way, Jonathan produced his FBI shield. "I'm a federal agent," he said. "This man was trying to attack a protectee. Please stay put until other agents arrive to take your statements." With that, he turned and headed toward the stairs.

He'd only taken a few steps when a beefy guy stepped out to block his path. The man presented a shield of his own. "I'm a cop, too," he said. "And I don't believe—"

"You don't want to start this fight," Jonathan said, attempting to sidestep around the cop.

But the cop blocked his way again. As he moved, his hand disappeared around the small of his back.

Jonathan didn't hesitate. He fired his left fist like a striking snake, nailing the would-be Good Samaritan squarely on the tip of his nose and launching a fountain of blood that sheeted down his lips and off his jaw. The guy dropped to his knees as if his wires had been unplugged.

A punch buys time, not safety. Jonathan took off running toward the exit to the emergency stairwell, where he was quickly consumed by the roiling crowd of anxious guests pushing their way to safety.

Jonathan's earbud popped as someone broke squelch on the channel. "Scorpion, Scorpion, Mother Hen."

"Go ahead."

"Be advised, a nine-one-one call just got out past the jamming signal," Venice said. "They're reporting an active shooter."

"What about the security cameras?" Gail asked over the air.

"I disabled them on your way in," Venice said. "ICIS is lighting up, too. Y'all need to get out of there as soon as you can."

Boxers said, "'Slinger and the PC are on board. We're just waiting for the boss."

Jonathan reached the bottom of the stairs and pulled himself together before he reholstered his pistol. As he stepped out of the door, he separated himself from the pushers and shovers and smoothed his clothes.

The armored black Suburban was right where he

thought it would be, idling at the curb directly across the street from the exit door. The panic out here was far less intense than it had been inside. Perhaps the great outdoors diffused the fear. Jonathan took his time getting to the vehicle and letting himself in.

"Jesus, why don't you just crawl?" Boxers said as Jonathan opened the back door and helped himself to the right-hand captain's chair in the second row. Gail and Hite shared the bench seat in the back.

"Running calls attention," Jonathan said. "So does speeding, so keep that in mind as you drive us out of here."

Once they were moving, Jonathan turned his chair around to face Hite. "Give me your phone."

"Why?"

"That's how they're tracking you."

"How do you know that?"

"It makes the most sense. Now, give it to me."

Hite seemed paralyzed by it all.

To Gail, Jonathan said, "Find his phone and take it from him."

As she moved to do just that, Hite shrugged away. "Don't. I'll do it." He fished his smartphone out of his pocket and handed it to Jonathan.

Jonathan opened the window and tossed the phone like a Frisbee into the surrounding woods.

"That cost me a thousand dollars!"

"And almost your life," Jonathan said. "Speaking of which, Captain, it's your turn. What is it about you that people are willing to kill for?"

Hite looked as though he might throw up. "Who are you? I don't believe that you're FBI agents."

Jonathan sighed. "We've already walked this walk. There's a question on the table."

"Okay," Hite said. "Okay, okay, okay." He was giving

himself a pep talk—settling himself, maybe. He reached into his floppy briefcase and produced a tiny blue memory chip. "This," he said. "They want this and anyone who knows about it."

"What's on it?" Gail asked.

"I recorded it when I visited Rocco LoCicero's cell and had a chat."

"Why would you do that?" Jonathan asked.

"It's the story he tried to tell the other FBI agents, the ones who visited him on the inside and shut him down."

"What does *shut him down* mean?"

"They wouldn't let him talk. They told me not to let him talk, and then they ordered him thrown into the hole. I saw their faces as he spoke, and I knew he was in trouble. He said something about drug cartels and the ability to bring down the White House, and they, like, panicked. That's why they put him in the hole. They had to shut him up and keep the story under wraps. If he's still alive, I don't think he will be for very long."

"Let me get this straight," Gail said. "The FBI ordered you not to let him talk, but you talked to him anyway?"

"What they did wasn't right," Hite said. "And the way they did it—throwing him into solitary—was all kinds of wrong. They don't have that authority, yet they were allowed to do it. That's when I knew his life was in danger, and I thought the only chance he might have to stay alive is to get his story out there. Once a secret's not a secret anymore, there's nothing to kill for."

Jonathan sighed. In a different world, that logic might hold, but in this one, given the likely involvement of the president of the United States, the logic was tragically flawed. As previous administrations had clearly demonstrated, conspiracy theories didn't resonate unless witnesses were caught holding smoking guns. In the current politically overcharged environment, without a witness, no amount of definitive circumstantial evidence was enough to convince leaders and the media to hold their side accountable, and no amount of exculpatory evidence would inspire them to declare politicians on the other side innocent of even the most outrageous rumor of misconduct.

At this level, if the story had the potential of going public, the witness would have to be killed.

"I hope you've thought this through, Captain," Jonathan said, "because there's no turning back now. You've come to the right place, but some very scary times lie ahead for you."

"Do you want this memory card or not?" Hite asked.

Jonathan took it from him. "Hey, Big Guy, do your fancy electronic toys allow you to play something as simple as a chip?"

Boxers held out his beefy hand, and Jonathan placed the chip in his palm. His eyes never leaving the road, Boxers opened the center console, found the right slot, and slid the chip home.

Over the next fifteen miles and twenty-three minutes, they all listened to testimony that would change everything.

When it was done, Boxers gave out a low whistle. "There's gonna be heads rolling up and down Pennsylvania Avenue."

"I got it all, too," Venice said in Jonathan's ear. "Want me to have Father Dom call Wolverine?"

"Oh, yeah," Jonathan said.

Chapter 12

As Grayson Buchanan climbed out of the dark hole of unconsciousness, the first thing he noticed was a stench of body filth. Then there was the heat and humidity and the realization that he was still alive. Right? Can dead people think they're still alive?

He lay on his back below a ceiling that looked like it might have been built from timbers and mud. For a few seconds, he thought that his head had been disconnected from his body. He couldn't feel anything, and he couldn't move. But then he could.

He turned his head first to the left, launching an ice pick of agony through his brain.

"Oh, shit." He brought his right hand up to keep his eyes from popping out of his face and in that motion realized that he'd collected more data points. His voice worked, and he could move his arms. For shits and giggles, he raised his legs to see if they were still attached and was rewarded with a wave of agony that shot through his abdomen and back, as if he'd been bench lifting four hundred pounds.

"Ow. Christ." He brought his hands to his belly and realized that he wasn't wearing a shirt. When he reached lower, he realized he wasn't wearing pants, either. "Seriously? I'm naked?"

Not quite. They'd given him a pair of old cutoff denim shorts. Why the hell couldn't they have let him keep his old clothes?

Shit, shit. What had they done to him while he was naked?

"Don't do this," he mumbled. Sometimes, when he spoke aloud, he could talk himself into things. What was done, was done. Don't forget the headline. He was alive. For now, anyway, that was good news.

Where's Sissy?

"Sissy?" he said aloud. He wasn't surprised when he didn't hear a response. Where the hell was she?

And did she wake up naked, too?

He couldn't think about that. Not now. Certainly later, but definitely not now.

What the hell had happened?

They were at that bar, the one with the belligerent guys. Javier and Lobo.

El Gallo Azul.

There was almost a fight. Grayson moved his hand to his crotch as he remembered the way Lobo had grabbed him. He took a few seconds to examine his sensitive bits. Everything was still where it was supposed to be. He decided to call that good news.

Tequila.

He'd been shamed into drinking the tequila. Forced into it, really. And after that . . . nothing.

He was there, and then he was here—wherever *here* was.

He raised himself first to a sitting position, then put his feet on the floor, moving oh-so slowly for fear of finding something broken that he didn't know about. So far, so good.

As he looked around, he saw that he was in a dormitory of sorts—a fifteen-by-fifteen-foot room with six cots in it. The others were all empty.

The door stood open to the bright sunlight outside, where the terrain glowed brown and yellow. Two windows with open shutters marked the front wall and the back wall. Neither of them featured glass or screens. It took him a bit to hear the hum of all the flies, but once heard, he could hear nothing else.

He noticed the toilet in the corner of the room just as he realized how badly he needed to use it. Still moving carefully, he pushed himself up from the cot and stood to his full height. As he moved, he realized that the terrible stench to which he'd awakened was his own sweat and dirt. He was disgusting.

He padded barefoot to the toilet, only to realize that it had no running water. It was merely a seat installed over a stinking hole in the ground. He did what he needed to do and continued his exploration of his new space. Could it be that he was the only occupant? He saw no signs of anyone else.

Whoever had placed him there had left a grey T-shirt that might have once been white hanging from a nail in a support pillar and a pair of flip-flops at the foot of his bed. He donned them both and walked to the door.

Was he free to walk around? He must be because there were no bars and no handcuffs.

He crossed the threshold and stepped onto a raised wooden-plank sidewalk—a deck, maybe—of the ilk he'd seen in every cowboy movie ever made. This was a world of sand and rocks and sunlight. At the base of the stairs, a rock-lined path led straight out for ten or fifteen yards, then forked, with one leg going straight out to the horizon and the other leg buttonhooking around to the right to disappear on the far side of the dormitory building.

The dormitory was but one of what looked to be a half dozen similar adobe buildings that were laid out in a wide horseshoe. Roughly a hundred yards ahead, the terrain transitioned from tamed, manicured desert to serious desert, marked with jagged rock outcroppings and vicious-looking plants and cacti.

He saw only a few people, all of whom wore versions of the clothing that had been left for him.

"You're awake," a voice said in heavily accented English. "Welcome to the hacienda." Thin and angular, the guy appeared to be a year or two older than Grayson and was trying hard to grow a beard that didn't want to sprout. Ray-Ban knockoff aviators shielded his eyes from the sun, as a straw cowboy hat shielded his eyes. His denim wardrobe hadn't been laundered in a while, but the guy was clearly proud of his appearance. Grayson could tell by the way he postured himself in a way to emphasize the gap in the shirt that he'd unbuttoned halfway to the belt buckle that was the size of some dinner plates.

Grayson said nothing. Silence was always best until all intentions were known.

"Are you feeling okay?" When he spoke, the man displayed a gold incisor.

"Where's my sister?" Grayson asked.

"You are confused," Gold Tooth said. "I ask the questions, you answer them. Are you feeling good?"

"I'm fine. Now, where's my sister?"

"Have you lost her? Where did you leave her?"

Gold Tooth's tone confused Grayson. He couldn't

tell if the man was being serious or obtuse. "We were drugged and kidnapped," he said. The words sounded harsher when he spoke them aloud than they did when they formed in his head.

"Who would do such a thing?" Gold Tooth asked, approaching closer. He was definitely trying to mess with Grayson's head. The new tone made it obvious.

As Gold Tooth came closer, Grayson stepped back. This was not the place to start a fight. He had no advantage on unfriendly turf, and Gold Tooth carried a sheathed six-inch blade on one side of his belt and a holstered pistol on the other.

"I must be mistaken," Grayson said. "I last saw Sissy in a bar. El Gallo Azul. Ever heard of it?"

Gold Tooth gave a low whistle. "That's a terrible place for gringos to go. That's over two hundred kilometers away. How did you get here?"

This guy was total bullshit. Grayson decided to play his game, anyway. "Where am I?"

"You are at your new home. As I said, welcome to the hacienda."

"Why am I here?"

Gold Tooth stepped even closer. "To serve your many masters." The predatory look prickled Grayson's skin.

Grayson retreated to the bottom of the steps to the pathway. "I have masters?"

"We all do, don't we?"

"N-not that I know of."

"You need to get used to the fact that, yes, you do. Until *el jefe* decides what to do with you in the future, you are a laborer, just like anyone else."

Now that he was away from the building, Grayson

could see people tending the grounds, moving rocks and clipping bushes. "I'm part of a landscape crew?"

"If that's what I want you to do," Gold Tooth replied. "I'll tell you if I want you to do something else." The predatory look never dimmed as he joined Grayson at the bottom of the stairs. "I like to see my workers sweat."

Grayson resisted the urge to step back farther and instead stood to his full height. "Dude, you are creeping me out. If you're thinking the thoughts I think you are, you are all wrong."

Gold Tooth's expression turned serious. "What did you call me?" He cocked his head and leaned in closer. "Dude?"

"It's just an expression."

"Dooood." He put his hand to his own chest and tapped it as he tried the word again in an even more drawn-out pronunciation. It came out sounding like "Do-o-o-o-o-o-d." He threw back his head and laughed at the sky.

Grayson took another step back. This guy was crazy—of the batshit variety.

Gold Tooth's demeanor snapped back to something close to anger. "I am not your dooood. I am Esteban, but to you I am Bebe or you can call me boss. At the right time, you will call me daddy. You will do whatever I tell you to do because I am me and you are you. Is that clear?"

Bebe closed the gap between them to bad-breath distance, but Grayson kept his feet planted. He wouldn't start the fight, but if it came, he would finish it. Or die trying.

"Oh, I like the tough guys," Bebe said. He shoved Grayson hard, nearly knocking him to the ground. By the time Grayson had recovered his balance, Bebe had drawn his knife. Its blade flashed in the sunshine. "I love it when they fight back and I can gut them like fishes." He swung the blade in a harmless horizontal arc.

Grayson jumped back, anyway.

"I like to do it when they're still alive," Bebe went on. "The flesh opens so easily, and the guts just slide out onto the ground. Or onto the mattress. I don't care which. Have you ever smelled shit when it is cut directly out of the intestine?" He inhaled as if he were in the midst of eviscerating someone now.

"It's disgusting, yet it's erotic at the same time. *Erotic* is the right word, yes?"

Grayson gaped. The last thing he wanted to do was spin the guy up by disagreeing with him.

"You are alive, Mr. Grayson Buchanan, because I wanted you alive. You are here because I wanted you *here*. The others wanted your Sissy as their prize, but you are mine. I may share you with customers, or I may not, but no matter what, you will do what I say. If I tell you to carry rocks, you will carry rocks. If I want to use you for other services, you will say, *Yes, Bebe. Thank you, Bebe.*"

"What have you done with my sister?"

"Sissy is fine."

"Where?"

"She is one of Paco's favorites, from what I hear." Bebe smiled. "You should be proud. Paco is the boss of bosses, and he is very particular in his choice of partners. Your Sissy will be very well taken care of."

"Where is she?"

"Suppose I don't want to tell you? What are you willing to give me to find out?" The gold tooth gleamed as Bebe made his eyebrows dance.

Grayson's mind reeled. He'd heard stories of things

like this happening, but he'd never . . . never in a million years . . .

If these people hurt Sissy . . .

If they so much as . . .

And if . . .

His stomach churned with an acid mix of anger, disgust, and fear—of *rage*. He literally could no longer see clearly. His eyes clouded with tears, but he knew that the tears conveyed exactly the wrong message. He knew that Bebe would see fear when what he actually was seeing was *resolve*.

"Is Sissy with Paco now?" he managed to ask.

Bebe spread his arms wide. "Come to me, Grayson Buchanan, and I will answer your question."

Grayson didn't move. There had to be another way. If he moved quickly enough, maybe he could grab the knife.

Bebe laughed again, way too loudly for the moment. "Oh, relax," he said. "Stop your crying. I don't like to see my slaves cry. It makes us all look so weak. Would you like me to take you to see your sister?"

Grayson kept his eyes steady, his feet planted for a fight. It took real effort not to clench his fists.

"You must answer."

"Yes."

Bebe threw his hands in the air and laughed again. "Nope, sorry."

Grayson's jaw locked. He couldn't do this for much longer.

"Oh, I'm just kidding," Bebe said. He clapped Grayson on the shoulder. "She's right over there." He pointed to one of the other dormitory buildings.

"Which one?"

"In the corner. The first door you can see."

Grayson squinted against the sun. "Why is the door closed?"

"The girls need their rest," Bebe said. "What is it that you gringos say? They need their beauty sleep."

"I want to make sure that she's okay," Grayson said. "I want to see her breathing and healthy."

"Are you calling me a liar?"

"I'm telling you that she's my twin sister. I need to know for myself that she's okay."

Bebe made a mocking pouty baby face.

"Okay, fine," Grayson said. "I'll let you do whatever you want with me—to me—if you just let me see her. I don't have to talk with her or anything."

Bebe feigned a lunge, causing Grayson to jump back.

"You will let me do whatever I want to you because I tell you to. I don't have to bargain with you. You will do it, or I will hurt you."

He'd stomped on a madman's ego. "Okay, fine. Whatever you say. I just need to see her."

"Oh, what the hell?" Bebe said. "Come with me." He whipped past Grayson and started down the path. "Have you noticed that you wear no chains?" he asked.

"Excuse me?"

"You're a slave, yet you have no chains. There are no bars on the windows. Do you know why?"

"Why?"

"Because you cannot run away. If you tried, it would be many kilometers before you even got to the edge of the Gomez hacienda. Even if you survived, you would die of thirst and starvation on the other side of the wall. I tell you this so you get no stupid ideas about running away."

Bebe didn't seem to want an answer, so Grayson didn't bother to offer one.

The dormitory buildings were identical on the outside. Adobe walls with tile roofs supported by jutting timber beams. Each had its little sidewalk porch. Bebe led the way to the third building to the right of Grayson's dormitory. The heavy wood door stood closed, but the open shutters lay pressed all the way against the wall for maximum circulation. As they passed the opening, Grayson smelled sweaty people.

"You people don't take many showers, do you?" He was surprised to hear that he'd asked the question aloud. That hadn't been his intent.

"You gringos and your perfume," Bebe said. "We romantics prefer the aroma of skin the way skin is supposed to smell."

Peering into the building, he saw only darkness made darker still by the contrast with the bright sunshine. "Are there people inside?"

"Only the ladies for now," Bebe said with a grin. "But when darkness falls, there will be many more."

Grayson felt the anger swell again.

Bebe turned the knob on the heavy wooden door and pushed the panel open. "Go ahead," he said. "Go see your sister."

As Grayson moved to push past, Bebe stopped him with a hand pressed to his belly, just at the belt line. "Remember your promise."

Grayson hoped his face remained impassive as he moved past his captor into the unlit space of the girls' dorm—into the brothel. Inside, the temperature spiked and the stench became nauseating. He started to cover his mouth but then abandoned the effort. He didn't want to give Bebe the satisfaction of seeing his revulsion.

He counted eight cots in the space, each separated

by old-school fabric-and-aluminum hospital divider walls. The cots lay equally spaced along both sides of a center aisle, and all were occupied by young ladies no older than twenty-two in various stages of undress. Even in the darkness, he could tell that they'd been drugged by the way their heads lolled on the thin pillows. The second one on the right lay on her stomach and had kicked her sheet onto the floor, leaving her bare flesh exposed. There was a time not too long ago that he would have found the sight titillating. Now it just made his heart hurt.

He thought about replacing the sheet but rejected the idea. He didn't want to trigger something weird in Bebe that would keep him from seeing his sister.

"Sissy?" he hissed. In the otherwise silent room, the word sounded like an angry snake. He tried it a little louder. "Sissy!"

Several of the girls stirred as they were startled.

"Gray?" The weak voice came from the cot that was one more spot down the aisle on the left.

After two quick steps, he was there. Sissy lay on her back, clearly naked under the sheet that she gripped under her chin. Her right eye was purple, but it hadn't swollen shut. She smiled and reached out for a hand, but her eyes weren't focused. They'd drugged her with something.

"Gray-Gray. You shouldn't be here."

He sat on the edge of the cot and nearly tipped it over, then moved to kneeling with one knee on the floor. He grabbed her hand. "What did they do to you?"

She closed her eyes, causing tears to roll. "You know what they did to me," she said.

"Are you hurt?"

Drugs notwithstanding, she was still able to give him *that look*.

"You know what I mean." Grayson lowered his voice to a nearly inaudible whisper. "I'm going to get you out of here."

She had a smile that matched *that look*. She pulled her hand from his grasp and patted his cheek. "Sure you will," she said. "When you do, I'll come along, I promise."

She didn't believe him. "I'm not kidding."

"Okay, then. But later, okay? I'm in no condition to run right now." With that, she laid her hand on the cot, and her eyes closed.

"I can see why Paco likes her so much," Bebe said from behind.

Grayson whirled and leveled his forefinger as if it were a spear. "You shut your mouth about her."

Bebe feigned a shiver. "Oh, I like it when boys defend their sisters."

Grayson stood, his jaw locked, and stepped closer to his tormentor.

Bebe put his hand on his knife. "Don't make me kill you before we've had a nice time."

Grayson did the math. If he struck quickly, maybe he could take this asshole down before he had a chance to defend himself. Once he got him on the floor, maybe he could get his knife and . . .

No, it wasn't worth the risk. Grayson was too sore and there was too much sunlight and he had no plan.

What had Bebe said? *When darkness falls, there will be many more.*

Darkness provided at least a little bit of advantage. Okay, it offered a little less disadvantage. Not the same thing, but close.

"You look like you're thinking of hitting me," Bebe said.

"Maybe if it was a fair fight," Grayson said. He figured that it would be senseless to lie. *Of course* he was thinking about hitting him. "But I don't want to die today. Or anytime soon for that matter."

Bebe closed the distance. "Oh, how I look forward to playing with you."

Grayson held his ground. Then his gut exploded as Bebe fired a bunch to his belly that he never saw coming. His legs folded, and then he was on the floor, braced on his hands and knees, struggling to make his diaphragm work so that he could draw a breath.

"I can read your mind, Señor Grayson Buchanan. You think you are better than me. Stronger than me, but the next time we meet, you will be begging me for less or begging me for more. Which it will be, will be up to you."

Grayson felt his T-shirt go tight as Bebe leveraged the fabric to pull him to his feet.

"But first you have to earn your keep, you shit-for-brains gringo. You dream of being the hero and of rescuing your sister. Maybe you even dream of killing me. But when this is over, within a week, you will either be my toy or you will be dead."

Still leveraging the fabric of the shirt, he flung Grayson toward the open door.

"For now, though, you earn your keep. Some work in the sun will clear your head and fatten your muscles for me."

Another figure had filled the doorframe from the outside. Grayson never saw him arriving, but he looked familiar.

"Javier," Bebe said. "Take our new friend to the wall and teach him to move rocks."

The bartender at the Blue Rooster.

"It's a mistake not to kill him," Javier said in English,

then he switched to Spanish and rattled off a paragraph that Grayson couldn't understand.

Whatever it was, it triggered a genuine laugh from Bebe. "As I said before, Señor Grayson Buchanan. Welcome to the hacienda."

Chapter 13

They met at the Compound, Jonathan's two-hundred-plus-acre hunting grounds in the hills outside of Charlottesville, Virginia. Equipped with nearly identical tools to the office in Fisherman's Cove, the Compound provided an extra layer of security—the kind that allowed the FBI director's helicopter to arrive unnoticed by looky-loos. It had taken the Batmobile a little over three hours to make the drive, bringing them to the front gate within minutes of Venice's arrival via her own vehicle.

The swirl of movement and activity left Michael Hite looking stunned. He moved where he was told and followed directions, but he looked numb, as if in a trance. Jonathan offered him a chair near the stone fireplace, under the watchful eye of a wild boar that Jonathan had killed on a hunting trip outside of Paris, Texas. Hite sat with both feet planted on the floor, his hands on his thighs, his expression neutral.

"Are you sure we can talk in front of him?" Irene asked.

"He's the star of the show," Jonathan said.

"Is he all right? He seems zoned out."

"I'm not zoned out," Hite said, finally making eye contact with the FBI director. "And I'm right here, so don't talk about me as if I'm not. And to be perfectly honest, I feel like I've never been in greater danger in my life."

"Probably because you haven't been," Boxers said. Ever helpful.

The hunting cabin on the Compound was essentially one huge room on the ground level, divided into three main parts: a sitting area dominated by overstuffed leather furniture and the river-stone fireplace that stretched all the way to the vaulted ceiling, a dining area with a massive black walnut table with seating for ten, and a chef's kitchen that spanned the entire width of the cabin. An open stairway led to an atrium that spanned the circumference of the interior and provided access to the bedrooms on the second floor.

Jonathan helped himself to the William and Mary rocking chair near the hearth. Something about the design made it the perfect choice for his ever-aching back. The others distributed themselves among the other chairs. Jonathan offered drinks to anyone who wanted them, and everyone but Boxers went for water or iced tea. Big Guy went for expensive scotch.

"You all are several steps ahead of me," Irene said, opening the conversation. "Captain Hite, why don't you start with the background of why we're here."

Hite repeated what he'd told the others about the concerning treatment of LoCicero inside the prison. As the captain spoke, he became more animated, as if the act of producing words made him more confident.

When Hite appeared to be done, Irene looked at Jonathan. "And you agree that the information on this recording spells the end of the world as we know it?"

"I agree that it spells the end of the Darmonds' world as they know it."

"Well, then. That seems worth listening to. I don't suppose anyone thought to make a—"

Before Irene could complete her question, Venice

thrust out a stack of papers. "Here's a transcript," she said. "I have copies for everyone, including you, Captain Hite." She passed them out.

As he listened to the recording again, Jonathan read along.

HITE: *Are you okay?*

LOCICERO: *What are you doing here?*

HITE: *I asked you a question.*

LOCICERO: *So did I. What did I do to get thrown in the hole?*

HITE: *To be honest, I don't know. This wasn't done through channels.*

LOCICERO: *I haven't done anything to deserve this. I've told the feebs everything they wanted to know. Answered every question from both teams.*

HITE: *Both teams? What does that mean?*

LOCICERO: *Just what I said. The team this morning and the one that just left an hour ago.*

HITE: *I didn't know anything about a second team. Did they meet you here? In your cell?*

LOCICERO: *Right where you're sitting. I made their friggin' day.*

HITE: *What did you tell them?*

LOCICERO: *I solved a whole goddamn crime syndicate. Those fibbies should be buyin' me drinks, yet here I am, still in the hole.*

HITE: *They don't have the power to put you here in the first place. Only the warden can do that, and he always goes through me when he does it. Not this time. Mr. LoCicero, I think you are in grave jeopardy.*

LOCICERO: *Why do you care?*

HITE: *Because I do.*

Jonathan held up his hand. "Stop."

Venice clicked the button.

"I think he asks a good question, Captain. Why *do* you care? There must be a thousand things that go on in that prison without you knowing it. What's so special about LoCicero?"

Hite's jaw tightened as his ears turned red. "You don't think much of corrections officers, do you?"

"To be honest, no, I don't. It's nothing personal. You might be the exception to the rule, but the COs I've interacted with are all about the power play. They enjoy bullying people in captivity that they would shit their pants if they ever met them on the streets." He saw the anger in Hite's eyes and added, "You asked. You were about to tell me why you are so interested in LoCicero's handling."

Hite still seethed. "Maybe you and I could meet each other on the street. Sometime when you're not backed up by King Kong."

Boxers rumbled out a chuckle. "You want to pick a fight with him, I promise you I won't intervene. Let me book the bets, though."

To be honest, Jonathan wasn't sure who Big Guy projected to be the winner, but he decided to take it as a win. "Captain, I'm not trying to piss you off. I'm just trying to figure out the dynamic here. Hell, LoCicero wondered the same thing. What's your angle?"

Hite clearly wasn't past his anger. He took a few seconds to settle himself by tracing the creases on his trousers with his thumb and forefinger. "Here's the truth of it, Agent Bonner. I am a professional at what I do. My corner of the criminal justice system isn't as glamorous as yours, but it's every bit as essential. COs on my watch do not abuse inmates, but they don't suffer abuse at their hands, either. I'm responsible for every life within those walls, regardless of which uniform they wear."

"I'm not sure you answered my question."

"No angle, Special Agent Bonner. Just a civil servant wanting to do the right thing. Whether you believe it or not."

"Please go on," Irene said, with a nod toward Venice. Mother Hen clicked her mouse, and the recording continued.

> HITE: *I'm telling you I've never seen this happen before. And this second team of agents. Have you seen them here before?*
> LOCICERO: *No, but I'm new here.*
> HITE: *Did you share a big secret with them?*
> LOCICERO: *Damn straight I shared a big secret. It's my ticket out of prison.*
> HITE: *You've got it wrong. The secret was your ticket into solitary, and through unofficial means. Is it the kind of secret that the government might want to keep hushed up?*

A long silence made Jonathan wonder if the recording had stopped.

"This is where LoCicero got really pale," Hite said. "A real *oh shit* moment of realization."

> LOCICERO: *I told 'em how to shut down the flow of drugs from Mexico. Most of it, anyway.*
> HITE: *It had to be more than that.*
> LOCICERO: *Hell yes, there was more than that. I told them how their bosses' bosses in DC were running the whole thing. All the way up to the asshole in the White House.*

Jonathan kept his eyes on Irene as she absorbed the details and tallied in her head the implications that his story would bring.

HITE: *You mean the Darmond administration?*

LOCICERO: *I mean the big man himself. Mr. Anthony Darmond.*

HITE: *Holy shit.*

LOCICERO: *Shit yeah, holy shit. Look, you've heard all this crap about a war on drugs, right? People whining and moaning about the cartels and fentanyl and addiction and shit? Ever wonder why a country as big and powerful as America can't win a damn war against a bunch of punk gangsters from the jungle? It's because the war itself is bullshit, and it's always been bullshit.*

HITE: *I'm not following—*

LOCICERO: *If you shut up and listen, you'll get it because I'll spell it out for you. You know what else is bullshit? The war on organized crime.*

Jonathan could almost see him using finger quotes on that last phrase.

LOCICERO: *The only hot wars against organized crime are the ones declared on the families that don't cooperate with the drug distribution machine that Tony Darmond inherited from his predecessor and fine-tuned into a friggin' ATM.*

HITE: *How do you know this?*

LOCICERO: [laughs] *You don't think Uncle Sam gets his own hands dirty, do you? Hell no. That's where we come in. Specifically, where I come in. I was the go-between, the guy who kept the money train on the tracks.*

HITE: *What does that mean?*

LOCICERO: *You gonna talk or you gonna listen? Honest to Christ, I'll spell it all out for you, but you gotta keep your trap shut. You think you can do that? Good. To know how it works, first,*

you've got to understand the ways it can all
go wrong. First of all, the product has to get
from the fields through the processors to the
distribution network, which almost exclusively
belongs to Los Muertos, which only continues to
gain in power, despite some pretty hard strikes
on their operations over the past couple of years,
including the sinking of one of their subs.

Jonathan was pretty sure that Irene caught the grin
and glance that passed between him and Boxers. They
were the ones who'd sunk the sub.

HITE: *Wait, the cartel has a navy?*
LOCICERO: *I'm not sure that's what I'd call it,*
but man, these guys got more money than
George Soros. They've got ships, submarines,
aircraft, you name it. This ain't some second-
class outfit. This is big business. So, how does
it get into the US of A? Right through the front
door under a bunch of different shell companies.
Care to guess who owns shares in pretty much
all of them?
HITE: *You didn't like it last time I chimed in.*
LOCICERO: *Oh, don't go pouty on me. They're*
owned by the Darmond clan and their buddies.
Christ, half of them are stupid enough to put
it on their financial disclosure forms. Problem
is, fibbies and the media see Save the Whales
LLC or some such, and it never occurs to them
to look past the cover sheet to verify that they
do what they say they do.
HITE: *I can't believe no one has looked into that.*
How many companies are we talking about?
LOCICERO: *Dozens, for sure. But they're sub-*
sidiaries of subsidiaries, you know? You'd have

to have wild detective skills to drill down to the actual ownership. Hell, we've been doin' the same thing in my business for years.

Jonathan said, "Stop the playback." To Irene: "Before you ask, the company names he's talking about go unmentioned in the recording." He couldn't stop himself from sneering at Hite for having forgotten such an important detail. He nodded for the recording to continue.

HITE: *What's your involvement in all of this?*
LOCICERO: *Me personally? I distribute the bribe money. On the government side, there's a DEA guy named Harold Standish.*

"He's a Darmond appointee!" Irene blurted. "And he's Homeland Security, not DEA per se. A much bigger job. Deputy assistant secretary or some such."

. . . He gives me a briefcase full of cash, and my job is to get it to the Customs and Border guys at the specific checkpoints where the big stashes of product will be coming through.
HITE: *You just wander up to the checkpoint with a bag full of—*
LOCICERO: *Of course not. That's not the way government payoffs work. It's the same as in Washington. You can't walk into a congressman's office and just hand him cash, right? Of course not. To give cash to a politician, you have to go through their chief of staff and do the handoff over drinks or coffee. It's the same thing here. I meet with Harold Standish at the Prussian Hotel in Shepherdstown, West Virginia—just on the other side of the Potomac from Maryland. He buys me dinner, we lay out a plan, and then when it's time to go, I walk*

away with the briefcase he brought. That will have the money in it. Very old-school stuff. Then, when I meet with the mules and the border guards and their supervisors, we repeat the process, but I'm the guy with the bag of money.

HITE: *How much money are we talking about?*

LOCICERO: *Each time? Five hundred. Maybe seven-fifty.*

HITE: *Thousand?*

LOCICERO: *Yeah. I think the record was a million two. That was a heavy briefcase. Then I drive the route across Texas, New Mexico, and Arizona like Johnny Appleseed, only my seeds are stacks of C-notes. I meet the senior muckety-mucks from CBP and repeat the same process.*

HITE: *How often does that happen?*

LOCICERO: *Every friggin' month. If I don't end up with a melanoma out of all this, it'll be just plain pure luck.*

HITE: *What does all this money pay for?*

LOCICERO: *Oh, hell, I don't know. I figure a lot of it goes to get people to look the other way. I mean this has been going on for a long friggin' time. It's a hell of a system. When was the last time you read a believable article somewhere about the war on drugs? You know, one that didn't sound like it was written by the DEA press office?*

HITE: *Um . . .*

LOCICERO: *A long damn time is the answer. Whenever someone tries, I get a call from my boss telling me to call my guy at Los Muertos, and somehow, either the story or the reporter disappears.*

HITE: *The cartels kill the reporter?*

LOCICERO: *Don't ask me to lie, 'cause I don't want to know. Those cartel guys make the Taliban look like Sunday school teachers. I don't want to know what they're up to.*

HITE: *Are there others like you working as distributors?*

LOCICERO: *I don't know. I don't want to know. But do the math. It's a big ass border.*

A buzzer sounded in the background on the recording. "That's shift change," Hite explained to the group.

HITE: *That's it. I've gotta go. Got work to do on my shift.*

LOCICERO: *That's it? I spill my guts and you just walk away? What about me?*

HITE: *Hang tight. I'm gonna see what I can do. I think I've got somebody I can talk to about this. What's happening here just ain't right.*

LOCICERO: *Who are you gonna talk to?*

HITE: *Sorry, Rocco. That's all the time I have.*

Chapter 14

As the recording wound down, Hite rose from his chair and walked to the window, where he watched the trees through the glass. When the recording was over, he asked, "Is it safe to stand in front of windows?"

Jonathan said, "As long as you're here on this property, you can stand anywhere you want."

"That was quite a story, Captain Hite," Irene said. Jonathan didn't like the look in her eyes. "What makes you think we can believe what a murderer says?"

Jonathan couldn't tell if it was an honest question or if she was working an angle of her own. He watched Hite turn from the window and rest his hands on his belt. "I don't know how to answer that," he said. "Other than to say that I believed him."

"The fact that we've been attacked twice lends some credibility," Boxers said.

"What are you thinking, Madam Director?" Jonathan asked.

"I'm thinking that this is the most explosive testimony I've heard in a long time. But I have to temper that with the source. LoCicero has a lot to gain by floating false stories that get a lot of people in trouble."

"Doesn't that describe every high-value snitch you

deal with?" Jonathan asked. "Everybody trying to get a deal by running their mouths."

"But the stakes are never quite this high." Her gaze narrowed as her eyes bored into Hite. "How about you? How trustworthy are you?"

He scoffed. "Now, how in the hell am I supposed to answer that question?"

"What's your background?" she asked. "Before Bureau of Prisons?"

"I was in the Army. Green Berets, if you must know. I played in the Sandbox for four tours, sending jihadis to paradise, and then when I separated out, I joined the police force in Joliet, Illinois. Didn't like the unreliable hours, so I signed on with BOP. That was fifteen years ago. That enough?"

"What are your concerns, Madam Director?" Jonathan asked.

"After all the shit we just learned, that's your question to me?" she said. "What are my *concerns*?"

"In this context," Jonathan said. "With Captain Hite."

"I'm concerned that the information that's flowing here is hotter than the sun and that we're going to have to trust someone we don't know to keep it all quiet until the time is right." She looked straight at Hite as she spoke.

"What, me? Damn straight I'm going to tell people. That's why we're here, isn't it?"

"There's a timing issue," Jonathan explained. "At this point, everything is just conjecture. A rumor. In the absence of evidence—at this level, a smoking gun— killing the rumor monger also kills the rumor."

Hite pushed away from the window and returned to his seat. "Shit."

"You said you met the FBI agents who told LoCicero to stop talking."

"Yes, ma'am," Hite said. "I was in the room with them. Their names were Caine and Hirsch."

"Do those names mean anything to you?" Jonathan asked.

Irene rolled her eyes. "I've got thirty-eight thousand employees," she said. "I've only been able to memorize thirty-four thousand of their names." To Hite, she asked, "You mentioned that one of those agents was different than the ones who've normally been interviewing Rocco LoCicero."

"Yes."

"Is it unusual for multiple agents to interview one prisoner at different times?" Gail asked.

Hite shrugged. "It happens, I suppose. Not every day or every case, but it happens."

"It's very rare," Irene said. "Especially when we're trying to leverage information out of an informant. They need that sense of consistency—a comfort level with the people they're dealing with."

"So, what happened here?" Jonathan asked.

"I've reached out to my assistant director—the one person in my office I know I can trust—to ask some questions. He should have some answers soon."

"I've got a question, Director Rivers," Boxers said, shifting in a chair that looked too small for him. "How do you know who you can trust on your staff? More important, how do you know who you *can't*?"

"I ask myself that same question five times a day," Irene said. "I don't have a good answer for you."

"Holy shit," Hite said. "Are you serious? Are things really that screwed up in DC?"

Irene looked at Hite and then to Jonathan, who could sense her unexpressed disbelief that she was saying these things in front of a stranger.

Jonathan arched his eyebrows. "In for a dime," he

said. "When he's in this deep, it doesn't make sense not to trust him all the way."

"I think you can trust him," Venice said, handing Jonathan her phone. "It seems that Captain Hite hasn't been entirely forthcoming."

Jonathan took the phone by its edges to keep from erasing the screen, and in a single glance saw what Venice had been referring to. "Green Berets, eh?" Jonathan asked. "Anything else you'd like to share?"

Hite shifted his eyes to the floor. "Only that I served with a good unit with a lot of very fine soldiers."

"You won the Distinguished Service Medal," Jonathan said. "Second highest valor award Uncle Sam can bestow."

"I didn't do anything anyone else wouldn't have done," Hite said.

Gail said, "What did—"

"I don't want to talk about it," Hite snapped. His demeanor left no room for negotiation. "You were saying, Director Rivers?"

At the mention of heroism, Irene's demeanor changed. "Yes, things are really that screwed up in DC," she said. "I don't yet know that Rocco LoCicero is telling the truth, but I wouldn't be surprised to learn that he is."

"Remember our previous conversation?" Jonathan reminded her. "This is the break we need to flush the toilet at sixteen hundred Pennsylvania Avenue."

"I need time to think about this," Irene said.

"We don't have time to think about anything," Jonathan said. "Let's take LoCicero at his word. And let's take Captain Hite at his. When word gets back to the White House through whatever channels they use, they're going to work overtime to make sure their tracks are all covered."

"I don't even know what that means," Irene said.

"Neither do I," Jonathan said. "But one thing's for sure. A lot of people should be sleeping with their eyes open for the next few days. The Darmond machine will kill anyone who gets in their way." He looked to Hite. "How safe is LoCicero in his cell?"

"It's the safest possible place to be as long as he stays there."

"Do you think they'll move him?" Gail asked.

"He doesn't belong there in the first place," Hite said. "Well, he does now, given what he told me, but there's no specific protection order to keep him out of danger."

"So, that means anyone can get to him whenever they want," Boxers said.

"Right."

"So, he's a dead man?" Gail asked.

"If the system wants him dead, he'll die," Hite said.

"That can't be true," Venice said. "There have to be safeguards."

"The fact that he's been put in solitary means that the safeguards have already been overridden," Hite said.

"Who does the warden work for?" Jonathan asked.

"The director of the Bureau of Prisons," Hite said.

All eyes turned to Irene.

"Bobby Sharpe and I are not on the best of terms," she said. "He seems to think that I got in the way of his nomination for attorney general."

Jonathan grinned. "Did you?"

"Yes, but I wouldn't have if I knew that Buster Norris was Darmond's next choice."

"Sharpe runs the Bureau of Prisons, I presume?" Venice said.

"Right."

"Can you give him a call?" Jonathan asked. "LoCicero is your best witness."

"Your *only* witness if I heard correctly," Venice corrected.

"We've still got Harold Standish," Jonathan said.

"We've got *rumors* of Harold Standish," Gail corrected. "Hearsay at best."

"We need to get him on the record," Boxers said. "And probably under cover somewhere. If the Darmond machine comes out full throttle, he'll be on their target list."

Jonathan held up a hand for silence. "Let's not get ahead of ourselves. Irene, are you willing to make the call to BOP?"

"For what purpose? What would I ask?"

"Tell him that you have information that Rocco LoCicero is in danger and that you want to put a guard on his cell."

Irene's phone buzzed and she looked at it. "Message from my deputy, Paul Boersky." She took thirty seconds to read the message, her concerned scowl deepening with every passing second. When she was done, she returned the phone to her pants pocket and stood.

"Trouble?" Jonathan asked.

Irene said nothing for another half minute as she wandered to the window and looked out at the same scene just surveyed by Hite. "The second agents who visited Rocco LoCicero in prison aren't assigned to the Schillaci case. In fact, they seem not to be assigned to any case. They are special investigators assigned to Buster Norris."

"Is that significant?" Jonathan asked.

"Not necessarily," Irene said. "But it means that they're not affiliated with ongoing investigations. They do *special projects* for the AG."

"You make that sound like a gestapo," Venice said.

"Do I? Hmm."

"Forgive me, Madam Director," Hite said. "May I call you Irene?"

"Absolutely not."

He seemed surprised but did not press the point. "All of this chicanery is going on in an agency that you're in charge of. Why can't you just stop it?"

Irene looked to Jonathan for backup.

Jonathan explained, "That's a long and complicated story. Suffice it to say that it's a tough, lonely job being one of very few honest political appointees." To Irene, he said, "You have to show your hand to Standish. Or more to the point, you need to make Standish understand that you've seen his hand."

Irene stood and headed for the door. "What I need," she said, "is a few minutes alone."

The room watched in silence as she stepped out into the afternoon.

"Is she okay?" Venice asked.

Jonathan said, "I think it must be very hard to realize that the only way to save the country you love is to walk away from the job that you love."

Irene adored autumn, by far her favorite time of year. The leaves out here were ahead of those in the DMV, but the thermometer hadn't yet stopped teasing people. Today would top out in the midseventies, yesterday it hit the high sixties, and tomorrow was projected to hit the high eighties. Such was the nature of Virginia weather.

Days like this made her wonder if she'd somehow squandered her life. In the early days, as a young special agent, she'd been the zealot of zealots, a true believer in the sanctity of justice and the Constitution and the rule of law. Then came the day when her own daughters were kidnapped by a fellow agent, and she learned that rules no longer mattered when people you love are in danger. She hadn't known Digger and Boxers before then, and every day since, she'd faced the reality that justice is relative. It's malleable. It can be twisted to serve the needs of powerful people, and such was her relationship with Security Solutions.

She told herself that when she bent the rules—except for that one time, that *first* time—she did it in service to innocents. Sometimes, the official wheels of justice turned too slowly, and when they did, shortcuts saved lives. The Security Solutions team, often with her help, *saved lives*. In the real world, though, when justice and legality could not coexist, the act of saving lives often meant taking lives. She'd approved that. Through Jonathan and his team, she'd been a part of that.

The Darmond administration, though, bent laws and ruined people, not for a greater good but to line their own pockets. They killed innocents through the scourge of narcotics that filled their pockets, and they killed innocents who might have gotten in their way and exposed all that they were doing.

Irene believed—*had* to believe—that she was better than them, but she was just as exposed as they were to legal catastrophe if her secrets were revealed to the world. She believed that she'd adequately covered her tracks, and she'd heard no rumblings that the forces of government were closing in on her, but how quickly would that change if she were to press Harold Standish as Jonathan had suggested?

Could she even force Standish to testify? As FBI director, she had no power to compel testimony. Under normal circumstances, flipping a witness included a potential plea deal that could only be offered up by the Justice Department, yet the Justice Department was itself neck-deep in the middle of the crimes to be prosecuted. This wasn't a Watergate-level high-altitude conspiracy that involved only a few political appointees. If the Darmond crime network was as wide and complicated as she believed it to be, the conspiracy would have to bleed past the level of patronage and down into the career ranks. There were just too many moving parts for it to be otherwise.

None of the ninety-three US attorneys appointed by Darmond could be trusted, and by extension, neither could any of the assistant US attorneys who were organized under them. Even as the thought passed through her brain, it made her feel ill. Surely, there were a few true believers among those hundreds of appointees, but how could she determine who they were? The choice would have to be risk free.

And then what?

Even if a plea deal could be arranged on the sly with a cooperative AUSA, it would still need to be heard by a judge, but that would mean selecting a judge who still put the scales of justice above political expediency. The new rules of the prosecuting world assumed that as political appointees themselves, judges and justices would ignore the rule of law in favor of the political leanings of the president who appointed them. It made her sick every time valuable information leaked out of the sanctity of a courthouse. Even the judicial palace of the Supreme Court had become infected by politics, with critical decisions being leaked without consequence to the press in a way to increase the likelihood of violence against unpopular justices.

Attorney General Buster Norris even doubled down

on the intimidation tactics by forbidding the Supreme Court police force and all other federal law enforcement agencies from interfering with the angry protests outside the justices' homes.

It was all very Third World, but few in the media or official Washington seemed disturbed by any of it.

The longer the infection was allowed to fester, the more gangrenous the corruption would become. As it was, half the country seemed ready to go to war with the other half over silly insults and societal memes. What would happen when the public finally came to realize how thoroughly they'd been lied to about so many things?

Some of the diehards who so loyally waved the president's banner would stick by him to the end. Violence could be the only result. The violence, then, would inspire the president's inner despot to declare martial law on the communities who oppose him, and thus trigger a new civil war, which could end everything.

In her mind, that dark future played out with the clarity of a motion picture.

Irene's time was running out. She had to take action. She had to confront Standish.

And then she had to keep him alive while the full force of the federal government would be trying to take him out. If Standish and LoCicero were both dead, there would be no evidence, and without evidence, there would be no case.

And here she was again, facing the same question as before: How was she supposed to make this happen? WitSec was an option for keeping other high-value witnesses alive, but witness protection would involve participation of the Marshals Service, another agency of the administration.

She'd never before realized how utterly clueless the framers of the Constitution were that the criminal element to be prosecuted could be the government itself.

Awash in incalculable variables, one thing was certain. She could not do this alone. The system would not let her. Unlike Jonathan and his team, she could not deploy blunt force methods. Whatever she did had to stay inside the established lanes of procedure if any of it had a chance of standing up in the courts.

When the time came to strike, she would have to strike quickly to head off the administration's inevitable attempts to kill her case by destroying witnesses and reputations.

The damage she planned to do would leave the political establishment in ruins and send powerful people to prison. They would go neither peacefully nor quietly. Instead, they would burn the country down to protect their fiefdoms. They would come at her with guns blazing— whether literally or figuratively. Perhaps both. And they would launch on her the instant they heard the *rumor* that their conspiracies were falling apart.

Irene heard the cabin door open and shut, then footsteps in the gravel behind her. Jonathan Grave's voice asked, "Are you all right?"

She more sensed him arriving at her side than saw him. She kept her eyes focused on the distant tree line. "Why does it feel like treason when your plan is to oust the real traitors?"

There was a smile in his voice when he said, "People are easy to gaslight. Sometimes, I think people crave it. Political parties make it even easier. They vilify people who ask questions, surround themselves with power brokers who profess to be true believers, and in an instant"—he snapped his fingers—" the Constitution is revealed to be nothing more than a piece of paper. What startles me are the numbers of people who just don't care, so long as they're getting their way. The rules only matter when they hurt the other team."

Irene pivoted her head to look at him. "You know, it's possible that you're even more cynical than I am."

"I have no doubt, Wolfie. I have no doubt whatsoever. What are you planning to do?"

She shook her head. "You first."

"I'm probably going to kill a lot of people and break a lot of things. I'm going to *end* the Los Muertos cartel."

"Do you even know who they are?"

"I'm confident I know people who do."

"And then what?"

He smirked. "Want a quick tour of the Compound?"

"Not especially," Irene said. "But I could use a little walk."

"Company?"

"Sure." The Compound, as Jonathan called it, wasn't much to Irene's eye. More forest than lawn, it appeared that some effort had been made to create paths by clearing grass and pouring gravel, but that had been some time ago, and the gravel was giving way to grass again.

"How often do you get up here?" she asked.

"Clearly, not often enough," Jonathan said. "There's a security team up here twenty-four seven, and they're able to keep the grass cut. As you can see, I haven't invested in a lot of cosmetic maintenance."

"My career as director can't continue when this is over," Irene said, getting right to it. "How are you going to get along without me?"

"I'm like a bad penny," Jonathan said. "You'll never be entirely rid of me."

"I'll have to be," Irene said. "For both of us. Darmond's going to dig deep. When they find out—"

"My team is invisible," Jonathan said. "You know

that. Don't worry about us being exposed. Venice's too good for that."

"Speaking of Venice, I need her for a task." Irene and Venice had always had an awkward relationship, and Irene wasn't sure why.

"That's for her to decide, not me," Jonathan said. "But I won't stand in the way. Can I ask what you need her to do?"

"I need her to use her badge one more time," Irene said. She laid out her plan for Jonathan in real time as it formed in her head. It only took a few minutes, and when she was done, Digger looked skeptical.

"This assistant US attorney," he said. "What's her name again?"

"Kresha Ruby. We went to law school together." They were also sorority sisters, albeit from different schools, but Irene held back that detail. She wasn't sure why.

"What makes you think she's trustworthy?"

"What makes you think she's not?"

Jonathan held up his hands. "I'm not picking a fight, Wolfie," he said. "I'm just helping you think it through. How ambitious is she?"

Irene got where he was going with this, but she wasn't going to justify her decision or invite an argument. The bottom line here was that Irene had to trust *someone*. For too long, she had witnessed the slow erosion in Washington from the safety of her office suite, playing the safe cards she held. Now, it was time to dive into the fray and get her hands wet and her face dirty.

"Tell you what," she said. "You do what you need to do, and I'll do what I need to do, and together and separately, we'll have plausible deniability."

Jonathan's impossibly blue eyes turned soft as he placed his hand on her shoulder. "You be careful, Wolfie.

We've worked together for a long, long time, and I don't want to see you get hurt. I sense that you're about to enter territory that you're not used to. You need to be very, very careful."

Irene smiled. She appreciated the sentiment but not the patronization. "You know I killed my first boss, right?" she said. "Peter Frankel, assistant director of the Bureau."

"Shortly after we met," Jonathan said.

"Yep. A long time ago. I spend more time in the office than I used to, but I'm still pretty fleet of foot." While it had been many years since Irene had been in a gunfight or applied a set of handcuffs, those were skills at which she had once excelled and that she continued to practice. "Besides, I have a hard time envisioning a circumstance where what I plan to do will go to guns."

Jonathan cocked his head. He didn't mouth the words that he thought she was full of shit, but his eyes spoke them for him. Desperate people were capable of desperate acts.

"I'll be prepared for whatever happens," she said.

"I can have my team back you up. We're a hell of a lot more experienced at—"

Irene moved his hand off her shoulder in a way that she hoped conveyed gratitude. "I appreciate your offer to help, Dig, I really do. But it won't work this time. I can get into the White House. You cannot. I can cause charges to be levied. You cannot. You like to believe that all problems can be solved by a frontal assault, and that is just not true. Not in Washington."

They'd stopped walking, and as they talked, they pivoted to face the cabin again. "How long is it going to take for you to do your thing?" Jonathan asked.

194   *John Gilstrap*

Irene ran the rough calculations silently. "Two days. Three at most."

As she watched Jonathan consider that, she asked, "How about you?"

"About the same, I figure. To be honest, we don't have much of a plan yet."

"Do you ever have a plan?"

"Usually better than what we've got now. But we'll get there."

They started walking back toward the front door. "Let me ask you this," Jonathan said. "In a perfect world, would you want Los Muertos to be screaming and on fire before you do your deal, or would you want us to hold till you're done?"

Irene chuckled at the notion of a perfect world, even a rhetorical one. "I don't want to coordinate our efforts, okay? I don't want you waiting for me, and I'm not going to wait for you. But in your perfect world, if you can blow them up an hour or two before I do my thing, that would be great."

"Gotcha," Jonathan said. "Now, I just have to figure out what my *thing* is."

Chapter 15

Time meant nothing in solitary. The lights never went on and never went off. They just *were*. Not so bright as to prevent sleep and not so dim as to prevent reading. Rocco had adjusted his mind to the notion that this six-foot by eight-foot slice of concrete real estate would be his home for the foreseeable future, but he held out hope that his long-term future might be a little brighter. If he played his cards right, not only would he be granted witness protection in the middle of nowhere, but he also might be totally free.

The Schillaci crime family had evolved away from the Hollywood cliché of the Mafia. In fact, that word, the M-word, had never once been mentioned in his presence. The Schillacis merely ran businesses that provided products that the government didn't *want* people to have but unofficially *needed* them to have in order for politicians and law enforcers to have the lifestyles that they desired. The way Rocco saw it, if the government didn't want their agents to accept trinkets and cash in return for looking the other way, they'd pay them better salaries to do the jobs they were assigned to do.

Most of the Schillaci family had dismissed the old man Giuseppe as a symbol of the past, a kind of anchor on the business, holding back progress. The case that Rocco would help the feds construct would be all about the old man. He'd give the feebs more of the information they already had, and even if Giuseppe ended up with a life term, that wouldn't equate to more than a few years. There was no way that Rocco would give up any of the side hustles run by Guiseppi's boys.

Except for the business with the cartel. Rocco was going to see to it that Rolo and Paco Gomez were done forever. How dare they kill his boy?

Rocco forced himself not to think about his son's demise. He was gone now. That was the hard fact. That was unchangeable natural law. He'd have never seen Giovanni again, anyway, not if they granted him WitSec. A reunion would have been too dangerous for all of them.

To concentrate on Giovanni's murder would be to invite anger, and nothing good or productive ever came from anger. Survival in Rocco's world required calm and detached analysis of every moment.

As he sat on the thinly padded concrete bench that served as his bed, Rocco reviewed in his mind the conversation he'd had with Captain Hite. The fear he saw in the captain's eyes was very real, but in Rocco's mind, entirely uncalled for. The information he had to share about the flow of drugs across the border would make the careers of every federal official who touched it.

When the time came—

The lock on the steel door to Rocco's cell turned, interrupting his thoughts. Without access to a clock or a watch, he had no idea how long he'd been ruminating, but it felt too early for his exercise period—his one hour in the chain-link cage that the prison had the balls to call the outdoors.

He stood to prepare to be handcuffed for the transfer, but when the door opened, the person on the other side wasn't like any guard he'd seen in the past. This one was dressed in riot gear, complete with a balaclava and helmet.

Rocco scoffed. "What the hell is this?"

The figure at the door said nothing. Instead, he raised a pistol to shoulder height and pointed it at Rocco's forehead. It was a small-bore weapon, maybe a .22. A suppressor had been threaded onto the muzzle.

"Well, shit."

Jonathan walked with Irene and Michael Hite as they crossed the lawn to board the helicopter that would take Irene back to her office and Hite back to . . .

"You seem to think you're coming with me, Captain," Irene said. "You know that's not happening, right?"

"I thought I was going into witness protection."

That's what Jonathan had been thinking, too.

"I can't offer that to you," Irene said. "Not yet, anyway." She explained the need for legal orders and the partic- ipation of the Marshals Service, which she was not yet sure she could trust.

"What the hell am I supposed to do, then?" Hite asked. "You need me to stay safe, or you don't have anything."

Jonathan thought he had a point. Hite wasn't nearly the prize witness that Standish would be, but Irene hadn't yet corralled the assistant secretary, and Jona- than wasn't at all sure that she'd be able to.

"I'm sorry, Captain," Irene said, "but the facts are the facts. You need to find a way to stay alive for a few more days."

Hite's face reddened. "Seriously? That's all you've got? I bring you this as a means to set things straight—"

"Don't bullshit a bullshitter," Irene interrupted. "Honesty matters. You came to Agent Bonner because you realized that you'd kicked a hornet's nest and you thought you'd found a way to stay out of danger for a while. It turned out to be a good plan, but don't overplay your hand."

An idea bloomed in Jonathan's mind. "Do you ever miss your Army days, Captain?" he asked.

Behind them, Boxers made an ugly noise. "What are you about to do, Boss?"

"Why do you ask?" Hite said. His warning radar was clearly spun up.

"Answer the question for me," Jonathan said.

"Parts of it, I suppose."

"What about the getting shot at part?"

"If I had to rank the parts I hated most, that would be right at the top of the list," Hite said.

"What about the flip side? Killing bad guys?"

Boxers got a little louder. "Please think this through."

Hite's eyebrows formed a solid straight line. "You're not telling me something."

"Screw it," Boxers said. "He wants to know if you want to travel to Mexico and kill cartel dickheads."

Jonathan hadn't expected that. Big Guy was precisely on point, but it wasn't the kind of thing he would normally say. Boxers valued his secrets.

Hite's jaw dropped. "Is that what you're going to do?"

"No," Big Guy snapped. "It's just a random question. That's my favorite thing."

Irene held up her hand for attention and silence. "You're getting to the parts I don't need to hear," she said. "I'm officially handing Captain Hite back to your protective custody."

"Who the hell are you to hand me over to anybody for any reason?"

Irene answered by spinning on her heel and advancing toward her chopper, whose pilot was beginning to spin up the rotor disk.

"Dammit!" Hite yelled. "Stop with the riddles, and give me a straight answer about something. This is my life we're talking about."

"Let's go back inside and talk," Jonathan said, gently touching Hite's arm.

Hite pulled away. "I'm not going anywhere." The way he'd planted his feet told Jonathan that he was serious.

"Suit yourself," Jonathan said. He moved past the captain and headed back toward the cabin door. "Don't try to climb the fence. Just go out the front gate and start walking."

"I don't know where I am."

Jonathan smiled but didn't look back when he said, "On the other hand, you can follow us back inside."

Boxers and Gail followed, and when Jonathan was nearly to the bar in the far corner, Michael Hite made his entrance. "You win. I'm here."

"Glad to have you," Jonathan said. "What's your poison?"

"I don't want a drink," Hite said.

"Oh, trust me," Boxers said through a rumbling chuckle. "You'll want a drink."

Hite looked to Gail and she nodded. "Yeah."

"White wine for me," Venice said.

Jonathan smiled. If anything in the world could be predicted, it was that Venice would want white wine.

"Bourbon on the rocks for me, then," Hite said. His tone was begrudging.

Jonathan called an audible and poured the captain a Maker's Mark, with Lagavulin for himself and Big Guy and a cosmo for Gail. Within five minutes, they were gathered around the coffee table in front of the fireplace.

"We're about to get to the details, right?" Hite said.

Jonathan leaned into his rocker, crossed his legs, and took a pull on the scotch. Lagavulin was as peaty as a drink could get, and he savored the mouthfeel. "You're among friends, Captain Hite. You're safe here and you're free to relax." He shifted his gaze to Boxers. "Give him the pitch, Big Guy."

Boxers looked startled to be called upon. "Okay." He took a long pull on his drink and set the glass on the table. "It's been a hell of a day, hasn't it?"

"That's putting it mildly," Hite said.

"Yeah, well, it's just beginning to get weird for you." Boxers lowered his basso voice to its most threating octave. "My role right now is to impress upon you how important it is to keep what you're about to hear a secret. You need to commit to that up front."

Hite said nothing, but his face screamed confusion.

"I need an answer."

"To what? You haven't said anything yet."

Boxers glared as the others waited.

"Fine," Hite said. "I'll keep your secret."

"The penalty for not keeping it is huge," Boxers said. "Think pain and misery for you. The kind of suffering that even I don't like to inflict but will if you betray us."

Hite's features grew pale. Big Guy had that effect

on people. "Okay, fine. I said *fine*. How about we cut through the bullshit and get down to—"

"We're not with the FBI," Jonathan said. "We're not with any government agency, in fact. We used to be, but we're not anymore."

Hite's confusion deepened. "But that was Director Rivers, wasn't it?"

"Yes, it was," Jonathan said. "Without getting into the details, we sometimes work together, but it's always, shall we say, off the books."

"I don't understand."

"You really don't need to," Jonathan said. "Not all of it, anyway. But here's the thing. The information you stumbled into during your interview with Rocco LoCicero only confirmed things that we've known but have been unable to prove. The fact that you know what you know about the administration puts your life in jeopardy. Your only path to safety is for Director Rivers to substantiate what you've learned and get it on the record within a time window that will allow a whole bunch of people to stay alive long enough to get it all done."

Hite gaped. His brain was getting full.

"You can ask questions as we go," Jonathan prompted.

"If you're not FBI, then who are you?"

"For now, think of us as Team America. You can call me Scorpion."

"Really?"

"It gets better," Jonathan said. "This is Gunslinger."

Gail offered a finger wave.

"That's Mother Hen, and the big threatening fella is, appropriately enough, Big Guy."

"No real names?" Hite asked.

"Not for you, no. And if you decide to stick around, your call sign will be Birdman."

Hite recoiled, then smiled as he got the joke. "Ah. As in Birdman of Alcatraz."

"Bingo."

"What's this about killing cartel members?" Hite asked.

"Before we get there, when was the last time you fired a weapon or set a detonator?"

"I compete at my local gun club almost every weekend. As for blowing shit up, well, it's been a while."

"Like riding a bike," Boxers said. "Physics and chemistry never change."

Jonathan said, "You heard LoCicero speak of the lack of a real war on drugs. There's lots of talk but never any meaningful action. Well, we aim to fix that."

"Meaning what?" Hite asked.

"Meaning that we're bringing fire, hell, and damnation to the Los Muertos drug cartel. We've taken a chunk or two out of it over the last months, but this time, we're going to kill it. I thought you might like to help."

Hite looked like Jonathan had grown a second nose. "Why on earth would I want to do that?"

"Because their product killed over a hundred thousand Americans last year," Gail said.

Jonathan added, "And it's the same product that caused us to have a shoot-out at the Hilltop Manor not that many hours ago. As Mr. LoCicero said in the tape, the cartel murders, maims, and terrorizes without pushback from their government."

"Because their government is afraid of them, too," Boxers said.

"The way I see it, Captain, you stumbled into a world of hurt here. Can I presume that you don't have a family?" He figured that had to be the case if Hite had up and left to run from the bad guys.

"No one here," Hite said. "I have a wife and two daughters, but they're living in North Carolina now." He looked down. "Apparently, I'm not the best husband."

"The separation is good," Jonathan said. "That will keep them safe, at least for the time being. If things go according to plan and we win this war, they'll never be the wiser. But if we don't, the administration won't hesitate to use Los Muertos monsters to do whatever is necessary to first silence you for what you know and then punish you for knowing it."

The early signs of realization crept into Hite's eyes. Maybe a touch of panic. He pointed to Venice. "You," he said. "Mother Hen. You don't say much. Is this for real?"

"It's very much for real," she said. "Not a week ago, my fourteen-year-old son nearly ate one of the candies that killed Giovanni LoCicero."

The room fell silent as Hite considered his options.

"You've got skin in the game, Captain," Jonathan said. "You can cross your fingers and hope that other people protect your family and your country, or you can help take the fight to the enemy. What's your call, Captain?"

Hite closed his eyes and settled his shoulders. When the eyes opened again, there was a new resolve. "The name is Birdman," he said.

Jonathan raised his glass. "Welcome to the team. Now, Big Guy, let's talk about your swarm of little Roxies."

"Little what?" Hite said.

"Hang on and listen," Jonathan said. "That's the best way to get with the program."

"I gotta go to the Batmobile," Big Guy said. "Follow me outside."

Jonathan's phone buzzed in his pocket. Never good

news. A glance at the incoming number confirmed his suspicions. "Hey, Wolfie. Missing me already?"

"I thought you should know," she said without pre-amble. "They got to LoCicero. He's dead."

"They killed him in his cell?"

Those words caused Hite's head to crank around.

"Two bullets to the forehead," Irene said. "No one heard a thing."

"Of course they didn't." The line went dead before he could finish his snarky remark.

"LoCicero?" Hite asked.

"Shot and killed," Jonathan said. "No witnesses."

Chapter 16

Jonathan, Gail, Venice, and Hite sat in matching rocking chairs on the front porch of the cabin while Boxers hauled two huge Pelican cases from the back of the Batmobile and placed them on the grass at the foot of the porch stairs.

"What is he doing?" Hite asked.

"We need a plan to invade Mexico," Jonathan said. "We need to make a surgical strike, take out the entire leadership of Los Muertos, and then get out again with our hearts still beating."

"Just the five of us?" Hite asked.

"Four, actually," Venice said. "I stay home and work the computers."

"That's not possible," Hite said.

Jonathan bristled. He got that they didn't know each other yet, but his skin puckered at the sound of defeatist language. "Everything is possible," he corrected. "You just have to plan properly."

Boxers opened the cases one at a time to display arrays of several dozen tiny rotor-powered drones, each of them maybe six inches wide by two inches long. They sat nestled in packing foam, their rotors folded and aligned with their fuselages.

"Meet my family of Little Roxies," he said. "All told, we have forty-eight of them."

"This is our air force," Jonathan explained. "Each one of those little bastards can be loaded with up to a quarter-pound of explosives, and they've got a range of . . ." He looked to Boxers.

"A couple of miles, give or take. The only limitation is the battery life. You can only have so much juice in such a small package."

Gail looked as confused as Hite. "You're not going to get a lot of damage a quarter pound at a time," she said.

"They're not about attacking property," Boxers said through a wide grin. "These guys are programmed to seek out and kill individuals."

"That shouldn't make you so happy," Venice said.

"Happy doesn't touch it," Big Guy replied. "Not when I think about who the soon-to-be-dead individuals are."

"How are you going to fly forty-eight drones all at the same time?" Hite asked.

Jonathan said, "Take it from here, Mother Hen. You've been in touch with Thor, right?" Thor was the call sign for Harry Dawkins, a career special agent with the Drug Enforcement Administration whom Jonathan and Boxers had not too long ago rescued from the talons of cartel torturers and who had subsequently helped the team out of other jams. His hatred for Los Muertos knew no bounds, and the administration's refusal to do their jobs left him in a continuing state of fury.

"I have," Mother Hen said. "He's on assignment that won't let him join you on this adventure, but he was able to send me the files we needed." She reached into

her purse and produced a tiny SD card. "It's all right
here. Images and social media data for every member
of the Gomez family and for every known associate and
enforcer. We know that the Los Muertos leadership
meets at Rolo's hacienda every third Thursday of the
month to do whatever they do."

"How do we know this?" Gail asked.

"Thor said he has intel sources. He didn't share what
they were, and I didn't press him because I didn't want
to put him in the position of telling me something I
didn't have a need to know."

"That seems like a bad idea to have a regular schedule," Boxers said. "Not the best security-wise."

"What security concerns can he have?" Jonathan
countered. "Hell, the military and police are often as
not enforcers for them. For sure, no public servant
makes enough money to bring cartel horrors down on
their own families."

Hite said, "But in the days of Pablo Escobar—"

"The US government gave a shit," Jonathan interrupted. "Maybe too much of a shit, in retrospect, but
Uncle Sam spent a fair amount of blood and treasure
to put his fat ass in the ground. And that was with the
cooperation of the Columbian government. Now, all
sides serve the same master, and the master's name is
Rolo Gomez."

"I don't know that I understand the plan," Gail said.
"We have these files from Thor. So, then what?"

"These Roxies are smart," Boxers said, swelling a
bit with a kind of parental pride. "After I arm the little
buggers, Mother Hen will upload the data, and then
we launch them outside the walls of the hacienda.
Once loosed, they will use their cameras and little

computer brains to hunt down and kill everyone they're programmed to hit."

"So, they each have their own target?" Gail asked.

"No, they'll all be programmed with all the targets. First come, first served."

"Jesus," Gail said. "That's horrible. What happens if they make a mistake? Not every face is that distinctive."

"That's where the social media element comes in," Venice said. "In this case, they'll be programmed to match at least three identifying criteria to go active."

"Suppose they miss?" Gail asked.

"They won't miss," Boxers said.

"Humor me. You've got a flying bomb with a load of explosives buzzing around. Even if you can guarantee that it won't hit the wrong target, you can't be sure that it will hit any target at all."

"We've got that covered," Jonathan said. "If a Roxie is still alive when its battery gets too low, it will zip up to altitude and blow up."

"How many people are we talking about?" Hite asked.

"Thirty or more," Venice said.

"There's no way they're going to drop everybody," Hite said. "What about the folks who are indoors?"

"Good question," Jonathan said. "Which brings us to the timing of everything. Roxies can fly through open windows, but they can't open doors. We have to hit these guys before they're settled into a conference room."

"That means we'll need eyes on," Gail said.

"Big Roxie will handle that," Boxers said. "I can put her in a five-hundred-foot hover with her lens zoomed to whatever we want it to be. We'll be able to see when people arrive. Or, if they're already there, we'll be able to see them mingling in the courtyard."

"Do we have pictures of this hacienda?" Hite asked.

Jonathan said, "Yes. When we go back inside, we can walk through those plans. But first, there's one more big element here, and that's the fact that we're going to have to follow the Roxies to do cleanup, because you're right that there will be some survivors when they're all done."

"That's a daylight operation," Boxers said.

"Yes. Not the best, but this is a case where we have to meet the bad guys on their battlefield on their terms."

"The good news is, they'll be in disarray," Gail said. "It'll be pretty unnerving to get attacked by kids' toys."

"And to leverage that disarray, we'll have to be pretty tight on their tails."

"How's *that* gonna work?" Hite asked. "My long-distance running days are behind me."

"Not to worry," Jonathan said. "We'll arrive by chopper."

Hite's jaw dropped. "Whose?"

"Not your concern," Jonathan said. The whole truth was that Jonathan himself didn't know the answer to the question. It was one of the promises made by Thor, and Thor never failed to come through.

"What about the pilot?"

"That would be me," Boxers said.

"Okay, then how do we get into Mexico in the first place?" Gail asked.

"Same chopper," Jonathan said. "The Gomez haci-enda is just twenty miles or so across the border from the Big Bend region of Texas. The rich folks who live on the American side have their own private enclave with their own private airfield. We'll park the jet there, transfer to the chopper, then fly under the radar to a spot in the desert to be named later—close enough to launch Big Roxie and her little children, yet far enough away to remain out of sight. After the little monsters wreak their havoc, we swoop in, park inside the wire, do our thing, and swoop out again. Easy peasy."

"Aren't the Mexicans going to see us coming across their border?" Gail asked.

Jonathan deferred to Boxers, who said, "We'll be very low—like fifty feet off the sand—and we'll be running dark."

"But it'll be daytime," Hite said.

"Term of art. The transponders will be off. Electronically, we'll be invisible. We've done this a million times before. While we might scare the shit out of some prairie dogs and set off a few car alarms, we'll be well below anybody's radar."

"What about locals?" Hite asked.

"What about 'em? The location of this hacienda defines *the middle of nowhere*. If Juan Valdez gets spooked and calls the cops, so what? They won't know where we're going, and even if they did, we'll be gone before the *federales'* engines warmed up."

"So, you don't anticipate any resistance?" Hite pressed.

"Oh, there'll be resistance," Gail said. "There's always resistance."

"And we've always dealt with it," Jonathan said. "The rules of engagement will be simple. Once we're in the compound, drop anybody you see with a weapon. No warnings, no questions. We'll have radios, and we'll be on VOX, so call out your hits when they happen. If you get hit, announce that, too, and fight on as best you can until we come and get you."

"What about staff?" Hite asked. "Other innocents?"

"Leave them alone," Jonathan said. "If they're not armed, they're not our concern."

"They've been known to use innocents as human shields," Gail said.

"You've got to make the call in the moment," Jonathan said. "Hopefully, the timing will be such that they wouldn't have thought that far."

"What do you anticipate the total time on the ground in the compound to be?" Venice asked.

"Too many moving parts to give you a hard estimate," Jonathan said. "Ten minutes, maybe? Certainly, no more than fifteen."

"When do we leave?" Gail asked.

"Tomorrow," Jonathan said. "We'll get to Manassas Airport for an equipment check, be wheels-up by noon. That'll put us back on the ground in Big Bend by three-thirty. Thor's arranged a safe house for us near the airfield, so we can be up and on our way to wreak havoc bright and early the next day."

"Are we bedding down here tonight?" Boxers asked.

"If you want," Jonathan said. "I know that fresh air gets to you after a while, so if you need to head back to the big city, suit yourself." Big Guy lived in downtown DC for the nightlife. "I plan to stay here and go straight to Manassas in the morning."

"That's my plan, as well," Gail said.

"Unfortunately, I can't" Venice said. "I've got that thing to do for Wolverine in the morning."

"You okay with that?" Jonathan asked.

Venice shrugged. "I am if you are. You guys will be the one with an unmanned command post."

"Only for a short while," Jonathan said. Irene wanted Venice to drive a getaway car of sorts for a mission he didn't fully understand. "The hot war doesn't start till the next morning." He stood. "Any more questions?"

"About a thousand," Hite said.

"I'll bet you do," Jonathan said. "Let's you and me go for a walk."

Boxers stood, too. "Want me to come along?"

"Not on this one, Big Guy." Jonathan could read Boxers' mind. He didn't like being closed out of any discussion that might impact a mission, and he especially hated being shut out of discussions that could affect mission security. Jonathan got it. But the simple fact of the matter was that his presence kept people from listening, let alone speaking their minds. This chat with Hite needed to be one-on-one. The mission on which they were about to embark was more hazardous than any of the bravado on the porch had indicated, and he needed to be sure that Hite was fully aware and onboard. As he retraced the steps he'd trod with Irene just a little while before, Hite followed close behind.

"You need to tell me what you're really thinking," Jonathan said. "There was a lot of bluster and blow in that planning session, and I know you were under a lot of pressure to say yes. And as much as I'd love to have you aboard, I need you to know that the mission is risky as hell."

"Isn't that always the case in a two-way shooting gallery?"

Jonathan smiled at the phrase. "How much action did you see over in the Sandbox?" he asked.

"Enough. I know how to clear a building if that's what you're wanting to hear."

"There are no right answers here," Jonathan said. "People are going to die on this thing, and I need you to know that. I need you to be comfortable with that."

Hite folded his arms across his chest and cast his eyes askance. "What are you people, really? What are you about?"

"That's complicated."

"If I'm going to risk my life in service to a group, I think I have the right to know something about it."

He made a very good point. "I'm sorry to be so vague, but you have to understand that for what we do to work, secrecy and operational security are paramount."

"I've kept a lot of secrets in my life," Hite said. "Under the circumstances, I don't know how you can hold everything back."

This was not the way things were done in Jonathan's world. You didn't go adopting operators on the fly in the middle of a gunfight and folding them into the organization. He had no idea what this guy's capabilities were, just as Hite knew nothing of theirs.

"Let me start with a question," Hite said. "Are you assassins?"

"Absolutely not," Jonathan said. That one was easy. "We don't do murder for hire. The missions we perform often involve violence, and in that violence, people die, but when the smoke clears, we are always on the side of the angels."

"Okay, now that I know what you're *not*, did that break the ice to tell me what you *are*?"

Jonathan inhaled deeply and rubbed the back of his neck as he tried to form the right words. "I am the president of a private investigation firm that gets things done for our clients in unusual yet very effective ways."

"What docs that mean?"

"It means that our clients pay us a lot of money not to tell them how we achieve our goals."

"You break the law," Hite said.

"We get results," Jonathan countered.

"By, say, invading a sovereign nation without authority or provocation?"

Jonathan had to laugh at the way he put it. "That's not an everyday occurrence, but I'd be lying if I told you this was the first time." He stopped and turned so they were facing each other. "Here it is, straight from the hip. Imagine your son or daughter were kidnapped. You maybe didn't have direct evidence, but you *knew*. Or you got a ransom note telling you that the child would die if you went to the police. What would you do?"

"I don't know how to answer that."

"I can tell you that if you *did* go to the police, they would move at a snail's pace, crossing *T*'s and dotting *I*'s to make sure they didn't do anything to offend a judge down the line that would get their case thrown out. They'd do their job in a world where all those dotted *I*'s were at least as important as getting your kid back, because if a single one went undotted, the kidnapper would skate out of court on a technicality."

Hite was clearly engaged, but he remained silent.

"As an alternative, you could hire me and my company to blast through the door of the hostage house, grab your kid, and bring him home again. If the bad guys cooperate and just give their hostages up, no one need be the wiser, and maybe they live on to kidnap another day. If they choose not to cooperate, well, like I said. We're on the side of the angels."

"And the police just look the other way?"

"Sometimes. Mostly, they quit when they realize that for many reasons—mostly affiliated with Mother Hen's ability to bend electrons to her will—my team and I are invisible."

"What does that mean?"

Jonathan shook his head. That answer would be a step too far. "Now, there's a thing you're not cleared to know," he said. He started walking again, still toward the wood line. "There you have it, Captain Hite. I've laid it all out for you. Now, I need a decision. Are you in or out?"

"I thought we already had this conversation," Hite said. "The name is Birdman."

Chapter 17

Harold Standish used a torn piece of buttered toast to wipe up the last of the egg yolk that lined the edge of his breakfast plate, then balanced his last piece of bacon on top before popping the whole thing into his mouth. As he chewed, he looked through the screened wall of his back porch down at the wooded slope that led to the edge of the Potomac River. In another forty-five days, with the leaves gone, he'd have a clear view of the river itself. Built in 1996 at the height of the McMansion boom in Great Falls, Virginia, this eleven-thousand-square-foot palace on its acre and a half of land had been quite the showpiece. Now, it looked dated, its internal columns defining that specific slice in time when those were the architectural necessities of the nouveau riche.

The temperature hovered in that October sweet spot where shirtsleeves were too light but jackets were too heavy. One of the things he disliked most about the chilly wet winters of the Northern Virginia suburbs was the need to close up the porch through the winter months. It was ironic, he thought, that the porch was his favorite room in the house when, in fact, it wasn't even a room.

As soon as he crossed his knife and fork across his

breakfast plate, his housekeeper, Trudy, appeared at the French door. She wore a modernized, trouser version of the classic black-and-white maid uniform. "Are you finished with your breakfast, Mr. Standish?" she asked.

Standish pushed the plate to the side, closer to her. "Yes, Trudy. Thank you. Delicious, as always."

"What time does Mrs. Standish arrive home from her travels?" Trudy asked.

"Not today, I'm afraid," he said. "Change in plans. Her aunt's health is not improving as quickly as we had hoped." By *aunt*, of course, he meant Allison's boy toy, Chico, he of wide shoulders and thirty-inch waist. Such was the price to pay when you choose a wife who is thirty years younger than yourself. To Allison's credit, she never lied about Chico. In fact, it was on Standish's insistence that the story of an aunt's ill health was born as the means to explain his wife's extended absences.

Washington expected cabinet secretaries to have arm-candy wives and rarely even feigned surprise when the truth behind political marriages became known. What was the old saying? Washington was Hollywood with ugly faces.

"I'm sorry to hear that, sir," Trudy said. "I'm sure you must get lonely at night."

When Trudy said things like that, Standish wondered if she was signaling that she knew the truth of the situation. Either way, he didn't care. He had far more important things on his mind than the gossip shared by his servants.

As was his daily habit, Standish enjoyed his breakfast with his Samsung tablet propped open to allow him to read the newspapers while he ate his food and sipped his coffee. Of the three morning papers he read, all carried the same headline, above the virtual fold, and it was a variation of "Shoot-out at Hilltop Manor Resort."

The details of the story hurt his stomach. What a ham-handed, unprofessional operation. Given the participation of former members of elite special forces units from here and elsewhere in the world, he'd assumed that the team sent by Nicky Mishin's people would have been more capable than this. First, there'd been that disaster in the motel parking lot, and now there's this shoot-out in a public place.

Standish had been assured that no evidence from the assault teams could be traced back to Operation Southern Hammer, but the fact that both bungled missions were triggered by visits to Big Sandy and the words of Rocco LoCicero was a serious issue. The fact of the shared link made every bit of discovered evidence that much more critical if and when it was found.

Earlier in his career, these kinds of chinks in the plan would have triggered a low-grade panic response, but not anymore. Standish had put more proverbial trains back on their tracks than he could count, and in each case, the odds at first seemed insurmountable, only to prove yet again that calm discipline will win the day every time.

Already, with LoCicero dead, Standish sensed that the genie was on its way back into the bottle. The runaway guard—Michael Hite—was still a problem, but a small one. If he was smart, he'd realize that by getting away in the Hilltop Manor, he'd both literally and figuratively dodged a bullet, and he'd go to ground and stay quiet. Los Muertos and the Schillacis wouldn't rest until Hite was dead, but the more time that passed while he was still alive, the less damage the details he'd been told could do.

Standish looked at his watch. Seven forty-five. It

was time to start his day. His driver would be out front by now, so all he needed to do was give his teeth a quick brushing and then he'd be out the door. The first order of business would be to meet one of Mishin's men at a diner in McLean, Virginia, where they would match notes, not just on the LoCicero business per se but also on the means by which to reinvigorate the flow of product across the border. Rolo Gomez was going to be angry at the disruption, and, together, Standish and Mishin would have to carefully cultivate a message that would pull the old man—and his psychopath son—off the ledge and relax them enough to start up the business again.

Trudy was waiting at the front door with Standish's briefcase in hand as he stepped off the sweeping curved stairway and onto the polished maple floor of the foyer. As he closed the distance, she opened the door for him. "Have a pleasant day, sir."

"Thank you, Trudy. Please do the same. And get my clothes to the cleaners. The laundry bag—"

"Is in your closet. Yes, sir."

The door closed behind him as he stepped out onto the stoop and trotted down the flight of seven stairs that took him to the waiting Suburban. He found it odd that no one was holding the door for him as he approached, but he was certainly more than capable of opening his own. "Good morning, Agent Dolan," he said as he slid into his seat and reached for the seatbelt.

"Good morning, sir," the driver said.

The voice was wrong. When Standish looked up, he saw a Black woman's eyes staring back at him in the rearview mirror.

"I'm not Agent Dolan," she said. "She has the day off. "I'm Agent Contata. Where to, sir?"

"We're going into McLean. The McLean Family Diner. Do you know it?"

The driver reached to the screen at her center console and typed in the name of the restaurant. "Yes, sir, I do now," she said.

Standish considered himself a good judge of people, and something about this new agent on this particular day didn't feel right. The same day when Mishin's hit teams had screwed up, what were the chances that his normal driver—who'd never once missed a day on his watch—would declare a day off?

"Are you with the Bureau?" he asked, but if the driver heard him, she made no indication. He raised his voice. "Excuse me, Agent . . . Comata, is it?"

"Contata, sir," she said. She kept her eyes straight, however, not looking at him through the mirror as he would have expected. "I'm pleased to meet you."

"You didn't answer my question."

"Question, sir?" Still no eye contact as she sped up a bit.

This was definitely wrong. He couldn't put his finger on it, but this was some kind of a setup. "Tell you what, Agent Contata. I need to return to my house for a moment. I forgot something."

"Yes, sir," the driver said, but when they passed the next intersection, she made no effort to change course.

"Are you not hearing me?" Standish asked. He felt a bubble of panic rising in his gut. They'd accelerated past the point where he could safely open a door and bail out onto the street. "I told you that I need to return home."

"I heard you, sir," the driver said. "But I have to wait for the appropriate intersection."

"Slow down," Standish demanded. "Better yet, stop this vehicle right now."

This time, the driver didn't bother to respond. Instead, her foot grew heavier on the accelerator.

Standish found himself transported in his head back to his days with the Agency during the Cold War years, when he'd received training for how to thwart kidnap attempts. But that training was a distant memory and his body was nearly forty years older. He didn't even carry a firearm anymore. How stupid was that?

"Are you taking me someplace, Agent Contata?" He heard an annoying shakiness in his voice.

The driver remained silent.

"Answer my goddamn question!" he boomed.

The driver jumped at the explosion of sound and, in the process, caused the Suburban to veer into the left lane and then back again.

"Please don't do that, sir!" the driver shouted back. "I have my orders, and I intend to follow them."

"Orders for what?"

"You'll know in a minute, sir."

"Look, Agent Contata, I don't know what you were told when you took this job this morning, but if you don't turn this vehicle around right now, I will see to it that your career—"

The driver slammed the brakes to slide a turn into a little roadside farmer's market that hadn't yet opened for morning business. A couple of miles an hour faster or another inch or two on the steering wheel would have caused the vehicle to flip. As it was, the applied physics tested the limits of Standish's seatbelt.

"Jesus!"

"Sorry, sir," the driver said. "The turn snuck up on me."

Standish didn't believe that for a second. "What are we doing here?"

"There's someone who wants to talk with you," the driver said.

"What the *hell* is going on?" As soon as Standish's demand for an answer had cleared his throat, that lump of dread he'd felt in his stomach bloomed to the size of a watermelon as an all-too-familiar woman climbed out of a Suburban of her own and started walking his way.

"This is the time for you to step out," the driver said.

Standish sat unmoving, seatbelt still on, while FBI Director Irene Rivers opened his door from the outside.

"Good morning, Harold," she said. Then, looking around him to see the driver, she said, "Well done, Mother Hen. As soon as we get Mr. Standish out of his seatbelt, you can be on your way. I'll take it from here."

"What is this all about?" Standish demanded. "You have no right—"

"Don't make me arrest you, Harold," Irene said. "You need to get out of your vehicle and come with me."

"Why would I do that?"

"Does the name Operation Southern Hammer mean anything to you?"

Something dissolved in Standish's gut. It was entirely possible that he was going to be sick.

"How about Nicholas Mishin, Rocco LoCicero, Los Muertos, and the president of the United States?"

Standish gaped. He knew he should be saying something—anything—to distance himself from those names and what they represented, but the words wouldn't form in his throat.

"Your poker face is letting you down," Irene said.

Standish's mind raced to comprehend the ramifications. Unless Director Rivers was bluffing, she had enough to put his ass away for ten lifetimes.

"We also know about the attempted missile installation in Venezuela."

Holy shit. Oh, my God. Oh, my God. Oh, my God.

"You really do need to come with me," Irene said. She placed her hand on his right wrist and squeezed it. "Please don't make me handcuff you. It's been a long time since I've had to do that."

"Am I under arrest?"

"Not necessarily," Irene said. "You really do need to come with me."

Standish felt as if his peripheral vision was collapsing in on him as he slid out and put his right foot on the gravel parking lot.

Wait a second. Where were the dozen armed agents and their SWAT gear? Again, none of this was going the way it was supposed to.

"What game are you playing here, Irene?"

"I think you're better off referring to me as Director Rivers, under the circumstances. And the game I'm playing is called let's-give-a-piece-of-shit-traitor-a-chance-to-save-his-ass. How does that sound?"

Chapter 18

The houses along Juniper Lane in Falls Church, Virginia, had been around long enough to witness at least one world war. A few had seen two. Originally built for the upper end of the working class, the neighborhood fell into hard times in the sixties and seventies, only to be resurrected in the early aughts. Now, the winding, tree-lined lane featured the full gamut of architecture, from pre-war Craftsman to the bloated twenty-first century version of that same iconic design to hideous wannabe mansions whose owners clearly had no sense of design.

One of the original Craftsman bungalows sat on the low side of a hill on three-quarters of an acre. The neighbors knew practically nothing about the residents of the well-maintained charmer, but because it was so damned cute, no one ever complained, either. Irene wondered if the local kids had devised any ghost stories to explain the absence of life in the place.

Because Washington and its suburbs were spooky places where spooky people lived, she imagined that at least some of the locals with appropriate experience would have guessed that the bungalow belonged to Uncle Sam and was used as a safe house when it was used at all. It was the nature of safe houses that they weren't occupied in a regular rotation. Predictability was the sworn enemy of intelligence operations.

At about eighteen hundred square feet, the bungalow was livable, but by modern standards, everything about the place was undersized. The ceilings were too low, the doorways too narrow. The bedrooms were big enough for a queen bed, but a standard would fit better and a king would be out of the question.

When people were running for their lives and living under the cover of lies, Irene supposed they weren't all that picky about their surroundings.

Irene and Standish sat in matching overstuffed chairs, facing each other across a slate hearth in front of a non-functioning fireplace. They both sipped from bottles of water retrieved from the kitchen fridge.

"May I ask what we're waiting for?" Standish said.

"You may ask whatever you wish," Irene said with a smirk. "The wild card is whether I'll answer."

"Whatever it is, will I have a chance to see the alleged evidence that you have against me for these supposed crimes?"

Irene noted with a mix of interest and amusement how Standish's attitude had morphed over the course of the last couple of hours. When first confronted with what he'd done, he'd looked as if he'd been slapped in the face. Now, he'd dialed it back into a prove-what-you've-got mode.

That's the way pros handled it, and Standish was nothing if not a professional. It was tragic how quickly and utterly the quest for power—even if it was only to touch the garment of power—corrupted otherwise good people.

The sound of an approaching vehicle beyond the drawn curtains eliminated the need for Irene to actively be rude. She rose, moved to the window, and parted the drapes with the thumb and forefinger of her left hand.

A polished black Suburban was navigating its way down the steep hill to park behind Irene's polished black Suburban. Any nosy neighbors now had to know that the bungalow was the site of either a high-level government meeting or a drug buy.

"Our guest is here," Irene said. She headed for the front door.

"And who might that be?" Standish asked.

"Kresha Ruby."

"The assistant United States attorney?"

"That very one. Now, be quiet and pay attention. This could be very good for you."

Standish held up his hands as if to surrender. "This is your show," he said.

The continued calm demeanor unnerved Irene a little as she walked to the door and opened it as Kresha was stepping up to knock. She'd clearly come from work, wearing a slightly dressy, slightly sexy pantsuit of the type that was still required of women in power.

"Thank you for coming, Counselor."

"I suppose I should say you're welcome," Kresha said as she accepted Irene's offer for a handshake. "But to be honest, I'm mostly annoyed. My day doesn't need more cloak-and-dagger shit than it already has."

As Kresha stepped all the way inside and allowed the door to be closed behind her, she made a show of checking out the surroundings. "Hey, nice safe house." Then she saw the other party in the room. "Mr. Standish?"

The man stood. "One and the same. Welcome to the execution."

"Excuse me?"

Irene gestured to the cushion she'd just vacated. "Please have a seat, Kresha. I'm in a bit of a pickle, and I'm leaning on you to help me out of it."

"What kind of pickle are you in?" Kresha seemed amused by the theater of it all.

"The kind that can topple a government and get a lot of people killed," Irene replied without irony.

"Well, okay, then." Kresha sat heavily in her chair. "Whatcha got?"

Irene pulled her laptop from her bag and inserted her copy of the chip from Hite's visit with LoCicero. "First, I need you to listen to something."

When the recording was finished, Kresha Ruby continued to stare at the laptop, as if expecting more, her elbows forming a tripod with her knees. After a few seconds, she rocked her head around to look at Standish. "Is the Standish referenced in the recording the same Standish as you?"

"I have no idea what that man is talking about," Standish said. "And for the record, I'd like a lawyer."

"I don't think you do," Irene said.

Kresha leaned back in her chair. "What do you want me to do with this?" she said. "It's all hearsay."

"It's direct testimony," Irene said. "First person from the guy who actually handled the money from Assistant Secretary Standish."

"Will he testify?"

"I'm confident he will," Irene said.

Standish scoffed, "How are you gonna get a dead man to talk?"

Kresha looked utterly confused. "That true? Rocco LoCicero is dead?"

"Killed in his cell," Irene said. "But there's been no announcement. You're surprised because the fact of LoCicero's death was never disseminated." She bored her gaze through Standish's head. "Yet somehow, you already knew. How is that?"

He showed that deer-in-the-headlights look again. It was there and gone in a couple of seconds, but she definitely saw it. "Lawyer," he said.

"Okay, Irene," Kresha said. "Come clean. Why are we here?"

"This is not the only evidence I have," Irene said. "I can prove multiple incidences where Tony Darmond and his surrogates have lent aid and comfort to our enemies, suborned drug trafficking and human trafficking, and, believe it or not, looked the other way while Russians attempted to install nuclear warheads in Venezuela."

Kresha's expression darkened. "Seriously, Irene?"

"I'm as serious as I can be," she said. "And I also have Michael Hite, the other person in the recorded conversation. He's in a safe house, despite several attempts on his life in just the past couple of days, and he is very, very willing to testify."

"Why is Captain Hite in a safe house?"

"Because a crew dispatched by Mr. Standish tried to kill him."

Standish laughed. "Did I kill JFK, too? What about Elvis?"

Irene ignored him, stayed focused on Kresha. "You've heard about the shoot-out at the Hilltop Manor?"

Kresha's jaw dropped, and she looked at Standish.

"She can say anything she likes," he said. "But saying it doesn't make it so."

Kresha's mind clearly wasn't yet processing it all.

Irene went on, "I can tie Harold Standish to everything." She shifted her attention to her target. "You know what you've done, sir, and you need to trust me that I can nail you to the wall with it."

"Then why is he here listening to this?" Kresha said. "Why aren't we drafting indictments?"

"Because he's not the one I want," Irene said. "And he's not the one the nation needs to indict."

"You want the president," Kresha said. "Of the United States."

"I want him and his family and God knows how many members of his administration. This conspiracy is unimaginably huge." She turned her gaze to Standish. "Harold, you need to understand that you face two choices here. You can go to prison for the rest of your life and then some, or you can cooperate with the United States Attorney's office and never see the inside of a jail cell."

"Whoa, whoa, whoa," Kresha said, pumping her hands in the air. "You're talking immunity. You can't offer that."

"I can't, but you can," Irene said. "That's why you're here."

"Why me?"

"Because I think I can trust you. I know I cannot trust the attorney general."

Kresha's arms dropped. "General Norris is a part of this?"

"Neck deep. Time is of the essence here. I know this is difficult to believe, but a hit team also tried to kill a team of my investigators who likewise visited Big Sandy."

Kresha cocked her head. "There was something in the news about a shoot-out in a hotel parking lot in Kentucky."

"The two hotel incidents are linked," Irene confirmed. "You sent that team, didn't you, Harold?"

He stayed silent.

"Good for you," Irene said. "The Fifth Amendment

is your friend today." To Kresha: "I need you to draft an order of immunity and get it blessed by a judge that you trust. With that, you can compel Mr. Standish to cooperate. If he refuses, we send him away forever."

"Let's say you're correct," Standish said. Irene knew he wouldn't be able to sit silently. Men with egos like his were somehow addicted to self-incrimination. It was a trait that made prosecutions so much easier. "I don't believe that you have all the evidence you claim to have linking me to any crazy conspiracy. If it existed, you'd have already arrested me. Instead, you need me to testify against myself and implicate others in this crime that never happened. Why would I do that?"

Fact was, Irene was largely playing a bluff here. The evidence she had almost exclusively came from the exploits of Jonathan Grave, and all of it was obtained by unconstitutional means. Standish was, in fact, her trump card.

She made a show of considering her answer, then smiled. "The decision is yours. If you want to walk away from immunity and roll the dice, I can share everything I've got and have you perp walked by morning."

"Bullshit. You're bluffing."

Kresha said, "As an alternative, you could tell the world that we all met. You could leak that Mr. Standish had agreed to cooperate." Finally, she was with the program.

"Interesting thought," Irene said. "If I'm totally off base, you'd have nothing to worry about, sir. There'd be no reason for those fictional hit squads to take aim at you."

The headlights look returned. This time, it was sustained.

"What do I get immunity for?" Standish said. Now, that was quite a course change.

"Everything you've ever done in your life that you should have been punished for," Kresha said. "If you give me reason, I'll make sure that your mommy and daddy reinstate the dinners you went without for disobeying when you were a child."

"You'd do that just on Director Rivers's word?"

"I've known Irene for a long time," Kresha said. "She's not a game player. If she says she's got it, she's got it."

"The only variable in this is how hard you're going to make everyone work," Irene said. "If any of us have to strain a mental muscle, it's easier to do the perp walk and fit you for a cell."

"Will the administration know that I'm cooperating?"

Kresha shrugged one shoulder. "Eventually, but not right away. By asking that question, are you confirming that crimes have been committed and that you're willing to cooperate?"

Standish shook his head aggressively. "Oh, no. I'm not testifying against anything until I have that immunity."

"And I'm not granting the immunity until I know that the payoff is worth the effort," Kresha said. "You need to work with me here. I know that trust is hard to come by in times like these, but here we are. You have my word."

"I want it on the record."

"I'm the witness," Irene said. "Full immunity if you confirm the details of the case."

"Chicken and egg," Kresha said. "That's the cycle we find ourselves in. If it helps, you'll note that there are no recordings being made." She glanced to Irene. "Right?"

Irene placed her right hand on her heart and raised her left. "I solemnly swear."

Kresha ostentatiously looked at her watch. "I have

other things to do if you don't want to play, Harold. But if I walk out the door, every offer that inures to your benefit is off the table. Call the ball."

Standish looked like a trapped animal. His eyes darted to every compass point before finally settling on Kresha. "Okay," he said. "I'll help. Full immunity, right? Say it again."

"Full immunity." Kresha and Irene said it together.

"So, let's get to it," Kresha said. "Is everything Mr. LoCicero said on the recording accurate?"

"Yes."

Kresha punted the questions to Irene, who asked, "Is Nicholas Mishin involved in drug-running operations in the United States?"

"Yes."

The way Standish answered that question didn't seem quite right. "Is there more?"

"Oh, God, yes. Rio Grande crossings are a super-highway for drugs and sex traffickers and weapons. If you've got enough cash, you can get anything across the border. Any*body* for that matter."

"What does that mean?" Kresha asked. "Any*body*?"

"Pick a definition that suits your imagination, and you're probably right. Did you know that the USA has a lot of enemies? Well, we're allowing them to pour in. We've got terror cells on top of terror cells here. You can pick from the menu. Hamas, Hezbollah, al Qaeda, not so much Taliban, but lots of Russians and Chinese. Where do you think the nationwide spike in crime is coming from? You really think a bunch of city dwellers and college kids woke up one morning with sponta-neous self-loathing? That's all organized. While Ameri-cans have the attention span of puppies, our enemies are patient. They fight the long game. It took a generation to capture academia and the media, but now it's self-sustaining."

"Wait," Kresha said, holding up her hand. "You want me to believe that the Darmond administration hates America? That they're trying to hurt Americans?"

Suddenly animated, Standish made a waving gesture with his hand. "You've been watching too much right-wing news. Nobody's a practicing traitor, and no one's trying to hurt Americans. You're thinking too hard. Ideology has nothing to do with anything. You two have been around the block enough times to know that. God, country, and apple pie stopped driving policy a long time ago. It's all about the money."

"How much money are we talking about?" Irene asked.

"You probably know the numbers better than I do. But I know I can't count that high. I mean, think about it. The president nominates a good buddy and big donor to a cabinet position. There's a few bucks right there. And by a few, you know I mean a *lot*. Ever wonder why a guy worth millions wants to work a job that pays a hundred and a half? It's because SecDef, say, gets to lead the charge for another big donor to build a billion-dollar manufacturing facility in a state whose congressional representatives also happen to be big fans of the president. Every one of those manufacturing plants has their *overhead burden*"—he used finger quotes—"that they guard with their lives. You don't have to spin all that many points off *billions* of dollars before you've got serious scratch."

Irene found herself staring with her mouth agape.

"About the cartels," Kresha baited.

"Multibillion-dollar business," Standish said.

"You sound excited by this," Irene said.

"I *am* excited by it. This shit has made me a very

wealthy man, and now I don't have to worry about ever getting caught."

"As hundreds of thousands of Americans die of over-doses," Irene said.

"Hey, I didn't get them hooked on the shit. I don't stick the needles in their arms. I don't even understand the desire to do that shit to your body, but a lot of people feel differently. I'm just a tiny cog in the supply chain. Again, follow the money. No one wants to turn off the spigot."

"We arrest cartel members all the time," Kresha said.

Standish smirked. "You arrest the competition. One of the biggest changes in recent years is the consolidation of cartel activity to just one major player."

"Los Muertos," Irene said.

"That's the one. Scary dudes."

"So, why the Schillaci connection?" Kresha asked.

"I think because it's always been that way," Standish said. "For sure, it goes way back before my time. I sus-pect it's because criminals prefer to interact with other criminals. *Federales Americanos* make them twitchy."

"That's just one more payment in the multilevel mar-keting platform," Irene said. "Why not keep it in house, so to speak?"

"I think of it as insulation," Standish said. "One layer between the government and the business. Plus, the mob is a constant. Administrations come and go, but all the institutional memory stays with the goombahs."

This was even more than Irene had hoped for. She decided to go for the kill. "Yes or no. Does this go all the way to the Oval Office?"

"Absolutely. I mean, it's not a part of the PDB, but it's a regular part of lunch discussions in President Darmond's private dining room."

Irene recognized the acronym for the President's

Daily Briefing, if only because she'd participated in more than a few of them. She looked to Kresha. "What do you think?"

"I think we've found a scary snake to wrestle," Kresha said. "And we need to find a way to document a lot of things while keeping it secret from a lot of people. Is it safe to assume that every cabinet post is corrupted by this?"

"I think it's dangerous to assume that any of them are *not* corrupted by something," Standish said. "I'm sure that some of them are Boy Scouts and straight shooters, but I can't tell you which one is which."

"So, what's the next step?" Irene asked.

"We need to find an honest judge to work with us on this." Kresha checked her watch. "But that'll have to wait till tomorrow."

"What about me?" Standish asked.

"I'll have an immunity declaration drawn up by tomorrow," Kresha said. "When it's as inclusive as this, the language is pretty easy."

"What about you?" Irene said to Standish. "What do we do with you?"

"Send me home to my own bed," he said. "I got nothing to run away from."

Chapter 19

Grayson Buchanan lay on his back, staring at the blackness of the ceiling, wishing that he were dead. He couldn't keep doing this. He hadn't been awake in this hell hole for twenty-four hours yet, but already he knew that he wouldn't be able to survive it. Even if the punishment and the labor didn't kill his physical body, the fact of being used at the whim of a psychopath would strip the life from his soul. He saw those same feelings in Sissy's eyes, and she'd always been the adult twin, the one who thought calm thoughts and acted rationally.

After his beatdown in Sissy's bunkroom, Javier had marched him through what felt like a mile of desert to a spot where four more men about his age were stacking rocks the size of bowling balls and larger four deep and six high to repair a fifty-foot section of a wall that stretched as far as Grayson could see. He presumed that the wall marked the property line of the hacienda, and he had no idea what had blown out this section. Their overseer had no name as far as he could tell, but he carried a pump-action shotgun slung from his shoulder and a short whip stuffed into his belt. No talking was allowed, and even grunting from the strain of the work met with a stinging rebuke from the whip to the back of Grayson's leg, right at the fold of his knee. Even now, five or six hours later, the welt still stung, no doubt made worse by the glaze of sweat that covered his body.

He wondered if his parents had figured out that they'd been kidnapped. By now, they must know that they hadn't been murdered on the street or hit by a bus, so what were the remaining options? Surely, they were working with the police to discover them and rescue them.

Or maybe not.

There were witnesses, of course, but Javier was one of them. Were the others in the bar in on the kidnapping, too? And to what end?

Well, that was obvious, wasn't it? He'd heard about human trafficking and sexual slavery, but he'd never given it a lot of thought. He'd certainly never considered that he'd be a part of it.

The anger he'd felt before when he was with Bebe had transformed into something toxic. Eighty-five percent acid, one hundred percent desperation.

He didn't have time to wait for rescue, if that was even in the cards. He needed to get away from this place, and he needed to take Sissy with him.

But how?

That was always the kicker, wasn't it? It was one thing to have the loftiest of goals and desires, but without a plan to achieve them, it was all kind of useless.

Roll out of bed and walk through the door.

Could that work? Would they chase him down or try to stop him? Would that be worth the effort? If what Bebe and Javier had told him was true, there were dozens and dozens of miles between him and the Rio Grande. No chains were necessary because to escape was to commit suicide.

Wasn't that better than a future of forced labor and rape?

If he ran, there'd be a chance of survival. But if he stayed . . .

Can it wait?

Suppose he put the decision off for another day? Or even another week? The risks of the desert would remain.

Sissy.

No, he couldn't wait. The fact of what Sissy was going through, obviously drugged into compliance, they'd already been here too long. One more night of trauma for her would be too much. The trauma that had already befallen her was too much.

He couldn't let her spirit be executed. Nor could he surrender his own.

So, this was the night.

Why not go now?

He didn't know anything about the surroundings here. Were there guards? Were they armed? He knew the Bebe carried a knife and a pistol, but what about the others? The nameless overseer had his shotgun and whip. If everyone had guns, it made sense that they wouldn't hesitate to use them to kill runaway slaves.

Did Grayson even have the right to make this commitment on behalf of Sissy? Suppose he grabbed her away but she was too drug-addled to assist in her own rescue? That could cost both of them their lives.

But that was the whole premise, right? Dying was preferable to subjugation. If he could find a way—

The door to the bunkroom slammed open, making Grayson jump and whirl to face the opening. He knew who would be there, and a quick glance confirmed it. The glare from a light pole somewhere in the compound cast a rectangle of light across the otherwise darkened room. Bebe stood as a silhouette in the doorway, canted a bit to the side, as if he'd had a few drinks before making his attack. His denim shirt was completely unbuttoned now, the shirttails pulled from his beltline.

"Good evening, Mr. Grayson Buchanan," Bebe said. His tone was clear, but his consonants slurred. "I hope you are a man of honor and remember your promises. I don't want to have to hurt you."

Grayson sat up on his cot and leaned forward, his weight on the balls of his feet.

"You still have clothes on," Bebe said, stepping inside and pushing the door closed behind him. "I thought for sure that you would be ready for—"

Grayson launched himself like a defensive lineman. He stayed low and caught Bebe in the midsection with his shoulder. The momentum drove them both into the wood panel of the door and from there down onto the floor.

Bebe launched a series of curses in Spanish that Grayson didn't understand and flipped around to his stomach, where he could get his hands under him and push up.

Using both hands, Grayson slammed the back of the other man's head and bounced his face off the tile floor. Then he did it again. And again, blood spattering after each blow.

That had to hurt like a son of a bitch, but Bebe still had all the fight in him. He executed the pushup he'd been trying for and flipped over again, this time throwing Grayson off-balance.

He saw a flash of steel as Bebe pulled the knife from its scabbard.

This shit was real now. A fight to the death.

Grayson lunged at the knife hand, grabbing Bebe's wrist and driving it to the floor. He sprawled himself across Bebe's chest, but it was like straddling a grounded seal. The other man wriggled and squirmed to regain advantage.

Grayson's vision danced as a fist contacted the back of his head, but it was only a glancing blow. Not enough to distract him from the knife. Soon, a pistol would be in play, too, but for now, survival was all about controlling the knife.

He dove on the fist with the knife, and he bit into the flesh of Bebe's fingers as if trying to eat a bony apple. He gagged as his mouth filled with the taste of blood.

Bebe howled. His grip loosened.

Grayson bit harder.

Bebe rotated again, nearly able to shake Grayson off, but Grayson clamped harder still. He could feel the bones in Bebe's fingers shifting as their joints hyperextended.

And then Bebe's hand pulled free from Grayson's jaws but the knife clattered onto the tile.

The pistol would be next, Grayson was sure of it.

Bebe had gained the advantage somehow. He was starting to sit up.

Grayson stiffened the thumb on his left hand and drove it with every ounce of force he could muster into the corner of Bebe's right eye. It entered at the man's tear duct, adjacent to the bridge of his nose, and with sickening little effort, Bebe's eyeball popped free of its socket.

Bebe and Grayson screamed together at the image.

But the fight wasn't done.

Grayson snatched the blood-slicked knife from the floor, closed it tightly in his fist with the blade extending past the pinky finger on his right hand, and he plunged it into the center of Bebe's face.

The screaming only got louder. How could that not have killed him?

He plunged it into the man's face one more time, then shifted his aim to the belly and chest. Three times. Five times.

Then it was over.

The entire world was smeared in blood. No turning back now.

Switching the knife to his left hand, he pulled the stubby revolver from the holster at Bebe's waist and stood. The dead man's remaining eye stared straight up at him—straight through him. It was as if he were threating Grayson, even in death.

He needed to move. All that noise—the clamoring and the screaming—had to have alerted someone that something bad was happening. They'd be here soon, and he needed not to be.

He pulled Bebe's corpse farther into the room to get the clearance that would allow the door to open to the front porch, then stepped over it to turn the knob.

He pulled the door open, squirted through, then shut it fast so as not to display Bebe's body to the world. Out here, the glow from the light pole in the compound was much brighter. Grayson's skin and clothing shimmered in blood. Anyone who saw him, even from a distance, would know that he'd been in a violent struggle. That felt like a license to die.

Grayson fought the urge to run as he stepped off the porch onto the pathway and started for the bunkroom that held his sister. Running attracted attention. He didn't stroll, either. Thirty seconds later, he was inside Sissy's bunkroom, where colored cloths had been draped over the lights to give textured colors to the brothel stalls. Hey, if you're a guy who wants to rape underage girls, maybe the atmosphere is important. Just inside the door, a guy in his twenties had already shed his shirt and trousers and was in the process of removing his second sock when Grayson leveled the pistol at his nose.

The guy surrendered instantly, raising his hands, terrified.

"Leave," Grayson said in English. "*Vete.*"

The guy didn't hesitate, didn't look back as he darted out the door half naked with the one sock streaming along the ground behind him.

The girl on the cot looked equally terrified as she pulled the sheet up close to her chin. Grayson thought he should say something, but the words wouldn't form.

"Sissy? Are you here?"

He hurried down the center aisle, pistol and knife clutched in his fists. Off to the right, he heard grunting as the sheet undulated, but he looked away. That was not his mission.

"Sissy!" He shouted it and instantly regretted just how loud he was.

"Gray?" The voice came from the darkness that was Sissy's bunk space.

He stepped to the bed, grateful that she was still alone. He didn't want to kill again. "We're going. Come on, get up?"

"Oh, no, just let me sleep," she said.

He grabbed her by her shoulders and pulled her to a sitting position. "Nope, come on. That's the drugs talking. We gotta go."

"Where?"

"Out of here. I'll tell you once we're out."

"Tomorrow."

"No, Sissy. Now. Right now. Stand up." He placed the pistol and knife on the cot and slung her feet to the side and placed them on the floor. "Put your hands around my neck."

She complied, but he wasn't at all convinced that she was awake enough to be coherent. He wrapped his arms around her chest and lifted her to her feet. "Come on, Sissy. You've got to do this. You've got to help me."

"Leave her alone," a male voice said from the shadows. The English was perfect, without accent.

Grayson ignored him.

Sissy wore a bra and panties and nothing else. That wouldn't do. Not if they had to traipse through the desert for a few days. "Stay right there," he said. "Don't sit back down."

Moving fast now that his eyes had adjusted to the light, he darted back to the first bunk, where he plucked the john's shirt and pants off the hook. He returned to Sissy and handed her the clothes. "Here, put these on."

It took some effort, but she slid her arms into the sleeves. That was good. She could hear instructions and take directions. That meant her brain wasn't completely fried.

"Paco's going to kill you two," the English speaker said.

Again, Grayson let it go. Sissy had trouble navigating the trousers on her own, so he bent slightly at the waist so she could steady herself with his shoulder. Everything was too big for her, even with the belt pulled tight, but it would have to do. This felt like it was taking forever, but they were probably done in under two minutes.

Grayson dropped the pistol into the right front pocket of his shorts and eased the knife into the pocket on his left. Putting an exposed blade into an open pocket felt like a bad idea, but he couldn't carry his sister and weapons at the same time.

"Okay, we're out of here," he said. "Can you walk?"

"Ever since I was a toddler." Humor was another good sign.

"Okay, put on your flip-flops." He held her steady as she donned them one at a time.

"Can I come too?" asked the girl from the first stall as they passed on the way to the door.

"You can do whatever you like," he said. "But don't follow me." He figured it would be hard enough to move and stay invisible when there were just two of them. More people meant more tracks and more opportunity for somebody to do something stupid. As if he knew enough not to be the stupid one.

Once out the bunkroom door, the whole world lay ahead of them, yet he had no idea which direction to start walking.

"What's the plan?" Sissy asked. She was coming back.

"To get out of here."

"And go where?"

"To someplace that's not here."

"Okay, then. Let's get going. Are we just going to walk?"

"Unless you've learned to fly. Sorry I don't have a more complete plan."

"I'll follow you wherever you want to take me," Sissy said.

As he led the way into the shadow of the bunk houses, he didn't know if her willingness to follow was a blessing or a curse.

Chapter 20

It had been a long time since Michael Hite had last sat in an aircraft on the way to engage an enemy. Back then, the interiors of the C-17s and various choppers had none of the opulent white leather chairs or carpeted decks. There, he needed a headset to hear or be heard. Here, the cabin was as quiet as a luxury car.

It had been about ten minutes since his ears had popped, and he felt their diminishing altitude. He figured that they would be on the ground soon, and after that, what would happen would happen. He understood the basics of the operation—it wasn't that complicated, after all—but he felt more like a hanger-on than an actual operator. These people said they knew their shit. While he had no reason to doubt them, he had no real reason to trust them, either.

"You okay over there, Birdman?" Scorpion asked from across the aisle, where he and Gunslinger sat facing each other, a teakwood table separating them.

"There's a lot to wrap my head around," Hite said. "I didn't know there was this much money in the private investigating business."

"I appreciate your willingness to come along," Scorpion said.

"I look at it as the best choice from among shitty

choices. Sitting around getting hunted doesn't suit me. Do y'all specialize in your field operations or is everybody a generalist?"

"I'm not sure I understand your question," Gunslinger said.

"I mean, do you have an explosives guy, a—"

Scorpion and Gunslinger laughed in unison. "Oh, yeah," Scorpion said. "Big Guy is the explosives guy. I mean, we all carry them, and we know how to use them, but Big Guy lives for it."

"Explosives and piloting," Hite said. "Interesting combination."

"He's interesting in a lot of ways," Gunslinger said. "But basically, we're all riflemen first. Strategy is basic SWAT doctrine. Overwhelming speed and threat of violence. When people comply, their day goes much better than if they don't."

"Meaning no disrespect, Gunslinger," Hite said, "you don't look like you're former military."

"Good eye," she said. "I'm a lawyer, a former sheriff, and before that I was part of the FBI HRT."

"She can shoot the wings off a fly at a hundred yards," Scorpion said.

Hite didn't challenge the hyperbole. He knew that the Bureau's Hostage Rescue Team set very high standards for their operators. "That's a lot of retiring," he said.

"She's living the dream with us," Scorpion said.

"Somebody has to counterbalance the boy's club," she said.

"About this other guy with all the contacts in Texas," Hite said. "Thor. What's the book on him?"

"You can't know that," Scorpion said. "I thought we already had this conversation. You should be happy that we don't share his bio with you. You can feel comfortable that we won't share your bio, either."

The speaker in the overhead popped, and Big Guy's unmistakable baritone said, "Attention, ladies and gentlemen, this is your captain speaking. Please fasten your seatbelts and hang on tight. We'll be landing in about thirty seconds."

Hite didn't like the ominous tone. "Hang on tight?"

"Big Guy has an interesting sense of humor," Scorpion said.

"Think of it as an acquired taste," Gunslinger added.

Once on the ground, things moved quickly. The Terlingua airport was more of an air*field* to Hite's eye, if that were even a real distinction. There was no terminal to speak of unless it was invisible in the obsidian darkness of the night. Big Guy taxied the jet over to a hangar at the end of the runway, where an SUV sat waiting, just as their friend Thor had promised.

Just beyond the disk of light cast on the asphalt from the gooseneck lights that arced out from atop the hangar doors, he thought he could see the silhouette of a helicopter. He didn't know one aircraft from another, but to his eye it looked like it might be a medevac chopper.

"Is that tomorrow's ride?" he asked Scorpion.

"Big Guy can tell you for sure, but I believe it is. Give us a hand with the equipment."

This was new territory. Hite hadn't seen the load-in because it was managed by the ground crew back in Manassas. When they opened the hold, he was greeted mainly with oversized duffels that must have weighed fifty pounds apiece, eight of them in total. He could tell from the feel that some contained long guns and ammo, but he could only guess at the content of the others.

They stacked the bags in the back of the SUV, but

before closing the hatch, Scorpion opened one of the duffels and spread the opening wide. He reached inside and came out with a stack of black boxes.

"These are our satellite radios. They're fully charged and ready to go."

Hite turned his over in his hands. It looked like every other portable radio he'd ever used, but this one had a thick foldable antenna. "Want me to turn it on?"

"Yes," Scorpion said. "Let's do a radio check here." He reached back into the duffel and retrieved more items—tiny square boxes. "These are the earbuds for your radio." He took fifteen seconds to explain how they worked and what their limitations were. When that was done and Hite had settled the buds into his ear canals, they tested the transmit and receive functions. Everything was working fine.

"Are we ready to go now?" Big Guy asked.

"Button it up and we'll be on our way," Scorpion said.

They closed the hatch and climbed inside. Big Guy drove while Scorpion rode shotgun. Gunslinger slid in behind Scorpion, leaving the passenger seat on the left for Hite. He had the sense that these positions were assigned, whether by diktat or simply by habit.

"Where are we going?" Big Guy asked as he started the engine.

Scorpion looked at his phone and read the address. "Looks like it's about a three-minute drive."

As they motored away from the airport, it became clear that they were in some sort of golf-course community. From what he could see in the darkness, the houses all featured a single story, but they appeared to be sprawling in their design.

"This is not your typical safe house community," Gunslinger said.

"All I got from Thor was that the house we're going

to is safe," Scorpion said. "Maybe that's a distinction from a safe house."

Hite smiled. The banter here was light and easy, the talk among friends. There was no sense of danger. He said, "The plan, then, is to sleep in this house and then head out in the morning in the helicopter?"

"Not a lot of moving parts," Big Guy said.

"What's the plan if one of us gets hurt?" Hite asked.

"The plan is to not get hurt," Big Guy said.

"We don't leave our people behind, if that's what you're worried about," Scorpion said.

"My worries are way more basic than that," Hite said. "If I get killed, feel free to leave my body. I won't give a shit. I worry about being shot and still alive."

"All of us have good combat medic skills," Gunslinger said. "We can patch you up pretty well and get you back across the border."

"There you go," Hite said. "That's what I was looking for. I deeply don't want to be wounded and left to the cartel."

"Not a problem," Scorpion said. "Remember the whole point of the mission is to make sure that there's no cartel left when we're ready to go home."

"They're not going to go easily," Hite said.

Big Guy laughed. "Lord, I hope not. Cartel assholes are way more fun to kill while they're fighting back."

"What about this hacienda where they live?" Gunslinger asked.

"We will burn it to the ground," Scorpion said. "We're going to take every one of those assholes out, and then we're going to destroy as much property as we can."

"Do you really think the drugs will stop?" Hite asked.

"Of course not," Scorpion said. "But with what's going to happen in Washington at the same time, the players and their methods will all change. If history is even half an indicator, wiping out Los Muertos will cause total chaos among the competing cartels. Rolo Gomez and his family have successfully sidelined all of them to build his empire. With Gomez gone, every one of those sidelined competitors is going to start killing the other sidelined competitors. The result will be cartel blood flooding the storm sewers."

"What about the Mexican government?" Hite asked.

"What about them?"

"They're gonna be pissed that Americans crossed the border and killed a bunch of their countrymen."

"How 'bout that?" Big Guy scoffed. "Killing their campaign contributors is just one more cause for celebration."

Scorpion pointed through the windshield. "Seven thirty-three," he said. "This is our place."

Gail said, "There's a trick to this line of work, Birdman. It's to not think too hard. Once we settle on the plan, you depend on the plan to work. Course adjustments have to be made along the way, but it's senseless to try to anticipate the unknowable variables."

None of this was new to Hite, but in the past, his teammates had been friends and colleagues with whom he'd trained for months. He didn't mean to come off as hesitant, but let's face it—the stakes didn't get a lot higher than risking your life.

"Remember, Birdman," Big Guy said, "there's always a chance to say no up to the point when we're wheels up tomorrow. After that, you're committed."

"I'm committed now," Hite said. "In it for the long haul."

Truth be told, part of him missed his days in the Sandbox. He missed the camaraderie most of all, and the clarity of purpose. The National Command Authority might not know its nostril from its asshole, but at the unit level, everyone had a job to do, and a good part of that job was to watch each other's backs. That clarity of purpose, in fact, was a contributor to why so many veterans had difficulty adapting back to civilian life. In war, despite the discomfort and the deprivations, you always had your team members. He'd hoped that by joining the Bureau of Prisons, he'd be able to recapture some element of the esprit de corps from the Army, but that proved impossible. The bar was set too low for corrections officers, and their shrinking numbers made it impossible to take the kinds of disciplinary actions that were necessary for the prisons to run safely.

And now, because he'd done his job the way the job was supposed to be done, he had a contract out on his life, ordered by the very people who were supposed to make sure that this kind of thing never happened.

"Do you guys deal with this level of government bullshit often?" Hite asked.

"Every day, it seems," Scorpion said. "Every damn day."

The house at 733 Country Club Lane looked like all the neighbors' places, except this one had lights on. Stained glass in the front door cast oddly shaped splashes of color onto the porch deck. "Did Thor say there'd be lights on?" Gail asked from the backseat.

"He didn't say one way or the other," Jonathan explained. "I never thought to ask."

"How do you want to do this?" Boxers asked.

In Jonathan's line of work, the quickest way to die young was to assume that anything that looked easy was anything but deeply treacherous.

"Body armor and pistols," Jonathan said. "We'll keep it low-key. Big Guy, you and Birdman go around to the back. When you're in place, 'Slinger and I will knock on the front door."

"Didn't your friend Thor give you a key code for the front door?" Hite asked.

"He did," Jonathan confirmed. "And if no one shoots at us through the door and no one goes running away out the back, I'll use the key code. From there, we'll have to clear the house. Birdman, you just do everything that Big Guy tells you."

"Roger that."

They spilled out of the vehicle and gathered at the front grill. "Stay on Channel Three," Jonathan instructed. "Big Guy, let me know when you're in position in the rear."

He and Gail watched as the other half of the team walked out of view. When they were alone, Gail asked, "What do you think of Birdman?"

"I wish he was more nervous than he seems," Jonathan said. "By the way, you're surprising me on this adventure."

"How is that?"

"We're invading a sovereign nation, and you're not advising caution."

"I don't see that we have a choice," she said. "I think of the number of times we've taken a nick out of the cartel's operations, only to have them come back to full strength afterward—maybe even stronger."

"Are you okay with the rules of engagement?" The specific mission to kill was new to his team. He wasn't sure how he felt about it himself.

"I think we'll all need some alone time with Father Dom when it's all over, but I think I'll be able to sleep okay."

This truly was not like Gail, Jonathan thought.

Normally, her moral compass was set five clicks higher than anyone else's.

As if reading his mind, she said, "They killed a little boy and almost killed Roman. And they did it in RezHouse. If it can happen there, then it can happen anywhere. These people just need to die."

Jonathan had no argument.

"Black side team in place," Boxers' voice said over the radio.

"All righty, then," Jonathan said. He led the way up the three steps that led to the concrete porch, then stood off to the right side of the glass panel while Gail stood off to the left. He rang the bell and followed it with a heavy rap against the door. Then they waited.

After thirty seconds, Jonathan keyed his mic. "No response yet. I'm going to use the key. Do you have access from the back?"

"I *always* have access," Boxers replied. "Depends on whether or not you want me to break things."

Fair point. "Hold off on excessive damage," Jonathan said. "But if you hear shouting or gunshots, I'd appreciate swift intervention."

A tap on the keypad mounted next to the door activated the backlit buttons. Jonathan keyed in the code from memory. The lock clicked, and he pushed the door open. As the panel floated inward, he scanned the left side of the foyer with the muzzle of his Colt from the outside while Gail scanned the right side with her Glock 19.

"Ready?" he said to mark the cadence. "In."

As they crossed the threshold, he swung right while she swung left. In a perfect world, this was an operation to be performed with SBRs—short-barreled rifles—for their additional firepower, but rifles drew suspicion from nosy neighbors.

The sprawling open-concept design made the sweep an easy chore. Fewer individual rooms meant fewer walls to provide cover for bad guys in hiding. In a minute and a half, they were done. "We're clear," he said over the radio.

Five minutes later, the gear had been moved from the SUV and assembled in the foyer.

"Good God," Hite said. "There's enough ammo and explosives here to destroy a whole town."

He was exaggerating, of course. Unless it was a small town. Or perhaps a large hacienda. On the explosive side of things, they had fragmentation grenades, flash-bangs, and thermite for throwing, and six pounds of C4 explosives for breaching walls and doors. The C4 would mostly be cut up into smaller chunks to create GPCs—general-purpose charges—that could be quickly deployed to punch holes in just about everything.

"Those are Claymores," Hite said. His tone was equal parts amazement and admiration. Claymore mines were essentially explosive shotguns that spewed high-velocity ball bearings in a lethal fan-shaped kill zone.

"Sometimes you want a little extra help on your exfil," Boxers said.

"Birdman, load up your ruck with whatever you're comfortable using," Jonathan said. "I'm going to re-quire plates in the carriers and Kevlar lids for everyone. After that, shop for what you think you can use and carry." Lord knew there was a lot to choose from.

Jonathan's load-out stayed the same with every op-eration. He carried an M27 carbine as his main gun, with his ever-present Colt on his right hip and a Heckler & Koch MP7 on his left. His plate carrier would have plenty of ammo to feed everything, and his ruck would carry the heavy stuff.

"Just remember, when the balloon goes up on this thing, we work as one primary team. If we need to break up, 'Slinger will come with me, and Big Guy, you and Birdman will pair up."

"Stay out of my way, or I'll run you over," Boxers said.

"I'll just let you go first to catch the bullets," Hite fired back. "If things go south, I can use your carcass the way cowboys used their horses."

The joke landed flat, but Jonathan was pleased that Hite had tried. Boxers could become a real pain in the ass if he thought you were afraid of him.

"It's twenty-two forty-five hours," Jonathan said after checking his Timex. "That gives us a solid eight hours before we have to do anything. Who wants first watch?"

They stared back at him.

"Color me paranoid," Jonathan said. "Invading foreign lands in support of an effort to topple our own government leaves me a little antsy. I want to have someone outside in NVGs to keep an eye out for surprises. I'll take three to five." As the leader, he thought it best to take the shittiest hours.

"I'm not even tired," Hite said. "I'll take twenty-three hundred to oh one hundred."

"I'm gonna be up anyway," Boxers said. "I'll take five to seven."

Fresh from the shower, Paco Gomez slid the short satin robe over his naked body and padded to the ornate portable bar that sat atop a chest of drawers that had been in his family for generations. The house staff knew to have spotless crystal glassware prepared in this place every night, yet force of habit drove him to hold the highball glass up to the light before committing ice or liquor to it. Fortunately for all, Samantha and her staff had done their jobs perfectly.

He lifted the stopper out of the decanter containing about a thousand dollars' worth of Pappy Van Winkle bourbon and poured himself about three fingers' worth. There would be no ice with Pappy. It would have been a sin to cut such nectar with even a thimbleful of water.

The new girl would be here soon, the one who called herself Sissy. Tonight, he expected her to be less inebriated and more full of fight. Overly compliant or complacent companions were boring to play with. He enjoyed the begging and the slapping. Last night, Sissy had been so unconscious that he'd sent her away and commanded that the redhead from El Paso be brought to him.

His orders tonight for Javier and Bebe could not have been clearer. Missy was to be conscious and functional by eleven o'clock. He wanted to see her cocked fists and snarling glare. As always, he'd left a pair of scissors, a letter opener, and heavy vases in clear view to entice her to violence, to which he would return *true* violence. The very thought of it aroused him.

Settling into his lounger at the foot of his king-size sleigh bed, he crossed his ankles on the ottoman and sipped his Pappy, reveling in every inch of the burn as it traveled down his throat.

All evening long, the peace of the night had been interrupted by the sound of vehicles as the leadership of Los Muertos arrived for tomorrow's conference. In general, he preferred silence over noise, but he wasn't obsessive about it. He could handle the drone of most vehicles for the short time he was exposed to them, but some of the council members and enforcers had leaned into the Mexican cliché of beefed-up engines and giant lifters in their pickup trucks, and that throaty growl irritated him at a visceral level. He hated them. And don't get him started on the screams of unmuffled Harleys. If it were up to him, they'd all be set afire and scrapped.

Of course, if it were up to him—as it soon would be when Papa finally gave up and died—these monthly meetings wouldn't happen in the first place. They were expensive, they drew important managers out of the field, and they posed an unreasonable security risk. Yes, for now, the cartel had the cooperation of the police and the military, but he worried that the cooperation was born only of recent memory. Current cops and soldiers saw the bloodshed and torture that befell the families of those who resisted their business, but how long would the memories last? Another two years? Five, perhaps? And as memories faded, social warriors would again seek election, and the violence would have to return. As that transition time approached, it made no sense to gather the entire leadership of Los Muertos in one spot, where a single bomb could ruin everything.

This particular meeting, however, was essential. With connection to the Schillaci family severed by the arrest of Rocco LoCicero, business was sure to suffer an interruption. Harold Standish could insist all day, every day that distribution of product would continue uninterrupted, but Harold Standish was a politician. He knew nothing of the difficulties of managing the transportation or the distribution chains that allow the business of Los Muertos to function.

He sipped at the bourbon again. An instant later, someone rapped lightly on his door.

He placed the glass on the side table and adjusted

his robe to be sightly open in the front—enough to tease, but not enough to satisfy.

"Enter," he said in Spanish.

The door floated open to reveal Javier standing next to the redhead from last night. The bruises on her face had barely faded, for God's sake.

Paco jumped to his feet. "What is this? I told you—"

"The girl you wanted is not there," Javier said.

"Is not where?"

"In the dormitory. Or anywhere else. Her brother is gone, as well."

Paco spread his arms wide. "Where could they possibly go?"

"I don't know," Javier said. "But there is more bad news. Bebe is dead."

Paco let his arms fall to his sides as he recoiled from Javier's words.

"He was murdered," Javier explained. "Apparently, with his own knife. My guess is that he made moves on Sissy's brother, and his entreaties were not well received."

"Damn. I knew this would happen one day. I *told* him this would happen one day." Bebe was a child in a man's body. A reasonably hard worker, he wasn't a complete waste of time and energy, but his loss would have exactly zero impact on the operations of Los Muertos. But killings could not be tolerated when they came at the hands of servants.

"Do you want me to chase them down?" Javier asked.

"Not tonight. Let them run and wear themselves out. Follow their tracks in the morning and bring them to me."

"Their bodies?"

"No. I want them alive. I will make an example of the boy. Perhaps he should watch while I play with his sister, and then she can watch as we cut her brother into small pieces."

"Yes, sir." Javier pressed the redhead across the threshold.

"And take that ugly bitch away from me. Bring me someone fresh."

When he stepped out onto the porch at 02:55, Jonathan found Gail on a wooden rocking chair, her M4 balanced across the arms.

"Welcome to the most boring street in America," she said. "I haven't even seen a rabbit."

"Under the circumstances, boring is good," Jonathan replied. "Go get some sleep. I got this."

"Have a seat first," she said. "I want to talk for a minute or two."

Jonathan felt a sense of dread. Conversations that started with those words rarely ended with happy chatter. "Don't really even need the NVGs, do we?" he said. The moon was huge and bright, casting sharp shadows. He crossed in front of Gail and took the rocker to her right. He planted the buttstock of his M27 in his thigh, the muzzle pointing harmlessly at the porch ceiling.

"Been thinking about tomorrow," Gail said.

"I figured. Happy thoughts?"

"Concerned thoughts about collateral damage. We don't really know what we're getting into. I worry about servants and hangers-on. If they're present, they're probably unwilling participants."

"Our rules of engagement haven't changed on that," Jonathan said. "Anybody who gives up and doesn't pose a threat goes on to live a long and happy life. The ones who point guns, throw rocks, or brandish knives get smoked. It's always been the rule."

"And I'm worried about these killer drones. Suppose they're wrong? Machines don't think twice. They just do what they're programmed to do. Suppose the programming got fat-fingered?"

"First of all, Mother Hen did the programming, so the likelihood of fat-fingering drops to about zero. And for your own safety, I won't tell her that you even suggested that as a possibility." The attempt to lighten the moment didn't work. "Don't forget that they're programmed to more than one criterion. It's not just physical appearance."

"It's not foolproof."

"Come on, 'Slinger. Nothing in this business is ever foolproof."

Gail fell silent. Jonathan recognized it as her tell that she was trying to form words that she didn't want to speak. "I've never felt this much like a terrorist," she said.

"I don't follow."

"It's the drones. We're using them to kill remotely, without any skin in the game. I can't explain why, but that feels wrong to me." Her head pivoted to look at him. "Do you ever think of retiring? Just walking away from the violence?"

"Not since about an hour ago," Jonathan said. He reached over and squeezed Gail's arm. She'd come a long way in her acceptance of Security Solutions' ethical ambiguity, but he knew that she'd never signed on with it completely. He admired her for that. He wished sometimes that he was capable of seeing shades of gray more vividly.

"I'm not going to give you the pep talk," he said.

She patted his hand with hers. "I appreciate that."

"What we do is important," he said.

"That sounds like the beginning of the pep talk." Her voice carried a smile.

"I've always thought that I was born to clean up other people's messes," Jonathan said. "Somebody's got to stand up for justice."

"I'm really not asking you to explain yourself."

"Maybe I need to," Jonathan said. "It's terrifying when I realize that I long ago lost count of the number of people I've killed, but the only deaths I remember are the good guys I couldn't save. I could name every one of them."

Gail squeezed his hand. "And you've slept just fine knowing that there will be more dead bad guys tomorrow. There's nothing wrong with that. Everybody's free to make bad choices, but when those choices harm other people—when they *kill* children—they have to pay."

Jonathan expected more. He expected to hear the part about how true justice comes from court proceedings, not from the muzzle of a gun.

"More and more," Gail went on, "it seems that the justice system that's evolved over the centuries is breaking down. Graft, misplaced priorities, intellectual laziness, God knows what else, has put the world in a place where people like that LoCicero boy go unavenged. That's just not right."

All of that was new territory for Gail. He wasn't sure what to say.

Another long silence. "Humanity's not going to make it, is it?" Gail asked with a wry chuckle. "It shouldn't be like this. We're not going to do anything that Uncle Sam couldn't have done years ago on his own."

"Cut Uncle Sam a little bit of a break," Jonathan said

through a smile. "There is the little matter of international boundaries and international law."

"We're talking Mexico," Gail scoffed. "What international boundary?"

Jonathan took his hand back and leaned into the back of his rocker. "Look on the bright side," he said. "This time tomorrow, the world will be different."

"Different, yes. But will it be better?"

"Ask me this time tomorrow."

Irene Rivers could not have felt more exhausted if she'd run a marathon. Despite all the progress of the day, things still felt incomplete. She didn't like that Harold Standish was still able to roam free, but she couldn't think of a better option. It was true that they'd built a box for him from which there was no escape, but somehow it didn't feel like enough.

She'd never been one to trust others to fulfill promises without a figurative or literal gun to their head, but on this of all nights, when her career—and arguably her life—hung in the balance, she had no choice but to trust Kresha Ruby to perform as she had promised.

Irene further had to trust that Kresha's choice of judges—Thomas O'Halloran—would be willing to sign off on the offer of immunity without passing it through all the required steps that were normally required.

She didn't fully understand why Kresha insisted on making the entreaty to the judge on her own, but again, she had no choice but to go along with that decision. Irene was a pretty powerful presence in Washington, after all. It seemed to her that having the director of the FBI on the same page as the assistant United States attorney might lend credence to the argument that a US attorney and the attorney general could be bypassed.

Irene's driver dropped her off at the top of her driveway and stood guard as she made her way to the front door. This little house on Thames Street in Fairfax County's King's Park development represented everything that was good and bad about homes constructed in 1964. The low ceilings, small, chopped-up rooms, and the existence of only two and a half baths would make it a hard sell in today's environment of open-concept great rooms and nine-foot ceilings, but it had the best thing possible going for it: It was paid for.

"Aunt Irene, is that you?" Twelve-year-old Wyatt Withrow pivoted in his chair in the family room to look around the Lay-Z-Boy lounger to get a view of the foyer. He'd been living with Irene for almost two years now, ever since Irene's sister Sharon had passed away from cancer. He swung the rest of the way over the arm of the chair and started walking toward her.

"You're home early."

Was that possible? She checked her watch. "It's eight-thirty."

He smiled. "Like I said, home early."

"And you're ready for bed already?" He still favored Ninja Turtles shorty pajamas, unless he was part of a sleepover, in which case the sleeping uniform switched to underwear to match the other boys.

"I spilled milk on my jeans."

"Where are the girls?"

"Ashley said she was going to the library, and Kelly got picked up by kids from school."

Irene cocked her head. Under any other circumstance, being picked up would not have raised an eyebrow. "Who were the kids?"

"I don't know. She's a big-whoop freshman now, so she doesn't exactly speak to me anymore."

Irene's mind conjured pictures she wished it didn't. "Did she seem surprised that they were coming?"

Wyatt scowled. "How would I know? Why don't you call her and ask?"

Maybe she would. The call would spark another lecture about bothering her when she was out with her friends, but such was the nature of things for kids who'd been kidnapped once before.

As she fished her phone out of her purse, she asked, "Did the girls fix dinner for you before they left?"

Wyatt laughed and turned back to the family room. "Yeah, right. Oh, we need more Honey Nut Cheerios."

Why did life have to be so hard? Why couldn't the kids learn to pull on the same oar in the same direction at least some of the time?'

Irene put her purse on the dining room table and was about to call Kelly's number when the phone vibrated in her hand. Caller ID showed a number she knew all too well.

She connected the call. "Director Rivers."

"Good evening, Madam Director. This is Patty Armistead." Irene recognized the name of President Darmond's personal secretary. "The president asked me to call and tell you he needs to see you in the Oval tomorrow morning at nine-thirty." That's the way it was when the White House called. No one asked about schedule conflicts because presidential audiences always took precedent over any other conceivable matter.

"I'll be there," Irene said.

"The president says thank you." The line went dead.

Irene stared at the phone for the better part of thirty seconds, wondering what this meant. It could just be coincidence, of course. Something happened in the world about which President Darmond wanted some level of input from her. It might have nothing whatsoever to do with Southern Hammer and the impending collapse of his presidency.

Sure it might. And pigs might fly.

The next twenty-four hours were going to be interesting.

She shook it off and pressed the speed dial for Kelly's phone. After five rings, Kelly answered with, "What, Mom? I'm fine. I'm with my friends. Nobody has kidnapped me. We're going to a movie, and you're ruining my life."

Irene allowed herself a smile. "Okay, honey," she said. "I just wanted you to know I love you."

"Of course you do." A pause. "Hey, are you okay?"

"I'm fine. You know I need to check on you from time to time."

"Leave me alone, then. I'm hanging up now."

"You know you're a brat, right?"

"I'm just doing my job. Are we done?"

"Don't be too late."

Chapter 21

Grayson didn't know how far they'd come through the night, but he knew that it wasn't far enough. Only two or three hours into their escape, it had become clear that Sissy could not go on until the drugs wore off. For what felt like the last mile, he'd been half carrying her until he no longer had the strength. He found a patch in the desert with enough rocks to provide a bit of shelter if not concealment, and they hunkered down to wait out the night.

He hadn't anticipated the cold. Deserts were supposed to be hot, for God's sake. Once they stopped and took shelter, the temperature fell like an anvil, leaving them both shivering and holding each other for warmth.

As he awoke, he realized that he hadn't realized that he'd fallen asleep. He lay on his right side with Sissy pressed against his back. The height of the sun in the sky surprised him.

"You awake?" Sissy asked.

He stretched as she pulled away from him. "I guess I am. What time do you think it is?"

"The sun's been up for a while. I'm going to guess around nine."

Grayson shot up to a sitting position. "Jesus, Sissy. Why did you let me sleep so late?"

"It looked to me like you needed it. Are you coherent enough to tell me where we are?"

He whirled on his butt in the gravelly sand to look at his sister. She looked terrible—drawn and disheveled, with darkness around her eyes. "You don't remember?"

"Sort of. I remember you coming in and . . . oh, my God, what happened to you?"

He looked down at his shirt, seeing clearly for the first time the gore that had been painted on his T-shirt. "Oh. There was a fight."

"Are you okay?" She reached over to help treat his wounds.

"The blood's not mine. It belonged to the other guy. Bebe."

She gaped.

"He's dead."

"You killed him?"

He told her the story, leaving out the part about the eyeball. "We had to get out of there."

Sissy teared up as she said, "You did all of that for me?"

"I did it for both of us."

"Where are we going?"

"Back to the United States, I hope."

"Do you know how far it is?"

"No."

"Did you bring food or anything?"

He pulled his stained T-shirt away from his body to let her see it more closely. "I didn't have a lot of time."

"Do you even know which direction to go?" Sissy asked. "Or which directions we're facing?"

Grayson felt anger building. Where was the *Thank you, Grayson, for saving me from a life of slavery*? He pointed to the sun. "It's morning, so that has to be east." He pointed ninety degrees to the left. "That makes this way north. I don't know a lot of geography, but I do know that the US is north of Mexico."

"What about water, Gray?"

He jumped to his feet. "Goddamn, Sissy. What do you want from me? I just saved our damn lives."

She held up her hands in surrender. "You're right," she said. "You're right, you're right. Thank you. Now, we have some things to figure out."

"How are *you*?" Grayson asked.

She also stood. "Like I've been beaten up and drugged and dragged through a desert." She sold that last part with a smile.

"Is your head clear?"

"Clear enough to be scared shitless."

"That sounds about right," Grayson said. He didn't want to admit that he felt like an idiot. All those things she talked about—food, water, a friggin' *compass*—had never occurred to him. All he knew was that they needed to get away. He still believed that was the case.

He just wished he'd thought through to Step Two.

"Don't worry," Sissy said. "We'll make it." She took his shoulders in her hands. "You did the right thing. And I'm sorry you had to kill the guy."

"He'd have killed me if I hadn't." It was important to Grayson that his sister understand that. Maybe it was even more important that he understood it himself.

"I think we should start walking," Sissy said. "Since it's not blistering hot, maybe we've got a few days before we have to start worrying about food and water. How far do you think we've come so far?"

Grayson squinted against the glare to scan the horizon. However far it was, it was enough to no longer be able to see the hacienda. "I don't know. I worry, though, that we haven't yet come to the wall."

"What wall?"

"They put me on a work detail yesterday to repair a wall that I figured was a kind of stone fence that surrounded the property. As far as we walked last night, I'd have thought we were past it, but I don't remember climbing it."

"You say it needed repair," Sissy said. "Maybe we walked through another part that was broken."

Grayson wanted to believe that, but the longer he looked out at the landscape, the more he could make out the tracks they'd left. They were not in a straight line. "Shit, Sis, I think I might have taken us in a big circle."

"Doesn't matter," she said. "We're away, and we have a direction to walk. Let's go that way. We'll head north."

"But look at our tracks," Grayson. "I think I took us south. That means we'll have to go back past the hacienda compound."

Sissy's shoulders sagged as she issued a wry chuckle. "You're making it hard to be positive here, you little shit. We'll find what we find and do what we have to do when we have to do it."

"I'm really sorry, Sissy."

"Stop. I'm the one who made us go to the bar where this all started."

Grayson smiled. "Oh, yeah, that's right. So, if we die, it's your fault, not mine."

"Absolutely. And that will make all the difference in the world."

They started walking again.

Thirty seconds into the journey, they stopped in unison. "What's that sound?" Sissy asked. It was a buzzing sound, like a mechanical insect.

He shielded his eyes with both hands and scanned the horizon. A feature of the geography made the

buzz sound as if it were coming from anywhere—
everywhere.

Then he saw the sources of the noise, and his heart
stopped beating for an instant. "There they are," he
said, pointing. "Dune buggies. They're coming to bring
us back."

In Irene's world, to be on time was to be late, so it
was no surprise that when she greeted the receptionist
in the West Wing waiting room she was offered a coffee
or water and directed to wait in one of the surprisingly
uncomfortable fabric chairs that seemed more scattered
than arranged in the small space.

She'd been here many times over the years, and on
each visit, she wondered yet again how the seat of
power for the entire Free World could look so tattered
and threadbare. Outside of the ceremonial spaces, the
working areas of the White House looked very much
like parts of the two-hundred-and-twenty-five-year-old
house that they were. Past the artwork and furniture on
loan from the Smithsonian and other museums around
the world, the carpet was worn and the decorative
moldings didn't always meet properly in the corners.
The ceilings seemed too low and the hallways too
narrow for the importance of the space. The heat and
air conditioning were often unreliable. Her visits to the
Oval started after the days when smoking in the building was banned. She couldn't imagine what the place
must have looked and smelled like in the days before.

Of course, President Darmond still smoked anywhere he wanted to, as did many of the presidents who
preceded him. It was one of those secrets the press
corps looked away from and never reported. Unless
the president belonged to the other party, in which

case he was widely savaged for threatening the lives of staffers with secondhand smoke.

As she sat in her seat and crossed her legs, Irene pretended to review emails on her phone as her mind focused on preventing her hands from shaking. If things went according to plan, thirty days from now—maybe sooner—Darmond and his cronies would be gone and as a result the world would fall into crisis. When the scope of the corruption was finally revealed, markets would tumble, and she could easily piece together a scenario where panic led to violence in the streets through cities and towns where such things never occurred.

In cities that had been overwhelmed with overdose deaths and crime waves that were tied to the organized flow of miscreants across the border, Irene imagined not just a flash of anger among the citizens but rather a volcano of acrimony. With the public safety net already weakened by political posturing that somehow morphed into actual political insanity, who knew what form that acrimony might take?

Now that they were on the brink—*this close* to the testimony that would finally end the corruption and bring justice to the Darmond crime syndicate—she was beginning to have second thoughts. That all she planned would result in widespread suffering in the ensuing panic and retribution was a sure thing, and while Darmond's crimes would be the true cause of the misery, Irene alone would live with the knowledge that she'd triggered it.

At what price justice? Was it possible that for purely practical reasons some people—say, the president of the United States—truly was above the law? Was the warm feeling of relief that Darmond was going to be held accountable worth the suffering and violence that the trial and punishment would cause?

Her inner Knight Templar told her that truth and justice were worth any price. The irony of the illegal means by which many of the details of Darmond's criminality had come to her was not lost on her. When *she* broke the law, it was to favor others—to favor the forces of good. What was it that Digger liked to say? She was on the side of the angels.

What would President Darmond say to that, she wondered. People saw themselves as the heroes of their own stories. No one is all evil, after all. She asked herself what lies Darmond had forced himself to believe that made right in his mind all the wrong things he had done. That the Darmonds had a troubled marriage was among the worst-kept secrets in Washington, as was the fact the Nicholas Mishin was an unhappy stepson. Perhaps the president found peace in the excuse that covering for Nicholas's transgressions was no more than the actions of a caring stepfather trying to keep his family out of trouble.

That made sense to Irene. She got it. She really did. But the rest of the operation was so much more, infecting and affecting so many senior cabinet-level office holders who in turn fattened their pockets by leveraging drug money and the lost innocence of trafficked prostitutes.

No, for that, they would have to pay.

"Director Rivers?" the receptionist said.

Irene looked up from the phone she'd never really been looking at.

"The president will see you now."

"Thank you." As she stood, Irene's phone buzzed with a text. A glance told her that the caller was Father Dom.

She opened the message.

Take heart. The future is about to change. In fact, it's changing now.

Well, there was no going back now. Digger had launched his war.

Jonathan wasn't a fan of flying, but he especially hated helicopters. His chronically sore back shot lightning bolts down the back of his legs just remembering some of the landings he'd endured. He'd learned that the difference between a combat landing and a crash were purely academic. The distinction without a difference had everything to do with the aircraft's ability to take off after the event and nothing to do with how many organ systems got bounced around on contact with the ground.

As they flew far too fast at far too low an altitude, Jonathan tried to focus on the electronic map on his lap that traced their location. "We're about three miles from the center of the hacienda," he said over the intercom.

"Copy," Boxers said. "Give me another mile and we'll set down for Phase One."

Thirty seconds later, the chopper slowed and flared to land. Big Guy set the bird down as gently as Jonathan had ever seen him do it. Jonathan considered saying something but realized that a compliment would only inspire Boxers to rattle his teeth on the next landing.

"Set up for Phase One," Jonathan said as he lifted the intercom headset away from his ears. He stepped out the door of the shotgun seat, and the others followed. They stayed out of the way while Boxers assembled his toys.

The first order of business was to get Big Roxie in the air to give them a look at what they were getting themselves into. Big Roxie featured the full gamut of imaging technologies, from light enhancement to thermal imaging. She normally did her work under the cover of darkness, so watching clear images illuminated by sunlight would be a treat.

"I'm going to take her to five hundred feet," Boxers explained to the other team members as they huddled around the viewing screen, watching over his shoulder at the edge of the cargo bay. He worked the controls, and Big Roxie's rotors spun up. "Don't let me down, sweetie," he said.

As the image of the ground dropped away, the screen filled with the vast expanse of the desert, all in color. As the drone approached its cruising altitude, a complex of buildings emerged in the far distance along the top edge of the screen.

"Over there is our target," Jonathan said.

"Wait," Hite said, leaning in to a closer point at the screen. "What's that over there?"

Boxers worked the controls, and Roxie's camera zoomed in on two dune buggies surrounding what appeared to be two teenagers, a boy and a girl. The men in the buggies were holding the kids at gunpoint.

"Looks like some kind of arrest," Gail said.

"Sure does," Boxers said.

"What the hell could you possibly do to get arrested inside a nest of cartel assholes?" Hite asked.

"They don't exactly look like terrorists," Gail said. "Looks like they're dressed for bed." She leaned in closer. "Lordy, look at the boy's shirt. Is that blood?"

"Or a lot of ketchup," Boxers said.

"He looks healthy to me," Jonathan said.

"Somebody else's blood, then?" Hite asked. "Could explain the arrest."

"Sucks to be him," Boxers said as he piloted the drone back to the target hacienda.

"The place is huge," Gail said.

"Mother Hen said it was designed to look like a

hotel," Jonathan said. "Kinda does." A two-story main building anchored the complex on the northern side, with lines of rooms extending south in parallel lines that flanked two central green spaces. The first line of green space dead-ended at a massive outdoor area that featured fountains and a pool, which then gave way to another stretch of buildings and green space.

"Thor tells us that those rooms along the green court-yards are for staff and bodyguards," Jonathan explained. "We're going to have to clear those before we're done."

"And those are our targets," Boxers said, pointing to the people gathered around a long table that had been set up next to the fountain.

The ground pulled away again as Boxers changed the view to feature what might have been a parade ground in a different world—a big field that was trying to be green but featured more sand and gravel than grass. One hundred yards distant from the field sat a series of small stucco and tile buildings arranged in the shape of an *L*.

"That field is our LZ," Boxers said. Landing zone.

"We're not sure what's in those buildings," Jonathan said, "but we're going to consider them nonessential to the mission."

"Why?" Hite asked. "Buildings hold people and people shoot back."

"According to Thor, his sources tell us that those buildings don't pose a threat. If he's wrong, then we'll be the first to know. What we're sure of, though, is that the hacienda buildings will be hot targets."

"We don't have enough people for this," Hite said.

"That's what the Little Roxies are for," Big Guy said. "With luck, they'll do all the heavy lifting."

"And whoever they don't eliminate will be scared shitless and off-balance," Jonathan said. Even as he spoke the words, he heard the unreasonable optimism they carried. Once an op went hot, nothing went as planned. Ever.

"Any questions?"

They looked back at him silently.

"Okay, then. Let's load up and fill the air with Little Roxies."

As the dune buggies approached, Grayson considered running, but he knew they wouldn't be able to outrun the vehicles. His toes were already bleeding from last night's run though the desert in flip-flops.

Sissy grabbed his arm. "Do you think maybe they're police?"

"I wish I could say yes."

"Are they going to take us back?"

"If they don't kill us here." He regretted how dark that sounded, but the truth was the truth.

"Should we run?"

"Do you think we can beat them?" They were only a hundred yards away now.

"Don't we have to do something?"

Yes, they should. Obviously, they should. Their parents had always talked the game that you never allow kidnappers to get the upper hand. But what could they do?

"Use your pistol," Sissy said, pointing to the gun on the ground.

"They've got rifles, and I bet they're way more experienced in using them."

Five seconds later, the window of opportunity to do anything had closed. The dune buggies slid to a stop ten yards away, and cartel dickheads stood and pointed rifles at them. They looked like M16s to Grayson, but he didn't know one gun from another. They were black and had carrying handles on the top. Of the four men in the vehicles, one of them was Javier.

"Get on the ground!" Javier yelled in English.

Grayson and Sissy held hands as they lowered themselves to kneel in the rocks.

"Where are the weapons?"

Grayson pointed with a twitch of his head. "On the ground over there."

"Is that the knife you used to kill Bebe?"

"Yes." What was the point in lying? He was drenched in the man's blood. "For what it's worth, he was trying to rape me."

No one seemed to care.

Javier pointed at Sissy with the muzzle of his rifle. "You. Girl. Stand."

She pressed off of Grayson's shoulder to rise to her feet. "You disappointed Paco last night. He is very angry."

Grayson watched as her jaw locked and tears balanced in her lids.

"You come first. Sit in the front seat of this cart." As Javier spoke, the other guy in that dune buggy moved around to sit in the rear, where he could shoot her in the back.

Incongruously, they made a point of fastening her seatbelt after she was seated. When the guy's hand got too close to her lap, she slapped it away, earning her a slap across the face.

Grayson reflexively jumped to his feet, but retreated when Javier brought his rifle tighter into his shoulder. "Give me a reason," he said. "Paco wants to kill you slowly, but please give me a reason to kill you right here."

Grayson raised his hands. Maybe there'd be a time for fighting, but this wasn't it. Not here, not now.

The gunman next to Javier cleared the front seat for Grayson, who sat down without being ordered and pulled the shoulder harness into place.

"You should have killed yourself when you had the chance," Javier said. "At the very least, you should give me a reason to kill you. You will not like what Paco does to people who murder his workers."

Grayson honestly didn't know how to process those words. They scared him—terrified him—but he wouldn't give the assholes the satisfaction of begging or seeing him cry. He . . . didn't know. His mind felt empty. He settled back into his seat and prepared for a long ride back to the hacienda.

When they were underway, Javier shouted over the engine noise, "Where did you think you were going?"

"Away. Back to the USA."

Javier laughed. "You were going the wrong way! You'd have died in two days. There is nothing but nothing for two hundred kilometers."

"Lucky me," Grayson mumbled. He hadn't intended for anyone else to hear him, and they didn't seem to.

Riding the dune buggy was a bit like riding a paint shaker in a hardware store. Even where the terrain looked smooth, bumps and irregularities tossed Grayson against his seatbelt. No wonder they were concerned about strapping them in.

"How far did I get?" Grayson shouted.

"About eight kilometers. Farther than I thought you would. But you left very obvious tracks in the sand. It was not a good night for you."

Grayson's sense of dread was spreading now, like a curtain over his soul. Life was never hopeless, but this was as close as he could imagine. Short of a miracle—

Far up ahead, where the outlines of the hacienda buildings were just coming into view, he could see a cloud of . . . birds? They flew as a disorganized swarm, swinging in different directions, some circling, some flying straight and level.

"What the hell is that?" Grayson asked no one in particular.

Javier's foot grew heavier on the accelerator as he sped toward the swarm. The other buggy kept up with them. Within a few seconds, they were hub-to-hub as they raced across the desert. The bumps became impacts, slamming Grayson from side to side in his restraints. "Hey! Slow down! You're going to kill us!"

If Javier understood, he made no indication.

"Why the hell are you driving *into* that?" Grayson yelled.

Again, no response.

Grayson pressed himself farther into the seatback and braced himself with his arms. Maybe immediate death was in his future, after all.

"Oh, shit!" Grayson yelled. "They're coming this way!"

A few of whatever-they-were had broken away from the swarm and were racing toward the dune buggies.

Javier yelled something in Spanish as he hit the brakes hard, sending the vehicle into a sideways skid.

Grayson looked across to Sissy, whose buggy had also stopped. Her mouth hung open as she watched the big black insects close in at surprising velocity.

The gunman in the backseat was yelling as Javier struggled to get the buggy moving again. Grayson didn't understand the language, but "Get us the hell out of here!" was clearly the context.

"Jesus, they're drones!" Grayson shouted.

As if they'd heard his voice, the four approaching machines split off from each other and sped in toward the dune buggies.

The backseat gunman's voice was an octave higher when he screamed this time.

When they were about twenty feet out, the drones accelerated to amazing speed and raced straight at Grayson's two escorts.

They hit their targets nearly simultaneously.

Javier's head exploded in a pink cloud that further drenched Grayson in gore. As he yelled and fumbled with his seatbelt, he looked back and saw that the other gunman's brain lay exposed across his forehead.

He finally got his belt undone and rolled out of the buggy onto the gravel, scrambling to his feet to get to Sissy, who was likewise scrambling out of her own seat. The two guys in her buggy had also been blown apart.

"What the hell!" she yelled. "Shit, shit, oh, holy shit, what the hell!"

Grayson felt lightheaded and sat down as he tried to make sense out of what he just saw.

Then, in the distance, from the direction of the hacienda, he heard faint pops and screaming voices.

"It's our miracle," he said.

Chapter 22

I rene knew the way down the hallway to the Oval. She'd walked it countless times over the years, yet some ancient protocol required that a White House staffer escort her past the Roosevelt Room to the door that was flanked by two Secret Service agents. She'd never interacted much with the Secret Service except at the very highest levels, where Ramsey Miller served as the director. To her eye, though, these agents at the door were new faces.

On a different day, the unfamiliar faces probably would have gone unnoticed. But today, she carried a burden of paranoia that felt like a lead blanket draped over her shoulders. She wondered how the likes of Aldrich Ames and Robert Hansen and other high-level traitors handled the pressure of looking into the eyes of the people who would soon come to loathe them.

Of course, in their cases, they were, in fact, traitors.

The escort from the lobby rapped twice on the closed door and then pushed it open without waiting for an invitation. It was the way it always worked.

The door from the hallway to the Oval was six inches thick and looked like it weighed hundreds of pounds, yet it floated open with practically no effort.

The Oval Office was the only element of the West

Wing that television and movies consistently got right, from the presidential seal on the carpet to the identical image along the parabolic ceiling. From this angle, the famous Resolute Desk sat ahead and slightly to the right, while the famous fireplace with its flanking sofas and chairs lay closer and on her left.

As she stepped off the polished hardwood onto the lush oval rug, she was startled to see that the chairs were all empty. She was alone. She turned to ask the escort what was going on, but the door was already closing.

What the hell was she supposed to do now? The president typically preferred to meet guests while seated on the near end of the conversation group, in a chair that faced the fireplace. But not always. Sometimes, particularly when it was a meeting between the two of them, he preferred to stay behind his desk while she sat in one of the two ornate wooden chairs in front of the spot on the desk where history will always remember the face of little John-John Kennedy peeking out.

She'd never been alone in this room. What was the protocol here?

Less than a minute later, a door opened behind her and to her right, and the president of the United States stepped into view from what she knew to be his private study. He carried two glasses containing a couple of fingers of brown liquor.

"Sorry to keep you waiting, Irene," he said, offering her one of the glasses. "Angel's Envy, right?"

"Yes, sir," she said. "A favorite bourbon of mine, though typically saved for the evening. Certainly not before noon. Sir."

He thrust the glass closer to her and smiled. "Come on, Irene. Humor your president." As if to clear her conscience of any doubt, he made a show of taking a significant pull on his own glass.

She accepted the drink, offered an air toast, and touched her lips to the drink. Good stuff, to be sure.

"You're handling that glass like I'm trying to poison you." He laughed a bit too hard and led the way to the fireplace conversation group. "Please, have a seat."

At six-two with a shocking head of hair that showed no gray, Tony Darmond looked like Hollywood's version of a president. He wore perfectly tailored suits and could fire off charming smiles like bullets from a gun.

He took his usual seat at the end of the coffee table, and Irene helped herself to the nearest cushion on the sofa to the president's left.

As she settled in, Darmond said, "You can't think of any reason why I might want to poison you, can you, Madam Director?"

Irene placed the drink on the coffee table and forced a chuckle. "I hope not, sir."

"Is something wrong, Irene? You seem . . . different today."

Irene tried to keep her features steady as she studied the president's face to get some glimpse into what he was thinking. "Just the pressures of the job, I suppose."

"Tell me about those," Darmond said.

"About what, sir?"

"The pressures of the job. Your job. Anything particularly hot going on that I should know about?"

Oh, this wasn't going right at all. "I'm not sure what you're looking for, Mr. President."

"Really?" He took another pull on his drink. "It's not that difficult a question, Irene. Are there any issues you're dealing with now that are more difficult or pressure-filled than any other day?"

Irene needed to calm her racing heart. She took a deep breath, settled into the sofa cushions, and crossed her legs. "Sir, why did you call me here this morning?"

Darmond finished the rest of his drink and set the glass down on the coffee table. "I called you here to answer questions," he said. "As your commander-in-chief, that is my prerogative."

Irene settled her shoulders. If he was going to get spun up, she needed to settle down. "Well, yes, sir, that is your prerogative, but only to a point. My office deals with matters that, frankly, are classified beyond your need to know. These are investigative matters."

"Cut the shit, Irene."

Clearly, the president knew something, but she didn't know what that might be. He seemed to be fishing for information, playing a bluff, perhaps, to maybe verify rumors he'd heard. "What shit might that be?"

"I've heard rumors that I'd like you to confirm or deny."

"I don't know that I can do that, Mr. President. For reasons already mentioned."

"Are you investigating me and my family for what you allege are crimes?"

Irene forced a smile. "Sir, if that were the case, it would be precisely the kind of rumor that I could neither confirm nor deny."

The president's smile morphed into something smug and ugly. He raised his head a little higher and yelled, "General Norris! Would you come in here please? And bring the others with you."

Irene uncrossed her legs and slid to the edge of the sofa. It wasn't until she'd done it that she realized she was preparing herself for a fight.

Attorney General Nigel "Buster" Norris had been a toady for Anthony Darmond since their days together at Harvard, and maybe even longer. Entirely unprincipled in his words and actions, the man stood for nothing and had the IQ of a bullfrog. At six-three, two seventy-five, his nickname apparently came from his days at Virginia Tech when he would bust offensive lines. Irene always wondered if he'd worn helmets.

Her heart flipped in her chest when she saw Kresha Ruby cross into the room, followed closely by United States Attorney Adele Krump. Kresha looked as if she'd been beaten, though there were no bruises. She made eye contact for only a second before looking away.

It was no surprise that Harold Standish brought up the rear. He stood tall again and smiled.

That was the instant when Irene realized that she was screwed. She'd somehow been outplayed.

Chapter 23

Rolo Gomez straightened his broken body as much as he could and braced himself against his desk, using his cane for support. There was no one at this monthly summit who did not know of his physical limitations, but those same people respected the fact that he overcame every one of them. He may not move as efficiently as he once did, but he could still get from here to there, and his mind was still as sharp as ever. His lieutenants knew him to be as rational and contemplative as they knew Paco to be reckless and impulsive.

When the day came for Rolo to move on—whether by choice or by death—the lieutenants within Los Muertos would eliminate Paco within days, if not hours. He was that reviled.

Now, here they all were, gathered at the hacienda not to speak of record profits and fresh alliances, but to find a way to untie the giant knot that Paco had tied into operations with his senseless temper tantrum.

The council would be furious, and they would expect action to be taken against Paco. Rolo would try his best to protect his son from harm, but even he questioned his influence to do so.

Some in the council would see this as a moment of weakness in Rolo's control of Los Muertos and try to

leverage it for their personal gain. It would not be the
first time his power had been threatened, and it would
not be the last, but it would almost certainly be the most
justified.

Wars within the cartel always proved more destructive
than any of the action-hungry youngsters anticipated.
Beyond the bloodshed and unnecessary loss of life, there
was the tragic loss of business and the damage done to
alliances within the United States government. That relationship had never been as perfect as it currently was
with the Darmond administration. That relationship
had taken nearly a decade to build and had cost countless millions of dollars to fund the right campaigns and
ruin the wrong ones. The stasis that existed now had
everything to do with the American administration's
comfort that Los Muertos was itself stable after the
many years of bloody infighting.

If the bloody infighting started again, all that progress
would be wiped away and Los Muertos would be fundamentally weakened. That weakness, in turn, would
inspire competing cartels to come at them to release
the stranglehold they held on the business of selling
chemical product and human beings.

He'd just now received word that the council members
were all seated, so now it was time to make his entrance.
Per Rolo's insistence, all would stand as he stepped out
onto the veranda, and they would remain standing until
he seated himself at the head of the long table. With
word of the council's arrival came word of a murder on
the hacienda. That word came from Anita, among the
most trusted of his maids, so he was confident that
the news was more than a rumor.

Rolo had thoughts about how that situation should
be handled, but if only to limit the angst of the day,
he decided to leave that matter to Paco's discretion. He

harbored little doubt what actions the young Gomez would take. Sometimes, it was disturbing to think about how much his son enjoyed torturing people.

As he crossed through the elaborate double doors that led from his office, every step hurt. His knees, ankles, and back all cried out for relief that he could not give. Given the opportunity, he would pay any price to be able to stand up straight again. But he would not complain. He'd always had a stern countenance, some of which was undoubtedly the projection of pain, but he forced himself to smile as he crossed through the grand salon, with its ornate tapestries and the menagerie of hunting trophies on the wall, to cross the next set of double doors and into the sunlight.

Squinting into the glare, he watched as Paco stood and said, "*El Jefe,*" causing the other council members to rise and then applaud. The show of respect was important.

Rolo nodded as he took his first few steps closer to the assembled council, but after only a couple of seconds, something went wrong. It started with distant odd noises. A low hum, followed by sharp pops and raised voices. Screaming. Beyond the gathered council members, Rolo sensed panic building.

People were running.

Someone he couldn't see yelled, "We are under attack! They are killing everyone!"

Paco whirled toward the chaos and yelled, "Everyone take cover! Under the table! Under the table!"

Rolo didn't wait. He was only ten feet from the doors to the main house, so he spun and headed back as explosions punched the air behind him. He didn't look because in his current condition, he couldn't afford the distraction.

Someone yelled something about drones.

As Rolo crossed the threshold into the grand salon, he pulled the heavy doors closed behind him. Through the diminishing crack between the closing doors, he saw what appeared to be a tiny plastic helicopter heading straight for him.

He pulled harder on the doors and got them closed just before the drone impacted and exploded, launching a spray of shattered wood into the grand salon and into the flesh of his shoulder and cheek.

"My God," he said. "What is happening?"

Jonathan watched, dumfounded, as the killer swarm spread out and hunted people down. Big Roxie caught much of it in high relief.

They hunted, they found, they destroyed. "Holy shit, Big Guy, that's amazing."

"I don't believe how fast they are," Hite said. "I mean, they start out fast and they get faster. Are they programmed only for head shots?"

"Apparently," Boxers said. "They're sure making a mess out there."

Jonathan looked at Gail, whose face was stone. He knew exactly what she was thinking. Dozens of machines were taking lives without mercy and without consequence.

He got it. Fascinating as it was, the slaughter was tough to watch. It was time to move on.

"Okay, team," Jonathan said. "Time to focus. Before we mount up, Big Guy, have Roxie identify the two power transformers again."

One of the great advantages posed by Roxie on hot operations was the ability to verify intel without risking harm to your troops. According to the plans that Venice had been able to find, the hacienda received electrical power from two feeder lines, each of which terminated at wooden posts on opposite ends of the hacienda compound.

It made sense to Jonathan that a cartel oligarch would have various forms of electronic security at his facility, but in the short time allotted to them, Mother Hen had been unable to find the source or the server. There was a good chance that the surveillance system was completely self-contained and not hackable. To be sure, that was the case with the surveillance system at Jonathan's facilities. He was hoping that by cutting the power, he could undermine the effectiveness of whatever security systems they had in place at the compound.

Boxers clearly knew where to look. As they all watched the screen, the desert dropped away as Roxie gained altitude, then it came back as she settled down. "There's the first one," Big Guy said, pointing to what appeared to be a standard telephone pole with a standard electrical transformer sitting near the top. "That will be on the right side as we come in, so that will be yours, Gunslinger."

Gail nodded. There was nothing here that she had not done before.

The image swirled again as Big Guy changed Roxie's course.

Big Guy pointed to the screen again. "Birdman, that one's yours. It'll be on the left side of the aircraft after we finish our circle. It's exactly where Mother Hen said it would be when she pulled up the map."

Michael Hite gave a thumbs-up. "Got it."

"All right, then," Jonathan said. "Mount up. I want to be airborne in one minute, and on our way home in no more than fifteen. Ten is even better."

* * *

Paco understood within seconds that they were under attack and that the technology of the attack was unlike anything he'd ever witnessed. The drones were tiny things, tinier even than the toys kids got at Christmas to buzz around their playgrounds. These things seemed to know who they wanted and where to find them.

"Everyone take cover!" he yelled. "Under the table! Under the table!" He dove under the heavy mahogany table just as he heard a loud *pop* from the direction of the main house. He looked back to see splinters flying from the explosive impact.

Somehow, these little monsters had been loaded with facial recognition software. That was the only way to explain the headlong, unhesitating attacks on his people. Even from under here, he saw the results as council members collapsed onto the concrete pool deck, their heads mangled from the explosions.

Within seconds, other members found their way to the same cover.

"What in God's name is happening?" yelled Simón Perez, one of the longest lasting and most loyal lieutenants.

"This is only the first wave!" Paco yelled.

Others were sliding under the tables now. One of the product managers, Soza, was nearly to safety when a drone made contact with his left ear and launched a fountain of gore into Paco's face.

He didn't have to time to explain his concerns or how he knew that human attackers would soon be on the way.

"The drones recognize our faces somehow," he announced. "Keep your faces covered and run to shelter inside. Arm yourselves and prepare for an assault."

"What about them?" Simón asked. "What about the machines?"

"Clearly, they don't have intelligence," Paco said. "They don't know to follow us under the table. I have to think if they cannot recognize our faces—"

"Have to *think*?" someone said. "If you're wrong—"

"If I'm wrong, we're all dead," Paco said. "But if we wait here till the human element arrives, we will be dead for sure."

Beyond and above the cover of the table, the sound of buzzing was intense. In Paco's mind, the little buggers had formed a swarm and were waiting for the first opportunity to blow off more heads.

"How many men have we lost?" Paco asked.

"At least six or seven," Frederico said. "I saw some of us running back toward the cars, but I don't know how many of them succeeded."

Paco counted heads. Seven others had gathered under the table. Adding his father, that gave them a total of nine survivors to hold off whatever assault force was on the way. Plus whoever else might have lived through the drone bombardment.

"I think we should stay here for a few minutes," Simón said. "They are small, and they have probably flown a long way. Their batteries can't last forever."

Paco thought that was a very good point. Perhaps waiting a few minutes would be a good idea. There was no way to know how sophisticated the drones' recognition software might be. Perhaps just covering their faces would not—

The sound of rotor blades churned the still desert air. At first, it was just a distant hum, but within seconds, the hum resolved into the distinctive *chop-chop* of an approaching helicopter. They were out of time.

"Now!" he yelled. "Grab your rifles and all the ammunition you can find."

"Who are we going to be fighting?" Simón asked,

seemingly on behalf of every other man who stared back at him.

"I don't know," Paco said. "But we will kill them all to find out."

Rolo Gomez hobbled into the ornate lift that would take him to the second floor of the hacienda, and as the heavy doors closed, he snatched the landline telephone from its cradle. He entered a phone number from memory.

The other party answered after the first ring. "Colonel Guiterrez."

"My hacienda is under attack." No need for introductions here. The commander of the local army post would recognize both the phone number and the voice.

"What do you mean?"

"Is it you?" Rolo accused.

"Attacking you? No. Why would—"

"Well, someone is. You get whatever resources you need out here right away, or I will see you and your entire family burned alive." He disconnected by slamming the handset down hard enough to crack the handle.

As the lift bounced to a stop on the second floor and the doors opened, Rolo stepped into the hallway that would take him to his bedroom, where his arsenal lay. By making his stand up here, he had more options than if he dug in downstairs. Multiple stairwells led to an escape tunnel where he could sustain himself for weeks if it came to that, or he could exit the tunnel through one of several escape doorways into various outbuildings on the compound.

These were the times when he was most aware of his twisted body. He needed to move quickly. In his heart, he was running. In reality, he wasn't moving any more quickly than any other day. He pulled his cell phone from his pocket and called another number—a forbidden number that the other party didn't even know he possessed.

The call connected after four rings. "Standish speaking."

"What the *hell* is going on, Harold? We are under attack."

The American's tone seemed overly casual, as if he were speaking where others could hear him. "I'm sorry, who's calling?"

"It's Rolo Gomez. Who is attacking my home?"

Silence.

"I asked you a question!"

The line clicked dead. Then Rolo heard the roar of an approaching helicopter.

Chapter 24

Irene stood as the others entered the room, not out of respect but because it was the thing to do.

"Why, Director Rivers," Standish said through a grin. "Imagine meeting you here."

"Eat shit and die, Harold," Irene said.

The president held up a finger. "Hey. I'll remind you that you're in the Oval Office. We'll not have that kind of language." He made a broad gesture with his hands. "Please, everyone take a seat."

Irene kept her gaze focused on Kresha as she settled into the sofa across from her, but on the far end. The AUSA would not look up from the spot she was staring at on the coffee table. In an odd violation of protocol, Standish took the seat closest to President Darmond while the senior ranking attorney general sat in the sofa's middle cushion. Seemingly minor issues like who sits where bear enormous significance among the ego-driven denizens of the West Wing.

The president nodded to Attorney General Norris to begin the show. "Director Rivers, I have to tell you that I'm worried about you. The US attorney has brought wild tales about your suspicions of misconduct in the administration." He looked to Adele Krump. "Perhaps you should take it from here, Counselor."

Adele Krump, United States Attorney for the Eastern District of Virginia, sat erect at the edge of her sofa cushion. Her back could not have been straighter if the rod up her ass was a real one. "At the insistence of Judge O'Halloran, AUSA Ruby came to me with a request to provide immunity for fanciful testimony from a member of the president's own cabinet, Harold Standish. Madam Director, the allegations—"

"Are all true," Irene interrupted. She sensed the onrush of a kangaroo court, and she wanted nothing to do with legitimizing it. She shifted her eyes to Darmond. "Mr. President, you and your family have been conducting illegal operations over the course of years, using the presidency as cover. You have not just suborned but facilitated the flow of illegal narcotics across our southern border, and these narcotics have demonstrably killed hundreds of thousands of Americans. That's just in the last two years."

"That's outrageous!" Darmond declared.

Irene smiled and looked to Kresha. "Counselor Ruby," she said. "Of the felons you've put away, how many of them declared that the accusations of crime were preposterous?"

Kresha didn't respond.

"What's the problem, Kresha?" Irene said. "Shame got your tongue?"

"Irene, I don't think you understand how much trouble you are in," Krump said.

"Adele, I don't think you understand how much evidence I have to prove my case."

"You don't have a case," Norris said. "Certainly not one that can be won in court. None of the evidence you have is real. And as I understand the state of things, you have no witnesses to present."

"I think that was what they wanted me to be," Standish said. "They wanted me to lie on the stand to make their case, on the cynical assumption that I must have committed some kind of crime in my life and that therefore by giving me unlimited immunity, I would dance to their—if I may—*preposterous* assertions."

"I have a recording," Irene said.

"Do you really?" asked the president. "I've heard this recording. All I hear is a crazed felon trying to make himself relevant. I'm told that there would be no way to corroborate any of the statements made by some dead wop."

Irene held up her hand. "Hey. I'll remind you that we're in the Oval Office."

No one smiled. She decided to press on. "I can also prove, sir, that you and your family have facilitated the unwilful and unlawful passage of young men and women into the United States for the specific purpose of forcing them into prostitution."

The president threw his head back to laugh at the ceiling in a gesture that was too big by half. "My God, you're crazy."

In for a dime, in for a dollar. "I can also prove that your involvement with drug cartels—specifically the Los Muertos cartel—has neutered your ability to enforce drug laws even if you wanted to. So extreme is their ability to extort policy from you that you very nearly allowed nuclear launch facilities to be installed in Venezuela."

"Nuclear missiles," Norris said. He looked like he didn't approve of the taste of the words. "Seriously, Irene?"

"I couldn't possibly *be* more serious," she said. "And in order to make that come to pass, Mr. President, you had to include senior military officers under your command. To be completely honest, I don't yet know who those officers are, but I think it's safe to follow the money that leads to the flag officers that you appointed. The wise place to start, I believe, is with the cadre of four-stars who were mere colonels at the beginning of your administration."

For whatever reason, that was the accusation that cut through the president's mask. Just a twitch, but it was there. It was an accusation he was not prepared for.

Irene read the room and saw nothing but fear and hatred. "I suppose this is where I'm supposed to offer my resignation."

"You can do that if you wish," the president said. "I would certainly accept it. But understand that nothing will end with a resignation. There will be no dignity for you. No cushy slots on the cable talk shows. My administration will see to it that you are exposed for this attempted coup and that you will be humiliated by it all."

"You really shouldn't make up lies, Irene," Standish said. "They always come back to bite you."

Irene stood.

"I didn't dismiss you yet, Irene," the president said.

"I don't give a shit, Tony." She turned her attention to Standish. "And you're absolutely right about getting bitten in the butt about lying." She sealed it with a smile.

She had no idea what she meant by that, but she knew she wasn't done with this fight.

Even if her career was over.

She'd only taken two steps toward the door she'd entered through when Standish's cell phone rang in his pocket, earning an angry glare from the president.

Standish fished out the phone, checked the caller ID, and blanched a little. He turned away from the group

and very softly said, "Standish speaking." He listened
for a few seconds. "I'm sorry, who's calling?" Even from
across the room, Irene could make out the buzz of a
panicky voice. Shaken, Standish clicked off and slid
the phone back into his pocket.

"Since when do you take phone calls in the Oval?"
the president asked.

Standish said nothing, and the president backed off.

Irene said, "Something wrong, Harold? Has there
been a glitch in your business model?"

They came in hot and low, a total projected ride of
less than two minutes. Michael Hite cinched the Velcro
on his ballistic vest a little tighter and examined the
chin strap on his helmet. As soon as they hit the ground
and he could shed the intercom headset, the Kevlar
lid would protect him from an AK-47 round to the
brainpan. Technology had come a long way since his
time in the Sandbox, but handling the gear was easy,
like muscle memory.

"We're thirty seconds out," Scorpion's voice said in
his ears. "We're gonna do a circular pass for the electrical transformers and to see what we can see, and
then we'll touch down and do the mop-up. On the recon
circle, keep an eye out for shooters. Smoke anybody
who has a gun."

"What about the remaining drones?" Hite asked.

Big Guy said, "The Little Roxies that didn't find
targets should be running out of juice about now. When
that happens, they'll pop up to twenty feet and detonate.
We shouldn't have to deal with them on the ground."

Shouldn't. Hite would have been happier with something more definite.

"Hey, look out to the left," Gunslinger said, pointing across Hite's face. "Looks like your little toys work."

In the near distance, a young man and a young woman stood over four bloody corpses that had collapsed in two dune buggies. "The same ones we saw a minute ago being rousted," Hite said. He waved at the kids.

They just stared back.

"Shows you that Little Roxies know their job," Big Guy said. The paternal pride in his voice struck Hite as odd.

"Fifteen seconds!" Scorpion announced. "Open the doors."

Hite slid the earphones off his head and replaced them with his helmet, strapping it down tight. Then he reached forward, unlatched the door to the backseats, and slid it back until it caught. To his right, Gunslinger did the same. The wind and rotor noise were not as loud as he'd expected, but he could feel the wind pulling at his clothing.

Below, the tan rocks and sand transitioned to some outbuildings and then the interior of the hacienda. Tile roofs, adobe walls, floors constructed of ceramic pavers. Blood. Corpses in contorted poses, most without heads. Many were scattered around a long table that could have seated fifteen or twenty people for a meal. Given the array of scattered papers and notebooks, this must have been the epicenter of the council meeting.

The hacienda compound's homage to a former hotel looked more obvious up close than it did from the maps and satellite imagery. He imagined there to be twenty-five or thirty contiguous rooms lining both sides of a manicured courtyard. He knew from the recon photos that the rooms were grouped in two sections arranged north and south, divided by a swimming pool in the middle and then a courtyard on the end before terminating in what must have been the main hotel building but was now the mansion that housed Rolo and Paco Gomez. If there was to be fierce resistance, that was where he expected it would occur.

"Movement on the left!" Gunslinger called over the noise.

As soon as he heard her words, Hite saw a man on his side of the chopper dashing for cover inside one of the sleeping rooms. Hite brought his rifle to his shoulder but didn't take the shot. The guy wasn't armed, at least not that he could see. For all he knew, the guy could have been a janitor.

Then the janitor brought an M4 clone to the door and took a shot. Hite didn't hear an impact, but the intent was clear. By the time Hite could reacquire his aim, the bad guy had already ducked back into his room.

"Coming up on the first transformer!" Big Guy yelled.

Hite watched as Gunslinger brought her right ankle under her left knee and braced herself against the seat-back. Her shoulder took the recoil as she fired a short burst. From somewhere beyond Hite's sightline, a secondary explosion flashed.

Scorpion held up his thumb. "Good hit, 'Slinger!"

"Birdbrain, you're up!" Big Guy yelled. "Call out when you have the target acquired."

Hite shifted in his seat and brought his M4 to his shoulder, pressing the buttstock into the soft tissue near his clavicle. Again, the years of training kicked in. "Target acquired!" he yelled.

With both eyes open, he settled the red-dot reticle on the trashcan-size transformer and pressed the trigger. Nothing happened.

"You gonna shoot or not?" Big Guy yelled.

Shit. The safety. So much for the persistence of training. Rookie mistakes don't come more basic than forgetting to switch off the safety before pulling the trigger.

Without looking, he moved his gloved right thumb, found the selector switch and spun it all the way around to AUTO.

"I can give you a baseball bat if you want to whack it," Big Guy shouted.

Birdman closed him out. He settled the reticle again and launched a five-round burst. Swear to God, the first round finished it. A flash and a boom were his reward.

"So you don't suck," Big Guy said. "Don't get cocky."

Tink. Tink. They were taking hits.

"To hell with this!" Big Guy said. He pulled on the controls, and the chopper gained two hundred feet in about five seconds. The aircraft spun on its axis, and the ground below returned to boring desert rocks and sand, which then rocketed toward them at terrifying speed.

Shit, we're crashing. Hite braced himself for a backbreaking impact.

At the last second, Big Guy pulled on the collective pitch lever and the big bird landed gently in a cloud of grit. As soon as they'd made contact with the ground, the pilot chopped the power.

"Okay, troops," Scorpion said as he opened his door on the shotgun side. "It's our turn."

Hite's gloved hands fumbled with the seatbelt while the others piled out.

"Sometime today would be nice," Big Guy groused.

Together, they jogged around the front of the aircraft and joined up at the starboard side, where Scorpion was already beginning to move. "'Slinger's with me. We're Alpha. Big Guy, it's you and Birdman, and you're

Bravo. Keep the radio clear except for emergencies. Mother Hen, are you on the net?"

"On the net and monitoring Roxie," Venice said. "I don't have hard numbers for you, but I'd guess there to be six to maybe ten survivors of the drone assault. All who scattered moved to the doors closest to the courtyard on the north end. I didn't see anyone moving in the buildings or courtyard south of the swimming pool. I advise you to keep those for last. No tangos are exposed at the moment, but I'll let you know if I see any." *Tango* was the radio alphabet letter *T*. It stood for *terrorist* back in the day, but in Jonathan's shop it had become the default designator for bad guy.

"Good work, Mother Hen," Scorpion said. "Keep an eye on the main house on the north end. I believe that's where we'll find the head of the snake. Call out if you see anyone leaving out of there and assign Roxie to follow."

"I copy," Mother Hen said. "Good hunting."

Scorpion looked at his teams. "You heard Mother Hen. For now, we'll bypass the doors south of the swimming pool. We'll catch them during mop-up."

"What if gunmen are hiding there?" Hite asked.

"If someone steps out, Mother Hen will let us know. It always makes sense to watch your six o'clock, but we'll hit them first where we know they are. Clear the old guest rooms first and then we move to the big house. Questions?"

No one raised a hand.

"Okay, Big Guy, you and Birdman take the right-hand line of rooms, and 'Slinger and I will take the left."

"It's you and me, Birdbrain," Big Guy said. "Try to keep up."

Given the man's size, Hite didn't imagine that would be a problem. He was wrong.

* * *

"That's our ride home," Grayson said. "Did you see they waved at us?"

Sissy gave him that look. *Are you out of your mind?* "Who are they?"

"Do you care? They've got a helicopter, and we're in the middle of a desert."

"How do we know they're not cartel assholes?"

Grayson barely heard what she said. Instead, he watched the chopper circle the hacienda complex, shooting and getting shot at.

"You know what they say," Grayson said, pulling Javier's body out onto the dirt. "The enemy of my enemy is my friend." He tried not to look at his attacker's mangled head as he yanked at the man's rifle to wrestle its sling free from his shoulders. "Sissy, grab their guns."

"Why?"

"So we have guns."

"What are we going to do with them?"

"Not go through this shit again. Please, just do it."

"I can't look at them."

"Don't. Just concentrate on the guns. Don't look anywhere near their faces."

Finally, he had Javier's rifle in his hand. He moved to help Sissy wrestle for the other guy's but saw that she didn't need him. "Great," he said.

"Okay," Sissy said with a huff. "Now we take the buggies over to the helicopter and try to hitch a ride?"

Over where the chopper had landed, the soldiers it brought were heading into the compound. They looked like they were ready for a fight.

What if they wouldn't offer them a ride home?

If not, then so what? They still had the dune buggies, and they knew the real direction to travel.

As he climbed behind the wheel of Javier's buggy, he looked over to the brothel buildings and hesitated. All those girls. Getting raped every day.

"You go ahead to the helicopter, Sissy," he said. "I'll catch up with you in a bit." He lurched the steering wheel to the left and launched a rooster tail of sand and stone as he raced toward the outbuildings.

This was the kind of operation Jonathan referred to as a sledgehammer op. No subtlety, no nuance. Just imprecise hammering.

He regretted taking the recon pass over the complex. It hadn't improved their knowledge over what they'd seen via Big Roxie, and it had given what was left of Los Muertos an extra minute to organize.

He pushed the thoughts aside. Regret had no place in the dynamic environment of battle. The past was gone the instant it happened. If you were still alive, only what lay ahead had any relevance.

The hairs on his neck stood like tiny telephone poles as he and Gail skirted past all those rooms south of the swimming pool without checking them. The decision to leave them for last was the right one to make, but his mind kept conjuring images of gunmen popping out of unchecked rooms and popping him in the back.

As they approached the swimming pool deck, this all got very serious.

"Alpha and Bravo hold tight," Mother Hen said over the air. "I've done some cross-checking by reviewing tapes from Roxie. Bravo, you've got known tangos in rooms nineteen, seventeen, and thirteen. Alpha, your knowns are twenty-two, eighteen, sixteen, fourteen, and eight."

"You've got more," Big Guy said over the air. "Want to trade?"

Chapter 25

Paco didn't know who these attackers were, but he knew they were organized and professional. They would not hesitate to kill. In fact, given their tactics, killing might actually be their primary goal. Hiding here in a dark guest room while other council members hid elsewhere would make the goal of killing them all many times easier.

The explosions and shooting had stopped, but he knew the peace would be short-lived. They didn't come by helicopter to not wreak havoc.

Paco hoped that the armament in the other rooms was as plentiful as the supply of weapons at his disposal here. Council members all tended to travel heavy, an acknowledgement that they would never again know true safety. Too many rivals and enemies wanted to see them dead.

He grabbed the M16 that had been propped in the corner near the fireplace and slid two spare magazines into the back pockets of his four hundred dollar designer jeans. That done, he slid his phone out of his pocket and texted the Disaster Group—the all-hands text group that he'd only used once before, after an incident in Venezuela that had killed a number of Los Muertos soldiers.

We cannot stay in hiding. We must fight back. Make your way to the covered walkway on the north end of the courtyard. We will make our stand there—together.

He returned the phone to his pocket and moved to the door. There was no need to wait for answers. Either the others would respond or they would not. He had work to do. He had to kill the killers who had invaded his home.

Grayson heard the sound of the other buggy coming up to overtake him. He looked right to see Sissy giving him a wide-eyed *are you crazy* stare. "What the actual hell?" she shouted.

"We can't leave them here," he said.

"I don't even know who they are. We're going to miss our ride home." As she spoke, gunfire erupted from the hacienda complex.

"Go then!" he shouted back. He might not know who they are, but he knew what they were going through, and he wasn't going to let that continue if he could help it. If serendipity had sent a ride for him and Sissy, they couldn't hog it from all the others who needed it even more than they did.

"I can't just leave you here!" Sissy shouted.

"Then come along." He smiled. He knew she couldn't abandon him. They were too close for that.

"Grenades through the windows," Big Guy said over the air. "That's quickest and easiest. Hit the rooms, then go back and mop up."

Jonathan thought that was a terrific idea. Hand grenades were the perfect solution in a situation where there were no good guys to worry about on the other team. Loud and lethal—even those who were not directly harmed by the fire and shrapnel were left dazed by the concussion and fear.

Jonathan keyed his mic. "Good idea." He and Gunslinger would get to their first room first, but Big Guy and Birdman would be on theirs only a few seconds later. These last few steps while closing in on a target were the most difficult not to hurry through.

Walking in an unintentional lockstep, with identical crouched postures, Jonathan and Gail crossed from the bright sunshine of the pool deck into the shadows cast by the timber-and-adobe-covered walkway that serviced the long line of rooms. He plucked an M67 fragmentation grenade from a MOLLE pouch on his vest and let his M27 carbine fall against its sling. Throwing a grenade was a two-handed operation.

The first room he passed on his left was Room 28. That meant in three more doorways—

The door to Room 22 flew open as one of the tangos dashed out onto the walkway and took off running north toward the main house. As he ran, he pointed a rifle behind him and shot without looking, let alone aiming. Reflexively, Jonathan and Gail dropped simultaneously to the concrete walkway as chips and bullet fragments went everywhere.

Across the courtyard, the same scenario unfolded, forcing Big Guy and Birdman onto the deck.

By the time Jonathan rose back to his knee and took aim, the guy from Room 22 was zigzagging between the heavy timber pillars that supported the sidewalk cover. Then, as if in a rehearsed effort, doors opened all the way down the walkway, disgorging armed men who ran as they fired, again forcing Jonathan and his team to dive for cover.

"What the hell?" Boxers yelled. At this stage, secrecy didn't mean much.

Behind and to Jonathan's left side, Gail fired a three-round burst from a kneeling position, and the nearest tango face-planted, DRT. Dead right there.

Across the courtyard, Boxers and Hite were throwing lead downrange, too, but not to great effect, from what he could see.

Jonathan keyed his mic. "Move forward. Stay together and shoot at anything you see. They're going for cover, for sure. I don't want a protracted firefight."

"Want it or not, it looks like you're going to get one," Boxers said.

They picked up the pace as they advanced on the main house as parallel twosomes, rifles up and ready to shoot.

"I don't see anyone," Gail whispered into her mic.

"If you see something, shoot something," Big Guy replied.

"Strike team, Mother Hen. Stop where you are. Your enemies have formed a line on the far side of the giant tree in the middle of the courtyard in front of you."

Jonathan and the others all took a knee. "Give me a count and locations," Jonathan said.

"They are definitely lying in wait for you. Three are hunkered down behind the masonry wall that defines the front of the back veranda."

Jonathan saw it in his mind.

"Others have taken cover behind the gaudy stone columns in the yard. They've all got rifles. As soon as you clear that hedgerow in front of you, you'll be in plain sight."

Damn. The enemy's setup was equal parts trap and ambush. In order to acquire a target, Jonathan's teams would have to expose themselves at a precise location that the bad guys had no doubt already sighted in.

There was only one way to go.

"We're gonna frag them," Jonathan said. "On my command, without exposing yourself to fire, lob two sixty-sevens over the hedgerow. After all eight are deployed, we'll move in for the gunfight. Get ready."

Grayson slid his buggy to a stop in front of the building he'd taken Sissy from and stormed inside, throwing the door open and flooding the interior with sunshine. "Everybody up!" he said. "Wake up. We're getting you out of here." He didn't know how to say any of that in Spanish.

The beds were all full, but the girls weren't moving. *Drugged.*

"Shit. Hey!" He nearly screamed it this time.

Some of them stirred as he counted heads. Six of them in here.

He headed back outside and encountered Sissy on her way in to join him.

"They're too drugged to respond," he said. "Have you looked into the other buildings?"

Sissy shook her head no.

Grayson pointed back inside. "See what you can do to get them to the buggies. Carry them if you have to."

Over at the compound, the fighting seemed to be picking up.

"We're going to have to leave them," Sissy said.

"Just *do it*. We've got time, just not a lot of it."

While Sissy stepped back into the building that so recently had been her prison, Grayson moved to the other buildings, checking them out. Lots of additional beds, but no people. Maybe they were out in the fields working, maybe they'd never been filled. He noted Bebe's bloodstains on the floor of the third building he checked out.

Somewhere in his gut, his conscience was telling him that he should feel some measure of guilt for having killed a man, but it wasn't in him. A good part of him wished he could go back in time and kill the son of a bitch a second time.

By the time he returned to Sissy, she was doing her best to guide a scantily clad, barely conscious teenager to the dune buggy. Both of them were crying.

Hite thought his heart might be leaving a dent in his plate carrier, it was hammering so hard. His hands shook as he pulled his only two fragmentation grenades out of the MOLLE pouches that attached them to his chest.

"You done this before?" Big Guy asked.

"In training." Hite saw no upside to hiding the facts. While he'd smoked his share of jihadis with his rifle and even a couple with his pistol, he'd never had an opportunity to toss a hand grenade in combat.

"If you've done it, you've done it," Big Guy said. "Nothing fancy. No counting down or none of that shit. Just pull the pin and throw the sonofabitch."

"Got it." That had been his plan all along. He'd heard stories of operators who would hold an armed grenade for a few seconds to bleed down the seven-second fuse and reduce the chance of it getting thrown back at them, but there were far too many ways for that to go the wrong way.

Scorpion's voice in his ear said, "Throw the first volley in unison. After that, in your own time. When we move forward, we move together and fast. On my count. One . . ."

"Pull the pin and stand by," Big Guy said. "If you drop it and kill us, your eternity is really going to suck."

Hite clutched the spoon safety tight as he hooked his finger through the ring of the safety pin and then yanked the pin free.

". . . two . . ."

"Get ready to throw it."

Hite remembered this well from training. It ain't a baseball, so you don't throw it like one. You used a locked-elbow, whole-arm throw. Like a human catapult.

". . . frags away."

Birdman didn't realize he'd been holding his breath until the grenade was arcing away from his hand and over the hedges.

He heard some yelling and scrambling from the far side as he snatched the second M67 from his MOLLE rig. He was about to pull the pin when the first volley detonated in a ripple of snappy booms. Next to him, Big Guy had already launched his second.

"Today, Birdbrain," he said.

Hite yanked the pin and threw the bomb. It was still in the air when everybody else's second grenades exploded on the far side of the hedge. He hadn't realized he'd been so slow.

"Okay," Scorpion said. "Here we go."

Hite keyed his mic to warn about his unexploded late throw when it went off.

Time to move.

Rising to a crouch, Birdman stayed on Big Guy's right while they advanced on the hedges and what lay behind. Big Guy started firing first, clearing his first thirty-round mag of 7.62-millimeter cartridges in seven seconds, max. His mag change was so fast and smooth that Hite could barely see it.

Splashes of blood on the grass and the pavement showed that the grenades had done some damage. One of the wounded bad guys writhed on the ground, holding his belly while blood fountained from a severed artery in his leg.

Big Guy shot him. "Dammit, Birdbrain, do your friggin' job."

To his left, Scorpion and Gunslinger were trading gunfire with at least one tango behind one of the giant freestanding pillars that Mother Hen had talked about.

Hite concentrated his fire on the masonry wall. He thought he saw the top of someone's head, but when he shot it, there was no blood spray. He took a knee to get a better aim and settled the buttstock deeper into his shoulder.

Big Guy grabbed him by the back of his vest and lifted him to his feet. "Keep moving. Be a fighter, not a target."

The bad guys on the porch had created a mess for themselves. Once they'd ducked behind the masonry wall for cover, they were stuck. If they raised their heads, their heads would go away.

Two of them raised their rifles over the top of the wall and fired randomly. All the rounds went high and wild. Hite shot one of them through the wrist, and the rifle went flying.

"Nice," Big Guy said.

"Bravo, Alpha," Scorpion's voice said in his ear. "We're in trouble over here. We've got three tangos behind the concrete pillars, and they've got us bracketed. Can you hit their flank?"

"Go, Big Guy," Hite said. "I've got this." He didn't look away from his remaining targets—if there were even any left, but if Scorpion called for help, he must truly need it.

"Remember to shoot anything you see," Big Guy said.

"I've got this. Go."

As Big Guy peeled off to the left to help Alpha, Birdman continued his approach to the covered porch. If he had any grenades left, he'd have pitched them over the masonry wall, but that was not an option.

He advanced on the four steps leading to the porch deck, finger on his trigger, ready to pound anyone—

A muzzle appeared over the top of the wall and sent a dozen rounds into the air on full auto, driving Hite back down to his knees on the steps. Reflexes are reflexes. The fact that the unaimed burst missed him by yards, not feet, only mattered two seconds later when he got his head about him.

He rose to a crouch in time to see the door into the hacienda closing.

Shit.

"Scorpion, Birdman," he said into his radio. "One bolted into the big house. I'm going in after him."

He didn't wait for a response. Given the volume of fire over at Scorpion's location, he had enough going on without acknowledging a transmission.

He scissor-stepped up the stairs, scanning left and right, ready to shoot. Halfway up, he could see the blood spray and portions of bodies as they exposed themselves to him. Two of the three were obviously dead from head wounds. The third was the man whose wrist Hite had shot. The guy jumped when he saw his attacker and reached for the pistol that he'd stuck in his belt. Hite shot him in the throat and the chin. Toast.

Holding his rifle to his shoulder with his right hand, he pulled the door to the house open with his left.

Borrowing Big Guy's tactics, when the door was open only a few inches, he stuck the M4's muzzle through the crack and emptied his magazine, raking it back and forth. Then he loaded a fresh mag and did it again in kind of a circular motion. He figured whoever was in there would be either hit or scared shitless.

Staying in a low crouch, he pushed through the doorway and entered a vast space of shredded timber and leather. Chunks of avulsed adobe marked where his bullets had chewed up the walls. Water gushed on the far side of the room from what looked to be a wet bar that featured shattered bottles of whisky, tequila, and rum.

He saw no bodies, though, and no blood trails.

This section of the hacienda must have been the hotel lobby in the building's original incarnation. Consisting of one continuous space that had been divided into different functional areas, he saw a massive fireplace and large, overstuffed sofas and chairs arranged as conversation groups. On the far side, the room terminated at a wall built of stacked logs, beyond which he had no idea what he may find.

The good news was that such a massive open room provided no useful cover or effective hiding places, so he was able to clear it quickly.

"Help me!"

The sound of a voice made him jump and drop to a knee again. "Who is that? Show yourself!"

"I can't," the voice said in heavily accented English. It sounded like an old man. "I am hurt."

The voice seemed to be coming from everywhere. "Where are you?"

"Upstairs. Near the top of the stairs."

"Who are you?"

"I am a nobody. A servant. Please don't hurt me anymore. I need a doctor."

Birdman scanned the railing at the top of the stairs for a sign of someone but saw nothing. Sensing a trap, he returned his eyes and his muzzle to the first floor and the timber wall.

"They're already gone," the man said. "They went to the tunnel. Please help me. It hurts so bad."

Hite keyed his mic. "Scorpion, Birdman. I could use a hand here in the house when you can spare one."

"Hold what you've got," Scorpion replied. "Two minutes."

The old man upstairs yelled, "Oh, my God! Help me!"

"Shit." He said it aloud this time. "What is wrong with you?"

"I've been shot. I'm bleeding to death. Please help me."

Hite looked at his watch as if that would mean anything. "Goddammit." He started up the stairs. "I swear to God, if I see a weapon, I will kill you."

"No weapon, I swear. Please come."

Hite advanced slowly, his muzzle pointed up the stairs while shifting his gaze periodically back toward the log wall in case someone popped out to fire a shot. Fully aware that he was exposing himself an inch at a time as he ascended the stairs, starting with the top of his head, he kept the rifle steady and both eyes open. Three steps from the top, he stopped and scanned the available compass points. A pretzel-twisted old man lay on his side on the blue carpet, his body turned away.

"Hey!" Birdman said. "Old man. You still with me?"

The man groaned, his consciousness ebbing.

Hite scanned the length of the hallway for hazards as he climbed the rest of the way and resumed his battle crouch. The doorways along the hallway all stood open. He considered that a good sign. If people were hiding in the rooms, they'd close the doors, wouldn't they?

"Just hang in there, sir. I'll be right there."

With his rifle up and scanning the corridor, he eased over to the suffering man and kneeled next to him. He let his rifle fall against its sling and put his hands on the man's shoulders. "Okay, take it easy. I'm going to roll you over. If anything hurts—"

The old man moved with terrifying speed, whirling onto his back.

Michael Hite didn't even see the six-inch blade the man had been concealing until it was buried deep in his belly, just below his vest. The impact drove the air from his lungs. And then the pain came, an overwhelming rush of agony that shot from his knees to his throat.

"Gringo shithead," the crooked old man said as he slid the blade deeper and cut a wider channel though Hite's belly.

Hite felt himself pitching forward as blood filled his throat. He couldn't raise his hands to stop his fall face-first into the tight nap of the carpet.

He knew he was dying. He had to be. No wound could hurt this much and not be fatal. He shifted his head until his right cheek was pressed against the blood-saturated carpet, and he watched as the man he knew to be Paco Gomez help the man he now understood had to be his father Rolo as they hurried down the hall and disappeared through the door at the end.

Michael Hite closed his eyes, grateful that the pain was finally beginning to subside.

Chapter 26

The firefight in the courtyard had lasted far longer than Jonathan had expected. The cartel shooters were both courageous and skilled, teaching Jonathan yet again the lesson he had learned so many times in the past: the instant you underrate your enemy, you triple your chances of getting killed. Thank God for Boxers. When he came from the enemy's left and opened fire, they got confused and their mistakes snowballed. As they pivoted in their positions to meet the new threat, they exposed themselves from their otherwise excellent cover, and that gave Jonathan and Gail targets to kill.

Now that the tangos were dead, it was time to go inside the main house and help Birdman.

"Why didn't you stay together?" Gail asked.

"Birdbrain's doing fine," Boxers said. "He just had a little cleanup to do."

Jonathn keyed his mic. "Birdman, Scorpion. We're coming in."

No reply.

"Birdman, Scorpion."

Nothing.

"Let's move," Jonathan said to the others. The silence

was concerning, but so was the absence of gunfire—the absence of any sounds of battle.

The door to the main room was still open, and the evidence of automatic weapons fire was impressive.

"I'm liking this guy more and more," Boxers said. "He reminds me of me."

"Upstairs!" The voice sounded strained and agonized.

"Hite?" Jonathan called.

"They got me good."

Jonathan pointed to the timber wall at the far end of the room. "Clear what's down there," he said to Gail and Boxers. He didn't know what they were getting into, but he knew that he was blind on that end of the structure. "Clear it and come upstairs."

He knew they'd object, but he didn't want to hear it. With his M27 carbine up and ready, he glided up the stairs, ready to shoot any nonfriendly face he saw. He was still four steps from the top when he saw Hite on the floor, surrounded by a growing aura of blood.

"Ah, Christ," Jonathan moaned. He hurried forward and kneeled next to Birdman. At a glance, he saw the severity of the wound. Amid all the blood, a loop of bowel drooped from under Hite's vest and onto the gore-soaked carpet.

"Did I really say *they got me*?" Hite moaned.

Jonathan keyed his mic. "Big Guy. Second floor. Now." Boxers' combat medic skills were better than any he'd ever seen, followed closely by those of Gunslinger. "We'll get you patched up, Birdman."

"They went that way," Hite said, pointing down the hall. "Jesus, I did it again. Too many cowboy movies in my youth."

"How many?"

"Two. It's the old man and his son. The door at the end of the hall."

"Boss?" Boxers' booming voice reverberated through the entire structure.

"Top of the stairs. Birdman's been cut bad."

"You need to get them," Hite said. "If I gotta die in this godforsaken place, I want those assholes coming with me."

Gail got to the top of the stairs first. "The rest of the downstairs is clear."

Jonathan stood. "Get Birdman back to the chopper and torch the whole compound."

"Where do you think you're going?" Big Guy asked as he appeared on the second floor.

"I'm finishing what we started," Jonathan said.

"You're not chasing down bad guys without us, Boss."

"Actually, I am. You save Birdman. I'll call if I need you. See you at the chopper."

Again, he didn't wait for an answer. He didn't know if Hite had a chance of surviving or not, but without immediate aid, he'd be dead. Jonathan had cleared spaces by himself before.

He placed his hand on Hite's head. "You're a good man, Michael. Godspeed."

Jonathan spun to his left and sprinted to the door that marked the end of the hallway. Weapon up and ready, he pulled the door open to reveal what might have been a closet, but there was nothing inside. With the electricity off, the space appeared as an eight-by-eight-foot black hole. He thumbed a switch on the left side of his M27 and brought his muzzle light to life, revealing what might have been an elevator car or the space into which to fit an elevator car sometime in the future.

He scanned up first, then the other three compass points before illuminating the floor. There, he first noticed that a rug had been pulled aside and shoved against the right-hand wall. He squatted for a better look, and then he got it. He saw the nearly hidden hinges in the floor and, opposite them, a recessed D-ring latch.

"They've got tunnels," he announced over the radio. "I'm going after them."

"For God's sake, Boss, wait for us."

"Follow your orders," Jonathan said. "Take care of Birdman and torch the compound. Save the main house for last, just in case. If I'm not back when you're ready, let me know."

"You'll be underground," Gail said. "How will we know anything?"

"Tunnels gotta come up somewhere," Jonathan said.

He swung his shoulders clear of his rucksack, opened the flap, and removed his NVG array. "Maybe I'll be able to see while they can't," he said, hoping to ease his team's misgivings.

He killed his muzzle light and turned on the NVGs. There was something comforting in the worldview through NVGs. He felt as if he'd spent half of his life navigating the world via the distorted colors of the display, and the technology only got better.

He activated the infrared muzzle light and laser sight on his M27, and then he was ready to go. Straddling the opening in the floor, he put his fingers through the D-ring and pulled. The hatch opened noiselessly. It was heavy—every bit of thirty pounds—but it moved smoothly.

The opening revealed a ladder that descended fifteen feet straight down into what would have been utter blackness had he not had the advantage of electronic vision enhancement.

If he did the math right in his head, Paco and Rolo had a five-minute head start on him. Maybe a minute or two more. They had the advantage of knowing where the hell they were going, but the disadvantage of not being able to move very quickly, given the absolute blackness of the space and the fact of Rolo's disability. In a perfect world, they would be using white-light flashlights to negotiate their path.

He moved his slung rifle around behind him while he climbed down the ladder. That way, the barrel couldn't trip him. The instant his feet touched the ground, though, he pressed the buttstock back into his shoulder. He took a few seconds to orient himself. He saw no signs of movement, but if he held his breath, he thought he could hear far away voices.

Whoever Gomez had hired to build the tunnels clearly had learned his trade in the mining industry. Maybe seven feet tall and four feet wide, a network of wooden beams held up the ceiling, and countless wooden slats kept the dirt from collapsing in and burying everything. Bare light bulbs dangled from wires in the center of the ceiling. Footprints were obvious in the dirt floor.

The tunnel extended straight away from the base of the ladder and appeared to have no turns or elevation changes within the range of Jonathan's IR flashlight.

"Big Guy," he mumbled, "you should be thanking your stars that you're not down here." Big Guy hated tight places, and down here, he'd have had to walk bent over like a human *L*. As it was, Jonathan had to rock his head from side to side to keep from hitting the light bulbs. He moved quickly, not quite running, but being less cautious with his movements than he ordinarily would. He wanted to catch up with the sounds that he thought he'd heard.

The worst concern he had as he advanced through the tunnel was that there might be traps built into the walls—cutouts on either side where someone could hide and ambush attackers as they approached. Battle was an inexact science, and Jonathan was betting that with just the two men trying to get away, they wouldn't take the time to set a trap for people they didn't know would be coming.

As he moved, he tried to orient the tunnel to the rest of the complex. Unless he was thoroughly turned around—which was possible, given all the changes in direction over the course of the past ten minutes—he was heading back under the courtyard in a direction that would take him under the parked helicopter and beyond that to God knew where.

Then he remembered the array of outbuildings that were located beyond the main compound. Tunnels all had to end somewhere, so it made sense that the buildings might be just the place.

Or not.

But that was a long hike. He picked up his pace, stopping every twenty steps or so to see if he could acquire the sound of the voices.

There. He heard it. A male voice, maybe two. He couldn't make out the words, but his imagination told him that they were speaking Spanish. Not a huge leap of faith.

He moved forward another twenty paces and stopped.

"*Vas demasiado rápido.*" You're going too fast.

The sound of the voice still sounded far away but spoken loudly—probably more loudly than the other party wanted because Jonathan thought for sure he heard a "*Callate*" in response—shut up.

Bringing his rifle from low-ready to a shooting position, he dialed more magnification into his scope, but whoever was out there remained beyond the reach of his IR light.

Jonathan became more careful of his foot placement now as he continued his advance.

He hadn't checked his watch when he entered the tunnel, so it would make no sense to check it now, but it felt as if he'd been at this tunnel chase for the better part of ten minutes.

The next time he froze in his tracks to listen, he thought he could hear footsteps. And then they stopped.

"*Estamos aqui.*" We're here.

Shit. Jonathan froze. Hearing was a two-way exposure. If he could hear his prey, then the prey could hear the hunter. He had no idea how well the Gomezes were armed, but a close-range gunfight in a tunnel wouldn't be good for anyone.

Crouching low, Jonathan raised his rifle again. Just as the scope acquired the forms of two men, an explosion of light washed out his NVGs, rendering him temporarily blind. He slammed his eyelids shut, but not fast enough. His night vision was fried for the next thirty seconds.

He lifted the NVG array from his face and looked again through his scope in time to see Paco Gomez pushing his father up the ladder into an open hatch in the ceiling. Seconds later, Paco was climbing up behind him.

Jonathan's finger found his trigger as he thumbed off the safety, but he didn't take the shot that would kill Paco. With the old man out of the tunnel, killing Paco would put Jonathan at a disadvantage. If Rolo retaliated—and of course he would—Jonathan had no maneuvering room. He'd be a stationary target.

No, he'd wait until Paco followed his father into wherever they were going, and then he would come up behind them. If they locked the access hatch, Jonathan still had a couple of GPCs that would help him handle that. But holy crap, that would be loud.

As Paco disappeared into the hatch in the ceiling, Jonathan heard the sound of people yelling. Then he heard gunshots.

Goddammit. It was time to run.

It sounded to Grayson that the war over at the hacienda seemed to have run its course. It had been silent there for a few minutes now. With five of the lady slaves loaded into the dune buggies, he sensed that time was running out for him as he and Sissy worked together to wrestle the last one out of her filthy bed.

They'd just gotten her to a vertical position, feet on the floor but legs wobbly, when the floor seemed to explode. Three feet away, a hatch flew open, slamming onto the floor with a bang that sounded every bit as loud as the explosions at the hacienda.

Sissy and Grayson both jumped, and as they lost their grip on the last girl, she slumped heavily onto the floor.

They gawked in unison as the hole in the floor disgorged the oldest man that Grayson had ever seen. The man seemed exhausted, and then when he made eye contact, he turned angry. As he rose to his feet, it became clear that he was forever stooped. He said something in Spanish that Grayson didn't understand. The tone was harsh.

"Who are you?" he said in English.

Before Grayson could answer, another face appeared in the hatchway. This man was much younger and moved far more easily as he cleared the door and stood straight and tall. When he saw the gringos the old man was talking to, he first showed surprise and then amusement.

He smiled as he reached down and shut the hatch cover in the floor.

"Why Papa, that is the murderer and his whore sister." As he spoke, he produced a pistol from somewhere behind his back.

Grayson grabbed his sister by both shoulders and bum's rushed her out the door and toward the dune buggies. Two gunshots rattled the world as chunks of wood flew from the doorjamb inches from his head. Then his right hip felt like he'd been hit with a baseball bat. He stumbled across the short porch and rolled down the four steps to the ground.

His right side betrayed him as he tried to climb hand over hand into the driver's seat, where he'd left Javier's rifle. As he reached for it, a gun fired again and the rifle skipped off the seat.

Grayson rolled onto his back, expecting to take the bullet that would kill him, but the attacker wasn't interested in him. Grayson followed his eyeline to see that the man was smiling at Sissy.

"Sissy from America," the man said. "At last, a bit of pleasure on such a bad day."

Jonathan pushed the latch panel hard, launching it open with a slam that shook the whole structure. He popped up like a jack-in-the-box and read the room in two seconds. The old man, Rolo Gomez, was standing in the middle of the room, listing off to the side. He looked . . . spent.

Beyond him, his son, Paco, disappeared through the door into the sunlight. The irritating smell of gun smoke hung in the air. Jonathan climbed the rest of the way out of the tunnel. A scantily clad teenager writhed on the floor as if trying to stand.

Rolo eyed Jonathan with equal parts fear and hatred. "Who are you?"

Jonathan said nothing as he walked to the old man, spit in his face, and launched a punch that dropped him in his own shadow.

"Leave her alone!" someone yelled from outside. The voice of a young male.

"No!" a girl's voice yelled. "Please!"

Jonathan darted to the open door. The young man sat awkwardly on the ground, bleeding from his hip, while a few yards away, Paco Gomez was manhandling a girl who looked enough like the boy to be his sister.

When she saw Jonathan, she screamed, "Please help me. Please!" A bruise was beginning to form over her eye.

Paco reacted without hesitation, swinging the girl and locking his elbow under her chin, with his pistol at her temple. He lifted her by her neck to bring his face next to hers as a human shield. Other girls in the same condition as the one on the floor of the shack seemed to be everywhere. Some seemed gorked, and others seemed to be trying to get away.

"I'll kill her," Paco said.

Jonathan moved with slow deliberation as he braced his M27 into his shoulder and rested his reticle on Paco's right eye. The shot was doable, but even at this range, it was high risk. If the girl twitched or if Paco anticipated the movement of Jonathan's trigger finger, the day could end in disaster. He'd come too far for that to happen.

When you're an experienced shooter and operator, you learn to walk without any bounce in your step. You learn to let your feet take you where you need to go without ever losing your sight picture.

Jonathan glided down the stairs to the rocky ground, closing the distance between himself and his target.

Paco reacted by stepping backward.

"Do you think I am bluffing, gringo?"

Jonathan didn't answer. Paco had only a couple of options here. He could move his pistol away from his hostage's temple to take a shot at Jonathan, in which case Scorpion would drill him the instant Paco's muzzle no longer posed an imminent threat. He could shoot his hostage, in which case Jonathan would kill him twice. Or he could surrender, in which case Jonathan would kill him slowly.

"Please don't let him kill me," the girl begged.

In his peripheral vision, Jonathan saw the wounded boy struggling to rise to his feet to get his hands on a rifle that lay on the floorboard. The boy launched himself up and over the seat, and that was all it took.

The noise was sudden and loud, and Paco couldn't help himself. He turned his head to look, and Jonathan's bullet drove a tunnel behind his eyes, entering the left temple and exiting with considerable fanfare out the right.

As Paco dropped away, the girl looked like she didn't know he was dead.

Jonathan walked to her and offered his hand to hers. "Hi, sweetheart, what's your name?"

"S-S-S." She couldn't get the word out.

"Her name is Sissy," said the boy. "She's my sister. I'm Grayson. Grayson and Sissy Buchanan."

Jonathan escorted Sissy to the steps and helped her sit before taking a look at Grayson's leg.

"Who are you?" Grayson asked.

"I get that question a lot," Jonathan said. "Call me Scorpion, and don't ask a lot of questions. Here, let me take a look."

As Jonathan leaned in to examine the wound, he made a point of leaning on Grayson's pelvis. When he didn't scream in agony, Jonathan knew it was a minor wound.

"Grayson, congratulations. You have officially been shot in the ass. Through and through. It'll hurt like hell for a couple of weeks, but you should be okay. Now, tell me about all these other girls."

Grayson worked through the details of the kidnapped girls being forced into sex slavery. "They tried it with me, too," he concluded. "I killed the guy."

Jonathan noticed with interest—but not judgment—that it was important to Grayson that that final detail be known.

"There's still one more girl inside."

"Yeah, okay," Jonathan said. "Let me make a quick phone call." He pressed his mic button. "Alpha and Bravo, Scorpion. What is your status?"

"Charges are all set, awaiting a heartbeat check from you," Boxers said.

"Birdman?"

A pause told Jonathan the answer before he heard it. "KIA," Gail replied. Killed in action.

Jonathan tensed his gut against the anger. "I copy," he said. "Hey, we're going to have some precious cargo with us for the flight across the border."

"Come again?" Boxers said.

"It'll make sense when you see it."

For now, he had one more young lady to bring to the buggy.

Jonathan pulled the last bench seat out of the chopper and placed it on the ground. The captain's chairs had already been removed.

"Thor is going to be very unhappy with you tearing up his helicopter," Gail said.

"Oh, I'm reasonably confident that Thor won't be the one who's upset," Big Guy said. "That'll be the guy who let him borrow the chopper in the first place."

They'd wrapped Michael Hite's body in sheets and a blanket found in a linen closet and duct taped everything so it wouldn't come apart.

The girls were mostly awake by now but not very responsive. In fact, they were damn near compliant, which made this last part of the task much easier.

"Hey, Boss," Boxers said, his voice low. "I'm not entirely sure that even with all the furniture torn out of the chopper, we won't be overweight."

"We don't have to go far," Jonathan said. "And we don't have to go high. Just get us back to Big Bend, and we'll be fine."

"I'm just sayin'."

"What's the alternative? We're already leaving a shit ton of ammo behind. That's a couple hundred pounds, anyway. We're not leaving any of these people behind."

"What about the piece of shit?" Boxers countered, nodding toward Rolo Gomez, whose twisted body had been zip-tied and his foul mouth gagged.

"That's a present to Thor," Jonathan said with a wink. "Maybe take some of the pressure off for returning a torn-up helicopter."

Gail said, "I'm surprised at you, Big Guy. It's not like you to worry about other people."

Boxers' neck turned red. "I think it's time to mount up," he said.

Jonathan didn't know the identities of any of his precious cargo—beyond the fact of Grayson and Sissy Buchanan, whoever they were—and he didn't want to know. Once they got to the other side, DEA and Border

Patrol and who knows who else would take care of the repatriations.

He just wanted to glow in the pride of finally killing the snake.

With the doors off and the PCs in-and-out comatose, Jonathan made sure that each of them had a rope around their waist that was tied off to something to keep them from somehow falling out of the aircraft. Such things didn't happen often, but they happened enough to take precautions. The exceptions were Grayson and his wounded ass, who got the copilot's seat, where he could hang one butt cheek over the side and tie himself in with a seat belt, and Rolo Gomez, because nobody cared.

As Boxers spun up the rotor disk, Jonathan made a point of sitting next to Rolo. He wanted to be there to watch his reaction to the light-and-sound show that lay ahead.

"I understand that this is your home," he shouted over the rotor noise. "This is your pride, your seat of power."

The rotor blades engaged, and the chopper lifted off the ground. The plan was that they'd climb to five hundred feet to watch the show, but Big Guy changed it to a thousand, based on the number and nature of the charges they'd planted. It didn't take long.

Through the intercom, Boxers said, "One thousand feet."

Jonathan pulled the initiator remote out of its pocket in his vest and held it where Rolo could see. The man's eyes showed pure fury.

"There it is," Jonathan said, pointing out the open door to the expansive hacienda compound. "Now, watch this." He pressed the button.

The explosions rippled from south to north, great bursts of energy that launched timber and stucco and dirt toward every compass point. An incendiary burst followed each detonation, ensuring that whatever had not been blown apart would be incinerated.

It took a full two seconds for the sounds of the detonations to hit, and when they did, they shook the entire aircraft.

The fireballs advanced like explosive dominoes, ending in a finale that vaporized the main house in one instantaneous, giant roiling cauldron of superheated gases.

"Hey, boss," Boxers said. "Make sure you're hanging on. Might get a good bump after that one."

As Jonathan leaned away from Rolo and wrapped his fist around a tiedown in the floor, the chopper did a one-eighty on its own axis, passing back over the fireball as the aircraft banked hard to the right.

Since he was not restrained, there was nothing to stop Rolo Gomez from sliding across the deck toward the open door.

"Big Guy!" Jonathan yelled.

It was too late.

If the twisted old man screamed as he fell into the fireball, no one could hear it through his gag.

"That one's for you, Birdman," Boxers said.

Chapter 27

Six weeks later

Harold Standish couldn't suppress his grin as he read the *Tribune*'s front page story for the second time. He'd pushed his yolk-smeared breakfast plate to the edge of the table to make room to open the paper all the way and place it on the space in front of him. He munched a wedge of multigrain toast as he consumed the news. The headline said it all: DISGRACED FORMER FBI DIRECTOR FACES GRAND JURY.

The political machinery had moved quickly after Irene Rivers resigned her position. The White House had launched the story of her failed coup attempt to the media even before she'd left the West Wing. Her party affiliations had driven her to do whatever it would take to harm the Darmond administration, even to the point of blackmailing Harold Standish, a longtime ally of the president, into concocting a false narrative about national security failures, bribes, and even human trafficking. None of these accusations were true, of course, though zealots from the other side of the aisle were likely to present bogus "proof" that only showed Irene Rivers's dedication to toppling the administration.

Within hours of her departure from the FBI, hordes

of media jackals were sicced on her tiny house in what used to be a quiet suburb. It was important not to merely ruin Rivers's reputation but to also make her a pariah among her neighbors and to disconnect her and her family from their friends. The drain on her finances came next as she was forced to hire expensive attorneys.

The two efforts at establishing a crowdfunding source were shut down within days, when their contributors were informed by federal officials that their assistance would be seen as aiding and abetting a traitor to the United States. Such a determination would never stand up under court scrutiny, but it would take a year or more for that ruling to happen, and by then, Irene Rivers would be broke and hopefully homeless.

Better yet, she'd be in jail, which was why this grand jury proceeding was such wonderful news. Standish happened to know that a murder charge was in the mix, dating back to the day she killed her boss in a shoot-out that was presumed to be self-defense at the time but was never adjudicated. If the grand jury decided, lo these many years later, that she had perhaps overreacted, second-degree murder could be on the table.

When would these social justice rubes ever learn that it was useless to enter a fight with the government? When you're that outmanned and that outgunned, your role as a citizen is to shut up and do what you're told. Go through the charade of electing officials and sending them to Washington, then sit down and let Washington take care of its own.

This wasn't the country Thomas Jefferson had envisioned, but who cared? Tommy owned slaves and was irrelevant now. This was a new USA. Capitalism 2.0.

While he would never say it out loud, he had to give Irene props for shutting down Los Muertos. He assumed, after all, that the obliteration of the cartel leadership was accomplished on her order. The irony was not lost on him that of all the life-destroying charges she was facing, an illegal war against the cartel would probably be the easiest to prove, but it was the place they could not go.

With Rolo and Paco Gomez and their disciples dead, Mexico and much of Central America had become a killing field as the rival cartels fought to establish hegemony over the flow of product. It would be years before an efficient and profitable pipeline could be reestablished across the border, if it ever happened at all. The flow of drugs would continue, of course. The ocean cannot be kept from the shore, after all, but the coyotes and mules would have to deal with the laws as they were written. What that really meant was negotiating individual deals with individual American officials along the border. Standish had confidence that Nicky Mishin would find a way to get his fingers into those pots eventually, but the Good Old Days were definitely in the rearview mirror for a while.

A glance at the clock told him that it was time to head to work for the day.

"Trudy! Can you clean the table for me, please?"

His cell phone buzzed, showing a 202 area code, Washington, DC. That was not unusual, of course, given his job, but most of the Washingtonians who called him were in his contacts list and would have shown up with a name.

He connected the call. "Yeah, Standish here."

"Good morning, Mr. Standish," said an energetic voice. "This is *Harold* Standish, right?"

"It is, and I'm busy. What do you want?"

"Yes, sir. I understand, and I'm sorry to bother you

so early. My name is David Kirk. I'm a reporter for the *Washington Tribune*, and I'm wondering if I could talk to you about a story we're posting later this afternoon. It'll be in the print editions tomorrow."

Trudy arrived at the kitchen door, wiping her hands on a towel. He gestured to the breakfast dishes as he leaned back into his chair and crossed his legs. "I presume this has something to do with the Irene Rivers debacle?"

"Sort of, I suppose, but only tangentially. Do you have a few minutes, or should I call back?"

"Now is fine."

"Great. Thank you. The story I'm posting is the result of a month-long investigation into the accusations leveled by former director Rivers."

"Oh, good Lord, not again. All of that has been debunked. It's all fake news."

"And that's precisely why I'm calling," Kirk said. "I want to give you a chance to respond to the accusations against you, specifically."

Standish felt a flutter in his stomach. "I'm not familiar with such accusations," he said.

"I figured as much, sir. Let me read the first paragraph of the story, and then you can tell me what you think. You okay with that?"

"Certainly," Standish said. What else could he say?

"Excellent. Here goes: *According to multiple sources independently verified by the* Tribune, *Harold Standish, special assistant secretary of Homeland Security, for years served as the point man for a sweeping criminal operation involving the transport of narcotics and sex slaves across the United States' border with Mexico.*"

Standish stared straight ahead as he listened, focusing

on controlling his racing heart. When it was his turn to speak, he couldn't form words.

"Mr. Standish?" Kirk said. "Are you there, sir?"

"That's preposterous," Standish said. He heard the tremor in his voice.

"Okay, got that," Kirk said. "Anything else?"

"That's flat-out not true."

"Which parts are not true, sir?"

"There's no part of it that *is* true. Who are your sources?"

"I'm afraid I can't share that, sir, but I have to tell you that the evidence against you is very compelling. Tell you what. I'll email today's story to you so you can give it a good read, but if you want to make additional comment, you need to do it before noon. That's the absolute limit for my deadline."

Standish remained silent.

"Okay, then. I'll use the email posted on the Homeland Security website to send you the story."

"No!" Standish said. He gave the reporter his personal email and listened as the line disconnected.

"Are you all right, sir?" Trudy asked. "You don't look well."

"I'm fine."

"Seriously, sir. Your face is—"

"I'm *fine*, Trudy. See to your own business."

It took effort to calm his shaking hands enough to manipulate his phone to open his email. There it was. All of it. Every detail of Operation Southern Hammer, down to the names of the Border Patrol supervisors who were paid off. The most frightening details of the piece were the first and last lines. The top of the article read, *The first of a seven-part series.* The teaser at the end read, *A path that leads to the White House.*

How was this possible? Everybody with this level of knowledge was dead.

"What's that syrupy saying from the nineteen seventies?" the old man asked Jonathan. "Today is the first day of the rest of my life."

As Jonathan watched Guiseppe Schillaci drink his best scotch, he kept reminding himself that killing the sonofabitch would accomplish nothing. He wondered how he would go about exorcizing the man's evil from the Compound's living spaces after he left.

Even as the thoughts went through his mind, he knew he was being unfair. He just had a hard time grappling with the notion that this wizened old murderer was actually doing the right thing—and doing it for the benefit of other people. That was not in the mob playbook that Jonathan recognized.

Okay, and Schillaci got immunity out of the deal, too.

"Can I be completely honest with you, Jonny?"

Jonathan bristled. He glanced at the federal marshal who sat in the chair next to Schillaci, but the guy remained stone-faced. "Only if you stop calling me that."

"Oh, give an old man a break. The last time I saw you, you were, what? Eight years old?"

"Something like that."

"You should visit your father," Schillaci said. "He misses you."

Jonathan glared. Simon Gravenow, Jonathan's father, had called a Supermax prison his home for many years now. He deserved to be there, and he deserved to die alone. "That's what you wanted to be honest about?"

"No. Well, yeah. Now that I've got immunity, I want

to be honest about everything. It's like being able to breathe free."

"Free breathing would have come a lot sooner if you'd decided not to kill people and commit crimes," Jonathan said. He was gratified to see the marshal crack a smile.

"Don't be cruel, Jonny. It doesn't become you. I was going to say—again—how entertaining it is to think of what Tony Darmond and all the rest are going to think when they realize that killing Rocco LoCicero put the nails in their own coffin."

At that, Jonathan had to smile, as well. With LoCicero dead, the case against the Schillaci family had collapsed. Giuseppe had seen in that an opportunity to keep himself and selected family members out of prison. He knew even more about Operation Southern Hammer than LoCicero. The end was near for the Schillacis, anyway.

"I've always been a fan of chaos," Giuseppe said. "Law and order bores me. That's why me and your dad was such good friends. I can't wait to see what comes after this story blows Washington apart."

Allowing David Kirk exclusive access to Giuseppe's testimony had been Kresha Ruby's idea, as was the plan to stay out of the way of the stories that had pummeled Irene Rivers. It was their way to keep the administration complacent. There was a less organized plan to help Irene rehabilitate her reputation, but everyone knew that she would never fully recover. In Jonathan's mind, she would always be a hero.

He'd offered his Compound as a safe house and sanctuary on the single condition that he was allowed to attend the meetings. The next step, as Jonathan understood it, was the convening of a grand jury sometime today at which Irene would testify against Harold Standish.

"What about you, Mr. Marshal?" Schillaci said. "You're awfully quiet today."

"Yep."

"Any idea when I get transported away from here?"

"Yep."

"Care to share it with me?"

As if in answer to his question, the sound of an approaching helicopter crescendoed in the distance.

When Irene heard the throaty growl of an approaching sports car, she knew who it was without looking. She finished ratcheting the tension strap closed around the wall of boxes that defined the tail end of the U-Haul and hopped down to the driveway to greet Jonathan Grave.

"Your timing is perfect," she said as he approached. "We just finished loading the truck." She offered her hand, but Digger turned it into a hug.

"I've never seen you in work clothes," he said. "Not real ones, anyway."

"This is the fashion of my future," she said.

"Where are you headed?"

"The Mountain State."

"Colorado?"

"West By-God Virginia," Irene said. "There's family property out there that I inherited ten or twelve years ago. Thought a total change of pace might be in order."

"Are you running to or running away?" Jonathan asked.

"Seeking change," she said. "I know the crap about

me has been wiped away, but the stains remain, if you know what I mean."

"I'm not sure that running away will help with that."

Irene closed her eyes and heaved a deep sigh. "I know you're trying to be helpful, Dig, but I really need you to shut up now."

He laughed. "As if it's the first time someone has said that to me. What do the kids think about the move?"

"Ashley, my oldest hates me for it, but in all fairness, she's eighteen and hates me, anyway. Kelly says she's willing to give it a try. Gracious of her, don't you think? And Wyatt's all-in. He heard we can hunt on the property."

"Is he a hunter?"

"He's a good shot at the range, but he hasn't actually hunted yet."

"What about you? What's your plan?"

Irene had thought about this a lot. None of the answers were particularly good. "Ask me in six months after we're settled. I've got my retirement, so money shouldn't be a problem. It goes a lot farther out there than here."

"Maybe join the local police force?"

She laughed. "Oh, hell no." She started up the front walk toward the porch. "I don't want to do anything important. Maybe get a job as a checker at the grocery store."

"Do they have a grocery store?"

"Yes, they have a grocery store."

"Is it more than a half hour away?"

She laughed again. "A grocery store is a grocery store." Truth be told, where she was going, *nothing* was less than half an hour away. That was part of the charm. They arrived at the porch. "Want to come in?"

"Nah. I just wanted to come by and give you my best."

It was turning awkward.

"Look, Irene, we've been through a lot. I—"

She touched his arm. "Don't," she said. "Yes, we have. A moment or two of those times were actually fun."

"I'm gonna miss you, Wolfie."

She held up an admonishing finger.

"I know," he said. "I just wanted to say it again. Call me sentimental."

"That's you, Digger, all the way. Mr. Sensitive." After a beat: "What did you do with the FBI credentials I gave you?"

He cocked his head. "Do you care?"

"Not really. In fact, I don't even want to know."

"That's a relief."

And then there was nothing left to say.

"Thanks for coming by, Dig. If I need anything, I've got your number."

Author's Note

If you've followed my writing journey for any time at all, you know that nothing happens in my life without the love and support of my wife, Joy. Forty-two years is a long time to put up with me, and not a day goes by that I am not grateful that she's by my side.

2023 marked our first four seasons in our new house in the woods in West Virginia. Every day brings new light and new shadows and new shifts in color that highlight the vibrancy of nature, along with new sets of chores that were not a part of our former citified lifestyle. I can testify for a fact that working a chain saw and slinging an axe work unique muscle groups and lead to a very deep and satisfying sleep.

Now that the pandemic madness has grown miniscule in the rearview mirror, I'm relieved that life for me has returned to normal. For the first time since 2019, I was able to return to the SHOT Show to reacquaint myself with the likes of Jeff Gonzales and Steve Tarani and Robbie Reidsma, who so generously share their wisdom and experience with me and help to lend verisimilitude to my fiction. It was great to see everyone again in person.

I owe special thanks to my friends Reavis and Shana Wortham for their guided tour of the Big Bend region of Texas where much of *Zero Sum* is set. If you get a chance to travel to that area, do it. It's beautiful—and different than anyplace I've seen before. Do yourself a favor, though, and don't go during July as we did. I don't care to endure 134 degrees Fahrenheit again.

One of the great windfalls of our move to the Mountain State was scoring a regular cohost spot on *Eastern Panhandle Talk*, a morning radio/TV show hosted by Rob Mario on WRNR/TV10 in Martinsburg. The show is mostly about local politics, with interviews of legislators and other elected officials. We also have segments on new books on the market and the local county fairs, and the station broadcasts local high school football games live, including a pregame show. I feel like I've finally moved to Real America. My experience on the radio has provided a fast track for me to get to know dozens of people who affect the lives of West Virginians in a very personal way. Plus, working in radio has always been a dream. Thanks, Rob, for giving me the chance. Special thanks also to the Mogul, Mike Hornby, who owns the place and doesn't override Rob Mario's kindness. Additional thanks to my regular fellow cohosts in the mornings, retired admiral and former president of the Berkeley County Commission, Bill Stubblefield (Mondays) and Jefferson County Prosecutor Matt Harvey (Thursdays). If you're interested in watching or listening live between 8 and 10 a.m. on weekdays, we stream the show on Facebook and we live forever on YouTube. In either case, search for *TV10 Martinsburg*, and we'll be there.

Everyone owes a hearty round of applause to

Michael Hite of Martinsburg, West Virginia, who donated serious money to the Hospice of the Panhandle to have a character named after him. I'm sorry the story didn't end well for him, but he knew what he was getting into when he placed his bids. His generosity aids one of the finest charities I've ever been associated with. Good on you, Mike!

Thanks also to Kendra Goldsborough at Four Seasons Books in Shepherdstown, West Virginia, for serving as my anchor bookstore. It's a beautiful store in a beautiful town, and there's nothing like working with people who deeply love reading and selling books.

I grow closer to my family at Kensington Books with each passing year. In this era of turmoil in the publishing business, the Big Guy in the Big Office, Steve Zacharius, manages to keep the trains on the track and on schedule. Michaela Hamilton has been my editor *extraordinaire* for at least twenty books now, and while I suppose I will never truly understand the function of commas, she has finally awakened my senses to the evils of adverbs. She *gets* my stories and characters and understands sometimes better than I do what motivates them and how they would react in certain circumstances. That's pretty special for an editor these days. Also at Kensington, I would like to express my thanks to Jackie Dinas, Lynn Cully, Ann Pryor, Lauren Jernigan, Alexandra Nicolajsen, and every other player on the team.

Speaking of my publishing team, I owe special thanks to my friend and agent, Anne

Hawkins of John Hawkins and Associates in New York. She's forgotten more about this business than I will ever know, and I am grateful for her guidance, encouragement, and skills.

Perhaps most important of all, I owe thanks to you stalwart readers who have taken time out of your day and money out of your pockets to run with my imaginary friends. I am deeply grateful. You might have noticed that things did not go well for Irene Rivers in this story, but worry not about her future. In 2025, you'll get to read the first book in her own series, separate and apart from the Jonathan Grave series. That will be very fun to write!

John Gilstrap
Berkeley County, West Virginia
November 21, 2023

Think you've seen the last of Irene Rivers?
Think again!

We are proud to announce the launch
of the Irene Rivers Thriller Series!

Keep reading to enjoy the first chapter of

BURNED BRIDGES

Coming soon from Kensington Publishing Corp.

Chapter 1

Irene Rivers believed that life was too short to swing an axe. That's why God invented chain saws. Last night's winds had taken down two, forty-foot hardwoods, one of which had fallen across their quarter-mile-long driveway through the forest and it had to be moved. After she'd cut the trunk of the roadblock into fireplace-friendly lengths and rolled them out of the gravel driveway bed, it was time for her daughter Kelly to split them. Irene rolled the wooden cylinders onto their sides and used the chain saw to cut halfway through the width longitudinally, then Kelly finished the trimming with a splitting wedge and a sledgehammer.

Rinse and repeat. They'd been at it about an hour, and the woodpile was beginning to look good.

Despite an air temperature in the mid-fifties, mother and daughter had both tossed their jackets onto the ground and were still sweating through their T-shirts.

"Where's Wyatt?" Kelly asked as she placed the sledge head on the ground to await her mom's next assault on a log.

"He's out exploring with Ruger," Irene said.

"I thought splitting wood was boy's work," Kelly objected. "I know that's what he would say."

"He's twelve," Irene countered. "And I thought you didn't believe in gender roles."

"He's almost thirteen, and he skates on every chore."

"Do you want to get this done in ninety minutes or three days?"

Kelly rolled her eyes. In her years since puberty, she'd mastered the whole eye roll thing. "I just think if he's going to be part of the family—"

Irene placed the chain saw on the gravel driveway and whirled on Kelly, forefinger extended at her nose. "Wyatt *is* a member of this family," she snapped. "Unconditionally and one hundred percent."

Kelly took a step back. "Jesus, Mom. It was a figure of speech. I *know* who he is and how he got here and what his status is. I also know he doesn't have to do anything he doesn't want to do."

Irene wanted to engage but knew that her daughter had a point. Her eldest, Ashley, called it survivor's guilt. Wyatt had never known his father thanks to an Islamist's bullet before they'd gotten to know each other, and his mother—Irene's sister Maggy—had been taken by a surprise aneurism in her forties, leaving the boy an orphan.

It had been a stressful couple of years.

"I don't want to push him too hard," Irene said.

"Maybe push him a little?" Kelly said. "I'd like to have a life, too. This whole *Green Acres* deal is your thing, not mine."

"A point you make at least four times a day."

"Ash is the lucky one," Kelly said. "She gets to live on her own."

"In no small measure because she's eighteen and has a job," Irene said. "And she has to do all her own chores."

Irene lifted the chain saw again and revved the motor. If nothing else, the noise eliminated the ability to talk.

Kelly had just lifted the next section of log onto the cutting block when she pointed toward the end of the driveway. "And he shall appear," she said.

At the far end of the driveway, Wyatt straddled his four-wheeler, motoring up the gravel hill. Ruger trotted alongside, her ears flapping and her tail wagging. The fifty-pound black Lab had been Maggie's last birthday gift to the boy, and she was his shadow. More ominous was the Jenkins County Sheriff Department Ford Expedition that followed fifty yards behind. Together, they raised a rooster tail of gray dust.

"Oh, this should be fun," Kelly said.

Gail ignored her. She killed the motor on the chain saw, placed it on the cutting block and pulled off her gloves a finger at a time. She felt her nascent lawyerly instincts coming to life, even though she couldn't imagine what Wyatt might have done to attract the attention of the sheriff's department. He was a peacemaker, not a troublemaker.

She stood at the top of the driveway apron, arms folded, waiting for the mystery to reveal itself. Maybe it had something to do with Wyatt not wearing a helmet, though helmets were not required on private property.

Wyatt slowed at the top of the apron and swung behind Irene, placing her between the sheriff's vehicle and himself. "Aunt Irene, I need to tell you something."

"I'll bet you do," she said. "Let's hear what the deputy has to say."

"It's important."

She held up a finger for silence. She had no idea what he wanted to tell her, but under the circumstances, saying anything in front of a cop couldn't help his cause.

She strolled to the Expedition's window as the vehicle coasted to a halt. The driver—a good looking guy in his forties with a high-and-tight military haircut—seemed startled by her presence. After throwing the transmission into Park, he killed the engine and opened his door. Irene stepped back to keep the distance between them friendly.

As he slid out and stood to his full height, the cop adjusted a Smokey hat just so on his head. "Good afternoon, ma'am," he said. He extended his hand. "Nate Monroe. Jenkins County sheriff."

She shook. "Irene Rivers."

The sheriff scowled and cocked his head. "*The* Irene Rivers? The FBI Irene Rivers?"

"The name is still current," she said. "The job assignment is not. I'm retired now."

Monroe chuckled. "You sure are," he said. "And you took a lot of people with you. I'm guessing you're not on President Darmond's Christmas card list anymore." His chuckle morphed into a laugh.

Six months ago, Irene had been the longtime director of the FBI, and Anthony Darmond had been president of the United States. In proving him to be the corrupt sonofabitch that he was, Irene had blasted two barrels into her own career. Last time she looked at the polls, the nation was split down the middle on whether she was a hero or the spawn of Satan. The media, which never liked her all that much in the first place, treated her revelations as a political vendetta. The vote for Darmond's impeachment had been close, but it cut against the president and now he was as unemployed as she.

Unlike Darmond, though, she wasn't facing the prospect of dying in prison for graft, human trafficking, and treason.

"I didn't realize we had a celebrity in our community," Monroe said.

"And I'm fine with that," Irene said. "I'd like to keep as low a profile as possible."

"Good luck with that. This is a small town." Monroe placed his fists atop his Sam Browne belt and craned his neck to look past Irene to see the two-story farmhouse that was now her home. "You buy this from the Waller estate?"

"Inherited it. My mother and father were Wallers."

"Big spread?"

"A hundred seventy-two acres. Big enough."

"I liked the Wallers. My parents knew them better than I did, but they seemed like nice folks. They've been gone a long time."

"Almost twelve years," Irene said. She'd been in law enforcement long enough to not enjoy undirected small talk with law enforcement officers. "Can I ask why you're here?"

"Place has been empty over a decade," Monroe said, ignoring her question. "How is it inside?"

"Musty as crap," Kelly said.

"Perfectly livable," Irene corrected.

"You got any proof that you're who you say you are?" Monroe asked.

"Seriously?" Irene scoffed. "You're the one who recognized *me*. Now, are you going to get to the point of your visit?"

Monroe showed his palms and took a step back. "Whoa. Are we a bit testy?"

"We're a bit busy."

Monroe cocked his head. "The boy told me his last name is Gordon."

"That's because his last name is Gordon. I'm raising him for his mom."

"And where is she?"

"Raising him was my last promise to her before she passed." Irene felt her patience fraying. "You were about to tell me why you're here."

"Why don't you ask the boy?"

"Because I'm asking you, Sheriff. We're big believers in the Fifth Amendment here. The fourth, sixth, and seventh, too."

Monroe eyed the baby Glock on Irene's hip. "And the second."

"That one especially," Irene said. She turned and headed back for her chain saw. "It's been a pleasure, Sheriff."

"Call me Nate. Everyone does."

"Good to know."

When Irene made eye contact with Wyatt, the boy looked like he was about to burst if he didn't talk. She shook her head no.

"Four wheelers aren't allowed on the public roads," Monroe said. "That's why I stopped him. That's why we're here. As a courtesy, so I didn't have to impound his ATV."

Irene avoided giving Wyatt a glare. "Where was he?"

"Out on Carriage Trail."

"Carriage Trail cuts through our property," Irene said. "How is he supposed to cross it?"

"The law doesn't have exceptions," Monroe said.

Irene felt herself puffing up. "It's a three second traverse on a road that sees ten cars a day."

"Unfortunately for him—and for you—mine was one of them." He pulled a citation book from his belt and started to write out the summons. "For what it's worth, he was not crossing the road. He was driving down it. And too fast for his age if I'm being honest."

This time, the glare had to happen.

Wyatt mouthed, *That's what I need to tell you.*

Irene signaled with her hand to stay silent.

After two minutes, Monroe handed the citation book to Irene. "Sign at the line. This is not an admission of guilt. It's merely a commitment—"

"To appear in court on the date cited," Irene said, finishing the sentence for him. She pointed to the fine print at the bottom of the page. "Is this the number to call if I want to protest the citation?"

Monroe smiled at a joke she couldn't hear. "It is," he said. "I understand that you don't like me all that much right now, but I do have some advice if you're in the mood to listen."

Irene nodded for him to proceed.

"Judge Stephens don't like friction too much. Bein' new and everything, it might be best for you just to pay the forty bucks and walk away."

"Duly noted," Irene said. "Are we done now?"

Monroe touched the brim of his hat. "Yes, ma'am. Pleasure meeting you."

Irene forced a smile and watched as Monroe's Expedition U-turned and headed back down the driveway. He was nearly to the road when Irene turned on Wyatt.

"Now, you," she said. "You know better than to take the ATV on the road."

"But I had to," the boy said. "That's what I've been trying to tell you. I had to get back here in a hurry, and the road was the quickest. I didn't know a cop—"

"Why?" Irene interrupted. "Why was there no choice? What made you so much in a hurry?"

Wyatt pointed past the big field to the woods beyond. "Out there," he said. "I found a dead body."

Visit our website at
KensingtonBooks.com
to sign up for our newsletters, read
more from your favorite authors, see
books by series, view reading group
guides, and more!

BOOK  CLUB
BETWEEN THE CHAPTERS

Become a Part of Our
Between the Chapters Book Club
Community and Join the Conversation

Betweenthechapters.net

Submit your book review for a chance to win exclusive
Between the Chapters swag you can't get anywhere else!
https://www.kensingtonbooks.com/pages/review/